LEVIATHAN FALLS

By JAMES S. A. COREY

The Expanse
Leviathan Wakes
Caliban's War
Abaddon's Gate
Cibola Burn
Nemesis Games
Babylon's Ashes
Persepolis Rising
Tiamat's Wrath
Leviathan Falls

The Expanse short fiction
The Butcher of Anderson Station
Gods of Risk
The Churn
Drive
The Vital Abyss
Strange Dogs

LEVIATHAN FALLS

BOOK NINE OF THE EXPANSE

JAMES S. A. COREY

orbit

orbitbooks.net

ORBIT

First published in Great Britain in 2021 by Orbit

1 3 5 7 9 10 8 6 4 2

A CIP catalogue record for this book
is available from the British Library.

HB ISBN 978-0-356-51039-2
C format 978-0-356-51038-5

Printed and bound in Great Britain by Clays Ltd, Elcograf S.p.A.

Papers used by Orbit are from well-managed forests
and other responsible sources.

Orbit
An imprint of
Little, Brown Book Group
Carmelite House
50 Victoria Embankment
London EC4Y 0DZ

An Hachette UK Company
www.hachette.co.uk

www.orbitbooks.net

Nine books later and you're still here,
so this one's for you.

Prologue

First there was a man named Winston Duarte. And then there wasn't.

The last moment had been banal. He'd been in his private study at the heart of the State Building, sitting on his divan. His desk—Laconian rainwood, with a grain like sedimentary rock—had an inset screen showing the thousand different reports vying for his attention. The clockwork of the empire ground slowly forward, with every revolution of the wheel making the mechanism a little smoother and more precise. He'd been reviewing the security reports from Auberon, where the governor, responding to separatist violence, had begun recruiting locals into the system security forces. His own daughter, Teresa, had been on one of her illicit adventures outside the grounds. The solitary nature hikes which she believed to be outside the watchful eye of Laconian Security were developmentally important for her, and he looked on them with not only indulgence but pride.

He had only recently told her about his ambitions for her: to join him as Paolo Cortázar's second patient, to have her awareness opened and deepened as his had been, to live perhaps not forever but at least indefinitely. A hundred years from now, they would still be guiding the human empire. A thousand. Ten thousand years.

If.

That was the terrible pressure behind it all. The overwhelming *if*. If he could push back against the human habit of complacence. If he could convince the vast, incoherent scrum that was humanity that they had to take action to avoid the fate of their predecessors. Either they did whatever it took to understand and defeat the darkness on the third side of the ring gate, or they died at its hand.

The experiments in Tecoma system were like all the critical steps that had come throughout human history. Ever since the first mammal decided to rise on its hind legs to see above the grass. If it worked, it would change everything again. Everything changed everything that had come before. It was the least surprising thing in life.

He had reached for his tea in those last moments, but noticed through one of the weird new senses Dr. Cortázar had given him that the pot had already gone cold. The awareness of molecular vibration was analogous to the physical sensation of heat—it measured the same material reality—but the merely human sense was like a child playing a whistle compared with Duarte's vast, symphonic new awareness.

The last moment came.

In the instant between deciding to call his valet for a fresh pot of tea and then reaching his hand out for the comm controls, the mind of Winston Duarte blew apart like a pile of straw in a hurricane.

There was pain—a great deal of pain—and there was fear. But there wasn't anyone left to feel it, so it faded quickly. There was no consciousness, no pattern, no one to think the thoughts that swelled and dimmed. Something more delicate—more graceful, more sophisticated—would have died. The narrative chain that thought of itself as Winston Duarte was ripped to pieces, but the flesh that housed him wasn't. The subtle flows of energy in his body fell into a storm of invisible turbulence, whipped past coherence. And then, without anyone being aware of it, they began to slow and still.

His thirty trillion cells still took in oxygen from the complex fluid that had been his blood. Those structures that were his neurons fell into association with each other like drinking buddies bending their elbows in unconscious synchrony. Something was that hadn't been. Not the old thing, but a pattern that took up residence in the empty space it left behind. Not the dancer, but a dance. Not the water, but a whirlpool. Not a person. Not a mind. But something.

When awareness returned, it first appeared in colors. Blue, but without the words for blueness. Then red. Then a white that also meant something. The fragment of an idea. Snow.

Joy came to be, and it lasted longer than fear had. A deep, bubbling sense of wonder carried itself along without anything to carry it. Patterns rose and fell, came together and came apart. The few that fell apart more slowly sometimes came into relationship with each other, and sometimes that made them last even longer.

Like a baby slowly mapping touch and sight and kinesthesis into something not yet called "foot," scraps of awareness touched the universe and something like understanding began to form. Something felt its own lumbering, brute physicality as it pushed chemicals into the vast gaps between cells. It felt the raw, open vibration that surrounded the ring gates that connected the worlds, and it thought of sores and ulcerations. It felt something. It thought something. It remembered how to remember, and then it forgot.

There had been a reason, a goal. Something had justified atrocities in order to avoid worse ones. He had betrayed his nation. He had conspired against billions. He had condemned people who were loyal to him to death. There had been a reason. He remembered it. He forgot. He rediscovered the glorious brilliance of yellow and devoted himself to the pure experience of that.

He heard voices as symphonies. He heard them as quacks. He was surprised to find that a he existed and that it was him. There was something he was supposed to do. Save humanity. Something ridiculously grand like that.

He forgot.

Come back. Daddy, come back to me.

Like when she'd been a baby and he had slept at her side, he refocused on her by habit. His daughter mewled, and he roused himself so that his wife wouldn't have to. His hand was in hers. She'd said something. He couldn't remember the words, so he looked backward in time to where she spoke them. *Dr. Cortázar? He's going to kill me.*

That didn't seem right. He didn't know why. The storm in the other place was loud and soft and loud. That was connected. He was supposed to save them from the things in the storm, that *were* the storm. Or from their own too-human nature. But his daughter was there, and she was interesting. He could see the distress flowing through her brain, through her body. The pain in her blood scented the air around her, and he wanted. He wanted to soothe her, to comfort her. He wanted to make right everything that was wrong for her. But more interesting, for the first time, he *wanted*.

The strange sensation of feeling these things plucked at his attention, and his focus drifted. He held her hand and wandered. When he came back, he was still holding her hand, but she was someone else. *We just need to scan you, sir. It won't hurt.*

He remembered Dr. Cortázar. *He's going to kill me.* He waved Cortázar away, pushing at the empty spaces between the tiny motes that made him a physical thing until the man swirled like dust. There. That was fixed. But the effort tired him and made his body ache. He gave himself permission to drift, but even so, he noticed that the drift was less. His nervous system was shattered, but it kept growing together. His body kept insisting that even if it couldn't go on, it could go on. He admired this stubborn refusal to die as if it were something outside of himself. The sheer mindless and physical impulse to move forward, each cell's determination to churn along, the obdurate need to continue existing that didn't even require a will. All of it meant something. It was important. He just had to remember how. It had to do with his daughter. It had to do with keeping her safe and well.

He remembered. He remembered being a man who loved his child, and so he remembered being a man. And that was a stronger rope than the ambition that had built an empire. He remembered that he had made himself something different than a human. Something more. And he understood how this alien strength had also weakened him. How the brutish and unapologetic clay of his body had kept him from annihilation. The sword that slew a billion angels had only inconvenienced the primates in their bubbles of metal and air. And a man named Winston Duarte, halfway between angel and ape, had been broken but not killed. The shards had found their own way.

There was someone else too. A man with dry riverbeds in his mind. Another man who had been changed. James Holden, the enemy who had shared his enemy, back before Winston Duarte had broken, and in breaking, become.

With infinite effort and care, he pulled the unbearable vastness and complexity of his awareness in and in and in, compressing himself into what he had been. The blue faded into the color he had known as a man. The sense of the storm raging just on the other side, of the violence and threat, faded. He felt the warm, iron-smelling meat of his hand, holding nothing. He opened his eyes, turned to the comm controls, and opened a connection.

"Kelly," he said. "Could you bring me a fresh pot of tea?"

The pause was less than might have been expected, under the circumstances. "Yes, sir," Kelly said.

"Thank you." Duarte dropped the connection.

A medical bed had been put in his study with an aerated foam mattress to prevent bedsores, but he was seated at his desk as if he had never left it. He took stock of his body, noticing its weakness. The thinness of its muscles. He stood, clasped his hands behind him, and walked to the window to see whether he could. He could.

Outside, a light, tapping rain was falling. There were puddles on the walkways and the grass was bright and clean. He reached out for Teresa, and he found her. She wasn't nearby, but she wasn't in distress. It was like watching her traipse through the wilds again, only without the artificial lens of the cameras. His love and indulgence for her was vast. Oceanic. But it wasn't pressing. The truest expression of his love was his work, and so he turned to it as if this were any other day.

Duarte pulled up an executive summary the way he had at the start of every morning. Normally it was a page long. This one was a full volume. He sorted by category, pulling out the thread that addressed the status of traffic through the ring space.

Things had, putting it mildly, gone poorly in his absence. Scientific reports of the loss of Medina Station and the *Typhoon*. Military analyses of the siege of Laconia, the loss of the construction platforms. Intelligence summaries of the growing opposition in the widely scattered systems of humanity, and of Admiral Trejo's attempts to hold the dream of the empire together without him.

There had been a time not long after her mother passed when Teresa had decided to make him breakfast. She had been so young, so incapable, that she had failed. He remembered the crust of bread heaping with jam and a pat of unmelted butter perched on top of it. The combination of ambition and affection and pathos had been beautiful in its way. It was the kind of memory that survived because the love and the embarrassment fit together so perfectly. This felt the same.

His awareness of the ring space was clear now. He could hear the echoes of it in the fabric of reality like he was pressing his ear to a ship's deck to know the status of its drive. The rage of the enemy was as apparent to him now as if he could hear its voices. The shrieks that tore something that wasn't air in something that wasn't time.

"Admiral Trejo," he said, and Anton startled.

It was the fifth week of Trejo's combination press tour and reconquest of Sol system. He sat in his cabin, spent from his long day of glad-handing and speech-making with the local leaders and officials. He was the visible face of a nearly toppled empire, making sure no one knew how close he'd come to losing it all. After the hard weeks-long burn out from Laconia, it was exhausting. He wanted nothing more than a stiff drink and eight hours in his bed. Or twenty. Instead, he was on a video call with Secretary-General Duchet and his Martian counterpart, both of them on Luna and near enough that light delay didn't interfere. The politicians were lying through their smiles. Trejo was threatening through his.

"Of course we understand the necessity of getting the orbital shipyards up and running as quickly as possible. Rebuilding our shared defenses is critical," Duchet said. "But given the lawlessness that has followed the recent attack on Laconia, our first concern is security for the facilities. We have to have some guarantee that your ships will be able to protect these valuable assets. We don't want to just paint a target on ourselves for the underground to aim at."

You just got the shit kicked out of you, had your factories blown up, lost two of your most powerful battleships, and are scrambling to hold the empire together. Do you have enough ships to force us to work for you?

"We've suffered setbacks, that's true," Trejo drawled, the way he sometimes did when he was angry. "But there's no need for concern. We have more than enough of the *Pulsar*-class destroyers to provide total security for Sol system."

I just reconquered you with two dozen of those ships, and I have a shit-ton more of them I can call in if I need to, so fucking do what I tell you to do.

"Excellent to hear that," the Martian prime minister said. "Please let the high consul know we will spare no effort to meet his production schedule."

Please don't carpet-bomb our cities.

"I will let him know," Trejo replied. "The high consul treasures your support and loyalty."

Duarte is a drooling moron, but if you give me the ships to hold the empire together, I won't have to glass your damn planets, and maybe we all win.

Trejo killed the connection and leaned back in his chair. The bottle of whiskey in his cabinet called to him gently. The freshly made bed was much louder. He had time for neither. The underground was still running riot in thirteen hundred systems and more. And that was just his human problem. After that, there were the gates to deal with, and whatever within them kept turning the minds off in whole systems at a time as it sniffed for ways to exterminate humanity.

No rest for the wicked. No peace for the good.

"Connect me to the Association of Worlds rep, Sol system. I don't remember her name," he said. No one heard him but the ship.

CONNECTING Now flashed on his screen. Time for more smiling lies. More veiled threats. More—and he used the word as an epithet—diplomacy.

"Admiral Trejo," said a voice from behind him. It was familiar but so unexpected that his mind scrambled to place it. He had a brief, irrational idea that his attaché had been hiding in his room this whole time and had only just now chosen to reveal himself.

"Anton," the voice said, lower and as intimate as a friend. Trejo turned around in his chair to face the room. Winston Duarte stood near the foot of his bed, hands behind his back. He wore a loose casual shirt and black trousers. He wasn't wearing any shoes. His hair was mussed, as if he'd only recently woken up. He looked like he was actually there.

"Security alert," Trejo said. "This room. Full sweep."

Duarte looked pained. "Anton," he said again.

In milliseconds, the ship had swept every inch of his cabin looking for anyone or anything that wasn't supposed to be there. His screen reported to him that the room was free of listening devices, dangerous chemicals, unauthorized technology. He was also the only person in it. The ship asked if he wanted armed security personnel to respond.

"Am I having a stroke?" he asked the apparition.

"No," Duarte said. "Though you should probably be getting more sleep." The ghost in his room shrugged its shoulders, almost apologetically. "Look. Anton. You've done everything that could have been asked of you to hold the empire together. I've seen the reports. I know how difficult this job has been."

"You're not here," Trejo said, asserting the only possible reality against the lies his senses were telling him.

"What *here* means has become strangely flexible for me," Duarte agreed. "As much as I appreciate your work, you can stand down now."

"No. It's not over. I'm *still* fighting to hold the empire together."

"And I appreciate that. I do. But we've been running down the wrong road. I need a little quiet to think this through, but I see things better now. It's going to be all right."

The need to hear those words—to believe them—rushed through Trejo like a flood. The first time a lover had kissed him, it had been less overwhelming than this.

Duarte shook an amused and melancholy smile. "We built an empire that spanned the galaxy, you and I. Who'd have imagined we were thinking too small?"

The image, illusion, projection, whatever it was, vanished so suddenly it was like a skipped frame in a film.

"Fuck me," Trejo said to no one. The security alert was still flashing on the screen over his desk. He slapped the comm link with one hand.

"Sir," the duty officer said. "We've got an active alert from your quarters. Do you want—"

"You have five minutes to prep for a max burn to the ring."

"Sir?"

"Sound the alarm," Trejo said. "And get everyone in their couches. We have to get back to Laconia. Now."

Chapter One: Jim

"It pinged us," Alex said. His voice was a light almost singsong that meant he thought they were screwed.

Jim, sitting on the ops deck with a tactical map of Kronos system on the screen and his heart going double time, tried to disagree. "Just because he's knocking doesn't mean he knows who's home. Let's keep acting like what we're acting like."

The *Rocinante* was acting like a small-haul freighter, a class of ship thick on the ground in Kronos system. Naomi had tuned the Epstein to run just dirty enough to change their drive signature without generating too much extra waste heat. A set of extra plating welded to their hull at an underground shipyard in Harris system had altered their silhouette. A slow dribble of liquid hydrogen was pumping out across the top of the ship and changing their thermal profile. When Naomi had gone over the plan to layer on camouflage, it had seemed comprehensive. It was only the threat of violence that made Jim feel exposed.

The enemy frigate was called the *Black Kite*. Smaller than the *Storm*-class destroyers, it was still well armed and had the self-healing outer hull that made Laconian ships hard to kill. It was part of a hunting group scouring all the inhabited systems for Teresa Duarte, runaway daughter of High Consul Winston Duarte, heir apparent to his empire, and, for the time being, apprentice mechanic on the *Rocinante*.

This wasn't the first time they'd seen it.

"Any follow-up?" Jim asked.

"Just the ladar ping," Alex said. "Think I should warm up the peashooter, just in case?"

Yeah, let's do that was on the edge of Jim's mind when Naomi's voice answered instead. "No. There's some evidence that their next-generation sensor arrays can recognize rail-gun capacitors."

"That feels unfair," Jim said. "What a crew does with its rail-gun capacitor in the privacy of its own ship shouldn't be anyone else's business."

He could hear the smile in Naomi's voice. "While I agree in principle, let's keep the guns offline until we need them."

"Copy that," Alex said.

"Still no follow-up?" Jim asked, even though he had access to all the same logs Alex did. Alex checked anyway.

"Comms are dark."

Kronos wasn't quite a dead system, but it was close. The star there was large and fast-burning. There had been a habitable planet in the goldilocks zone there at one point—at least enough that the protomolecule had been able to hijack the biomass needed to build a ring gate. But in the strange eons since the gate's formation and humanity's stumbling into the alien ruins, the goldilocks zone had moved. The original life-bearing planet hadn't quite been engulfed by the star yet, but its oceans had been boiled to nothing and its atmosphere stripped away. The only native life in Kronos was on the wet moon of an outlying gas giant, and that wasn't much more than viciously competing continent-sized sheets of slime mold.

The human inhabitants of Kronos were around ten thousand miners on seven hundred thirty-two active sites. Corporations, government-sponsored interest groups, independent rock hoppers, and unholy legal hybrids of all three were stripping palladium out of a nicely rich scattering of asteroids and sending it out to anyone still building air recyclers or working on adjustment-terraforming projects.

Which was everyone.

Kronos had been the edge of the Transport Union's reach back in the day, then the ass end of the Laconian Empire, and now no one really knew what it was. There were hundreds of systems like it, all through the gate network: places that either weren't self-sufficient yet or didn't plan to be, more focused on digging out their own little economic niche than any broader coalition. The kinds of places where the underground could usually hide and repair their ships and plan for what came next. On the tactical map, asteroids marked by orbit, survey status, composition, and legal ownership swirled around the angry star as thick as pollen in springtime. The ships were clumped around the excavation and survey sites by the dozen, and as many more were on lonely transits from one little outpost to another or on errands to gather water for reaction mass and radiation shielding.

The *Black Kite* had come through the ring gate three days before, torpedoed the underground's radio repeater at the surface of the gate, and then burned gently to remain in place like a bouncer at a pretentious nightclub. The ring gates didn't orbit the stars so much as remain in fixed position as though they'd been hung on hooks in the vacuum. It wasn't the strangest thing about them. Jim had let himself hope that blowing up the underground's pirate transmitter would be all the *Kite* did. That the enemy would finish its little vandalism and fuck off to cut the metaphorical telegraph wires on some other system.

It had stayed, scanning the system. Looking for them. For

Teresa. For Naomi, functional leader of the underground. And for him.

The comm display lit up the green of an incoming transmission, and Jim's gut knotted. At their present range, the battle wouldn't come for hours, but the rush of adrenaline was like someone had fired a gun. The fear was so present and overwhelming that he didn't notice anything odd.

"Broadcast," Alex said over the ship comms and from the deck above Jim. "Weird it's not a tightbeam...I don't think he's talking to us."

Jim opened the channel.

The woman's voice had a clipped, emotionless formality that was like the accent of the Laconian military. "...as offensive action and treated as such. Message repeats. This is the *Black Kite* to registered freighter *Perishable Harvest*. By order of Laconian security forces, you will cut your drive and prepare for boarding and inspection. Refusal to comply will be viewed as an offensive action and treated as such. Message repeats..."

Jim filtered the tactical map. The *Perishable Harvest* was about thirty degrees spinward of the *Roci*, and burning toward the wide, angry sun. If they'd gotten the message, they hadn't complied with it yet.

"Is that one of ours?" Jim asked.

"Nope," Naomi said. "It's listed as property of a David Calrassi out of Bara Gaon. I don't know anything about it."

With light delay, they should have received the *Black Kite*'s command ten minutes before the *Rocinante* did. Jim imagined some other crew in a panic because they'd received the message he'd been dreading. Whatever happened next, the *Rocinante* was out of the crosshairs for the moment at least. He wished he could feel the relief a little more deeply.

Jim unstrapped from the crash couch and swung around. The bearings hissed as it shifted under his weight.

"I'm heading down to the galley for a minute," he said.

"Grab a coffee for me too," Alex said.

"Oh no. Not coffee. I'm maybe up to some chamomile or warm milk. Something soothing and unaggressive."

"Sounds good," Alex said. "When you change your mind and get some coffee, grab one for me too."

On the lift, Jim leaned against the wall and waited for his heart to stop racing. This was how heart attacks came, wasn't it? A pulse that started fast and then never slowed until something critical popped. That was probably wrong, but it felt that way. He felt that way all the time.

It was getting better. Easier. The autodoc had been able to supervise the regrowth of his missing teeth. Apart from the indignity of needing to numb his gums like a toddler, that had gone well enough. The nightmares were old acquaintances by now. He'd started having them on Laconia while still a prisoner of High Consul Duarte. He'd expected them to fade once he was free, but they were getting worse. Being buried alive was the most recent version. More often it was someone he loved being murdered in the next room and not being able to key in the lock code fast enough to save them. Or having a parasite living under his skin and trying to find a way to cut it out. Or the guards on Laconia coming to beat him until his teeth broke again. The way that they had.

On the upside, the old dreams about forgetting to put on his clothes or not studying for a test seemed to be off the rotation. His weirdly vindictive dream life wasn't all bad.

There were still days when he couldn't shake the sense of threat. Sometimes a part of his mind would get trapped in the unfounded and irrational certainty that his Laconian torture team was about to find him again. Others, it was the less irrational dread of the things beyond the gates. The apocalypse that had destroyed the protomolecule's makers and was on the path to destroying humanity.

Seen in that light, maybe he wasn't the broken part of the equation. Maybe the larger situation was bad enough that feeling as whole and sane as the man he'd been before his Laconian imprisonment would have been a sign of madness. Still, he wished he could tell whether the waves of shuddering were a resonance effect of running the drive dirty or if it was just him.

The lift stopped, and he stepped out, turning toward the galley. The soft, rhythmic thump of dog tail against deck told him Teresa and Muskrat were already there. Amos—black-eyed, gray-skinned, and back from the dead—was there too, sitting at the table with the same placeholder smile he'd always had. Jim hadn't seen him shot in the head back on Laconia, but he knew about the drones that had taken the pieces of human flesh and reconnected them. Naomi still struggled with whether the thing that called itself Amos really was the mechanic they'd shipped with for so many years, or if he'd become an alien mechanism that only thought it was Amos because it was made from his body and brain. Jim had decided that even if he looked different, even if he sometimes knew things that were scraps of the ancient alien world, Amos was Amos. He didn't have the spare energy to think about it more deeply than that.

Besides which, the dog liked him. Not a perfect critical guide, but probably the least imperfect.

Muskrat, sitting at Teresa's feet, looked up at Jim hopefully and wagged her tail against the deck again.

"I don't have any sausage," Jim said to the expressive brown eyes. "You'll have to make do with kibble like the rest of us."

"You spoiled her," Teresa said. "She's never letting you forget that."

"If I go to heaven, let it be for spoiling dogs and children," Jim said, and headed for the dispenser. Without thinking, he keyed in a bulb of coffee. Then, realizing what he'd done, he added one for Alex.

Teresa Duarte shrugged and turned her attention back to the tube of mushroom, flavorings, and digestive fiber that was her breakfast. Her hair was pulled back in a dark ponytail, and her mouth had a permanent slight frown that was either a quirk of her physiology or her character. Jim had seen her grow from a precocious child to a rebellious adolescent in the State Building in Laconia. She was fifteen now, and it was sobering to remember who he'd been at her age: a thin, dark-haired Montana boy with no particular ambitions beyond the knowledge that if nothing else worked out, he could join the navy. Teresa seemed older than adolescent Jim had been, both more knowledgeable about the universe and angrier with it. Maybe the two went hand in hand.

She'd been afraid of him when he'd been her father's prisoner. Now that she was on Jim's ship, the fear seemed to have evaporated. He'd been her enemy then, but he wasn't sure that he was her friend now. The emotional complexity of an adolescent girl socialized in isolation was probably more than he could ever really understand.

The dispenser finished both his bulb and Alex's, and Jim took them, appreciating the warmth against his palms. The shuddering was almost gone now, and the bitterness of the coffee was more calming than tea would have been.

"We're going to need a resupply before much longer," Amos said.

"Really?"

"We're okay on water, but we could stand to re-up the fuel pellets. And the recyclers ain't what they used to be."

"How bad?"

"We're solid for a few weeks yet," Amos said.

Jim nodded. His first impulse was to dismiss it as a problem for another day. That was wrong, though. Fuck-it-if-it's-not-happening-right-now was crisis thinking, and if he couldn't break out of it, it would only lead to more crises later on.

"I'll talk to Naomi," he said. "We'll figure something out." *Assuming the Laconians don't find us. Assuming the gate entities don't kill us. Assuming that any of the thousand other catastrophes I haven't even thought of don't kill us all before it matters.* He took another sip of his coffee.

"How're you doing, Cap'n?" Amos asked. "You seem a little twitchy."

"Fine," Jim said. "Just covering near-constant panic with light humor, same as anyone."

Amos had a moment of eerie stillness—one of the hallmarks of his new self—and then smiled a little wider. "All right then."

Alex broke in over the ship comms. "We got something."

"Something good?"

"Something," Alex said. "The *Perishable Harvest* just dumped some kind of liquid, and it's burning like hell for the big trade station in the outer Belt."

"Copy that," Naomi said—also over the comms—in the new staccato calm that Jim thought of as her Commander Nagata voice. "Confirming."

"The *Black Kite*?" Jim asked the wall.

Alex and Naomi were silent for a moment, then Alex said, "Looks like they're going after them."

"Moving away from the ring gate?"

"Yes indeed," Alex said, and the pleasure in his voice was unmistakable.

Jim felt a surge of relief, but it didn't last more than a moment. He was already thinking about the ways it might be a trap. If the *Roci* turned toward the ring too soon, it would draw attention to them. Even if the *Roci* evaded the *Black Kite*, there might be another Laconian ship risking itself by waiting inside the ring space, ready to intercept any ship fleeing the system.

"Why are they running?" Teresa asked. "They don't think they're going to get away, do they? Because that would be stupid."

"They aren't trying to save the ship," Amos said. He had the same patient, almost philosophical tone as when he was walking her through how to do a good weld in microgravity or checking the seal on a pipe. It was the voice of a teacher walking his student through a lesson in how the world worked. "Whatever they had on that ship that Laconia was going to get pissed about, they can't hide it. Not in a system as thin as this one. And there's no way they're slipping off and swapping transponders, so their ship's fucked. The trade station's big enough they can maybe get the crew off and sneak onto other ships or pretend they were on the station all along."

"Running to where the hiding places are," Teresa said.

"And the more lead time they have, the better the chances they can find a good spot," Amos said.

That could be us, Jim thought. *If the* Black Kite *had decided that we looked a little sketchier than the* Perishable Harvest, *we would be sacrificing the* Roci *and hoping we could get small enough to overlook.* Only it wasn't true. There was no hiding place in Kronos or anywhere small enough that Laconia wouldn't look there. Plain sight was their best hope, because their plan B was violence.

He didn't think he'd said anything aloud or made any kind of noise that would show his distress, but maybe he had, because Teresa looked at him with something between annoyance and sympathy. "You know I won't let them hurt you."

"I know that you'll try," Jim said.

"I'm still the daughter of the high consul," she said. "I've gotten you out of trouble before."

"I'm not leaning on that trick," Jim said, more harshly than he'd intended. Muskrat shifted, hauled herself up to standing, and looked from Jim to Teresa and back in distress. Teresa's eyes hardened.

"I think what the captain's saying," Amos said, "is that using you as a meat shield isn't something he's a hundred percent comfortable with. It's not that you wouldn't do it, since you already did. But the people on the other end of that gun? We don't know them, they may not be the most reliable, and the less we have to count on them, the better."

Teresa scowled, but less.

"Yes," Jim said. "That was much more eloquent."

"Sometimes I'm good that way," Amos said, and it might have been a joke or it might not. "You want us to get the ship ready to rabbit? We've got enough reaction mass for a decent burn."

"I thought we needed fuel pellets."

"We do, but we can spend 'em getting out of Kronos, put water on the grocery list, and call it good. Recyclers are really going to be our limiting factor."

The pull of the thought was stronger than gravity. Light the drive, put nose toward the ring gate, and get the hell out before the enemy could get hold of them. Jim intentionally loosened his grip on the bulbs. "Naomi. What do you think?"

A moment of silence, then, "Sorry. I wasn't listening. What was the question?"

"Should we prep the *Roci* for a mad dash out of here? As soon as the *Black Kite*'s fully committed to its burn, we could make a break."

"No," she said, the way he had known she would. "They haven't identified us. If we go too soon, it'll only make them suspicious. Better if we look like bystanders. Alex? Plot an intercept with the *Whiteoak*. It's the big ice hauler at the second gas giant."

"Got her," Alex said.

Amos shifted on his bench. "Captain?"

"I'm fine."

"If we need to run," Naomi said, "we'll run."

We'll always need to run. We'll never get to rest, Jim thought. There didn't seem like any point in saying it.

Chapter Two: Tanaka

Aliana pressed the button on her vaporizer and inhaled deeply. The mist tasted like vanilla and hit her lungs like a soft warm cloud. Nicotine and tetrahydrocannabinol mixed with just a touch of something more exotic. Something that tempered the THC sleepiness with a vivid hyperawareness. The shades in her room were drawn, but the hint of light at the edges shifted the dust into a rainbow of sparks. She moved one leg, and the silk sheet caressed it like a thousand tiny lovers.

Tristan was asleep next to her, his small muscular butt pressed up against her thigh. He snored gently as he slept, punctuated by the occasional twitch and sigh. Aliana knew that she found the noise charming and sweet because she was high and postcoital. The minute his snoring became annoying, Tristan would have overstayed his welcome.

There were, in her experience, two ways to thrive in a rigid, authoritarian regime. The first—the one most people reached for—was to be what power wanted you to be. Mars had wanted loyal soldiers, and they had produced them like they were printing machine parts. She knew, because she was old enough that she'd been one of them. She'd seen her cohort try to strangle or excise from their collective souls anything that wasn't sufficiently Martian, and sometimes they'd managed.

The other mode of survival was to enjoy having secrets. Enjoy the power of seeming to be one thing while being another. And then be good at it. Even when it didn't involve fucking her junior officers, it was a kind of sexual perversion. The thrill of knowing that a wrong word or an unexpected slip could put a bullet in the back of her head was more important to her than the actual sex.

A permissive, open society where she could have done all the same things without fear of consequences would have driven her crazy. She'd loved being part of the Laconian experiment from the beginning because Duarte's vision—first as a capital offense against Mars and then as a permanent engine of danger—fed her kinks. She felt no shame about that. She knew what she was.

"Wake up," she said, pushing her fingers into the young man's back.

"Sleeping," Tristan slurred at her.

"I know. Now wake up." She jabbed him again. She spent ten hours a week boxing and wrestling. When she stiffened her fingers, they were like iron bars.

"God dammit," Tristan said, then rolled over. He gave her a sleepy grin. His tousled blond hair and clean-shaven face with its deep dimples made him look like a cherub in a classical painting. One of Raphael's putti.

Aliana took another hit off the vaporizer and offered it to him. He shook his head. "Why'd you wake me?"

Aliana stretched luxuriously under the soft sheets, her long frame barely contained by the oversized bed. "I'm high. I want to fuck."

Tristan flopped onto his back with an exaggerated sigh. "Allie, I barely have any fluid left in my body."

"Then go get a glass of water, take a salt pill, and get your ass back into my bed."

"Aye, aye, Colonel," Tristan said, laughing.

The laugh ended in a sharp *oof* when she rolled over on top of him and slammed down onto his belly, locking his thighs to the bed with her ankles and feet, and gripping his wrists in her hands. He looked up at her with surprise, then thinking it was sex play, started to struggle. His arms and chest were well formed but soft, more like a healthy teenager's than a man in his twenties. Her arms were thin and ropy, the muscles of a long-distance runner, burned down to their essence through constant hard use, and strong as steel springs. When he tried to move, she easily shoved him back down, squeezing her hands until his wrists popped and he squealed.

"Allie, you're—" he started, but she squeezed again and he shut up. She was angry, and he saw it. She liked that she was angry. She liked that he saw it.

"In this room, I am Aliana. You are Tristan," she said, speaking slowly, making sure the drugs weren't slurring her words. "Outside that door, you are Corporal Reeves, and I am Colonel Tanaka. Those things can never be confused for us."

"I know," Tristan said. "I was just kidding."

"No kidding. No jokes. No slipups. If you make a mistake, if you forget the strict discipline that allows this to exist, I will at minimum be dishonorably discharged."

"I'd never—"

"And you," Aliana continued as if he hadn't spoken, "will not like the version of me that comes calling on you then."

She stared down at him for a moment, waiting until his sudden fear turned into understanding. Then she let go of his wrists and climbed off of him, lying back down on her side of the bed.

"Get me some water too, would you?" she said.

Tristan didn't answer, just got up and left the room. Aliana watched him go, enjoying the clenching of his thighs and ass as he walked, the gentle V of his back and shoulders. He was very,

very pretty. When the thing they had inevitably ended, she was going to miss him. But that didn't change the fact that it would end. They always had before. That was part of the joy.

A few moments later, Tristan returned carrying two glasses of water. He paused at the foot of the bed, looking unsure. Aliana patted the sheets next to her.

"I'm sorry if I hurt you," she said.

"It's okay," he replied, then handed her a glass and sat down next to her. "I'm sorry I slipped up. Still want to fuck?"

"In a minute," she said. They both gulped water for a while.

"Will I see you again?" he eventually asked. Aliana found herself gratified by the hopefulness in his voice.

"I should be on Laconia for a while this time," she replied. "And I do want to see you again. We just have to be careful."

"I understand," he said. And she knew he did. She liked her toys to be much younger and much lower rank. It kept things simpler that way. But she didn't waste her time with stupid men.

Her thirst gone, the warmth in her lungs was spreading down to her belly in a very pleasant way. She reached over and put her hand on Tristan's thigh. "I think we should—"

The handheld on her nightstand chimed. She'd set it to do-not-disturb, which meant the device thought the incoming call was important enough to ignore that. She'd had it a long time and trained it well, so it was probably right. She lifted it to check the connection request. It was coming from the State Building. She accepted the connection without visual. "Colonel Tanaka here." Tristan slid out of bed and reached for his pants.

"Good afternoon, Colonel. This is Lieutenant Sanchez with scheduling and logistics. You have a debriefing at the State Building in two hours."

"First I've heard of it," she said, reaching for the side table and her sobriety meds. "Can you tell me the agenda?"

"I'm sorry, Colonel. I don't have access to that. You were added to the attendees by Admiral Milan."

The party was over.

When she reached the State Building, a light rain was falling. Tiny droplets turned the paving dark and shiny at the same time. The low mountain at the edge of the grounds looked like something from an ancient ukiyo-e print. Yoshitoshi or Hiroshige. An attaché from the Science Directorate was waiting to meet her with a cup of coffee and an umbrella. She waved both away.

Tanaka knew her way around the State Building. Most of her assignments were in the field, but she'd made enough friends and professional connections in the highest ranks of power that when she was on Laconia, she was often here. She hadn't been back since the siege of Laconia, the destruction of the construction platform, and the maybe-kidnapping, maybe-autoemancipation of Teresa Duarte. There weren't any physical changes to the building. The poured concrete was as solid as ever, the cut flowers in the vases as fresh. The guards in their razor-pressed uniforms were as stolid and calm. And everything felt fragile.

The attaché guided her to an office she'd been in before. Yellow walls of domestic wood with the blue seal of Laconia worked into them, and two austere sofas. Admiral Milan—acting commander in chief while the high consul was in seclusion and Admiral Trejo was in Sol system—sat at a wide desk. He was a broad man, with a heavy face and salt-and-pepper hair shaved tight. And a crusty old sailor from the Mars days, impatient with bullshit and quick-tempered as a badger. Tanaka liked him immensely.

At one sofa, a lieutenant with a signal intelligence insignia on the standard Laconian blue naval uniform stood. Beside him, Dr. Ochida of the Science Directorate sat with his hands on his knee, fingers laced together. The silence had the awkwardness of an interruption.

Admiral Milan was the first to speak. "We're running a little long here, Colonel. Have a seat. We'll be done soon."

"Yes, sir," Tanaka said, and took the other sofa for herself. Admiral Milan looked to the standing lieutenant—Rossif, to judge by his nametag—and drew a circle in the air with his finger-tip. *Get on with it.*

"Gedara system. Population just shy of two hundred thousand. High concentration of fissionables in the upper crust, so they've been trying to get deep-crust mining operations going for the last several years. Agriculture exists but it's a decade away from self-sustaining."

"And the incursion?" Admiral Milan said.

"Twenty-three minutes, eleven seconds," Rossif answered. "Total loss of consciousness. Some accidental fatalities, some damage to infrastructure. Mostly people crashing vehicles or falling off of things. And logs show that just seconds before the incursion, two unscheduled heavy freighters passed through the ring and went dutchman."

Dr. Ochida cleared his throat. "There was something strange this time."

"Something stranger than everyone's brain shutting off for twenty minutes?" Admiral Milan said.

"Yes, Admiral," Ochida answered. "A review of instrumentation during the event shows a different kind of time loss as well."

"Explain."

"Short version," Ochida said, "light went faster."

Admiral Milan scratched his neck. "Did the word *explain* change meanings and no one told me?" Tanaka suppressed a smile.

"Simply put, the speed of light is a function of basic properties of the universe. Call it...the fastest causality can propagate in vacuum," Ochida said. "For twenty-some minutes in the Gedara system, the nature of space-time shifted in a way that altered the speed of light. Made it faster. The light delay from the ships at the Gedara ring to the planet at the time was slightly less than forty minutes. Logs of the event show that during the incursion, it decreased by nearly four thousand nanoseconds."

"Four thousand nanoseconds," Milan said.

"The nature of space-time *changed* in that system for twenty minutes," Ochida intoned, then waited for a reaction he wasn't getting. He looked crestfallen.

"Well," Milan said. "I will certainly have to think about this. Thank you for the briefing, Lieutenant. Doctor. You're both dismissed. You stay, Colonel."

"Yes, sir," Tanaka replied.

Once the room was empty, Milan leaned back. "Drink? I've got water, coffee, bourbon, and some herbal tea shit my husbands both drink, tastes like grass clippings."

"Am I on active duty?"

"I don't think you need to concern yourself with breaking protocol, if that's what you mean."

"Then bourbon sounds great, sir," Tanaka replied. Admiral Milan spent a minute fussing at his desk, then came back with a cut crystal glass and two fingers of smoky brown liquid swirling in it.

"To your health," Tanaka said, then took a sip.

"So," Milan said, and sat with the unconscious grunt of an old man with a lot of bad joints. "What do you think that lightspeed shit means?"

"Not a clue, sir. I'm a shooter, not an egghead."

"This is why I've always liked you," he said, then sat back in his chair, steepling his fingers. The silence was different this time, and she wasn't certain what it meant. "So just between the two of us—one old sailor to another—is there anything you want to tell me?"

She felt the adrenaline hit her bloodstream. She didn't let it show. She was too practiced at deception for that. "I don't know what you mean."

He tilted his head and sighed. "I don't either. I find this whole thing pretty fucking mysterious. And I'm not as good at swallowing my curiosity as I was when we were young."

"Still genuinely unclear what we're talking about. Was someone supposed to tell me why you wanted me here?"

"It wasn't me that wanted you. Trejo made the request, and he had me do a little paperwork on your behalf." He pulled out a physical folder of red paper with a silver string to close it, and handed it to her. It seemed so out of place, it was like being handed a stone tablet. She drank the rest of her bourbon off in one shot before she took it. It was lighter than she expected, and the string came undone easily. Inside was a single sheet of three-layer security parchment, the document verification circuits crisp as lace. Her picture was on it and her biometric profile, her name and rank and identification record numbers. And a short passage granting her Omega status from the Laconian Intelligence Directorate at the personal request of the High Consul's Office.

If it had been a severed head, she wouldn't have been more surprised.

"Is this..." she began.

"Not a joke. Admiral Trejo has instructed that you be given the keys to the kingdom. Override authority on any mission. Access to any information, regardless of security classification. Immunity from censure or prosecution for the duration of your deployment. Pretty sweet. You really telling me you don't know what it's about?"

"I assume there's a mission?"

"Probably, but I'm not cleared to know what it is. You just keep your seat. I can show myself out."

When Admiral Milan closed the door behind him, the office system threw a comm message on the wall screen. After a moment, Admiral Trejo appeared. She'd known him for as long as she'd known anyone living. His eyes were still the same uncanny green, but now there were dark bags under them. His hair was thinning and his skin had an unhealthy waxy shine. He looked haunted.

"Colonel Tanaka," he said. "I'm reaching out to you with a critical mission for the empire. At present, I am taking a break from a hard burn from Sol system, and if this could wait until I arrived on Laconia, I'd brief you in person. It can't, so this will have to do."

She stared into her bourbon glass. It was empty, and the bottle sat just a meter away, but suddenly she didn't want it anymore. She felt her attention sharpening.

"I'm sure that you, like everyone else in the empire, are wondering what exactly the high consul has been doing in seclusion. How he has been spearheading the fight against the forces that are threatening us from within the gates. I know there's been some speculation that he was somehow injured or incapacitated. So, candidly, I need you to know that when I left for Sol system, the high consul was a drooling, brain-damaged moron who couldn't feed himself or wipe his own ass. He has been that way since the attack that destroyed the *Typhoon* and Medina Station."

Tanaka took a deep breath and let it out through her teeth.

"Dr. Cortázar had altered the high consul's biology considerably by using modified protomolecule technologies. It left the high consul in possession of certain…abilities that were not fully documented or explored before Dr. Cortázar's death. And in fact, Duarte killed him. Waved his hand and splattered that crazy fucker across half a room. I've never seen anything like it. Right now, the only people who know this are you, me, Dr. Okoye of the Science Directorate, and Teresa Duarte, who ran away with the underground's assault forces after they cleaned our clock. So, pretty much the whole fucking enemy.

"Given that for background, you'll understand how confused I was when the high consul appeared to me eighty…eighty-five hours ago in my office in Sol system. He didn't register on the sensors. He didn't interact with any physical object or leave any evidence of his presence that could be verified by an outside observer. But he was here. And before you get too happy with the Anton-Trejo's-having-a-psychotic-break theory, there is some external evidence. Just not here in Sol.

"Shortly after I experienced what I experienced, Duarte disappeared from the State Building. Not popped-out-of-reality disappeared. He put on his pants and a fresh shirt, had a cup of tea and a polite conversation with his valet, then walked off the grounds. Every planetary sensor we have has been sweeping the landscape since then. No one has seen him.

"We've got over a thousand colony systems that are wondering if there's anything left of the government. We have extradimensional enemies experimenting to find ways to snuff us out wholesale. And I am convinced that the answer to both of those issues is Winston Duarte, or whatever the fuck he's turned into. I've known you for a long time, and I trust you. Your mission is to find him and bring him back. You've heard of carte blanche, but I promise you have never seen a check this blank. I don't care what you spend—not in money, equipment, or lives—as long as you bring Winston Duarte back from wherever he's gone. If he doesn't want to come, convince him nicely if you can, but this only ends with him in our custody.

"Good hunting, Colonel."

The message ended. Tanaka leaned back on the sofa, stretching her arms to her sides like a bird unfurling its wings. Her mind was already ticking away. The strangeness of it, the shocking revelations, the threat it posed. All of those were in her. She could feel them. But there was also the calm of a job that needed doing and the pleasure, deeper than she would have guessed, at the power she had just been given.

The door opened quietly, and Admiral Milan came back in.

"Everything all right?" he asked.

Tanaka laughed. "Not even close."

Chapter Three: Naomi

They waited until the *Black Kite* was far enough from the ring gate that an intercept burn would have been difficult if not impossible. Then they waited a little more so that they wouldn't seem suspicious for starting their transit burn at the first possible moment. And then Naomi couldn't stand waiting anymore.

Three hours after that, the Laconian frigate hit them with a tightbeam demanding in official language and harsh tones of voice who they were and where they thought they were going.

"This is the *Vincent Soo*, independent freighter on contract with Atmosphäre Shared Liability Corporation out of Earth. We are carrying ore samples for quality control testing. Our public contracts and permissions are attached. Message repeats."

The voice was built from samples of ten different men, slip-mixed by the *Roci*'s system so that even if the Laconians realized the message was false, they wouldn't be able to track the voice patterns back to anyone. The *Vincent Soo* was a real ship with a similar drive signature and silhouette to their present modified version of the *Roci*, though it didn't work outside Sol system. The contracts the message included would come back as real unless someone started digging into them. It was as plausible a mask as Naomi could fashion.

"They aren't responding," Alex said.

They were both on the ops deck. The lighting was low, though she noticed that Alex had started keeping even the low settings a little higher than he had when they'd both had younger eyes.

"Could be good, could be bad," Naomi said.

"Sure wish I could tell which it was."

"If they start chasing us with their guns blazing, then it was bad."

Alex nodded. "Yeah. That makes sense. I just wish they'd say 'Hey, we decided not to chase you down and kill you.' Just out of courtesy."

"At this range, we'll have plenty of time to watch violent death barrel down on us. You won't miss anything."

"Well, thank God for that."

With every minute the *Black Kite* didn't answer and didn't turn its drives in pursuit, Naomi felt the fear of capture or destruction fade, and the fear of transit grow. It was hard to believe that there had been a time when her life hadn't been moving from one trauma to the next like walking on stepping-stones in an ornamental garden. There had been whole decades when passing through the ring gates hadn't been more than a passing unease. Yes, if there was too much traffic, the ship could go dutchman— quietly vanish from existence for who-knew-where or no place. But it had been the same scale of threat as anything. They could hit a micrometeor that broke their drive. The magnetic bottle could fail and spill a free fusion reaction into the body of the ship. She could have a stroke.

Once, there had been rules about how the gates worked.

Human rules about what traffic was allowed through. Inhuman rules about how much matter and energy could pass through in a certain period of time without angering the dark, ship-eating gods.

All of that was gone now.

"How many ships you think they have looking for us?" Alex asked.

"You mean how many ships do they own, or how many are in the specific hunt group tasked with trying to find us?"

Alex was silent, then made a soft clicking sound with his tongue. "Probably wouldn't like either answer, would I?"

"How long until we reach the gate?"

"If we don't brake before the transit, about eighteen hours."

Naomi unstrapped from her crash couch and stood up. The deck rose up under her, thrust gravity at just over half a g. "I'm going to get some rest. Call me if someone decides to kill us."

"Will do," Alex said as she headed for the lift. And then, "How's Jim?"

Naomi looked back. Alex's face was tinted blue by the light of his screen. The thin white stubble of hair clinging to the side and back of his head reminded her of pictures of snow on rich soil, and the gentleness in his eyes told her the question hadn't really been a question.

"Yeah, I know," she said. "But what can I do?"

She made her way down to the crew decks, listening to the reassuring hum of the ship around her. After so many years in close company with the *Roci*, she could judge the health of the ship by its sounds. Even if she hadn't known already that they were running the drive just a little out of balance, she'd have been able to pick up on it from the way the decks muttered and creaked.

When Jim had been taken prisoner by Laconia, Naomi had mourned him. Mourned the version of herself that had him at her side. When, against all odds, he'd come back, she hadn't really been ready. It was something she hadn't let herself hope for, and so she hadn't thought deeply about how it would be.

The crash couch was rigged up for the two of them to share. For extended hard burns, one or the other of them might take one of the spare cabins or—more often—a couch on the ops deck. The doubled couch wasn't built for optimum function so much as quality of life. The pleasure of waking up at someone's side. The intimacy of watching them sleep, feeling them breathe. Knowing on a cellular level that she wasn't alone.

Jim was sleeping when she came into the room. He still looked thinner than she remembered him being before his time in prison. Before her time in self-exile. It might only have been the graying of his hair, but the skin of his eyelids seemed darker than it had been before, as though he'd been bruised in a way that wouldn't heal. Even in sleep, there was a rigidity to his body, like he was braced against an attack.

She told herself that he was recovering, and that was probably true. She could feel the passing days and weeks changing her too. Letting her expand a little bit more into a place she hadn't had access to when they had all been apart. It was different than it had been. Bobbie was gone. Clarissa was gone. Amos was transformed in ways that made her skin crawl if she let herself think about it too much. And Teresa and her dog were there, half permanent passengers and half threat. Even so, this was closer to the life she'd had than she had any right to expect. A version of her family, back together. Sometimes that was a comfort. Sometimes it was just a way to be nostalgic for what hadn't returned.

If they could stop, recover, decompress, who knows what else they might have been able to salvage, but they couldn't.

She lay down beside him, her head pillowed on one folded arm. Jim shifted, yawned, cracked open one eye. His smile was the same—boyish, bright, delighted to see her. *This time is a gift*, she thought. And she smiled back.

"Hey, sexy lady," Jim said. "What did I miss?"

Years, she thought. *We missed years.* Instead of the truth, she smiled.

"Nothing critical," she said.

"I really want to slow us down," Alex said.

Naomi, in the galley, was putting the remains of her meal into the recycler. They had cut thrust, and the whir of the vacuum sucking the stray bits of food into the system was almost as loud as Alex's voice over the comms. On the wall screen, the Kronos ring gate hung against a wide field of stars, the weird dark, twisting mass at its perimeter visible only because of the *Roci*'s enhancements. With each passing second, the magnification dropped. The ring was a thousand klicks across, their transit was counting down from twelve minutes, and it still would have been invisible to the naked eye.

"You can tap the brakes if you want to," Naomi said. "But if there's unfriendly company in the ring space, it'll just make us easier to hit."

"I want to charge up the rail gun," Alex said. "But you won't let me, so I'm sublimating."

"You could recheck the torpedoes and PDCs."

"Amos and Teresa are doing that already. I don't want to seem like I don't trust them."

"You could arm the hull charges and be ready to blow the disguise plates off."

Alex was silent for a long, slow breath. Across the little room, Jim gave her an approving thumbs-up.

"Yeah, I'll do that," Alex said. "Really want my rail gun up, though."

"When we're on the other side, you can charge it to your heart's content," Naomi said.

"Promises, promises." A click said that Alex had dropped the connection. The magnification on the ring gate continued its slow fall. Naomi called up a little inset window pointing back. The noise from their drive cone made the image blurry, grainy, and approximate, but even so, she could see that the *Black Kite* wasn't moving toward them.

"I'm not seeing a repeater," Jim said. "They blew ours up, but it doesn't look like they dropped one."

"I noticed that. They aren't worried about coordinating with anyone on the other side. So there's at least a chance we aren't burning straight into a trap."

"Yay!"

Ten minutes remained.

"Ready?" Naomi asked. In answer, Jim pulled himself to a wall handhold and pushed off toward the central lift. Naomi opened a connection to Amos. "We're taking stations on the ops deck. Not that we're expecting any trouble, but if there is some..."

"I hear you, Boss. I've already got the pup in her kennel. In case we bang around a little."

Bang around a little meaning *evade incoming fire*. "And Teresa?"

There was one of his odd pauses before he answered. "We're strapping down in engineering. You have a need, just say the word."

Naomi dropped the connection and followed Jim. The lift was at the bottom of the shaft, locked down until someone called it, and they swam through the empty air of its shaft until they reached ops. They went to their usual stations, pulled the straps across their bodies, shifted the screens to the controls they would each take if the transit landed them in danger. The combination of fear and familiarity turned it into a ritual, like brushing her teeth before sleep. The ring persisted, but the lensing of the telescopy put fewer stars around it now.

"Ready in ops," Naomi said.

"Flight deck," Alex said.

"Yeah," Amos said. "We're good. Do your thing."

The counter reached zero. Jim took a sharp breath. The gate blinked to the grainy trailing image—the same structure, but behind them now and receding. The stars all went out at once.

"And we are through," Alex said. "No threats on the board so far as I can see, but shit howdy, are there too many people in here. I'm flipping us around and putting the brakes on until we know where we're headed."

The thrust gravity warning went on even though he'd just said it, and after a moment of vertiginous rotation, up and down returned. The gel of the couch pressed into Naomi's back. She had already brought up the tactical map.

The ring space—what she still thought of as the slow zone even though there hadn't been the hard limit on velocity here since Jim and a protomolecular echo of Detective Miller had turned it off decades ago—was a little smaller than the sun in Sol system. A million Earths could have fit in it, but the only things it contained now were 1,371 ring gates, the single enigmatic station at its center, and fifty-two ships including the *Roci*, all of them on transits of their own. Alex was right. It was too many. It was dangerous.

"How many do you think we've lost?" Jim asked. When she looked over, he had the same screen open before him.

"Just underground ships?"

"No, I mean the big we. Everyone. Laconian. Underground. Civilians just trying to get supplies where they're needed. How many do you think we've lost?"

"No way to know," she said. "No one's keeping track anymore. There's a war on."

She set the *Roci* to identify the ships by transponder, drive signature, thermal profile, and silhouette, to note any discrepancies and flag any ships that were known to be associated with the underground or the Laconian Empire. It took the ship system three seconds to produce a compiled list with cross notations and a navigable interface. Naomi started the human work of paging through. The ships most closely allied with Laconia were a freighter called *Eight Tenets of Bushido* that operated out of Bara Gaon and a long-range explorer called the *Flying Buffalo* that was based in Sol but owned by a corporate network that had embraced Duarte's rule the moment Earth and Mars had surrendered. Neither were warships, and both struck Naomi as being allies of convenience more than true believers in the Laconian cause. They weren't part of the official Laconian hierarchy, anyway.

The only ship on her known underground contacts was an

independent rock hopper out of Sol that was flying as the *Caustic Bitch* but was listed in the registry as *PinkWink*. There was probably a story there, but Naomi wasn't sure she wanted to know what it was.

There was also a bottle on the float.

"One of yours?" Jim asked.

"Hope so," Naomi said. "We'll see."

Once, humanity's comm network had been a fairly robust thing. In-system radio signals hit repeaters at the ring gates that were either strong enough to shout over the interference in the gates or actually physically penetrated them with transceivers on both sides. Medina Station, at the heart of the ring space, had maintained them and monitored the comm traffic. For decades, a message from Earth could reach Bara Gaon and receive an answer back within a day even if the signal queuing was swamped. But with the death of Medina and the rise of the underground, that was gone.

Now the thirteen hundred worlds communicated in a shifting patchwork of relays, ships carrying messages, and the modified torpedoes she called bottles. This one in particular was an advanced design, set to wait and gather incoming messages from the underground that were meant for her and keep them until it was triggered. It was an imperfect system, and she was certain she'd lost more than a few along the way, but it was easy to verify, difficult to fake, and difficult if not impossible to trace.

She pulled up the Epstein drive controls and dropped in a slightly altered feed pattern. To anyone besides the bottle, it would be unremarkable—well within the range of normal drive fluctuations. To the sensor array on the surface of the bottle, it would match a pattern.

It did.

The bottle shouted a dense blip of tightly packed data, putting it out broadcast for any ship in the slow zone to hear. A tight-beam would have pointed a finger if anyone had caught backscatter from it. This could be meant for any of the dozens of ships that could hear it. And every now and then, the underground set false bottles to sneak into the slow zone or a gate to spit out faked data and confuse the patterns.

The *Roci*'s system sucked in the radio burst and set quietly to work decrypting it, while at the edge of the ring space the bottle lit its own drive and zipped out through one of the gates. Naomi's underground knew to watch for its detonation as the sign to place another one when they could. If the Laconians saw it—even if they knew what it meant—there still wasn't anything for them to do about it.

It was all run like an OPA cell writ large, and Naomi was the one who'd designed it. The sins of her past, finding a use.

"Well, that could have gone a lot worse," Jim said. "I guess the question now is where we go next."

"That will depend on what's in the data," Naomi said. "I don't like spending more time in the ring space than we have to."

"I would also hate to be eaten by forces from beyond space and time before it was my turn." The lightness and humor she'd always known were still there, but there was an emptiness behind it. Not nihilism, she thought. Exhaustion.

"If we need to," she began, "there's always—"

Teresa's voice cut in on the ship-wide comms. "I need help. In the machine shop. I need help now."

Jim was unstrapped before the girl had finished speaking. All the weariness was gone from him. He didn't wait for the lift to engage, dropping down the handholds in the shaft like climbing down a ladder. Naomi was barely behind him. Some part of her was almost relieved to see him moving with certainty again. Like catching a glimpse of the Jim from before. Even if a lot of him was in hiding, he was still in there.

"What's going on?" Alex asked from the flight deck.

"Something's happening to Amos," Teresa said. She had the tense calm of an emergency responder.

"We're on our way," Naomi said. Jim didn't respond at all. When they reached the engineering deck, Naomi heard something.

A voice, Amos' voice, but not with words in it. It was a low wet sound, half growl, half gargle. Something about it reminded her of drowning. She and Jim strode down to the machine shop together.

Teresa was sitting on the deck, her legs crossed and cradling Amos' wide, bald head in her lap as he jerked and shuddered. A pale foam dripped from his mouth, and the pure black eyes were wide and empty. A sickening smell—as much metallic as organic—filled the air.

"He's having a seizure," Jim said.

Teresa's voice trembled when she spoke. "Why? Why is this happening?"

Chapter Four: Elvi

Get her out," Elvi said. "I'm pulling the plug."

"No," Cara replied. The girl's voice was still shaking, but the words were clear. "I can do this."

Cara's brain function showed in seven different datasets on twice that many screens. The data from the BFE—the technicians' pet name for the Jupiter-sized block of green crystal that was the only feature of Adro system—showed beside it. Advanced pattern-matching protocols mapped the two together in six dimensions. The instability had passed in both datasets, the seizure—if that's what it was—falling back from turbulence to a more stable flow.

All around the lab, the researchers and techs turned wide and uncertain eyes toward Elvi. She could feel the desire to keep pushing forward from her whole staff. She felt it herself. It reminded her of being the RA in her graduate dorm house and having to shut down the hall parties.

"I am the lead researcher. She is the test subject. When I say we're pulling the plug, we're pulling the plug." As her team sprang to life, closing down the experiment, she turned to Cara, who was floating over the bed of imaging sensors. "Sorry. It's not that I don't trust you. It's that I don't trust any of this."

The girl with the pure black eyes nodded, but her attention was on something else. Cara's visual and audial cortices were lit up like Paris at New Year's, and a deep, slow pulse was passing through the girl's postcentral gyrus that matched the energy readings coming from the BFE's southern hemisphere. Whatever Cara was feeling just then, it was taking up more of her attention than Elvi was. She had the sense that she could scream in Cara's ear right now and still be a tiny minority of the information flooding the girl's brain.

Or for that matter the girl's body, which was part of the issue. Elvi had studied somatic cognition theory, but the degree to which the BFE seemed to want to present its information to Cara's whole nervous system—muscles and viscera included—was complicating things. She spooled back through the data as her team ran the shutdown procedures and brought Cara back to merely human reality.

The *Falcon*, Elvi's private and state-sponsored science ship, was the most advanced single-function laboratory in thirteen hundred worlds. Which sounded really impressive until she remembered that most of those thirteen hundred worlds were the equivalent of 1880s European dirt farmers trying to grow enough food to not slaughter half their cattle at the start of every winter. The *Falcon* was the only ship that had survived the attack that killed the *Typhoon* and Medina Station, and the scars showed everywhere. The decking was subtly mismatched where threads of darkness that had been somehow more real than reality had ripped a third of the ship's mass away. The power and environmental systems were all patchworks of the original and rebuilt. Her own leg had a line across it where the new skin and muscle had grown in the softball-sized scoop that had vanished in the attack. Working on the *Falcon* was like living inside a trauma flashback. It helped Elvi when she could focus on the data, and on the BFE, and on Cara and Xan.

Dr. Harshaan Lee, Elvi's second lead, met her eye and nodded. He was an energetic young scientist, and she liked him. More than that, she trusted him. He knew what she wanted to do, and with a gesture, he'd offered to make sure Cara's re-emergence from the experiment went according to protocol. She nodded back, accepting the offer.

"All right, people," Lee said, clapping his hands together. "By the numbers and by the book."

Elvi pulled herself through the air to the lift shaft, and aft toward the engine and the isolation chamber and Cara's younger brother Xan.

Fayez floated against one wall, his left leg tucked behind a wall grip and his hand terminal glowing with text. Beside him, the thing they called the catalyst—the body of a woman infused with a contained but live sample of protomolecule—was strapped in its gurney. The catalyst's sightless eyes found her, and Fayez followed its empty gaze.

"How'd he do?" Elvi asked, nodding toward the containment chamber and therefore Xan. Most of the time, the catalyst was stored there, but for the periods when they used it to activate the old, alien technologies, she put Xan in its place. The only time the young boy and the protomolecule interacted at all was during the changeover.

Fayez pulled up a screen with the security camera. Inside the isolation chamber, Xan floated. His eyes were closed and his mouth was just slightly open, like he was sleeping or drowned.

"Listened to some music, read a few issues of *Naka and Corvalis*, and went to sleep," Fayez said. "For all the world like the preadolescent boy he appears to be."

Elvi pulled herself to a stop at her husband's side. The data on his hand terminal was the feed from the lab laid side by side with the monitors trained on Xan. She could tell at a glance that there wasn't a correlation between them. Whatever Cara was going through, Xan wasn't being subjected to it along with her. Or at least not obviously. She'd still feed everything through pattern matching.

She wasn't conscious of sighing, but Fayez touched her arm as if she had.

"You heard about Gedara system?"

She nodded. "Lightspeed change. Dark gods banging around in the attic. Feels like that's happening more often."

"We'll need more data points for a good frequency analysis," he said. "But yeah. It does. I hate the feeling that something vast and angry is scratching at the corners of reality and looking for a way to kill me."

"It's only scary because it's true."

He ran a hand through his hair. He'd gone silver, and when they were on the float, he tended to look like something out of a children's cartoon. Elvi's hair was well on its way to white, but she kept it short. Mostly because she hated the compression fluid in the high-g crash couches, and it took forever to get the smell of it out of longer hair.

"You shut down early?"

"There was some instability when she synced up with the BFE."

Now it was Fayez's turn to sigh. "I wish they didn't call it that. It's a *diamond*, not an emerald."

"I know. Sorry."

"And anyway, BFD's funnier," he said, but there wasn't any heat to it. Their marriage was a vast tissue of in-jokes, light comic bits, shared curiosity, and common trauma. They'd built it like a code between them over the course of decades. She knew the inflections that meant he had something that was interesting him, and how it sounded different from when he was angry about something. When he was trying to protect her and when he was struggling with something he was seeing but couldn't understand.

"What's on your mind?" she asked.

"You didn't notice the sync?"

"What sync?"

Fayez pulled up the dataset again. On one side, the brain and body of a teenage girl fixed at the age when she'd died and been "repaired" by alien technology. On the other, the particle scatter and magnetic resonances of a vast crystal that—if they were lucky—held the history of a galaxy-spanning species whose tracks they were following toward extinction. She could trace the similarities with her fingers. Fayez lifted his eyebrows, waiting for her to notice something. She shook her head. He pointed to a tiny indicator on the side of the readout: IN-FRAME LIGHT DELAY CORRECTION OFFSET: -.985S.

She frowned.

"We're point nine-eight-five light seconds from the diamond," Fayez said. "Matching orbit around the star, neither moving toward nor away from it. The last times we tried this, Cara and the diamond were talking back and forth. Call and response. Now they're singing in harmony. No light delay."

Elvi felt the implications running through her mind like water spilling down a creek. They'd always known that the protomolecule was able to do strange things with locality, but they'd thought it was related to quantum entanglement of particles. Cara and the BFE hadn't exchanged any particles that she knew of, so this pseudo-instantaneous information transfer was something new. One of the fundamental hypotheses of protomolecule technology had just taken a profound hit.

It also meant that their reaching out to the artifact had gotten it to reach back. Her experiment was working.

She'd expected success to feel less like fear.

When Elvi had started working for the Laconian Empire, it had been under duress. Winston Duarte had taken over all humanity with the speed and thoroughness of a plague. When he'd invited her to a senior position in his Science Directorate, the answer was yes. It would have been a dream job, except for the consequences of refusing it.

Then Duarte's plan to confront the forces that killed off the civilizations that built the ring gates went wrong. Duarte was crippled by it. And Elvi's immediate boss, Paolo Cortázar, was reduced to a thin, heme-stinking mist. Elvi, who'd wanted the job but not the employer, found herself receiving a field promotion to the head of the Laconian Science Directorate with the understanding that her primary task was to figure out how to stop the attacks that were knocking out consciousness, sometimes in single systems, sometimes all through the empire. Unless her primary task was to find a way to fix Duarte's scrambled mind. Or maybe to prevent any more ships from vanishing in the transit between the normal universe and the weird nexus of the ring space.

She had the nearly infinite resources of the empire behind her, the survival of humanity on her shoulders, and a research protocol so streamlined it would have failed out of an ethics review board from just the table of contents.

There were two levels that she had to figure out. First was the civilization that had built the protomolecule and the gates, then the forces that destroyed them. On her best days, she'd thought of herself like a medieval monk struggling to understand the saints to better see the face of God. More often, she felt like a termite trying to explain dogs to her fellow Isoptera so that they could all speculate about fusion jazz.

She understood the protomolecule engineers and what had killed them better than anyone else in all of humanity. Except, if this worked, for Cara. And Xan.

"It was like being in a dream," Cara said, "only bigger. I don't remember really tasting things in dreams, you know? This was tasting things and hearing things, and the shape of my body seemed like it was changing. It was...everything."

"I didn't feel anything," Xan said. He sounded disappointed.

Originally, Elvi had done the debriefings with the two siblings separately, talking first to Cara and then to Xan. The idea being that by keeping them from hearing each other's accounts she could keep them from influencing those reports, but it stressed both of them to be apart.

Now, she brought them into her private lab together, the two of them on the float while she braced herself at her desk and wrote up her notes. The décor was rich psychiatrist's office: blond grass-colored padding on the walls, spider plants in capillary-fed niches, the low pulse of a dedicated air recycler. Everything about it was designed to say that the woman who used it was a very important person. She hated it more than a little, but she didn't spend the energy to examine why.

"Was it different from the last time?" Elvi asked.

"There was a…stutter? Like a moment when everything fell apart, and when it came back together, everything was brighter and more immediate? That's not the right word. There may not be a right word."

"How did it compare to your experience of 'the library'?" Elvi asked.

Cara went eerily still for a moment, the way she and Xan did sometimes. Elvi waited for a breath, and then Cara came back. "The library isn't sensory at all. It's just knowing things. But this? It isn't the library, but it's where the information all comes from. I'm sure about that."

Xan made a soft noise. Cara put a hand on his arm and pulled him close to her. A primate's instinct to comfort by cuddling unchanged by its translation across light-years of vacuum into a bubble of ceramic, steel, and carbon lace.

"Were you able to interact with it at all?"

"I think so," Cara said. "I mean, I didn't understand what I was doing, but I think I can figure it out. I feel fine. I'm ready to go back in."

Elvi typed SUBJECT SHOWS STRONG DESIRE TO RETURN TO INTERFACE CONSISTENT WITH DROP IN DOPAMINE AND SERO-TONIN LEVELS POST-EXPERIMENT. ADDICTIVE?

"That's good," she said out loud. "There are a couple recalibrations we need to make, but we should be ready for another run in a couple shifts. And I'm going to want to run a scan or two while we're doing that. Check your baseline."

"Okay," Cara said, almost hiding her impatience. "Whatever you want."

Xan fidgeted against his sister's arm, setting both of them turning a little. "I'm hungry."

"Go ahead," Elvi said. "I need to write this up, but you two should eat and rest. I'll be along in a little bit."

Cara nodded once, gathered Xan close to her. "Thank you, Doctor." She pushed off Elvi's desk with one long, graceful leg. The children—or test subjects, or human-alien hybrids, or however Elvi thought of them in the moment—closed the door behind them. Elvi pressed her palms against her eyes until colors bloomed, and she let out a sigh. Her body was rattling with exhaustion and excitement and anxiety. It felt like drinking too much coffee, and she hadn't had any at all.

She wrote down the rest of her observations of Cara and Xan and attached the raw data to the report. Then it was just her summary still to go. She shifted the interface to Dictation and let herself float away from her desk. Her leg wanted her to stretch, but it also wanted to cramp. Ever since she'd regrown the hole in her thigh, it did this sometimes.

"We are seeing definite progress," she said, and the words laid themselves out on her screen. "The triadic relationship between protomolecule catalyst, conscious subject, and the BFE—" Elvi scowled and made a clicking sound with her tongue that backed out the last two words. "—the presumed alien data core seems to be finishing what we're calling its handshake protocol. I am concerned that the primary subject and the interface weren't designed for each other, and the interaction between them might be—" She clicked twice again. "—has the potential to be destructive to one or both of them."

Her office door opened, and Fayez floated in. She raised a hand, asking for silence, as he stopped himself on a handhold. She waited for the door to close before she went on.

"The next phase will be trying to confirm information we already have. Specifically, I'm going to ask the subject a set of simple questions about details from the research into artifacts and archaeology from several systems that she wouldn't plausibly have had access to. If she can confirm information we already have, that will let us move forward with some confidence that what we get from her further on will be trustworthy. But since she was present in Cortázar's private lab, and we don't know what his information hygiene was with the subjects, I'm having to be very careful in choosing test questions.

"Neither subject seems to have been affected by the events in Gedara system. The staff here, myself included, haven't had any blackouts or losses of consciousness since the all-systems attack months ago. Without knowing what constraints the enemy is working under, I can interpret the limited scope of the Gedara attack as an indication that it is still in an experimental phase, looking for interactions that will be effective in disabling us. Or that the new attacks required more effort, and the enemy doesn't want to expand them. Or that we just don't have enough information yet to know what we're seeing and I'm just talking out my ass."

She clicked her tongue to delete the sarcastic editorial at the end, and then finished the report. She started spooling through the text to look for errors and typos. Fayez shifted over to her side, watching the screen over her shoulder.

"You didn't say, 'And if we don't get a handle on it soon, the bad guys will figure out how to snuff out all our minds like so many billions of candles, and the cockroaches will have to evolve enough to take over before we get an answer.' "

"Ants, I think, before the cockroaches," Elvi said. "Predatory superorganisms. Cockroaches are just mobile food pods to them."

"You've given this a lot of thought."

She routed copies of the report to Dr. Ochida at the Science Directorate back on Laconia and privately to Admiral Anton Trejo, who was at the moment the closest thing Laconia had to a controlling intelligence for their own predatory superorganism.

Somewhere on the *Falcon*, a tightbeam stuttered on and off, spilling light to the repeaters they'd dropped behind them on the assumption that they were still up and functioning. At the speed of light, it would take the information almost an hour to reach the ring gate, then across the cobbled-together, war-ravaged, unreliable communications network that laced the ring space, and then she didn't know how long to reach Trejo.

She packaged another copy of the report, flagged for easy interception by the underground and addressed to Naomi Nagata. She sent it too.

"That's going to get us in trouble someday," Fayez said.

"We're already in trouble."

"Yeah, but it's cosmic-forces-beyond-space-and-time-kill-us-all trouble. Feeding all our data to the underground is ship-security-shoots-us-for-treason trouble."

Elvi laughed, but it was a tight, angry laugh. "What we're doing here is bigger than politics."

"I know," he said. "I just keep hoping the politicians see it too."

As if in response, her system chimed. A high-priority message from Laconia. Elvi's eyes only.

"That's fucking eerie," Fayez said. "You want privacy?"

"No," she said. "But I'd better take it anyway."

The door closed behind him, and she started the playback. Kelly, Winston Duarte's personal valet, leaned in toward the camera. His lips were thin and gray. Whatever it was, it looked like bad news.

"Dr. Okoye. I have been authorized by Admiral Trejo to brief you on a security matter that may touch on your work. There's been a change in High Consul Duarte's status..."

Chapter Five: Tanaka

The Laconian Mechanized Infantry Suit: Special Reconnaissance, or more affectionately the Stalker, was a marvel of design. Built for extended recon, it was lighter and faster than the standard suit, and instead of bristling with weaponry, it was covered with sensors and tracking systems. It wasn't meant for front-line fighting. Its job was to slip in, spot the enemy and mark the targets, then slip away before the heavily armed shock troops arrived to take care of business. The small-caliber rapid-fire Gatling gun on the suit's right arm meant a Stalker could still handle a little business of its own, should the need arise.

In her many decades of service, first in the Martian Marine Corps as a member of the elite Force Recon Battalion at Hecate Base, and later as a combat officer in the newly created Laconian Marines, Tanaka had worn just about every model of power armor made. The Stalker suit was her favorite. Long and lean, fast as a greyhound and tough as nails, she'd always fancied that the suit looked like a robotic version of herself.

The one she wore now was currently a gentle mottled green, the color-shifting surface changing to match the rolling forest and Laconian brush that the suit's three-sixty optics were picking up. It didn't make her invisible, but it meant the suit's camouflage was always appropriate for the environment. Two large battery packs rode on the back, giving her a ninety-hour range. The gun was loaded with a belt of mixed armor-piercing and high explosive. She loped through the forest at an easily sustainable twenty kilometers an hour, scattering the small animals before her. There was no reason to move cautiously. Unless she actually found the high consul out there, nothing in the wilds was a threat to her.

She'd started her work by reviewing some of the files and background previously closed to her.

Actual information about the high consul's personal life and data was thin, even with Omega status to unlock files for her. His medical records were sketchy and vague. Much of his privacy had been preserved over the years by never recording data in the first place. Everyone else on Laconia, on the other hand, was well documented. She'd taken the high consul's laundry and locked it in a room with her suit's sensor package while she prepped for the trip. When she put the suit on, it had identified the chemical markers of every human who'd come in contact with the fabric. All but one of them were identifiable. Process of elimination made the remaining signal the high consul. Negative space for hunting animals.

Now she had a scent.

From the security records, she could track Duarte to the edge of the State Building's grounds, and then a little beyond it. The track after that was thin. Wind had scattered the scents, rain had washed them away.

Laconia wasn't a huge planet, but it was still an entire planet. Duarte had left days before on foot. Best-case scenario he was still walking, and she'd be able to find him in a long afternoon.

But the colony worlds had a habit of sprouting ancient transportation networks—methods the aliens who'd engineered the place had used to move shit around. If he'd tapped into one of them, he could be anywhere on Laconia or miles under it. If she could find where he'd accessed it, she'd have the next step. That was all it took: one step after another until the mission was done.

She was moving fast enough to surprise a family of bone-elk digging for food in the soil with their impressive racks of horns. They startled at her sudden appearance, then all bolted in different directions trying to get away. Her suit tracked them all, marking their threat level as low. If she overrode that and changed the threat to high, the gun on her arm would turn the entire herd into paste in seconds.

She chose not to.

At first, she followed the vague signs. A 15 percent match, hardly better than an educated guess, led down a particular animal trail lined by silver-leaved bushes. A 20 percent match went directly up a sheer rock wall, and she discarded it as a false positive. As she crisscrossed the landscape, her mind relaxed into the experience of the search, and time became less concrete. She'd heard about a similar kind of flow with artists when they fell deeply into their work. It was a lovely way to be—alone in her head with the pure focus of the task.

She made steady speed through the narrow band of forest and into the rocky foothills of a mountain. When she reached it, she had a pretty good hunch where she was going. Topographical maps led her through a twisty box canyon and up to the entrance of a cave. It was well hidden from casual view. No wonder no one had found it without a concerted effort. Teresa must have thought she'd found the best hiding spot in the world.

A pair of large rodent-like creatures—black fur and eyes, callused mouths, and ears like seashells—were in the entrance, fighting or mating or some combination of the two. They stopped and hissed at her as she approached, baring brownish hook-needle teeth. She kicked them out of the way. They hit the cave wall with a wet thud, and stopped moving. She considered the little bodies for a moment and ducked into the darkness below the stone.

The tunnels near the entrance were where the enemy spy had lived for years. His stink was still everywhere. The suit also found traces of Teresa and a dozen other Laconians. The extraction team that had killed Timothy or Amos Burton or whoever he'd been, and then the search team that came looking for his corpse and his equipment. The report said he'd been sitting on a backpack nuke the whole time. The prevailing theory was that he was waiting to see if he could extract James Holden before using it. She had a certain respect for that. There was a purity about someone who could casually hold death in his hands, just waiting for the right moment.

The suit thought it had Duarte's scent, but if the high consul had come through here, his trail was either too faint or too muddled up with everyone else's for the suit to track it with certainty. She moved through the cave, trying to recapture the pure state she'd felt in the forest, but something about killing the little not-rats and finding the evidence of the spy's nest had gotten her thinking. The pure and beautiful moment was gone, even if the hunt was still on.

The stone here was pale, flaking, and weak. She could have dug a passage through it with the powered gloves of her suit. It made her more than a little worried about cave-ins, especially after she got past the entry area where the camp had been and the tunnel system turned into a maze. Her suit's inertial tracking meant it could create a 3-D map of everywhere she went in real time, but the mountain was large. If the tunnels carved their way through the whole thing, she could be there for days. If she was right and Duarte had come here, it was going to be hard getting him out.

The efficient thing would have been to call for a swarm of micro drones and flood the tunnels with them. But Trejo had impressed on her the need for strict operational security, and including a tech team to run the drones felt like an unnecessary risk. Still, if she couldn't put her hands on the man, that could be her plan B.

She wasn't ready to give up, though. Not yet.

The farther into the caves she got, the less natural they seemed. Near the entrance, they had felt like accidents of geology, but here and there strange textures and protrusions began dotting the walls and grew up from the floors in the larger caverns. Black and silver spirals that seemed to carry their own light. Tanaka had spent enough time on Laconian warships built by the strange orbital shipyards to know protomolecule builder tech when she saw it.

This place had definitely been one of their installations, but its purpose was lost to time. The report from the investigation team had marked the location as needing further study, but with the attack on Laconia, everyone seemed to have just forgotten about it. No one's first priority. Unless maybe Duarte's.

She passed through a complex junction—an east-west tunnel above intersecting with a curving north-to-southeastern one below, and the suit alerted. She checked the display. Seventy-five percent match in the upper passage.

"Got you," she said.

Only maybe she didn't. She followed the suit's prompting through the twists and turns of a section of the tunnels, the chemical signal staying between 75 and 60 percent match, and came out into a large room filled with elaborate crystalline growths. They rose from the floor like delicate five-meter-high towers of glass lattice, glowing in soft pastel colors when her suit's lights hit them. In another context, they'd have been breathtakingly lovely. A kind of post-revivification abstract sculpture. She wondered if they were made by alien intelligences or the blind, idiot forces of nature. That she couldn't tell was either beautiful or damning, but either way, beside the point.

The suit was sure the high consul had been in the room. Her first 100 percent hit. Whether he was still in there or not, Duarte had definitely stood where she was or very close to it. Had seen the crystals with his weirdly altered eyes. Her heart rate increased a little as the realization struck that she might actually be able to find him. The relief at a real prospect of success showed her how carefully she'd been ignoring the possibility of failure.

The trail led her around the base of one of the towers. A pair of doglike constructs were worrying at a shard of crystal lying on the ground next to it. Tanaka could see the gap at the top of the tower where it must have broken off and fallen. In the files, Laconian intelligence called these things repair drones and indicated that they were nonthreatening. Occasionally they'd wander into the fringes of the city and steal broken things, only to later return them repaired, but altered. Researching what they chose to fix and how they went about intuiting original function was one of the projects that the Science Directorate was going to get around to one of these days.

The suit indicated that the high consul's scent was on one of the drones. Tanaka scowled to herself. If Duarte had left his scent on the thing by touching it—if that was the trail she was following— she was screwed. They could have interacted anywhere before the dog came here, and she'd have no idea where Duarte and this thing had met up.

She was about to go searching for another trace of the scent when one of the dogs said *ki-ka-ko*, then picked up the broken crystal shard in its weird puppetlike mouth and wandered off. She followed it.

After a confusing series of twists and turns, they emerged into another chamber, ten times the size of anything she'd seen before in the tunnels. It was like stepping into a cathedral. A fluting sound like wind over the top of empty bottles muttered through the space with no clear origin. Strange, almost organic-looking mechanisms grew up from the floor and towered over her, ten or fifteen stories high. For a moment, she felt something like awe.

In among them were half a dozen pits filled with viscous brown fluid, like sewer water mixed with petroleum oil. The dog walked over and dropped its broken bit of crystal into one of the pools, then waited motionless. The suit warned her that there were eleven other mobiles in the cavern. Each of them another one of the weird dog things. None seemed hostile. As she watched, they brought things into the room and dropped them in the pools. One time, a dog took something resembling a half meter of water pipe out of the pool and then left with it.

"This your machine shop, puppy?" she asked. "What are you doing here?"

Tanaka raised her arm and fired half a dozen shots into one of the motionless dogs, blowing it apart. She waited. After a few moments, three of the other dogs came over and began gently picking up the pieces of their dead comrade and dumping them into the pools.

"Ah-ha," Tanaka said to them. "Fixing your friend up, aren't you? All right. I'll wait."

They just looked back at her with their big eyes as though they were embarrassed at her outburst.

One said *ki-ka-ko* but didn't move.

There were a lot of strange chemicals in the air in the chamber, and the suit took a while sorting through them all, but after a few moments it popped up an alert. Duarte's scent. It was a significant trace. She had a hard time believing that it was just contact with a repair drone. If he'd passed through that room, had he been hurt or killed and the dogs brought him there? Had he figured out the same thing she just did, and used the sewage pools to fix something? Her hands itched a little bit, and she grinned. She felt the impatience of the chase, like she was a dog straining at its leash at the smell of rabbits. The joy of the hunt.

Slowly, methodically, she moved around the perimeter looking for the strongest match. Tracing Duarte's movement inside the room was probably pointless, but knowing where he'd come from and what direction he'd left would be enough. The best hit was a tunnel leading off the large cavern and gently sloping up.

She followed it, the chemical scent growing stronger as she moved. Half an hour later she emerged into a large room with an open window to the outside.

The chamber was shaped like a half circle, with a flat wall nearly sixty meters across. The middle twenty meters of the wall were missing, creating a large opening to the outside. Sunlight streamed in. Sky glowed oxygen-blue between the draping strands of vine and branch.

He'd been here. More than that, he'd spent time here. Duarte's scent marker was everywhere.

"High consul?" she said, the suit amplifying her. "This is Colonel Tanaka. If you're here, I just want to talk with you, sir."

No one answered.

On either side of the outside opening were spindly cradles growing up from the floor, with fifteen-meter-long egg-shaped objects held in them. The eggs had the same mother-of-pearl gleam she'd seen in the interior of a *Gravitar*-class battleship. Like something made at the alien construction platform. And the high consul's most recent scent track moved up to the empty cradle in the center. She walked slowly around the cradle, but no track led away.

"All right, little buddy," she said to the egg that had been there and was gone, "what the fuck are you?"

"A ship," Dr. Ochida said.

Tanaka leaned back in her chair. She'd taken over an office in the State Building as her base of operations with a staff of ten and high-priority access to everyone of any importance to the empire. The décor was generic politician, but she'd put a print of Ammon Fitzwallace's *Artemis the Hunter* on the wall where she could see it, all vibrant green with shocks of bright and bloody red.

"You're sure?"

"Well, no," Ochida said. "We have a team going to the site now, as you requested. We'll know more once that's complete, but we have seen similar structures elsewhere. Persephone system. Bara Gaon. Swarga Loka. Seven Kings. It's not the most common, but it's certainly not unprecedented. A fair proportion of the artifact tree seems focused on material transport, and especially in the Seven Kings data, we see—"

"Probably a ship."

"That's oversimplifying. We believe they were material transport pods," Ochida said. "But—"

"Did it fly?"

"The location and design seem to indicate yes," Dr. Ochida agreed with a nod.

"Then how do we track it?"

Ochida leaned forward. His chair creaked under him, and he blinked like an owl. "Track it?"

Tanaka clenched her fist where the scientist couldn't see it and kept her voice even. "If I wanted to find where the ship went. Is there a drive signature I can search for? Some kind of energy profile?"

Ochida shook his head like she was a little girl who'd asked him for a unicorn. "The native propulsion systems aren't something we've cracked yet. Not for want of trying. But we've known since Eros moved that it involves decoupling local inertia from frame inertia. That's not something that has a drive. It seems more like a controlled gravity where a nonlocal area falls *through* normal space—"

"Okay," Tanaka said, not punching the grinning scientist in the face only through great effort of will. "No drive plume. Then what can I use to find it?"

"Eros was also invisible to radar, you'll recall."

"You're telling me a lot of things I can't do. Start telling me what's on the 'can' list."

Ochida shrugged. "Eros was at least always visually available. If the ship passed through any light telescopy, you might find it that way. Of course, after the attack the planetary defenses are compromised, so..." He pressed his lips together in a universal gesture of impotence.

"All right," Tanaka said. "Thank you."

"You're quite welcome."

"No," she said. "I mean you're dismissed."

Ochida blinked in surprise, but then he left. So that was good.

Tanaka ached. She'd barely begun, and her search area had just expanded from Laconia at or near a transport network to literally anyplace in 1,300 systems and no obvious path to narrow it down. The raw frustration of it was a knot between her shoulder blades. She pulled up a notepad and started thinking her options through. Signal intelligence was obvious. Images of the remaining egg-ships had to be put out to anything with visual telescopes. Stations. Ships. Anything near a ring gate.

The *Voice of the Whirlwind*—the only surviving *Magnetar*— was acting as ersatz planetary defense. It would be the priority. If it had seen the egg-ship, that would at least give her an idea what direction it was going. It was possible, after all, that Duarte had been going someplace in-system. She didn't know for sure he'd been headed for a gate.

And then...what? Hunting a ship that couldn't be tracked on radar, that didn't leave a drive plume. That ran dark. If she knew what he'd been going after, maybe it would give her a smaller list of possible destinations. She'd need to talk to the valet and Admiral Trejo to see if Duarte had given any hint where he might be heading.

Or...maybe hunting wasn't the right model. Maybe trapping was. Maybe it wasn't a *place* Duarte was heading for. If the high consul was looking for something, that thing could be used as bait.

The records of ongoing operations were highly restricted. Trejo was probably the only one who could access everything, but he'd given her the keys. There were five active groups trying to recover Teresa Duarte. She read over their operating reports, but half of her mind was probing the strategy. Before his resurrection, the only sign Duarte had given that he was still conscious was his slaughter of Paolo Cortázar. That, according to Dr. Okoye, who had been there at the time, had been out of concern for his daughter. Was it such a stretch to think that the girl would be the first person he reached out to now? Wasn't she the best available bait?

It sure as hell seemed like better odds than tracking the missing ship.

The most promising lead was an intelligence counter-op. A distant cousin of Duarte's dead wife ran a boarding school on New Egypt, and there had been some chatter between her and known underground contacts. If Tanaka had the girl, it was the sort of place she'd have found to park her. And the school's new term was starting soon. Hiding a teenage girl in a place with a lot of other teenage girls made sense.

Tanaka pulled up the command structure. The operation was being run through a hunting frigate called the *Sparrowhawk*. Captain Noel Mugabo was in charge.

Or had been, anyway. Until now.

She opened a connection to her aide and didn't wait for him to speak. "Contact the *Sparrowhawk* and let them know I'll be taking over direct operational command of their New Egypt mission. And find me a fast transport. Something with the breathable-fluid crash couches.

"Put me on New Egypt now."

Chapter Six: Naomi

Amos—or the thing that had been Amos—smiled and waited for the autodoc to finish its run. Naomi, braced at a handhold, watched the values and scans as they spooled out. Red and amber and occasionally green, they were the medical equivalent of a shrug. The machine thought he was a basket full of different kinds of strange. Some was the strange he'd been ever since returning from Laconia. Some was new strange that deviated from previous measures. Whether any of it was significant was anybody's guess. There was no comparison data for an animal like him, no others of his kind apart from the pair that Elvi Okoye had. There was no context.

Naomi felt that way a lot these days.

"I'm feeling fine," he said.

"That's good. You should stay here for a while anyway. In case it happens again."

The pure black eyes shifted. It was hard to tell if he was focusing on her or something else in the room. Without iris or pupil, he could appear all-seeing and blind at the same moment.

"I don't think I'll be getting the wigglies again anytime soon," he said.

"You've been pretty shaken up. Not just this. All of it. Better that we get an idea what's going on with you now so you don't have another seizure while you're doing something dangerous."

"I get that. But it's not going to happen again."

"You can't know that unless we know why it happened."

"Yeah."

They were quiet for a moment. Only the hum of the air recyclers and the muttering of the autodoc. "Do you?"

"Do I what, Boss?"

"Do you know why the seizure happened?"

Amos lifted a wide, grayish hand in a gesture that said *maybe, maybe not*. The little widening of his smile was exactly the one he'd have used before, but half a second later than he would have used it. "I got a feeling. There's stuff running in the background with the new head. There was a hiccup. Don't think it'll happen again."

She tried to smile back, but it felt forced. "That's not as reassuring as you think."

"You don't think I'm him, do you?"

She noted the pronoun. *Him*. Not *You don't think I'm me*. "I don't even know what that question means."

"It's all right. I get it. I went away like I used to be. I come back with these eyes and this blood. And my brain doing things it didn't use to do. If you weren't at least wondering, that would be weird."

"Are you?"

"Am I?"

"Are you still human?"

His smile could have meant anything. "Not sure I ever was, really. But I know I'm still me."

"That'll do then," she said, and made herself lean over and kiss his wide smooth scalp the way she might have if she hadn't had doubts. If it was true, and he was Amos, then it was the right thing. If it wasn't, and he wasn't, better that whoever he was believe she accepted him. "Still, wait an hour before you get back to work?"

He sighed. "If you say so."

She squeezed his shoulder, and it was solid. Had it felt like that before? Amos had always been strong. He'd spent as much time in the ship gym as Bobbie, and Bobbie had damn near lived there. Naomi couldn't tell if this was a change or just her mind looking for discrepancies. Building them whether they were there or not.

"I'll check on you," she said, because it wasn't a lie, no matter what she meant by it.

The ring space wasn't somewhere to relax. There had been a time when it had been the hub of humanity's great spread to the stars. It had seemed safe then, or relatively so. Anything that found its way to the edge of the sphere defined by the ring gates vanished and was lost, but nothing reached back.

Until it did. And then it had been annihilating. Now most ships moved through it fast and hot, setting the angle of their transit before they came in and getting out the farther gate as quickly as they could. It was exactly the wrong thing to keep from going dutchman, but it minimized the time spent in the uncanny space.

Other ships passed in and out of the rings, the traffic of more than a thousand systems, all of them relying on trade to one degree or another. All of the ships on their own errands with no particular interest in or awareness of Naomi and her burdens. The *Roci* stayed there, on the float. Every hour courted the danger that reality itself would start boiling again and everything in the ring space would be killed. But before they could go anywhere, they needed a place to go and a plan that was more fleshed out than *Don't die.*

She worked on the ops deck, floating just over her crash couch with her legs folded in the lotus position. The straps shifted around her like kelp in a vast water recycling tank, and the web of the underground spread out on the screen before her. It had been easier when she'd been focused on attacking Laconia. Breaking things was always easier than building them up.

In the aftermath of Laconia's defeat in its home system—on its home planet—the empire had moved to consolidate the power it still had. Trejo was locking down shipyards and supply lines as best he could with the forces that remained to him. Naomi was trying to leverage the influence and organization she'd gathered for the battle into some kind of sustainable self-governing network. The newsfeeds from Sol, Bara Gaon, Auberon, and Svarga Minor chattered about increased Laconian presence. Though why anyone was worried about a backwater like Svarga wasn't entirely clear. The message queue was as long as her arm, it felt like.

"Their objection is the same one we're seeing over and over again," Jillian Houston, the captain of the underground's stolen flagship, said from Naomi's screen. She looked like a child. She was older than Naomi had been when she'd signed on to the *Canterbury* a lifetime ago. "Báifàn system is on the edge of being self-sustaining, but which side of the edge is debatable. They don't like anyone saying when they can and can't trade, and they're absolutely not going to accept constraints that other systems aren't abiding by. And I have to say, I'm sympathetic. We're here to protect people's freedom. I'm not sure what liberty is if you're not permitted to decide what chances you're willing to take."

Naomi turned her head, trying to ease the knot at the base of her skull. She'd watched the report three times now, each time hoping she'd find a graceful and diplomatic response that had eluded her before. It hadn't happened.

Instead, she felt herself growing taut and angry. The tension in her neck, the tightness across her chest pulling her shoulders forward into a hunch, the ache at the corners of her scowl. They were the physical manifestations of an impatience that reached far beyond Jillian's message or her own still-uncomposed response.

She kept coming back to the uncharitable thought that if the underground were just made up of Belters, the problem would have been tractable. Or if not that, at least she'd have been sure a solution existed. Belters were viciously independent, but they also understood what it meant to rely on the community around them. Skipping a seal replacement didn't only risk the life of the slack bastards who'd cheaped out on their work. Failure meant the death of everyone on the crew.

The colony worlds were acting like their safety could exist separate from the well-being of all the other systems and ships. It couldn't be so hard to see how accepting a little restriction and regulation benefited everyone. But inner-worlds culture didn't measure it that way. For them, being better meant being better than the person next to you, not both of you sharing the same increase.

She knew it wasn't fair or even really accurate. Her frustration was leaking out as tribalism and spite. Which was why she hadn't responded yet, even though as the de facto leader of the underground, she had to. What she really wanted to do was put a camera on Jim and have him give one of his heartfelt little sermons about how they were all one people, and that by pulling together, they'd get to the other side of their struggles. It was his genius that he could still believe that, even after everything they'd seen and been through.

But she'd just gotten him back. If she let herself get into the habit of seeing him as a useful tool for her work, it would betray the chance they'd been given. She needed to have the connection between them as something separate, something sacred, that the rest of the universe didn't have claim on.

So maybe there was a thread of selfishness in Belters too.

She started the recording.

"Jillian. Thank you for the report. Please let our friends in Báifàn system know that I hear and understand their concerns, and I absolutely understand their need for safety and equity in how trade is carried out through the rings. The goal has to be minimizing the need for ring transit by building up to sustainability for all the colonies as quickly as possible, and their goal for that is absolutely the same as ours. I'll include the presentation for why the protocols are the best, safest way forward for all of us, and you can pass that along too. Hopefully, they've already seen it."

But maybe this time they'll actually pay attention.

Or maybe the builders' ancient enemy would figure out how to end all human life and none of this would matter. Fatalism had its dark attractions, after all. Hopelessness and despair could almost look restful.

She played back her message, decided that it sounded too pat and rehearsed, and redid it another four times before she gave up and sent it out. The message queue still waiting looked like forever.

She massaged her hands, digging into the aching muscles at the base of her thumbs, while the next message played on her screen. Governor Tuan had thin, terrier-sharp cheeks, frog-wet eyes, gray-black hair, and a tight, officious smile. She wondered whether she would still have thought he was ugly if he'd had a different personality. She'd probably have been more forgiving.

"On behalf of the governing council of Firdaws, I would like to thank you for submitting your proposal. I am very interested in returning to a schedule of reliable and mutually profitable trade."

"But," Naomi said to herself as Tuan scowled theatrically on the screen.

"There are, however, some very real concerns about the document as it stands that will require some thoughtful conversation. In that spirit, I would like to propose a summit meeting. While Firdaws is not yet entirely self-sustaining, we do have certain amenities that we will be happy to offer. Our state-of-the-art luxury villas can be set aside for you and your associates for as long as the negotiations take."

She slid it into a secondary queue. There was only so much explaining to people how cooperation would keep them all from dying she could manage in a single sitting.

The next entry stopped her. It was from Sol. It was from Kit.

The only child of Alex's second marriage was a grown man now, but she'd seen him as a newborn and known his mother, Giselle, as well as any of the *Roci* crew had really gotten to know her. Now here he was, looking into a camera. He looked more like his mother—Giselle's high, sharp cheekbones and regal forehead and brows. When he moved, she could see Alex in him.

"Hey," he said. "So I know it's been a while. And things...I know it's not like we could be in touch more. But I wanted to let you know something."

Naomi's gut tightened, and she braced for a hit. That Kit had come to her had to mean it was something about Alex, or something that would hurt Alex badly enough that Kit wanted to be sure there would be people there to comfort him, even if he decided to keep it to himself.

"Well," Kit said, "there aren't a lot of planetary engineering gigs in Sol system, and the ones there are they have fifteen people applying for every spot. I know that we talked about me keeping a low profile—"

Naomi frowned, trying to remember when she'd said something like that.

"—but we got offered a contract with a geological survey on Nieuwestad. It's a good company. Jacobin-Black Combined Capital. They're doing a lot of industrial construction and microclimate engineering, and I think it could be a really good move for us. But it will make it harder for you to come visit, and I know with Rohi pregnant, you'd want to see your grandson."

Kit grinned like he'd just delivered the punch line to a joke, and Naomi stopped the playback. Relief was like a drug in her veins. She leaned back in her crash couch, the gimbals hissing under her, and called up toward the flight deck.

"Alex! I think I got some of your mail. I'll send it up."

But he was already coming down the lift ladder. "What's up?" he said.

"I got some of your mail. It's in the intelligence packet, but it's yours. From Kit."

His smile was quick and automatic. "Well, play it."

Naomi scrubbed the message back to the start and let it play. Knowing what was coming, she watched his face, and saw the shock and the joy and the tears in Alex's eyes when the news landed. Kit went on for a time, telling Alex about the dates they were shipping out for Nieuwestad and the due date for the coming child. And some news of no real importance about Giselle and life on Mars. And then the message ended with Kit saying *I love you, Dad* and Alex lowering himself into the crash couch at Naomi's side.

"Well ain't that a kick in the nuts," Alex said through a wide grin. "I'm going to be a granddaddy."

"Yes, you are."

He considered it for a moment, then shook his head. "I was going to say I'm too young to be anyone's grandfather, but I'm not, am I?"

"No," Naomi said. "You aren't. If anything, you ran kind of late."

"Took a while getting it right. God. Kit's a good kid. I hope he's better at keeping a marriage together than I was."

"He isn't you. I'm not saying he won't fuck it all up, but even if he does, it'll be however *he* fucks it up. Not how you did." For a moment she thought of her own son, dead along with his father and the rest of the Free Navy. The memory almost didn't hurt. That wasn't true. It would always hurt, but now it was a low-level ache instead of a knife to the belly. Time had done its healing, or at least let the scars go numb.

The piloting subsystem chimed, and Alex hauled himself up out of the couch. "I guess Giselle's going to be a grandmother." He grinned. "And she's going to hate the shit out of it, isn't she?"

"The title may not fit her self-image," Naomi said.

"You make a good diplomat," Alex said, and headed back for the lift. When she was alone again, she separated Kit's message from the rest of the packet and copied it over to Alex's message queue. She thought about keeping a copy for herself, but it hadn't been meant for her, and she didn't want to presume.

A soft clicking alert, and a new message popped up on her queue. She'd built a system of flags to help her keep track of her cascading responsibilities. This flag was the deep gold color that she'd chosen to mean Home. Issues specific and peculiar to the *Rocinante* and her little family. What remained of her little family.

The message was the one Naomi had been waiting for. Its tracking headers showed the subtle signs and countersigns the underground used to confirm authenticity. The repeaters echoed back to New Egypt, as she'd hoped. Nothing looked amiss. Anything that touched on the daughter of High Consul Winston Duarte, Naomi treated like it was made from snakes and plutonium.

Once she was certain of the message protocols and origins, she isolated her comm system, offered a silent prayer to the universe, and decrypted the message. It was a single line of text:

ADMISSION APPROVED FOR FALL SEMESTER.

Chapter Seven: Jim

"Why am I only hearing about this now?" Teresa asked.

Jim couldn't tell if the tension was anger, fear, or something else, but it had settled around the girl's shoulders like a shawl. Her eyes were focused someplace just over Jim's right shoulder, fixed and glaring in a way that he knew from his time on Laconia was her way of listening intently.

It was strange to think that of all of them, Jim had spent the most time with Teresa. They'd lived in the State Building for years, her as the child of the high consul, and him as his prisoner. Or maybe both as his prisoner, just in different ways.

"That was me," he said. "I didn't want to float the possibility if it didn't come through."

Her gaze flicked to him with a question.

"I didn't want to disappoint you," he said.

"But it came through. It's here. A possibility."

"It's a boarding school in New Egypt system. Sohag Presbyterian Academy—"

"I'm not interested in a religious education," she said.

"It's not really specifically religious. I mean, there are religious classes and services, but they aren't mandatory."

Teresa took a moment, processing that like she'd taken a bite of food and was deciding whether to spit it out.

"A cousin," she said.

"Elizabeth Finley. She was your mother's cousin, and apparently doesn't think much of your father. It's kind of perfect. She knows who you are, and can take steps to keep you safe, and she's not interested in bowing before Laconia for personal reasons, so we don't have to worry about her deciding to hand you over for a bounty."

"And you've vetted her?"

"The underground did what it could. She seems to check out. There's not a big presence in New Egypt, Laconian or underground. That's another part of the appeal."

Teresa's gaze floated back over his shoulder as she thought.

Like all the cabins in the *Roci*, Teresa's had been designed for Martian military back when that had still meant something. Jim was used to the spartan design for himself or the others. Putting an adolescent girl in the same setting made it seem more like a prison. At fifteen, Jim had been a sophomore at North Frenchtown High. The issues he'd struggled with were how to sleep an extra twenty minutes in the mornings, how to cover over his profound disinterest in Mr. Laurent's chemistry lectures, and whether Deliverance Benavidez would go out with him. Back then, all of Montana had seemed too small. Teresa only had a few square meters.

"What about Muskrat?"

"Finley says it won't be a problem. There are other students who have pets too. Mostly they're service animals, but it won't stand out enough to cause trouble."

"I don't know," she said. "I like it here. Amos is teaching me things. And there are fewer variables here. I wouldn't know the people there. I don't think I'd trust them."

"I hear you," Jim said. "But this is a warship. And we're at war. And while you did pull us out of the fire, I'm not comfortable using you as a shield."

"I'm a good shield."

"Yeah, but I'm done with that play."

"Why?" she asked. "I know you don't want to, but it worked. And it'll keep working, at least sometimes. Why don't you want something that works to keep you safe?" The sincerity in her voice surprised him.

"Shields take the hit," Jim said. "Shields get shot. That's what they're there for. And someday, someone is going to think that they can disable the *Roci* by putting a round through our drive cone. Or that it's worth the risk to drop a few rail-gun rounds through us. There's a calculus here, and yes, you make them less likely to shoot us down. But I don't want to be the guy you died for. I'm not okay with it."

She tilted her head like she was hearing a new sound. "You care about this."

"Yeah. Kind of do."

If he'd expected an outpouring of emotion from her—gratitude or admiration or just respect for the morality of his position—he'd picked the wrong girl. She considered him like he was an unexpected kind of butterfly. It wasn't quite contempt, but it wasn't not-contempt either. He saw something occur to her and waited until she was ready to say it.

"If I went, and I didn't like it there, could I come back?"

"Probably not," he said. And then, a moment later, "No."

The sorrow in her expression was brief, but it was deep. He understood a little better the loss he was asking her to embrace.

"I need to think about this," she said. "When do you need my answer?"

When Naomi had come to him with the news, she'd asked him to tell Teresa. Not ask permission, not negotiate with. The verb had been *tell*. And yet, here he was. Jim scratched his neck.

"It's weeks until the term starts. I'd like to get you there early enough to have you situated, but if we make it a relatively hard burn…"

"I understand," she said. "I won't take too long."

He pulled himself out of the room, skimming down the corridor. He heard the door close behind him. The ship was quiet. Naomi was waiting for him on the flight deck. He was going to have to tell her that a fifteen-year-old girl had maneuvered him into giving her the choice of going to boarding school or…staying on the ship, he guessed. Doing something that wasn't Naomi's plan. It was barely his responsibility, and he still felt like he'd screwed it up.

He passed Alex's cabin and heard the familiar voice drifting through the door. *But it will make it harder for you to come visit, and I know with Rohi pregnant, you'd want to see your grandson.* Alex had been smiling a lot since the message came through, but he knew there was something else there too. Jim wanted to be happy for him, and he thought he was faking it pretty well. He'd slapped Alex on the back and made grandpa jokes that made his old friend grin.

The truth was, Jim was astounded by Kit's optimism. And by *astounded*, he really meant *horrified*. When Alex talked about his grandson, working out whether he'd been born yet, how big he was likely to be, speculating on the names that Kit and his wife might choose, all Jim could see was one more body on the pile when the end came. Another baby who'd stop breathing when the deep enemy solved its puzzle. Another death.

Maybe that was unfair. There had been any number of endtimes before this: black plague, nuclear war, food web collapse, Eros moving. Every generation had its apocalypse. If they made humans stop falling in love and having babies, celebrating and dreaming and living out the time they had, they'd have stopped a long time before.

It was just that this time, it was different. This time, they weren't going to make it. The only other one who knew, who understood, was Amos. And so Amos was the only one he could talk to.

He made his way down toward the reactor and the drive. The smell of silicone lubricant sweetened the air, and Muskrat's soft bark drew him toward the engineering deck. The dog was floating in the air, her tail a circular whirl that left her head shifting in a circle a few centimeters across. Her lips were pulled back in a wide canine smile.

"Still no sausage," Jim said, and the dog barked softly.

"She doesn't actually care about that," Amos said. "She just likes having you around."

Jim steadied the dog with one hand and petted her with the other. "You know, I would have said dog on spaceship was a very bad plan, but I do kind of like having her here. I mean, more when we're under thrust."

Amos rose from a workstation, a small welding torch in one hand and dark goggles to protect his eyes pushed up onto his forehead. A hydraulic valve was clamped at the station with a line of scorch marks along the ceramic where the metal sealant was still cooling. "She does get embarrassed when I have to take her to the vacuum fire hydrant."

"The what?"

"It's the idiom for where dogs piss," Amos said. "I don't make this up. I just follow the network groups."

"Because there's a lot of floating puppies," Jim said to Muskrat. "You're not the only one."

"They cope with atrophy better than us too," Amos said as he stripped off the goggles and fit them into his tool case. "Something about having more legs on the ground, I think."

"Probably. I will miss her when she's gone," Jim said, then nodded at the valve. "Is there a problem with the water feed?"

"Nope. And there isn't going to be. Mineralization was messing with the seal, and you wait until that's bad enough for a little erosion, you might as well print up a new one, y'know?"

"I at least have it on good authority. That's close enough for me."

Amos snapped the welding torch into its place and pulled a

polishing cloth out of his pocket. "We need to get the fuck out of the slow zone. Hanging out here like this is making my scalp crawl."

"Yeah. As soon as Naomi gets through her data, decides for sure where we're going," Jim said. "I'm worried about the kid."

"Yeah. Me too."

"It's easy for me to forget how much she's lost, you know? Her entire experience was curated to the millimeter before she came with us. A few months here—just enough to get comfortable and find her feet—and now another total change. It's a lot. She's fifteen. Can you imagine facing all that at fifteen?"

Amos looked over at him like he'd said something funny. "You stressed over Tiny? She's going to be fine."

"Is she? I mean…What do we even know about this school we're taking her to?"

"We know it gets shot at less than we do."

"Besides that."

Amos put the cloth over his thumb, took a firm grip on the valve, and started rubbing away the scorch marks as he talked. "Tiny's working out who she is. Shit, *what* she is. It's what she was doing on Laconia. It's what she's doing here. When she goes to that school, it's not like the job changes. The question is, does she have more to learn from a boarding school at the ass end of nowhere or getting missiles thrown at her with a bunch of old-fart revolutionaries?"

"I don't think we're really revolutionaries."

"And," Amos went on, raising his voice to keep Jim from changing the subject, "it's not what's really eating you. We both know that."

Before Jim could reply, Alex's voice came over ship-wide. "Hey, everybody. I was hoping…I kind of need to call a little group meeting? In the galley. If you can. Um. Thanks."

Amos squinted at the valve, turning it one way and then the other before giving it a last, satisfied swipe with the cloth. He set it back in its clamp.

"Do you need to put that back in place?"

"Nah," Amos said. "I got a spare holding the line for now."

"Then I guess we should go see what's up with Alex."

"He wants something, but he needs to apologize for a few minutes before he asks."

"Well, sure," Jim said. "I mean, I wonder what he's going to ask for."

If there had been gravity, Alex would have been pacing when they came through the galley door. Teresa was already there, floating beside the wall without touching it. Her arms were crossed, her mouth was tight and small, and every now and then she moved her jaw and made some brief expression. If he had to guess, Jim would have said she was deep in conversation with herself and barely paying attention to them. Amos took a place at the table, rooting himself by his mag boots to keep his hands free to steady Muskrat. The dog seemed perfectly at ease, reassured by having so much of its pack together.

Naomi came last and pulled herself a bulb of tea while motioning to Alex that he could start.

"So, yeah," Alex said. "You all heard about Kit and Rohi, right?"

"You may have mentioned it," Jim said, teasing him, but gently. Alex grinned.

"So I did the math, and I'm pretty sure that the baby's already born. Now, I know that we've a lot on our plates here. The work we're doing is really important. And risky. I didn't sign on to any of this thinking it was like a normal contract. This has never been a normal contract."

Amos' sigh was almost inaudible. Alex heard it anyway, and Jim could see the old pilot dropping minutes of talking around the subject.

"Communication is dangerous, for him and for us, but I would really like to...to send my boy a message, you know? Maybe get a picture of my grandson. I don't know what we have or what the underground needs from us. If we can't...I just had to ask. You know, if it was something we could, and I just didn't..."

Jim turned to Naomi and lifted his chin, asking. She took a sip from the bulb.

"It would mean poking our nose through the Sol gate," she said. "We could get a tightbeam through trusted repeaters from there."

"Any gate's just about as far as any other one right now," Jim said. "I mean, we'd just have to keep pretending we were on the same fake contract as before. Even if Laconia has forces in the system, there's no better system to get lost in the traffic. Sol's got a few centuries' worth of ships and infrastructure to blend in with. It's not like we'd be trying to go unnoticed in Arcadia or Farhome."

"It would be more risk," Alex said, but he was just trying to tell them that he wouldn't be angry if they said no. Jim, Naomi, and Amos had all shipped with him long enough to know that was true. He wouldn't be angry, but he would be sad. And if they were all going to die anyway, there was no reason to miss the chance.

"I think we should go," he said.

"I was hoping we could drop Teresa off at school and then head for Firdaws," Naomi said.

"The Sol gate's right here," Jim said. "A quick burn. If there aren't any guard ships right at the ring gate, we can flip as soon as we've passed through the gate."

Amos scratched his neck. "We got enough water out of Kronos. We're not hurting for reaction mass. We could probably make up the time by burning a little longer to and from New Egypt. We are still hurting on fuel pellets and recyclers, but a little detour like that won't matter for those."

"Fine," Naomi said. "Sol gate for long enough to contact Kit, then New Egypt. We resupply in Firdaws."

"That work for you, Tiny?" Amos asked.

Teresa snapped back to the room from wherever she'd been. There was a bright sheen of tears over her eyes. Not thick, but present. "Yes. Fine. Yes."

Alex's relief melted him. When he spoke, his voice was reedy and thick. "Thank you. Really. If we hadn't, I'd have lived with it, but...just thank you."

"Family's important," Naomi said, and Jim couldn't tell which of the thousand things she could have meant by it were in her mind.

It took less than an hour to get the *Roci* ready to go, even with Amos swapping and testing the repaired valve. Alex, on the flight deck above them, was singing to himself like a finch at dawn. There wasn't a melody to speak of, just the musical lilting of pleasure and anticipation. Amos, Teresa, and Muskrat were in engineering, and Jim was thinking about all the things the girl might be feeling. Abandonment. Anger. Rejection. He hoped it wasn't like that. Or that at least there were other things—anticipation, curiosity, hope—to leaven them. He hoped without any reason to hope that it would matter and that Teresa would by some miracle live long enough to work through the complications of her own heart.

As they started the burn for Sol ring at half a g instead of the usual third, Naomi sighed. At first, he thought her mind was on the same things as his.

"Too many fucking ships going through the rings," she said. "And here we are, not exactly leading by example."

He looked at the tactical. She was right, of course. Just in the time they'd been at a relative stop so that she could read through the data, ten more ships had passed through gates, burning on one errand or another that someone decided was worth the risk. Or didn't understand that there was a risk. Or didn't care.

"You saw there was another event?" Naomi asked. "There was a message from Okoye. It happened in Gedara system."

"How many does that make?"

"Twenty? Something like that."

Alex, above them, burst into a little run of melody. Something bright and jazzy, and as full as springtime. It was like listening to a message from a different universe.

"She'll figure it out," Naomi said, answering Jim's silence. "If anyone can, she will."

As they dove down toward the fluttering interference surface that was the gateway to Sol, a fast transit ship burst through the Laconia gate behind them, flipped, and started a punishing maneuvering burn. Jim watched them, waiting for the tightbeam demanding their surrender. It didn't come.

"Looks like we skipped out at just the right time," Naomi said.

"Another near miss," Jim said. "Don't know how many more of those we're going to get."

They passed through the Sol gate before they could see where the fast transport was headed.

Interlude: The Dreamer

The dreamer dreams, and her dream carries her and hers flowing backward into a time before minds. Like grandmothers telling the stories their grandmothers told about their grandmothers before them, she falls gently and forever into black oceans the size of everything. The other two are and aren't and are again, with her and within her like humming to the memory of songs she never quite forgot. She broadens like a sunbird spreading its wings to catch the warming light, but there is no sun and no light—not yet—and the cold darkness is wide and comforting as a bed.

And she knows things.

Once and gone so far away no one was there to think it, the *it* was like this: Down was the hardness of heat, and up was the hardness of cold, and between those two implacabilities was the universe. The dreamer dreams the currents of flow and force, and her blood is the ocean's blood. Her salt is the ocean's salt. With a hand as wide as continents and softer than her skin, she caresses the burning heat below her and the soothing cool above. Long eons, and nothing is alive until something is. Maybe many things are, but the dream is a middle dream, and she dreams the middle because the path that crooks her swimmingly on begins there, but slowly slowly slow.

The dreamer drifts and the others drift with her, and more now: little bulbs of pastness around her and within, drifting on the same flow that she is and that she *is*. Two touch and become one; one thins itself into two and two and two and two. She watches the languid, lightless stuttering in the blessed cold as the grandmothers whisper that here is the birth of lust. Here, the puppy-wise gambol of making for the joy of making, with nothing to make of but from self more self.

The dreamer forgets, and is the slowness. She reaches over timelessness and invisibilities, thirsty for something richer than water. Thimble feasts rise from below and sate her for decades, and she dreams that she is dreaming, safe inside the eternal flow. Her hand reaches up to her heel, fingertips stretching ahead to brush her toes. She is a child made of saltwater bubbles, and one of the others says so, *like cells?* but the words are another place and she is voluptuous now, outside all language.

There is no light—not yet—but there is heat far far below, stuttering and buzzing and raging. It boils up the strange taste of stones that draws her and drives her away and becomes her. Above, the cold where nothing flows, the endless curving wall around the universe. And the ripple, now the always-ripple of a flow inside the flow that only some things feel. A handhold in the waters, a something made from nothing that she shimmies wrigglingly along. She presses herself against it, and lusty, she improvises. The little bulbs of pastness complicate and reach, one for another. And for the first time in all of time, she is tired.

Watch watch watch, the grandmothers whisper. *Feel that one that falls, slippingly down too far into the heat and riot; that mindless genius. This is important*, they say, and the dreamer draws herself down too and others how many with her sink. The bubble rises, full of thrum and fever and ill, and when it cools, it is butterscotch on the tongue and a billion insects choiring joyful in the summer night. It is a thousand new toys wrapped in gauze and ribbon. It is coffee and candy and the first awkward kiss, the almost-almost-almost shuddering against the skin. And she knows she will go again, that she who is a child of bubbles will send herself away again to be burned and then cherish her blisters. She longs to be made strange by the hotness and the hurt.

This is how it was when we were girls, the grandmothers say, and the dreamer dreams that she understands.

That's enough, someone says. *All right, people. By the numbers and by the book.*

Chapter Eight: Elvi

Fayez, floating at her private desk, scrolled through the notes. Whenever he was confused or skeptical, a little line appeared between his eyebrows. "So does this make any fucking sense to you? Because I'm baffled."

The notes had the scans of Cara's brain and body and the ones of the BFE, but the important part for Elvi was the interview and subject report with Cara. It had taken them hours to complete, Elvi asking questions and Cara answering verbally or writing out her reply, and while it was the least objective thing in the report, it was also the thing that excited her most.

"It does. I mean, I think it does," Elvi said, and paused. "I have some ideas."

He shut down the window and turned his attention to her. "Maybe you better tell me, then. Because I don't know what I'm looking at here."

She gathered her thoughts. Exobiology hadn't been Elvi's first field of concentration. Back in the dim and ancient times that were really just a few wild and change-filled decades before, she'd gone to Sejong World College because it had the best medical genetics program that she could afford. When she was being honest with herself, it wasn't even that she loved medical genetics all that much. When she was fifteen, she'd seen Amalie ud-Daula play a medical geneticist in *Handful of Rain*, and she spent the next year trying to get her hair to look the same. She never really managed. The weird alchemy of adolescent imprinting transformed her unconsidered identification with an entertainment feed actor into an interest in how strands of DNA turned into pathologies.

The idea of a flaw as tiny as a missed base pair translating itself into a slightly different curve on a protein and then into a leaking heart valve or a nonfunctional eye was compelling and creepy in more or less equal degrees. She thought that it was her passion, and she'd followed it with the dedication of a woman who believed she was on the path the universe wanted for her.

She'd taken a course on non-terrestrial fieldwork because her advisor had pointed out how many more postings there were for newly graduated medical geneticists on Mars and the stations on Jupiter's and Saturn's moons than there were on Earth. Elvi had taken the hint.

Lectures had been held in a small room with yellow, water-stained carpet and a wall screen with a burned-out pixel that made it look like there was a fly on it. Professor Li was three years into his retirement, and only came back to teach the class because he liked it. Maybe his enthusiasm had been infectious, or maybe it had all been the universe's way of putting her in the right place at the right time. Whatever the reason—or lack of reason—Professor Li had done a section about the first explorations for extraterrestrial life in the oceans of Europa, and Elvi's brain had lit up like someone had put euphorics in her breakfast cereal.

To the dismay of her mother and her academic advisor, she changed her focus to the then-purely-hypothetical field of exobiology. Her advisor's exact words had been *From a work perspective, you'd be better off learning to tune pianos.*

And that had been true right up until Eros moved. After, everybody in her program had jobs for life.

She was older now than Professor Li had been when he told her about Europa and those first tentative efforts to show that Earth's tree of life wasn't alone in the universe. She'd seen things she hadn't dreamed of, been places she hadn't known existed when she was a girl, and found herself—thanks to chance and James fucking Holden—at the razor's edge of the most important research projects in human history.

Strange then, how it all cycled back to Professor Li's lecture about Europa. Cold dead Europa, which had turned out to never have had any life in it but opened up the universe to her anyway.

Elvi steadied herself with a handhold. She'd been on the float enough that it came almost naturally now. She still missed being able to pace. "Okay. How much do you know about the slow life model?"

"I am now aware that there is something called a slow life model."

"Right. Basics. Okay. So, there's a range of metabolic rates. You can see that in animals. You have something fast with a high reproduction rate like rats or chickens on one hand, and tortoises with a really long lifespan and a much slower metabolism on the other. The whole tree of life is on that spectrum. It predicts that you'd see things evolving in very low-energy environments that, y'know, needed very little energy. Low metabolisms, low reproduction. Long lifespan. Slow life."

"Space turtles."

"Ice turtles. Actually, very cold saltwater slugs. Or jellyfish. Probably something pretty near neutral buoyancy. That's not the point. You could in theory have something evolve in an environment with very little available energy, and with a very...let's call it 'leisurely' sense of time. It's what the Tereshkova missions were looking for."

"And that's awesome," Fayez said, blankly.

"Tereshkova One and Two were the first long-term crewed surveys of Europa? They were looking for extraterrestrial life."

"Which they didn't find."

"Some amino acid precursors, but no life."

"So the space turtles weren't from Europa."

A brief flash of annoyance rose in her and faded. They were both tired. They were both in the only ship in an unpopulated solar system with help weeks away at best. And she wasn't explaining herself that well. She swallowed, set her shoulders, and went on.

"They weren't. But maybe they were like what we were looking for. And here's the other thing. The other form of life the Tereshkova missions were looking for was deep vent organisms."

"Those I know. Worms and things that live near volcanic vents. They use the energy from the vent instead of sunlight."

"And they also get a bunch of biologically interesting minerals, but yes."

"Start talking vulcanism, and I know my way around," Fayez said.

"That's what Cara's describing. That biome. Look. She talks about the cold above and the heat below. Like the ice shell of a water moon with a hot core. And free water in between. The part where she says she felt it starting to make more of itself. That's... I don't know. Some kind of reproduction. Mitosis or budding."

"And the thing where she tasted stones," Fayez said. "Minerals and nutrients floating up from below. You're thinking they're both there. These slow life turtles—"

"Jellyfish."

"—and vent organisms too, but lower down."

"Like what we were looking for on Europa."

The line on his forehead erased itself. She wanted to keep going, but she knew her husband's rhythms. He was working something through, and if she talked now, he wouldn't hear her. The hum of the ship around them and the ticking of the air recycler were the only sounds until he laughed once, like a cough.

"Okay, I know what I was thinking of," he said. "The part about the thing in the water."

"The handhold?"

"Yeah, that. It happened after the...fuck...tasting stone? Seriously, I feel like we should have brought a poetry grad student along. This is bullshit as data."

"You were thinking of something?"

"Right, sorry. If that was some kind of impressionistic, experiential description of iron uptake leading to magnetic navigation. Maybe that's the handhold in the water?"

"And that thing at the end," Elvi said. "When something went down into the heat and came back up scarred, but with this... revelatory whatever it was? If that's the slow life intentionally reaching for a nutrient-rich environment for the first time. Seeking out food instead of just bumping into it. I think Cara is experiencing this organism's evolutionary history. The diamond—"

"Thank you for not calling it an emerald."

"—is showing her how they came to exist. Like if we were explaining life to something that had never seen anything like us by pushing down to organic chemistry and building the story up from there so that we'd have a common context."

Fayez went quiet. The line on his forehead came back. Elvi pushed off the wall, turning to take the edge of her desk in her fingers and pull herself to a stop. He saw her expression and shook his head.

"No, it makes sense. Sort of. I see why that would be the best information-sharing strategy and all that. It's just. Okay, say the protomolecule engineers have gotten us up to the part of their story where they were like hamsters avoiding the dinosaurs. I don't mean to be an asshole, but...so what?"

Elvi didn't know exactly what she'd been expecting him to say, but it hadn't been that. "So we know something about what they are. This could be the origin of the species that established a vast galactic presence and overcame a bunch of things we always thought were laws of physics? That's a big deal."

"It is. I hear you. But it's so far back, sweetie. If Cara could ask the diamond maybe the top five ways to keep vast monsters from beyond time and space from killing everyone, that might be a better place to start."

"Only if she can understand the answer."

"And if they knew. Which evidence suggests they didn't. I mean that elaborate gamma-ray burst trap in Tecoma system was just them wiring a shotgun to a doorknob. Even if we know everything about the space jellyfish, is that going to be enough?"

They fell silent. Elvi knew the solid feeling at the center of her gut. It was always there these days. The only thing that changed was how aware of it she was. She anticipated what he would say next—*What are we doing here?*—and her own reply—*The best we can*. But he surprised her.

"It's going to be okay."

She laughed, not because she believed it but because it was obviously untrue. And because he wanted to comfort her, and she wanted to be comforted. He took her arm, drawing her across the open desk, and pulled her beside him. His arms enfolded her, and she let herself curl against him until they were floating together, his head at her shoulder, his thighs under hers, like twins in the same amniotic sac. It wasn't an image she thought other people would find heartwarming, but she did. And when she was alone with Fayez, other people weren't important. His breath smelled like smoky tea.

"I'm sorry," she murmured. "Baby, I'm so sorry."

"For what?"

"All of it."

"It's not your fault."

She pressed her cheek to his head, felt the scratch of his hair against her cheek. Tears were sheeting across her eyes, making the office swim like she was underwater. "I know. But I don't know how to fix it, and I'm supposed to."

She felt the subtle expansion and collapse of his sigh. "We are hailing an awful lot of Marys, aren't we?"

"We're making progress. We already know so much more."

"You're right. I'm frustrated. I didn't mean to piss on the project," Fayez said. "If the answer's anywhere, it's here."

She nodded, and hoped that was true, and that the growing sense she felt that there was something important—critical—in her notes that she'd missed was right. And that whatever it was, she could find it in time.

Later, when Fayez had gone to get some sleep, she went through a packet of reports from Ochida. The high-energy physics workgroup had their most recent data ready for review. The latest complex modeling outputs mapped possible connections between the attack on the *Typhoon*, the uptick in virtual particles in Tecoma system, and the initial loss of consciousness after the *Tempest* had destroyed Pallas Station. A surveying company that usually did mining operations around Jupiter was trying to find the weird magic bullet that had been frame-locked to the *Tempest* when it was destroyed. Her own computational biology group was setting up a distributed study that would put subjects in NIRS imaging around the clock in every populated system in hopes of catching good data the next time the enemy flicked consciousness off. And all the reports were being dumped through massive virtual pattern-matching arrays on Earth, Mars, Laconia, and Bara Gaon in hopes that machine intelligence might catch something the humans had overlooked.

It was the broadest, best-funded research effort in the history of the human race. A million people searching through a haystack the size of 1,300 planets and hoping there was a needle in there someplace.

She sometimes wondered if this had been Duarte's plan all along. Push and push until solving the ring entity problem was forced into first position for all humanity. He'd always held that it was a problem they'd have to solve sooner or later, and humans did tend to do their best work when survival was on the line. But whether it had been the high consul's intention or not, humanity had one problem it was trying to solve now. And James fucking Holden had somehow managed to put her in charge of it.

She didn't know whether looking over the vast effort calmed her or keyed her up. Maybe both.

When she reached the end of the packet, she closed down her screen. There were a couple dozen things that she, as head of the Laconian Science Directorate, needed to authorize or comment on, and she would. But after she'd had some food and maybe a nap. If she could sleep.

She pulled herself through the ship, floating down the corridors. Cara and Xan were in the galley with Harshaan Lee and Quinn de Bodard, and Elvi watched them as she decanted herself a bulb of lentil soup.

"Major," Harshaan Lee said, nodding to her as she floated over.

"Doctor," Elvi said, and took a mouthful of soup. The *Falcon* made good food. The lentils tasted almost fresh—like nutrition and mud and comfort—even though they were probably made from textured fungal proteins.

"We were just talking about *Koenji Wizard*," Quinn said. "It's an entertainment feed out of Samavasarana system."

"I don't know it," Elvi said, and Xan, spinning slowly about his z-axis, launched into a description of the story. It involved a hidden space station built by angels that were also human desires in physical form. And apparently there were a lot of songs, one of which Xan sang. Cara joined in for the chorus. Elvi listened and, to her surprise, felt herself beginning to relax. Xan's enthusiasm and the benign, childlike narcissism that drove him to the center of every conversation were actually a joy. For a few minutes, Elvi was out of her own head. It was easy to forget that he'd been a seven-year-old for over forty years now.

She almost regretted coming back to herself.

"Cara?" she said, nodding toward the other side of the common room. "Could I borrow you for a second?"

The girl who wasn't a girl froze the way that she and Xan did sometimes, suddenly going as still as stone. It only lasted a moment, but it was eerie every time. Then she nodded and pushed gently off in the direction Elvi had indicated. Elvi tossed her empty bulb in the recycler and floated over to meet her. Xan, still with Quinn and Harshaan, blinked anxious black eyes at them, and Elvi waved what she hoped was reassuringly.

"What's on your mind, Doc?" Cara said. Her casual informality left Elvi feeling warm toward the girl every time she heard it. For someone who'd been imprisoned and experimented on for decades by an induced sociopath, Cara had given her trust to Elvi quickly.

"Couple things. I wanted to see how you were feeling. The last dive was... There were some interesting readings. It looked like you were in a different kind of sync with our big green friend. It was looking more like a nonlocal reaction than something with light delay."

"Yes," Cara said, so quickly it was almost interrupting. "I felt like that too."

"And since we don't know what this is, I need you to tell me how you feel. Are you all right?"

"I'm fine," Cara said. "Going in there like this seems... I don't know. It feels good. It feels *right*."

Which Elvi knew already. She'd seen the scans and knew what the connection was doing to Cara's endorphin levels. It was anthropomorphizing to say that the BFE wanted Cara to come back. There was no reason to think it had any will or intentions. But it wanted the girl to come back.

Somewhere deep in her mind, Elvi knew that what came next was a mistake. And that she'd chosen to make it.

"Given that," she said, "I'd like to consider accelerating the session schedule. If we could take a day or two less between the dives—"

"That would be great," Cara said. "I don't think there's any reason not to. I can handle it."

Her grin was so genuine—so human—that Elvi couldn't help grinning back. "All right then. I'll talk with the team, and we'll get a new protocol schedule out. Maybe we can try another run as soon as tomorrow?"

Cara gave a little shiver of excitement, and from across the common room, Xan frowned and looked anxious. More than anxious. Melancholy. Elvi took Cara's hand, squeezing her fingers, and Cara squeezed back. A human gesture of connection, as old as the species.

"It's going to be all right," Elvi said, not realizing until she heard herself that she was echoing Fayez. That she hadn't believed it when he said it.

"I know," Cara replied.

Chapter Nine: Kit

His father looked out from the screen, eyes red from happy tears. Probably, Alex Kamal had wept over Kit the same way once, but Kit had been a baby then. He didn't remember it, and so seeing it now felt like the revelation of something new.

"I am so proud of what you and Rohi are doing. The life you've put together. It's—it's—it's hard to understand what it means to make a family. To bring a new person into the world. But now that you have, I hope you can see that's the love we had for you. Me and your mother both. It's overwhelming. This is everything I hoped you could find. And I know—I *know*—that you'll be a good father. A better father than I was."

"Oh, fuck, Dad," Kit breathed. "Are we doing this again?"

"The bad things that happened were never about you. About how much I loved you. How much I do love you. I am so full.

What you've done, it just leaves me feeling so full. I'm so happy. I'm so happy for you."

The message ended. It was five full minutes long, and Kit wasn't sure he had the stamina right now to listen to it again. It was easy for his father to romanticize Kit's life. Distance and the political dangers of their contact meant Alex could only see a small part of a very large picture.

He checked the time. There wasn't much to say, and most of it wasn't something he'd want to put on Alex's shoulders anyway. If Aunt Bobbie had still been alive, maybe he'd have turned to her. She'd had a way of seeing to the heart of a thing. Compassion without sentimentality. His father was carrying too much baggage for that, and Kit still couldn't help protecting him.

He started the recording.

"Hey," he said into the camera. "I want you to know that I really appreciate you coming close enough to swap these messages close to real time. More often than not, I send you something and I just have to hope you even got it…Shit."

He stopped the recording, deleted it. He didn't want this to devolve into another round of Alex whipping himself for not being more present in Kit's adolescence. The issue carried more guilt for his father than any resentment from Kit. It was just that he had too much right now to add on the burden of one more person's emotional well-being.

But he had to say something.

The door chime saved him for the moment. He dropped his comms and told the door to unlock. His mother breezed into the apartment the way she always did. She was a stately, strong-jawed woman who wielded the nobility of her features like a club. Kit loved her and he always would, but he liked her more when she was on a screen.

"Where's my baby?" she said with a grin. She didn't mean him.

"Rohi's changing his diaper," Kit said, gesturing toward the back room with his chin. "She'll be out in a minute."

"Rokia!" Giselle said. "Grandma's come to help."

Rohi hated it when people not from her birth family used her full name. From the day his mother had found that out, she'd never called her anything else. Kit understood that she meant it as a statement of love and acceptance. He also understood it was a power play. The apparent contradiction of being both things at once made sense to him in a way it didn't to Rohi, but he'd been raised with it. The dysfunctions and idiosyncrasies of childhood became the self-evident norms of adulthood.

He listened to their voices—Giselle's and Rohi's and the gabble and fuss that was Bakari. He couldn't make out the words, but he knew the tones. Mother's imperiousness compensating for her insecurity. Rohi's polite kindness that masked her annoyance. And the baby's vocalizations, still too new to mean anything to Kit but his own joy and exhaustion.

A minute later, the three of them came out together: his mother, his wife, and his son. Giselle already had Bakari on her hip. Rohi's smile was strained but patient.

"Grandma's here," his mother said. "I am in control. You two lovelies go off and enjoy your date night while I play with my perfect baby boy."

"We'll be back after dinner," Kit said.

"Don't hurry," Giselle said with an airy wave. Rohi's eye roll was so small it was almost subliminal. Kit bowed to his mother, kissed his confused son on the top of his head where the bones hadn't yet fused, and then he and Rohi walked out to the public corridor and closed the door behind them. The last thing he heard was Bakari starting to wail as he realized they were leaving.

"Date night?" Rohi asked as they walked down toward the local hub.

"It was easier than 'Rohi and I need to have an uninterrupted conversation,'" Kit said. "It would have been half an hour of her telling me why divorce is bad. This way, there was no lecture."

He had hoped she would laugh, but her nod was sharp, short, and businesslike. She didn't take his arm, and her gaze stayed locked on the walkway before them. The common corridor was bright, and the plants on the median shifted their broad leaves in the breeze of the recyclers. They'd taken positions at Aterpol on Mars with the understanding that it was both a center of research, second in the Sol system only to Earth, and a more congenial place for pregnancy than any of the deeper stations except maybe Ganymede. Giselle had been delighted, and Rohi had too, at first.

They came to the noodle bar that had been their habitual off-shift hangout. A young man with an untreated acne problem and a dombra sat on a little dais, plucking a gentle melody and being ignored by the people eating at the tables. Kit sat, Rohi sat across from him, and they ignored the music too.

"Do you want to order first?" Kit said, careful to keep his voice neutral.

"Yes," Rohi said. It didn't take more than a moment to key their preferences into the table and have the system confirm them. They sat in silence for the three minutes before old Jandol came out with their bowls—lemongrass and egg roll for him, com chiên cá for her. That she'd ordered one of her comfort foods meant something to him. Jandol nodded to them both, missing the tension or else ignoring it, and went back to the kitchen. Rohi leaned in over her bowl.

"Well," Kit said. "What's on your mind?"

"Hear me out, all right?"

He nodded her on.

"I think we should look at postponing the contract again."

"Rohi—"

"No, hear me out." She waited until she was sure he'd be quiet. "I know Mars is only a third of a g, but it's a consistent third. Always-on gravity is really important in the first few months of development. His inner ear is still forming. His bone growth is starting. He'll be going through a lot of fundamental changes in the next year, and even if we're on one of the fast ships, we'll still be on the float for months. I don't want him to grow up with any of the low-gravity syndromes. I don't want to start his life by changing his body in ways that give him fewer options later on. Not if I don't have to."

"I hear what you're saying."

"I've looked at the schedule. There's three other parts of the team who could take our berth on the *Preiss*. We'd still be in the date range if we switched to going out on the *Nag Hammadi*."

"Assuming we got on it," Kit said.

"I'm not saying don't *ever* do it," Rohi said. "I'm not saying *cancel* the contract. That's not what I *meant*."

A fat, slow tear drifted down her cheek, and she wiped it away like it had betrayed her.

Kit took a deep breath, and let it out. When he spoke, he spoke carefully. "You're crying."

"Yeah. Well, I'm scared."

"What are you scared of?"

She looked at him, incredulous. Like the answer was obvious. It was, but he thought it was important for her to say it out loud anyway.

"I'm suggesting that you compromise your career," she said. That she'd said *your* career, not *our* careers, was everything. Kit thought he'd understood the dynamic between them, and now he knew he was right. The corners of her mouth tugged down, and he could see for a moment what she'd looked like as a child, long before he met her.

"Okay," he said. "My turn?"

She nodded.

"Here's the first thing," he said. "I'm not my father. And I'm not your mothers. I'm not going to make the decisions they made. You and Bakari are my first choice, every time. I'm not going to leave, even if it means cutting off a career path."

"I just—"

He took her hand. "Hear me out?"

She nodded. The next tear, she ignored.

"I know this isn't the perfect time," he said. "But there's never going to be a perfect time. There will always be something.

Bakari's development or my mother's health or a conference we won't be able to come back for or something. There's always something."

"Until Laconia decides to start another war to prove a point. Or the aliens kill us all."

"I can't control any of that," Kit said. "All I can do is keep acting like the universe is going to keep existing and planning for a future in it. Nieuwestad is one-point-two g. It's going to be hard on him, and us too. Jacobin-Black Combined Capital is a good company doing the kind of work we want to do, but that doesn't mean we have to do it. We can break the contract and find something else. Or we can go and do the best we can. If we go, there are a lot of good programs for helping kids and babies with gravity transitions. And I'll get up to go to the gym with you every day if you want. If we stay here, there are other jobs. We can do anything. But we're going to be doing it together."

Rohi's eyes were red now, and she wicked the tears away with her napkin. "This is stupid."

Kit took her hand. "You get scared when we talk about balancing the family and work, and it's okay that you do. I get it, and I love you, and a good cry is just part of the way we talk about this stuff. And you never judge me when it's my turn to be the weepy one."

"I just don't want to mess things up," she said. "What if we mess things up for him?"

Kit stroked her knuckles with his thumb the way he did when she couldn't sleep. "We will, though. No one's perfect. Everyone's carrying something that their parents would have done differently if they'd known. Or if they'd been better people. Or if things had just been different. That's all right. It's normal. Part of why I am what I am is all the bad choices my mom and dad made, and if they'd done differently, they'd still have made some mistakes somewhere along the line, and those would be part of me instead. They weren't perfect, and we aren't perfect."

"He is, though," Rohi said. "Bakari is."

"He is, isn't he?"

They were quiet for a little while. Jandol came out and offered to take their leftovers away. When Kit shook his head, the old man shrugged and puttered back to the kitchen.

Eventually, Rohi hauled in a breath, and when she sighed, she folded forward. When she spoke, her voice had lost its tightness. "All right. Thank you."

"Don't say 'I'm sorry.'"

"I didn't."

"You were about to."

She smiled, and he could see the storm had passed. "I was about to."

He sucked up a mouthful of noodles and chewed. The lemongrass tasted real, and the noodles were soft and salty. If they'd gone a little cold, he didn't care. Rohi sighed and relaxed into her chair.

After dinner, they walked home slowly. She took his hand, and he leaned against her. For a while, it was almost like they were courting again, only deeper. Richer. Fuller. This was the life that both of their parental groups had given up, and Kit didn't understand any of them at all.

At the rooms, Giselle was sitting on the couch, spooling through entertainment newsfeeds on her handheld. As they came in, she lifted a finger to her lips and pointed toward the nursery.

"He fell asleep ten minutes ago," she said. "Ate well. Shat out his bodyweight. Giggled, played, cried for fifteen seconds, and out."

"Thank you, Mama," Kit said, and Giselle stood up and wrapped him in her arms.

"It's not for you," she said, quietly enough that only he could hear. "I'm soaking in all the grandbaby I can while I have him. Storing up for winter."

After she left, Rohi went to her office, walking softly to keep from waking the baby, and he sat at his own desk and pulled up his message queue.

He started the camera.

"Hey, Dad. I love you too. Thank you for coming close enough to send the message. I know how hard that can be. And I love you for it. Having a kid is the scariest thing I've ever done, and I love it. I love having a kid. I love being a dad.

"I know you and Mom didn't have things go the way you'd have picked. But no matter what happened, I always knew you cared about me. I learned that from you. If that's the only thing I manage to pass on, it'll be worth it. It's a great legacy. Seriously the best."

He tried to think of something more, but exhaustion was seeping in at the corners of his brain, and he didn't really know what else there was to say. He reviewed it, sent it, scrubbed his system the way he always did when he'd gotten something from the underground's network, then showered and got ready for bed.

Rohi wasn't there. He found her standing over the crib, looking down at the new little life they'd made together. Bakari's soft, round belly rose and fell as he slept. Kit stood there with her and with him.

"He's a strong little guy, isn't he?" Rohi said.

"He is. And his parents love him."

"Okay, then. Let's go."

Chapter Ten: Fayez

Planetary geology wasn't the sort of degree people usually went into looking for a career as a kingmaker. There wasn't a lot of crossover between freshman analysis of sedimentary patterns and having people vie for your influence over issues of life and death. Add in political sway over a galaxy-spanning empire, and the overlap was pretty narrow.

But without intending to, Fayez had stumbled into it.

He was floating in Lee's private cabin with a bone-colored bulb of whiskey in one hand. It was a thick, peaty distillation that was too harsh for him when they were under thrust. A couple weeks on the float did something to deaden his taste buds, and so at times like this, it was perfect. Lee, Elvi's second-in-command, was queuing up a message from home. Or, at least, from Laconia. Which despite having lived there for years, Fayez still didn't think of as home.

"Here," Lee said, pushing back from his station.

"Okay, who am I looking at?" Fayez said.

"His name is Galwan ud-Din," Lee said. "He's a senior researcher in extrapolative physics."

"Right. So I'm not going to understand this at all, am I?"

"I told him to give you the educated layman's version."

The screen flipped to an image of a thin-faced man with a vast and well-trimmed beard and a collarless formal shirt. He nodded to the camera in not-quite-a-bow. "Thank you for your time, Dr. Sarkis. I want you to know how much I appreciate it."

Since it was a recording, Fayez sighed.

"I wanted to share with you some thoughts my workgroup has put together. I think you will find them very promising," the thin-faced man said, then visibly gathered himself. His expression settled into the thing Fayez expected on grade-school teachers who were trying to be approachable. "Light, as I'm sure you know, is a membrane phenomenon on the surface of time."

Fayez drained the bulb of the last drop of whiskey and put his hand out for another. Lee had it ready.

For half an hour, ud-Din made what in the end was a surprisingly comprehensible case that Elvi's slow-life jellyfish had ended their evolutionary arc as a complex, vastly distributed brain-like structure that relied on the counterintuitive truth that time dilation put photons in a state of instantaneous emission from a distant star and absorption by an observing eye even if they seemed to outside observers like Fayez to travel for years in between. The rate-limiting step on a system like that would always be mass, and so technologies for moving mass—inertia manipulation, "shortcut" ring gates—would be prioritized, which evidence suggested they had been.

By the end of the presentation, Fayez felt almost as excited as ud-Din seemed to be, and he hadn't even finished his second whiskey.

"You see, I hope," ud-Din said, "why I am so hopeful for this path of research. Which is why I need to ask your help. The new orders from the Science Directorate putting us at the beck and call of Colonel Tanaka...I don't dispute that the high consul has the absolute right to direct our efforts as needed, but you have his ear. If you could encourage him to refrain from interrupting our research unless it is critical to the empire. I...I only say it because I feel we are on the verge of a breakthrough, and I would hate for the high consul to make his decisions about our workgroup without a full understanding of our situation. Thank you. Thank you for your time."

Ud-Din licked his lips anxiously and the message ended. *How charming to pretend there's still a high consul running this bumblefuck*, Fayez thought, but didn't say aloud. Some things were too dangerous, even for a kingmaker.

"I have half a dozen like this," Lee said. "Workgroup and research leads who got the message to do whatever Tanaka asks. Several of them, she has already retasked."

"They know we can't do shit about it, right? Because we literally can't do shit about that. You got the brief about what Tanaka's doing?"

"I did," Lee said, and then pointedly didn't expand on it. "We have a great many absolute top priorities. We can't do them all."

"I get that," Fayez said. "But Elvi's not the one setting them. She's been very open about letting expertise place the goalposts."

"But she is the adoréd saint to Duarte's Holy Ghost," Lee said. "People want her to intercede for them."

"And so they ask you to ask me to ask her," Fayez said. "No, one more. So that she'll ask him. Or, functionally, Trejo."

"Yes."

"The way we do things, it's amazing humans ever figured out shoes. I'll talk to her, but you know how she is right now."

"I do. Thank you, Dr. Sarkis."

"Keep plying me with drink, and you'll wind up turning my head, Dr. Lee."

Lee's thin smile was as close to emotional intimacy as the man got. Fayez liked him.

The halls of the *Falcon* hummed and glowed. He navigated his way through them from handhold to Laconian-blue handhold. Some of the younger members of the crew launched themselves like Belters, zipping from intersection to intersection without touching a wall in between. He wasn't that guy. Getting where he was going with all his cartilage intact had become a more interesting prospect in the last couple decades.

The thing about expertise was that it wasn't actually transferable. Winston Duarte had cut his teeth in the MCRN's logistics department, where he had apparently been an underappreciated genius. It was easy to see how his brilliance there had helped build his breakaway empire. He'd pulled it off, and by grabbing up samples of the protomolecule and the experts who could use it, he'd tamed enough of the alien technology to put all humanity under his heel. For a while, anyway.

Being good at something—even the best that humanity's billions could offer—didn't make him good at everything. It just made him too powerful to say no to. And so when he decided to make himself into an immortal god-king, not for his own benefit, but to selflessly provide the human race with the continuing stable leadership that it needed in order to storm heaven and kill God, he'd already talked himself and everyone around him into thinking he was as impressive as the story about him claimed.

Only a few people officially knew how badly that plan had gone. Elvi was one. Fayez was another.

He heard Elvi and Cara talking as soon as he came into the corridor for her lab. The door to Elvi's office was open, and Cara was floating in the open space between the workbench and the medical scanners. The young woman's—girl's—face was bright with excitement, and she gestured as she spoke, as if she needed to stuff more meaning into the words than mere syllables could hold. Elvi was strapped into her crash couch, taking notes as they spoke. Except for the part where they didn't look even vaguely genetically related, they reminded Fayez of a grandmother and granddaughter bonding through solving some great puzzle. Even before he could make out what they were saying, the tones of their voices told the story. Giddy and enthusiastic was the good spin. Fevered and manic also fit.

"Then there was this sense of…of light?" Cara said. "Like we were eating eyes and it made me able to see."

"That actually fits," Elvi said.

"It does?" Fayez said. "What does it fit into? Because I just learned a lot about light, and it was really weird."

Elvi's smile wasn't annoyed at all, and Cara's was only a little. "I think our sea slugs hit a milestone," Elvi said. "They already had a method of exchanging information through direct physical transfer, like bacteria trading plasmids. If we're getting this right, they formed a mutualistic relationship or successful parasitism with a little goo cap that could go down to the volcanic vents and come back up."

"Ooh. Dirty," Fayez said, pulling himself fully into the room. With all three of them, it was a little tighter than comfort, but Cara grabbed the wall and made space for him. "How did the eyeballs come into it?"

"They harvested evolutionary innovations from the faster ecosystem. Something down by the vent figured out a rudimentary infrared eye so that it could navigate the vent. The slugs got it, put it on the signaling protein mechanism, and all of a sudden they didn't need to stick plasmids into each other to share information anymore. They could do infrared semaphore."

"No, it was light," Cara said.

"Maybe bioluminescence," Elvi agreed. "At that point, the very slow things started being able to talk very very fast. And they start looking a lot less like jellyfish and a lot more like free-floating neurons. Plus we already see the deep strategy of sending out semi-biological runners to inhospitable biomes and implanting instruction sets into whatever life they find there. Which—I'm stretching here—starts sounding a lot like the protomolecule's mission on Phoebe…" Her voice trailed off. Her smile shifted to something more rueful. "But that's not what you came to talk about, is it?"

"There's a briefing you should totally listen to, but no," Fayez said. "I needed to talk about something else."

"Cara? Could we take a quick break?"

The black eyes were still for a fraction of a second, then flickered up to Fayez and away. "Sure. No problem."

Cara pushed herself to the doorway and out into the corridor, closing the office door behind her as she went. Fayez drifted to the medical scanners. Cara's readouts were still on the screens. He traced the curve of her stress metabolites. He wouldn't have known what they were, except Elvi had explained them.

"They're not as high as they look," she said, a little defensively. "We don't even really know what the upper boundary is for someone who's been modified like her."

"I didn't know you were doing another dive today," Fayez said.

"She felt up to it. That's not what you came for either, is it?"

He shut down the screens, rotated back to face Elvi, and braced on a foothold. "The Tanaka thing is a problem."

She had looked tired before he said it. She looked worse now. "What are we seeing?"

"She's reallocated and retasked four workgroups. Instead of doing deep background scanning, they're searching for an artifact that may or may not have left from Laconia and doing deep brain scans of Trejo looking for . . . I don't know what."

"Traces of manipulation," Elvi said. "Something that would show evidence that he'd had a direct neural link like the one James Holden and the remnants of Miller did on Ilus."

"So you know about this?"

Elvi made a vague, helpless gesture. "She outranks me."

"But you're the administrator of the Science Directorate."

"And that used to matter," Elvi said. "Not anymore. Right now, her orders might as well say, 'from the desk of God.' "

"These scientists want you to protect them from the bureaucracy."

"What they want is for me to talk Duarte into overriding Trejo and getting her clearance pulled," Elvi said. "There's a problem with that plan."

"That Duarte doesn't exist?"

"That Tanaka will need to find him before I can ask him any favors, yes."

Fayez was quiet for a moment. He didn't want to go to the next place, but he had to. "Do you think that's really what's going on?"

Elvi's sigh meant she'd had the same thoughts and suspicions. "You mean do I think Tanaka's really searching for a version of Duarte that came out of his coma and disappeared?"

"Or is Trejo feeding us a story and seeing if it leaks out to the underground? This could all be a test. Duarte could be back at the State Building right now contemplating his oatmeal. We wouldn't know until Dr. Lee gets a quiet order to put a bullet in the backs of our heads. We're high in the food chain, but Trejo's still an authoritarian despot, and there's a lot of precedent for shit like that."

"I can't care about it," Elvi said. "I can't play the game. I don't have the focus or the energy."

"You can stop feeding our results to Jim and Nagata."

Elvi nodded, but not in the way that meant she agreed.

Fayez pressed his fingertips into his closed eyelids. "Babe," he said, but she stopped him.

"It's happening more than we thought."

"What? What's happening?"

"The incidents. Like Gedara. We've only been seeing the near misses. We always catch the ones that turn off consciousness, but I had Ochida run through pattern matching for other anomalies like Gedara's lightspeed thing? They're happening all the time."

"What do you mean, all the time?" Fayez said, but his gut had gone suddenly cold.

"Changes in virtual particle annihilations in Pátria, Felicité, and Kunlun systems. Lightspeed variations in Sumner and Farhome. Electron mass changed in Haza system for almost two minutes. *Electron mass.* Sanctuary system had gravity increase by a tenth of a percent throughout the system for six seconds."

"Okay, every single thing you just said fucks me up."

"This was one twenty-four-hour period. The things that are

doing this are rattling all the windows looking for the way to make us die, and I don't know how we guard our physical fucking constants against attack. It's just a matter of time before they figure out how to trigger vacuum decay or something. So I'm going to keep doing exactly everything I can, and yes, that means sharing data. Because if that's how we catch a break on this, it will be worth it. And if poor Dr. Lee needs to assassinate me because of it, at least it won't be my problem anymore."

"Okay. I get it."

"Trejo's fighting to hold on to an empire. I'm fighting to have something that's recognizable as the universe with living things in it."

"I get it," he said again, but now that she'd started, she couldn't stop. Not until the pressure was vented.

"If there's a chance—one chance in a billion—for me to figure this out, I'm taking it. If there's a price that I have to pay, that's fine. Not even going to think about that. Just opening my wallet, and whatever the universe needs to take from me, it's welcome to. That's what we're playing for. So yes, I really, really hope that Duarte snapped out of his fugue state and ran off to do whatever the fuck half-protomolecule former emperors do in their retirement, because that would mean Trejo wasn't playing court intrigue games with me while I'm at work. But who knows? I don't."

She went quiet, still shaking her head in a tight, angry motion. Fayez steadied himself on the handhold.

"How do I help?"

"Just keep doing what you're doing. Help me keep doing what I'm doing. Hope that we catch a break in time."

"All right," he said. "Can do."

"I'm sorry. I didn't mean to—"

"I do not accept your apology. You're right. I get it."

She took his hand. She felt cold. Her skin was dry. She'd grown thin enough that he could feel the individual tendons shifting over her bones. "I'm so sorry I pulled you into this."

"It's hellish, that's true. But the company's good."

"No one I'd rather face the end of everything with than you."

"It's because I have a cute ass, isn't it? That's my secret power." She managed a smile. "You got me."

"I can crack a walnut with these cheeks," Fayez said. "I mean, you wouldn't want to eat it afterward, but—"

"I love you," she said. "Stop cheering me up. Send Cara back. I need to get some work done."

He found Cara in her quarters with Xan. They were floating together in the space between their bunks, with Xan chattering excitedly about something from his entertainment feeds. Cara's face was the polite boredom of older siblings throughout history. It was weirdly reassuring to see something normal, given their context. When Fayez cleared his throat, the pleasure on the girl's face was as clear as the disappointment on her brother's.

"Is Dr. Okoye ready?" Cara asked, and there was a hunger in the question that left Fayez a little uncomfortable. He swallowed it.

"She is. Sorry I interrupted. Just had some stuff I needed to talk with her about."

"It's okay," Cara said. "But I should go."

Fayez pulled himself aside and let the girl haul herself out. As she floated down the corridor, he had one of those moments he had sometimes where his sense of balance tried to wake up. For just a moment, Cara wasn't floating away to the side, but falling headfirst down the hallway. He grabbed the handhold to steady himself, and after a few breaths, the feeling passed.

"Is something wrong?" Xan asked.

"No. I just...I'm never going to get used to living on the float. Spent my formative years down a gravity well, and some things are baked in."

"I've heard that," Xan said, then turned and touched the ceiling to press himself down toward the floor. It was hard to read his expression. The kid had been a little boy for several decades now, and between his child-stuck brain and the depth of his experience, he wasn't really one thing or the other. His sister was like that too. It was impossible to see them as children, and it was impossible not to. Xan's mag boots locked onto the deck, and he turned almost like he was walking in gravity.

"What about you?" Fayez said. "All well in your world?"

"I'm worried about Cara," he said without hesitating. "She keeps coming back different."

"Yeah? Different how?"

"Changed," Xan said. "The thing that's teaching her? It's making her too."

The chill that ran through Fayez had nothing to do with temperature. He kept his tone light and jovial. "What's it making her into, do you think?"

Xan shook his head. An *I don't know* motion. "We'll find out," he said.

Chapter Eleven: Teresa

At fifteen years since the first permanent settlements, New Egypt was a younger colony system. It had two planets with large habitable areas. The school where she was going to live, like most of the other established settlements, was on the smaller of them, the fourth planet out from the sun. The planet—called Abbassia—had a little under three-quarters g and a thirty-hour day. For reasons that hadn't been investigated in depth yet, the magnetosphere was very strong, which was important given the very active and frequent solar flares. Even near the equator, the auroras were supposed to be magnificent.

The total population of the two planets together was less than the Laconian capital, and it was spread across half a dozen small cities and a score of mineral extraction sites. Only a third of Abbassia was covered by ocean, and most of the land surface was arid, though with extensive cloud forest analogs at upper elevations in both the northern and southern hemispheres.

Sohag Presbyterian Academy was nestled in a river valley in the south, a few hundred kilometers from Nouvelle École, with which it cooperated academically. Sohag Presbyterian's grounds were a little under a thousand hectares of terraformed soil and agricultural cultivates. The buildings had been designed by Alvaro Pió shortly before his death, and they were listed in the top thousand most significant architectural sites in the new worlds.

Teresa had looked at pictures of the campus filled with smiling young people her age and a little older. She tried to imagine herself among them. Tried to imagine who she would be if she were in those images. *This is going to be my home now. Unless something goes wrong.*

And it seemed like something might be going wrong.

The whole crew was gathered at a screen on the ops deck that showed the tactical display of the New Egypt system. Their focus—and so Teresa's focus too—was the ship that had just passed through the ring gate 6 AU behind them and was burning hard for Abbassia.

"I don't have it on any of the transit schedules from the underground," Naomi said. "But that's exactly the problem. There isn't a single coordinated set of flight plans, and even if there were, people are smuggling all the time now."

"Nothing on the drive signature?" Jim asked.

"Doesn't match anything in the records," Alex said. "But that doesn't mean much either. Could be something that was built or had the drive swapped out at a shipyard in Bara Gaon or Auberon. There's more and more decent yards in other systems too. It's not like it was back when everything was just Sol system."

"I know," Jim said.

Alex increased the size of the image, but the ship was still too small to make out—a black dot against the brightness of its drive plume. A few dozen meters of ceramic and carbon-silicate lace as seen from almost nine hundred million kilometers. It was a miracle they could make out as much as they could. "Chances are decent that its coming through now is just coincidence."

"Yeah," Jim said in a voice that meant he disagreed. Amos crossed his thick arms over his chest and smiled. He wasn't smiling about anything. Teresa still thought of him as Timothy sometimes. Timothy always smiled, even when he'd been hiding in a cave. Jim hauled in a wide sigh and let it out again. "But if it is a Laconian ship—"

"It still probably wouldn't be tracking us," Naomi said. "We've kept radio silence. We're not even passing data with the local repeater network. They'd have to know we were coming here."

"Probably it's what it looks like," Amos said. "Freighter hauling freight. Or a pirate. Pirates are good too."

"It's not the chances that bother me," Jim said. "It's the stakes. I don't want them tracking us down to the surface."

"I can make landfall when the site's on the far side of the planet," Alex said. "Zip in, drop Teresa and the pup off, and get back up above atmosphere before they'd see us taking off. Even if they're watching, they won't know where we went. Might not even know we landed at all."

Teresa listened with a sensation growing in her belly. It was like a tightness. Or a stone. It had a taste too. She unbuckled herself from the crash couch and pulled herself down the lift. She wasn't sure where she was going, but the crew of the *Rocinante* talking through the details of how they were going to drop her off made staying in place unbearable.

She passed by the galley to the crew quarters, including her own. She heard Muskrat bark an inquiry as she passed, but she didn't answer, just kept going down. The machine shop was as close to a safe and comfortable place as she had anymore. She had a list of tasks from Amos and she pulled it up. It was time to check the water supply's chemical sensors. She'd never done it before, but the instructions were linked to the entry. She read them, gathered up the tools, and made her way to the tank feeds. Her jaw ached. She made herself stop clenching her teeth.

Travel between systems was slow. The *Rocinante* didn't have any of the breathable-fluid crash couches that would let bodies sustain long, very high-g burns. The duties that Amos assigned her to keep her engaged filled the gap that Ilich and other tutors had left, and she clung to them now not because she particularly enjoyed them, but because they were familiar. And because it felt like laying claim to something.

She was about halfway done with a bubble of escaped water the size of her fist adhering to her arm when Amos pulled himself in beside her. He didn't say anything, just took a little hand vacuum and cleaned the spilled water off her wrist. He handed her tools when she needed them and stowed them for her when she didn't. It went faster with him there. In the end, she found that two sensors out of sixty were showing periodic faults. Low-voltage shorts. Harmless. And they could be down half the sensors and not really have to worry about water quality. She tagged both of them for replacement anyway. Amos' philosophy was to replace things before you needed to, not after. She found it a sensible rule.

"So," he said, "this was back on Earth when I was younger than you are now. There was this guy I knew. His parents both OD'd the same night. Upside, he was a registered birth, so someone gave a shit. Downside, he got put into the foster system. It fucked him up pretty good."

"Abusive foster caregivers are a common issue in aggressively individualist social orders. I had a unit about civil service reform two years ago. We studied it."

"True, but that wasn't the only thing got him. He was one of those people that tried to put down roots, you know? Wherever he was, he'd find things and hold on to them. Put him in a new city for a week, and he'd already have a favorite park. That kind of shit. Only it was fostering, so every few months he'd lose it all again."

"Is this an uplifting story about how he found his real home inside himself?"

Amos went still for a moment the way he did, then looked chagrined. "Actually, he got addicted to a bunch of home-brewed narcotics and slow-melted his nervous system. So, nah, not really. I was trying to say that you're not the only one who has a hard time letting go. Moving on to the next thing. I don't know. Thought it might help to hear that."

"What about you?"

"I'm good wherever I am," he said. "But getting to that point was unpleasant. You don't want to be like me."

They were quiet for a moment. Her sleeve was still wet. It clung to her arm.

"I'm angry," she said.

"I know."

"I feel like he's throwing me away. Putting me aside because I'm inconvenient."

"I hear you."

"It's like who I am and what I want don't even matter to him. I know that's crazy. Or at least I know it's overblown, but it's like I have a splinter I can't dig out. It's just right there on my nerve ending, and every time I even brush up against it, it hurts."

"Yeah."

She sat still, feeling her blood pulse in her temple, her mind agitated. "I'm not really mad at the captain, am I? This is about my father."

"This school thing could be good for you, Tiny. A lot healthier than hanging around an old warship with nobody your own age."

"But I *like* it here. You like me being here, right?"

"No," Amos said. "I don't want you to stay."

It felt like a punch in the gut. "But—"

"Look, Tiny, I've watched a lot of people die. Some of them were my friends. I'm mostly okay with that now. But I ain't ready to watch you die. And if you stay here on this ship, you will. That's the kind of ship this is."

"That's what Jim said too," Teresa said.

"Yeah? Well, the two of us see a lot of things the same way."

"You seem very different to me."

"We are."

"You're going to be fighting for the fate of humanity. I'm going to be worrying about algebra assignments."

"Well, maybe you'll get lucky and we'll win and the algebra will matter. Then twenty, thirty years down the road, something else will show up to slaughter everyone, and you can take care of that one."

She didn't want to be crying. She didn't want to be sad. Amos leaned over and put a thick, ropy arm around her. He was strangely hot to the touch, like he was always running a fever. She leaned into him and wept anyway.

She said her goodbyes to Alex and Naomi on the ship just after they touched down. They'd landed far enough away from the school that they wouldn't damage the grounds, so there was still a little walk from her old life to her new one. She tried not to think about that. It was easier if she could pretend that this wasn't the last time she would be on the ship. That she didn't have to start her life over again. She just put one foot in front of the other as if this particular walk didn't signify anything in particular.

Jim and Amos went with her to make sure everything was all right, but she could tell their minds were more than half on the incoming ship. Like guards from the State Building, they wore light body armor and sidearms. She just had a duffel bag with a couple of folded flight suits and a few days' supply of dog food. Muskrat trotted along with them, her brown, worried eyes shifting between Teresa and Amos.

The sky was wide and blue with cumulus clouds on the horizon. The valley opened before them, gentle curves of land that looked like erosion and wind and the growth of plants. The local plants were tall and thin, rising up into the air like three-meter-high blades of blue-tinged grass. The breeze passing among them sounded like radio static. The school's grounds stood out from the world around it—straight lines and right angles. The air smelled like overheated metal.

There weren't any people.

"Term doesn't start for another two weeks," Jim said. "You're probably the first to arrive."

"Isn't it a boarding school?" Teresa asked.

"They still have breaks between terms. I mean, don't they?"

Amos shrugged. "Not a lot of private school types in my social circles. They know we're coming?"

"Finley knows to expect us, but Naomi was keeping the radio-silence thing pretty strict. You know, in case."

"Sure," Amos said.

The main path was crushed stone gravel, light gray with flashes of pink and blue and gold where the sunlight glittered off it. An earthmover stood idle at the side of the path. Its wide industrial treads had left tracks behind it half a meter across. The disturbed ground was dark and damp. The sun hadn't dried it yet. Amos smiled at nothing in particular, looking around like a tourist taking in the sights. Jim seemed tenser.

They walked up the path to a central courtyard three glass-windowed stories tall with a canopy stretched between the buildings. A stone fountain had lines of mineral deposits that showed where the water would have flowed if it had been flowing.

Teresa recognized it all from her reading about the school—the pale wood juxtaposed with the glass was apparently very interesting from an architectural perspective, but she just thought it looked awkward. The smiling kids and serious instructors that had filled the campus weren't there, though. Muskrat whined and pressed in against Teresa's leg.

"Yeah, dog," Amos said. "Putting my little hairs up too."

The wide double doors of the main building ten meters ahead of them swung open and a woman stepped out. Her arms were out at her sides, her hands open and empty. She was tall, long limbed, and thin, with high cheekbones and dark eyes. Her skin looked as taut and tough as if she'd been carved out of wood. Teresa couldn't guess the woman's age, but she wore a Laconian Marine uniform.

Jim muttered *fuck* to himself.

"I'm unarmed," the woman said. Teresa recognized her tone. An officer's voice. Brusque, and carrying an expectation of obedience. Her father's palace had been filled with voices like it. "I'm no threat to you. You don't need to escalate."

"What are you doing here?" Teresa said, loud enough to carry through the courtyard. "Do you know who I am?"

Amos put a hand on her shoulder and gently pulled her half a step back. Jim's eyes were wide, and his face was bloodless. If his expression hadn't been so calm, she would have thought he was having a panic attack.

"Yes, I know who you are," the woman said. "You're Teresa Duarte. I am Colonel Aliana Tanaka of the Laconian Marine Corps. And Captain Holden, if I'm not mistaken. I have to say that's a bit of a surprise. I'd have thought you'd have put her on a different ship. Eggs. Baskets. You know."

Jim stood silent. Frozen. *Oh*, Teresa thought. *He's* about *to have a panic attack.*

"I'm not here to hurt anyone," Tanaka said. "I need the girl's help."

"I am here of my own free will," Teresa said. "If my father—"

"At this point, I am considerably better briefed about your father's condition than you are," Tanaka said.

Amos reached down into his pocket, appearing to scratch idly at his leg while he looked up toward the canopy. Teresa heard a tiny, distant voice. Alex, saying *What's up, big guy?*

"If we're all friends and just talking," Amos said, his voice loud enough to carry, "how come you got a fire team on the roof up there?"

Teresa looked up. She wasn't certain, but there might have been shadows on the canopy. Her heart was tapping at her ribs like it wanted to get out. Muskrat whined, and she put a hand on the old dog's back.

"He's right," Jim said, his voice steadier than Teresa expected. "That doesn't seem friendly."

The woman didn't miss a beat. "You're correct. If I wanted to resolve this through violence, it would already be resolved. But I think we've all been through enough firefights to understand that when the bullets start flying, it gets very hard to be certain where they all end up. And I don't want anything to happen to the girl either."

"Where's the head of school?" Jim said. "The one who was meeting us?"

"She's safe. Honestly, I was hoping I'd find Teresa already here."

"We didn't know we were inconveniencing you, or we'd have scheduled things differently," Jim said. Despite the casualness of his words, his voice was like a wire under so much tension it was about to snap.

"In your position, I would have made getting her to safety a much higher priority. You can't imagine what a relief it is to discover I didn't waste my time coming out."

"You sure about that?" Jim said.

"Wouldn't play with this one, Cap," Amos said softly. There was a dangerous buzz in his voice Teresa had only heard once before. *Close your eyes, Tiny. You don't want to watch this.* The last thing he'd said to her before he'd been killed.

"This isn't a fight either of us need to have," Tanaka said, taking a few slow steps forward. Her arms were still out to her sides, fingers splayed to emphasize the emptiness of her hands. "I'm not looking to arrest you, Captain Holden. Or your crew. Or your ship. You're free to go. My mandate at present is very narrow."

Teresa glanced over at Jim, and he looked back. While their gazes were still locked, he shouted, "How do I know you won't open fire as soon as we don't have her?"

There was no reason for her to believe that Jim was bluffing. In the moment, Teresa was certain he would leave her with Tanaka, and relief complicated her fear. They didn't want to see her die. She understood that better now. She didn't want to see them die either.

"You have my word," Tanaka said.

"I was looking for something a little more solid."

"I don't have a habit of breaking faith. That's going to have to be enough."

Jim looked away from Teresa, back to the woman. Amos had started humming softly and tunelessly. The shadows on the canopy were larger now, and more clearly shaped like Laconian power armor.

"Not sure that it is going to be enough," Jim said, "but I'm willing to discuss other ways to make a handoff. You let us go back to our ship. Once we're in the airlock, we'll let the girl walk back by herself."

Tanaka's smile was hard. "Let me make a counteroffer. How about you do what I said, and no one dies?"

Jim tensed. He was on the edge of doing something stupid out of fear, and Tanaka was starting to escalate. Teresa had been trained in negotiation strategies, up to and including hostage situations. Jim was going to fuck this up. She had to take control. "I'm a little tired of being talked about like I was luggage. This isn't a conversation between him and you. This is a conversation with me. I decide what ship I leave this place on. Not him."

Muskrat, sensing the tension, started barking and hopping on her front legs. Tanaka smiled, and it was cold.

"All right," Tanaka said. "Please come with me. Do it now, and in return I won't kill your friends."

"You don't have to do this," Jim said, quietly enough that it was just for her to hear it.

Whatever happened, she would know that even now, having landed on this planet to get rid of her, he was still willing to die to protect her. The knot in her stomach was replaced by something warm and comforting. It had to be enough.

"I'll go," Teresa said, but no one heard her. Her voice was suddenly drowned out as the static hiss of the tree-sized grasses took on a deafening rumble. For a second, she thought of earthquakes or stampedes of cattle. Tanaka's neck worked. She was subvocalizing to someone.

"You have to the count of three," Tanaka shouted. "One—"

Amos said *Fuck it*, stepped in front of Teresa, and drew his gun.

Chapter Twelve: Tanaka

The girl was staring at her, arms crossed defiantly, so certain of her place in the natural order. Comfortable with the absolute necessity of her existence. Tanaka had seen that attitude before in other people, many times. She'd also seen the surprise and hurt in their eyes as they died.

Tanaka had no such illusions.

Anyone could die at any time, and the universe didn't give a shit. So while the girl stood in front of her shielded by nothing but the accident of having a powerful daddy, Tanaka wore an armored suit of woven carbon-silicate lace that would stop anything short of a rocket launcher under her clothes.

"I'm a little tired of being talked about like I was luggage. This isn't a conversation between him and you. This is a conversation with me. I decide what ship I leave this place on. Not him."

Oh, little girl, Tanaka thought, *you have no idea.* It made her hands itch to have Duarte's daughter so close and not just grab her. A dozen quick steps and she'd have the girl, the escaped prisoner, and the terrorist who was apparently not dead despite having been shot in the head back on Laconia. But killing the kid had a lot of downside, and the risk wasn't zero. So instead, she smiled and spread her hands a little wider, trying to seem as nonthreatening as possible. James Holden might be rounding the corner from middle-aged into old, but he was still dangerous. And the lump of gristle next to him that went by Amos Burton had more than one question mark next to him in her book. Tanaka didn't underestimate either of them. The dog started barking and bouncing up and down on its front paws. It wasn't a trained attack animal, just an old pet. She knew from the file that the girl would be easier to control if they didn't kill it.

We're all friends here, she smiled at them, willing it to be true. A large-caliber pistol loaded with high explosive rounds pressed into the small of her back in case it turned out they weren't.

"Venom One," a voice said in her ear. "Check check."

"Venom Two at southwest corner, I've got Holden," came a different voice.

"Venom Four northeast, I've got Bluto," said a third.

"Three covering south."

Tanaka smiled. Whatever happened from here in, her enemy was well and truly fucked.

"All right," Tanaka said to Teresa, playing for time. "Please come with me. Do it now, and in return I won't kill your friends."

The girl looked uncertain. She'd never believe a threat made to her. Not really. But threats to her friends she believed. Her file made it clear she had significant abandonment issues. If things like that didn't make you strong, they made you weak.

"You hearing this?" Venom One asked, his mic buzzing with background noise as he spoke.

A distant rumble was growing, the tall swordlike foliage whipping as something blasted toward them. The girl was talking, but whatever she was saying was drowned out by the noise.

"*Sparrowhawk*," Tanaka said, activating the bone mic in her jaw.

"Mugabo here."

"*Rocinante* is oscar mike," she said.

"On our way," Mugabo replied. He'd hidden her ship around the far side of the planet to avoid detection. She'd known that was a risk. She didn't regret it. Not yet, at least. "I'll be to you in twenty."

Tanaka's gaze flickered across what was about to be a battlefield. She probably couldn't stall for twenty.

"Forget me," she said to Mugabo. "Stay on the *Rocinante*. Do not let it leave this planet with the girl on board."

"Are you...authorizing force? Even if the girl is on board?"

Tanaka didn't answer. She needed to get her hands on the target before the *Rocinante* showed up. She couldn't risk losing the girl if the situation went violent. And when her team moved on the two adults and the *Sparrowhawk* showed up overhead, things were liable to go very violent indeed.

Out of time and out of options. Something like pleasure flowed through her. It was time for someone to make a decision.

"You have to the count of three," Tanaka shouted at the girl as she beckoned. *Come to me.* "One—"

Burton shoved the girl behind him and pulled his gun. The *Rocinante* blasted into view, barely skimming the tops of the foliage, the powerful landing thrusters in her belly flattening everything it passed over. Tanaka found herself impressed by the recklessness of the maneuver. Here she was, working so hard not to put the girl in any danger, and the *Rocinante* crew was willing to throw a spaceship at her to keep her away.

"Venom, take the girl," she shouted over the deafening sound of the ship, pulling her gun from behind her back in a smooth, practiced motion. Burton saw her do it and drew down on her as he continued pushing the girl back toward the approaching ship. Tanaka dove behind a low stone planter box just as he fired, the bullet blowing a fountain of soil into the air.

"Shots fired," one of her team said.

"Five millimeter caseless. Low threat," someone else said, as flat and emotionless as if he were placing a lunch order.

"They're firing at *me*," Tanaka shouted back. "Get the girl!"

"Free fire?" Venom One, the team leader, asked.

"No, no shooting. Pull the other two apart with your hands if you need to, but do not risk firing toward the girl," Tanaka yelled, then peeked up over the planter box. Holden, Burton, and the girl were about thirty meters away now, still backing up. The *Rocinante* had taken up position about two hundred and fifty meters farther away, still hovering on its landing jets. It would have to put down to let them board, but the pilot wasn't taking any chances.

A metallic-blue figure dropped into the courtyard between Tanaka and Holden, then darted toward the fleeing group in a blur. Three more figures dropped from the canopy above, surrounding Holden and the girl. Burton pointed his gun at one and started firing.

"Taking fire," Venom Two reported.

Her team moved toward the three, not returning fire but moving fast. Aggressively. The old-style Martian Navy sidearms Holden and Burton carried would never penetrate a modern suit of Laconian power armor. They could fire their guns dry, and her team would just walk up and snap their necks. Quick, neat, almost no danger to the girl unless Burton shot her. But the old mechanic was careful and methodical as he fired. Every shot hit one of Tanaka's team, and he kept the girl behind him.

Venom Three was the closest, only a few meters from Holden, when the world exploded. A blinding flash, and a concussion like someone had hit her in the chest. Tanaka dove back behind her planter box, her mind trying to make the detonation into her team having disobeyed orders and opened fire. But the guns on the Laconian armor weren't that loud. Nothing was that loud.

A quick look over the planter box told her that all four members of her fire team were down. No, not down. Literally blown apart. She could see the remains of Venom Two, an undifferentiated pile of meat and technology spread across a few meters of ground. In the distance, the barrels of the *Rocinante*'s point-defense cannons were fully extended, and swiveling as they looked for new targets.

PDC fire in atmosphere with their own people between the ship and its target. If she'd had time to think about it, she'd have been impressed by the audacity.

Tanaka jumped up to her feet and ran flat out toward one of the school buildings surrounding the courtyard, looking for cover. She imagined one of those PDC barrels snapping around with merciless machine speed to lock onto her. If it fired, she'd never hear the shots that ended her. Against a warship's PDC rounds, her fancy armored undersuit might as well be silk pajamas.

She made it to the wall of the school building. The *Rocinante*, hovering on its maneuvering thrusters, was completely blocked from her line of sight. She didn't think a pilot who flew for James Holden would shoot through a school to get her, but she displaced to another nearby building anyway. Once the shooting had started, people could panic and do things they would never have imagined themselves doing otherwise. Better not to risk it.

The roar of the ship's thrusters rose in pitch, then began to cycle down. The ship had landed. They'd blown her team apart, sent her running, and decided the coast was clear.

The coast is decidedly not clear, motherfuckers.

Tanaka sprinted out from behind the building and into the tall native grass. She ran parallel to the path Holden and crew were taking toward their ship, staying far enough away to hopefully hide the sound of her movement. If anyone could still hear anything after the ear-shattering blast of the *Rocinante*'s PDCs firing in atmosphere. Even if they caught something on thermals, they might think twice about accidentally shooting a bystander. Might. They were a pretty fucking reckless bunch. She was going to enjoy taking them down.

After thirty meters she slowed down and angled in toward the three fleeing shapes. She was still a dozen meters away from them when she caught a glimpse of Holden in his dark Martian armor heading toward the ship. He wasn't looking in her direction. Through the ringing in her ears, she was almost certain she could hear the dog barking, so the girl had to be nearby.

Tanaka angled away and put on more speed, staying low but getting ahead of them. The surface of the tall native grass was covered in tiny hooks that tugged at her clothes when she brushed against them. When she accidentally hit one with the back of her hand, it left a painful abrasion, like a rug burn. She ignored it. She had the scent of blood, and her prey was just a few meters away.

When Tanaka felt she'd gotten far enough ahead of them, she moved back to the edge of the grass and waited. The ship had gone quiet. The grass hummed its white noise around her. From farther down the path, the dog was barking. She heard Holden's voice. *Hurry. They'll have backup coming.* They were a dozen meters or so away and moving toward her. They were trotting, but she'd been faster. One step ahead.

Tanaka stepped out of the grass, leveling her pistol at Holden. The look of surprise on his face would have been comical in any other context. The girl shrieked with alarm and grabbed at her dog's collar as it barked furiously.

"I can't let you leave with that girl."

Holden had his gun in his hand, but it was down at his side. He shifted his weight like he was going to make a move, but Tanaka just shook her head at him and pointed her gun at his face.

"If I spray you all over that girl, she'll panic. If she runs, things get even less predictable than this. No one wants that."

Holden nodded and dropped the pistol, then his gaze shifted to Tanaka's left shoulder.

"Wait," she said, "where's—"

"Right here," said a deep voice from behind her.

Shit. She was one step behind.

She was already swiveling to bring her gun to bear before the second word was out. Something heavy slammed into the side of her head and sent her spinning to the ground. Amos Burton stepped out of the grass, his hands balled up into fists.

"Hi," he said, moving toward her.

The hit was solid, jaw to inner ear. Her world was swimming. Tanaka rolled away and found her gun on the ground. She was bringing it up when Burton's boot connected with her forearm and sent the pistol flying off into the grass.

"What are you doing?" Holden asked.

I'm getting my ass kicked, Tanaka thought, dazed enough to wonder why he was speaking to her.

"I think we might want to talk to this one," Burton said. "Let's take her with us."

Tanaka said, "No," and tried to stand, then let herself collapse again. *Look how hurt I am.* It was only half bullshit.

"Hurry up," Holden said, and started to lead the girl past her.

Burton reached down to grab Tanaka's arm and yank her to her feet. He was very strong. That was good. It would make him over-confident. Tanaka let him pull her up, pushing hard with her legs as she rose, and snapping her other arm up to drive her palm into the underside of the big man's chin. His head jerked back from the impact, but his grip on her left bicep didn't loosen.

He raised his other arm and threw a massive fist at her face. With his hand gripping her, she couldn't dodge, so she whipped her head to the right and slapped at the punch, shoving it to the left. It still grazed her cheek, and the impact was enough to make that side of her face go numb.

The motion brought him in closer, and Tanaka threw her-self backward, letting the momentum of the punch and her own weight yank Burton off his feet and on top of her as she fell.

He let go of her arm, trying by reflex to catch himself, and they both hit the ground. He landed on her like a falling tree, driving the air from her lungs. She was ready for it, though, and threw up an elbow that caught Burton in the throat as he dropped. He made a sound like an injured duck and rolled away, clutching at his neck. Tanaka bounced to her feet and looked for the girl. The swimming world whirled around her. She gritted her teeth and ignored it.

The girl was hiding behind Holden, clutching at her dog and staring at the melee, her mouth a round O of surprise. He was digging around at his feet, trying to pick up his dropped gun.

Tanaka could see hers, lying in the grass not too far away. Diving for it to take a rushed shot at Holden would be risky with the girl so close by. She raised a hand instead. "Holden, wait."

"Leave him out of it," Burton said behind her, "we're not done yet."

Tanaka spun on the ball of her foot and lashed out with a kick at the spot the sound was coming from. The big mechanic casually swatted it away. He looked none the worse for wear after a throat strike that would've killed most people. Something was wrong with his eyes. They were flat black. She remembered reading about someone with eyes like that. She didn't remember who.

"I've read your file," Tanaka said, backing toward Holden and the girl. She didn't have time for a boxing match with the strange-looking man with the eerie black eyes. Not when her best shots didn't seem to even faze him.

"Yeah?" he asked, moving toward her.

"It said we killed you," she said. "Any other time, I'd stay to figure that out." The girl was so close that, if she could just get her balance, she could take two steps, grab her, and be running before the others knew what had happened. Tanaka would place bets they wouldn't shoot at her if she had the kid in her arms.

"You've got time," Burton said.

Tanaka turned toward the girl and then stopped short. Holden was standing in front of her, his gun in his hand. The eyes that had seemed frightened a moment ago were now flat, emotionless, cold. *That's bad.*

"No," he said. "She doesn't."

Before Tanaka could even start to move, Holden's gun went off three times. She felt the three shots as hammer blows to her sternum. All three, center mass. Kill shots. She hadn't been certain until that moment that he had it in him.

Tanaka staggered two steps toward the edge of the path and

then collapsed on her face. The three slugs from Holden's gun pressed into her chest where the nanofiber undershirt had caught them, like daggers in the deep-tissue bruise they'd left in her flesh. She ignored the pain and lay very still, holding her breath.

"Shit, Cap," Burton was saying. "I think we shoulda kept her."

"We have to go. We have to get out of here. Now," Holden replied. He sounded angry. Based on her reading of his file, Tanaka would have bet he wasn't mad at the mechanic. He was angry he'd been forced to shoot someone. For all the shit he'd seen, the Laconian interrogator's psych evaluation said that Holden had never really grown comfortable with violence.

Don't come check my body, Tanaka willed at them.

"Let's get out of here before more of them show up," Holden said, and the three of them started walking away.

Moving as little as possible, Tanaka inched toward her gun. When she was able to put her right hand on it, she risked turning her head to see where they were. Holden and Burton were side by side, the girl between them. They were about forty meters away. Not a very long shot. Not for her. They were both wearing old Martian light body armor. The high explosive rounds in her pistol would go right through it. There was some risk of fragmentation hitting the girl, but it wasn't likely to be fatal. And fuck it. A little bruising might do the bitch some good.

Tanaka rolled onto her back and sat up. She aimed at Burton's back. He was the more dangerous of the two. Kill him first. She lined up her sights between the big man's shoulder blades. Took a long breath, let half of it out, and pulled the trigger.

The round slammed into his back and blew out his chest like someone had swapped his heart with a grenade. Tanaka shifted her aim to Holden, who was already spinning, gun in hand. The big man took a couple more steps and fell over. She lined up on Holden's chest, then jerked her head as something cut a groove across her scalp. The report of the gunshot arrived a split second later.

He figured out the body armor, Tanaka thought. *He's taking the headshot.*

She moved, scrambling for cover in the grass and trying to line up her next shot. Holden was standing still, pivoting slowly at the waist to put his sights on her. It was a race now, and she was sighted in on his head, ready to pull the trigger and end it, when someone slammed a sledgehammer into her cheek. The other side of her mouth exploded out. The pain barely lasted long enough to notice, and everything was gone.

Interlude: The Dreamer

The dreamer dreams, and her dream carries her deeper into intimacy with vastness. All through the wideness and flow, she sparkles and the sparkles become thought where there was no thought before. The great slowness remains, soft and wide as the icy cold and all-encompassing sea, and the slowness (drifting, languid) shuffles and reshuffles itself. The sticky and the slippery, the bright and the dark, the moving and the moving for there is no true stillness in the spark-filled substrate, and the sparks become a mind. The dreamer dreams, and others dream with her, not just the ones at her side, not just the bubbles of salt, but the dance that they make. She dreams the dance, and the dance dreams her back. Hello hello hello.

Once, and gone so far away there were only the first thoughts to think it, the *it* was like this: the ball at the center of down, and the shell at the edge of up, and between them the slow dancers and the sudden dance. *Watch watch watch*, the grandmothers whisper, and their voices become a chorus, and the chorus says something else. The dance wants, and it pushes to the edges of everything, the skin of the universe. The dreamer dreams the dance and the dance dreams and its dreams become things and the things change the dreams. Desire and longing for desire bumble over eager forward and make new things to dance with. A brain growing the wires that form itself, thoughts flow from one substrate into another, and the great curiosity spins and makes and spins and learns. It presses down into the heat at the bottom of everything. It presses up into the cold, and it cracks the vault of heaven. The cold and hard of up yields to the dance, and the lights that they are meet lights that they are not.

A new thing has happened. Light from *elsewhere*. The bright-singing voice of God, inviting and inviting and inviting—

The kick from behind blows through, carrying blood and bone and breath with it. The dreamer takes a step, and then another, and then falls, shrieking, and the grandmothers say *no not that, over here over here, look at what came next.* Death floods toward her emptier than darkness and the dreamer forgets, grabs for the brother who is always at her side except not here except not here and the other one is, pock-voiced and funereal, *it's all right it isn't you I've got you.*

She floats up faster than bubbles, the heat below and behind, the cold cracked open to the stars, and screaming, she launches up and out of the dream and into the body that is only hers, in a confusion of vomit and weep and a fading deeper than dreams could be.

What the fuck was that?

Chapter Thirteen: Jim

Amos was limp, his dark eyes closed. His mouth hung open and his lips were white. The hole in his back was about as big as a thumb. The one coming out his chest was wider than two fists together. The black meat of his flesh made the pale bone of his spine look like a worm someone had pulled apart.

"We have to go," Teresa said from very far away. She pulled at his sleeve. "Jim! We have to *go*."

He turned to look at her—her impatient scowl, her hair pulled back over her ears. Muskrat, at her side, was dancing on anxious paws and whining. Or maybe that was him. He tried to say *All right* but realized he was about to vomit just in time to turn away.

We have to go, he thought. *Come on. Pull it together.*

He went to Amos, putting his arms under the big man's knees and across his wide shoulders. On Earth, he'd never have been able to lift him. With the three-quarter g of Abbassia, he was heavy but manageable. Man, girl, dog, and corpse, they started running toward the *Rocinante*. Jim tried to yell *Hurry*, but the thing that had clenched up in his chest when he saw Amos blown apart wouldn't let him. He didn't look back. His peripheral vision started to narrow, like they were running down a tunnel that was slowly squeezing closed. He had to get to the ship. A wash of cold and wet stuck his clothes to his belly and his thighs. Amos' black blood spilling down him.

Ahead of them, the airlock opened. Alex was in it, a rifle in one hand, waving them forward. The dog reached the lock first, misjudging the gravity and skittering against the hull. Teresa grabbed Muskrat around the middle and climbed the ladder with her. The weight of Amos' body slowed Jim down, but Alex reached out to help with the last couple steps. Jim knelt, lowering the corpse to the deck. The eyelids had opened a slit during the run, and the eyes beneath focused on nothing. Jim closed them.

"Fuck," Alex said. "What the fuck?"

"Take off now."

"All right," Alex said. "Let's get stowed, and we'll—"

Jim shook his head and opened a connection to Naomi. "We're in. Get us up."

"Are you in a couch?"

"No, so don't bounce us around too much, but get us out of here." She didn't argue. The roar of the maneuvering thrusters rattled his teeth. He took Teresa by the shoulder, pulling her close to shout in her ear. "Get the dog to her couch and strap yourself in. I don't know how bad this is going to get."

She looked at him with an equanimity he couldn't feel. She was hurt, frightened, traumatized. She was a kid. How could she stand to see what she'd seen? How could he?

"He isn't secured," she said.

"He won't care. Go."

The deck lurched under them, shifting slowly as the ship went from belly-down to the usual engine-down orientation. Muskrat whined, and Teresa took her by the collar, leading her away.

Amos' body shifted and rolled. There was horror in Alex's eyes, and Jim felt a rush of anger. The distress in his old friend's eyes was too much. If he tried to comfort Alex, it would be too much. He was shaking as it was, and he didn't know if it was the vibration of the ship carving its way through the atmosphere, or his own body betraying him. Maybe both.

"We have to get to ops," Jim shouted. Alex took a step toward the spent clay that had been Amos, then caught himself, and they made their rocking, unsteady way toward the central lift. The deck shook and plunged under them as they went from handhold to handhold. Thrust gravity and the pull of the planet made his knees and spine ache. His vision, dark. He found himself on the edge of confusion, unsure for a moment whether they were fleeing New Egypt or Laconia. When they reached the lift, he sat down to keep from passing out. His mind pieced itself together as they rose.

Alex squatted beside him. "You okay?"

"They were there waiting for us. They knew we were coming."

"I'm sorry," Alex said. "I should have been there."

"She shot Amos in the back. Shot him in the back as we ran."

Alex was quiet, because there wasn't anything to say. Jim looked at his flight suit, smeared black from the gut to the knees. His hands were stained black too, but it still smelled like blood.

The lift pushed up, deck by deck. When they got to ops, Jim either had himself back together or he was fully dissociated. It was hard to know which.

The ride smoothed out as they reached the upper atmosphere. The winds were screaming past them, but with so little mass to the air that a ripping five-hundred-kilometer-per-hour current deflected them less than a breeze. The deck felt steadier under his feet. Naomi was in a couch, the flight controls on her screen. She glanced over as he lowered himself into the crash couch beside hers. He saw her register the blood and whose it was.

"Amos?" she asked.

He shook his head, not meaning that it wasn't. Meaning not now. He knew she understood.

Alex went up to the flight deck, his rifle still bouncing against his shoulder. "I'm taking the stick," he shouted down moments later.

"Copy that," Naomi replied. "I'm fire control." The screen before her shifted to status readouts on the ship's guns—PDCs, torpedoes, the keel-mounted rail gun. Jim pulled up tactical. On this screen an augmented map of Abbassia below them filled one side, a schematic of the nearby space of New Egypt system the other. And a sliver of red marked something the *Roci*'s threat detection thought he should be alarmed about. A stone in his chest, he selected it and pulled up the ship identification.

"We've got company," Alex shouted from above.

"I've got them," Jim answered.

Naomi's voice was sharp and matter-of-fact the way it always was in the teeth of crisis. "Is it a *Storm*?"

Jim looked at the analysis. Now that there was only one *Magnetar*-class ship left, stuck in Laconia guarding their homeworld, the *Storm*-class destroyers were the backbone of Laconian power. And even one would be more than a match for the *Roci*. But this was smaller, with a squat, broad design, and a drive cone that promised it was built for speed.

"No," he said. "Smaller. Maybe an explorer. I don't know."

"Well, it's coming our way," Alex said. "And it looks pissed."

"Can we keep the planet between us and them?"

"If I put us in a low, fast orbit, maybe for a little while. Long term? No."

"Give me a little while, then."

Naomi didn't speak, but she cycled through the PDC status checks. If it was a shooting war, they'd be as ready as a lone ship could be. Jim's first impulse was to turn their back to the sun and burn as hard as they could stand it toward the ring gate and out of the system.

It wouldn't work. The Laconian ship was made to be faster. And if they wanted Teresa, their best move was to punch a hole in the *Roci*'s drive cone and force a shutdown, then board and take her at their leisure. Turning tail and running would just make the shot easier. The alternative was to make it hard.

He closed his eyes. There was only one next step that he could think of, and he hated it. His mind shifted and slipped, looking for a better idea.

"Uh, Jim?" Alex said. "Your while's about up. What's the play?"

Fuck, he thought. "Keep our nose pointed at them. Make it so they have to put a hole through every deck in the ship to hit the drive."

Naomi and Alex were silent for a moment, then Alex said, "I'm on it."

The distant sound of the thrusters was totally different from the earlier roar. The shift of the crash couch felt almost gentle.

Naomi nodded, and checked power status on the rail gun. "Funny. You were saying before that the human shield thing made you uncomfortable."

"I've moved past uncomfortable to furious."

She nodded her agreement, then the screen lit up as the tight-beam request was accepted. A man's face appeared on the screen: broad, with round cheeks, dark skin, and a full and well-groomed mustache. He was wearing the blue uniform of Laconia with a captain's rank. He nodded at the camera, as calm as if they were in line together at the commissary.

"Captain Holden. I am Captain Noel Mugabo of the *Sparrow-hawk*. Please return to the planet surface. I mean you and your crew no harm."

"You people just put a bullet through my mechanic," Jim said, and Naomi stiffened.

"And you killed four Laconian Marines," the captain said. "I am here to help us both deescalate. My orders are to keep you here. We need Teresa Duarte's assistance, and for that, she must come with us. We will not hurt her, nor will we detain you."

"I don't believe you."

"Your doubt doesn't change our situation." Jim noticed the way the man said *our situation*. Building rapport. Making it harder to pull the trigger, but also not backing down a centimeter. He'd had conversations like this as a prisoner on Laconia. "Please return to the planet's surface, and we will take care of all this without any more violence."

His crash couch put up a low-grade medical alert. His blood pressure and heart rate were concerning. Not dangerous, but not not-dangerous. He turned off the alerts.

"No," Jim said. "I think we both know that's not going to happen."

Alex called down from the flight deck. "They're getting closer. Want me to break orbit?"

Jim muted his mic. "Not yet."

"What alternative do you suggest?" Captain Mugabo asked. "I am open to discussing this."

"I propose you land so we know you're not a threat. Then we leave. With the girl."

"May I have a moment to consult with my superior?"

Jim nodded, and Mugabo's eyes shifted down as if he were sending a text-only message. Jim pulled up a tactical window. The two ships whipping around the planet in a low orbit, pointed dead-on at each other like gunmen in a cheap entertainment feed. He didn't know what sorts of weapons the *Sparrowhawk* carried, but he knew for a fact they were all pointed at him right now.

Another window appeared. Fire control, with the rail gun charged and ready, the Laconian ship locked in with passive targeting so that it wouldn't seem like an escalation. He glanced over to Naomi. She mouthed the words *If you need it*. He nodded.

"All right," Mugabo said. "I accept your terms."

"What?"

"We both value the life of the girl. If we have to continue this negotiation another time, so be it. You can go."

Jim took two long breaths. "You're not beginning a deorbit burn."

"Did you expect me to?"

"I don't think you're telling me the truth," Jim said. "I think if I fire the maneuvering thrusters, start to turn a little bit, you'll send a round through my drive cone. I think the only reason you haven't already done it is that you'd have to shoot through the whole ship to do it, and the risk to Teresa Duarte is too high."

"I assure you that is not the case," Mugabo said.

"Then you go first. If we're free to leave, begin your descent. When I see you touch down, I'll know you were telling the truth."

"Yes," Mugabo said. "Of course. I very much understand your position."

"You're playing for time."

"I understand why you would feel that way, Captain Holden. Please believe me that we mean you and your crew no harm, and that my offer is sincere."

The tactical screen bloomed at the same moment that Naomi's calm voice reached him. "Fast movers. They've launched torpedoes."

Radar tracked the pair of torpedoes as they arced out away from the *Sparrowhawk*. Mugabo had been buying time while his people locked in a firing solution that sent the torpedoes out and around the *Roci* to arc back in and hit her from behind. Take out the drive and leave the rest of the ship intact.

Jim tapped the fire control, and the *Rocinante* dropped away beneath him for a fraction of a second as a two-kilo tungsten slug spat out toward the enemy without the main drive on to compensate for the kick. Mugabo vanished, the tightbeam connection lost. The rolling, deep chatter of the PDCs vibrated through the ship. One of the torpedoes blinked off his board.

"I'm lining up another shot," Alex said. The rail gun showed ready. The other missile blinked off the board. The *Roci* squealed a warning at them as two more torpedoes locked on.

"They're getting ready to launch again," Jim said.

"I've got the reactor set to dump core if the *Roci* thinks we're out of luck," Naomi said.

"Alex?"

The rail gun locked onto the *Sparrowhawk* a second time and fired without Jim's having to clear it. "I think you got 'em," Alex said.

Jim switched to the external telescopes. The *Sparrowhawk* was where it had been, curving around the planet toward them, its orbit unchanged. But now a cloud of gas and water vapor sprayed out of the ship along one side. The lock-on tone died as the *Sparrowhawk*'s torpedoes failed to fire.

"They may be playing dead," Naomi said.

"Alex, keep the rail gun trained on them."

"Copy that."

A tiny suggestion of up and down came, shifting the couches on their gimbals as Alex adjusted the ship's orbit to keep the *Sparrowhawk* lined up in their sights. No new lock-on warnings sounded. No active radar bounced off their hull. Jim pulled up the comms again, tried the tightbeam connection without knowing exactly what he'd say if Mugabo answered. He didn't. The Laconian ship drifted on in its low, fast orbit. Either the Laconian ship would repair itself, or in another few weeks it would fall back down into the planet's gravity well and burn up like a meteor. Or it was only playing dead, waiting for Jim to declare victory, turn the ship, and catch a rail-gun round through its drive.

"Alex," he said. "Pull us back on maneuvering thrusters. If they don't turn to match...Turn us, and let's break orbit. Get out of here."

"Copy that," Alex said, and the *Roci* shifted under Jim. They moved gently. Slowly. Waiting for the alarms that would mean the *Sparrowhawk* had only been playing dead.

The alarms didn't come.

"So what now?" Alex said.

"Now we plot the fastest way back through the ring gate and out of here."

"Any thoughts on where to?" Alex asked. "Firdaws is on the flight plan, but—"

"Freehold," Naomi said, her voice calm and authoritative. "We needed resupply before, and we're burning through a lot of reaction mass on the maneuvering thrusters. And I wouldn't mind being under the protection of one of our own while we figure out how this went pear-shaped."

"Yeah," Alex said, his voice grim. "This kindness-of-strangers thing isn't going so well for us."

Jim heard Naomi's restraints clattering free, and he felt her coming close. She stroked his hair, and he took her hand, kissing her fingers gently.

"That went very bad," she said.

"Yeah."

She waited a moment before she said, "What happened to Amos?"

Jim shook his head. *We lost him*, he tried to say. *I lost him.*

"Yeah," Amos said. "I got pretty fucked up all right."

He stepped in from the lift, his shredded flight suit as wet and black as if he'd poured ink on it. The exit wound on his chest was pale flesh around a flat circle of onyx. When he smiled, it seemed tentative.

Naomi's expression went empty.

"Hey, Cap. We got Tiny back safe, didn't we?"

It took a moment to understand this was really happening, but then Jim said, "Yeah. We did."

"And the dog?"

"Her too."

Amos stepped into the ops deck and lowered himself into an empty crash couch, grunting like he was sore. "Good. Tiny really likes that dog. There's a hell of a mess in the airlock. I'll get it cleaned up, but I gotta get some food first. I'm really hungry."

Alex, drawn by the sound of Amos' voice, came down from the flight deck. His face was pale. "Amos?"

"Hey," the big man said, lifting a hand in greeting. "I think I must have took kind of a hit down there. I'm missing some of what happened."

Jim wanted to feel joy, and he did. But there was something more with it. A sense of wrongness that came from trauma after trauma followed by something that violated his inborn sense of how the universe worked. What was possible.

"You died," he said. "You took a round to the back, and it blew most of your chest out. I saw your spine. It was in pieces."

Amos went still in that unnerving way he sometimes did, and then frowned, nodded. "Yeah, okay. I think I knew that part."

Jim laughed, and it was disbelief. And maybe relief. And something else he couldn't put a name to. "Is there anything that kills you anymore?"

"Pretty sure I'm starving to death," Amos said.

"Well," Alex said. "God damn."

Naomi still hadn't spoken. Amos touched the black circle of his wound, exploring it. It didn't look like skin anymore. Whatever it was, it was what Amos' resurrected corpse made when it replaced his injured flesh. Jim wondered what the inside of the wound looked like. For the first time it occurred to him that the changes the drones on Laconia had made to his old friend hadn't stopped when they escaped the planet. Amos hadn't become something different. He was in an ongoing process of becoming. Something about the idea was chilling.

As if Amos had read Jim's thoughts, he frowned. "I don't know how this whole thing works. But we'd be better off not doing it too often."

Chapter Fourteen: Elvi

Elvi missed gravity. She wanted to be able to sit by Cara's medical bay and feel the weight of her exhaustion bearing her down. The long, slight stretch along the back of her neck when her head hung forward. The heaviness in her arms and legs. She understood intellectually that she was near collapse, but the familiar somatic cues weren't there on the float. The only one that seemed to remain was the trembling in her large muscles, and by itself that felt like fear.

Cara was strapped into the bay with wide, white bands that kept her from drifting. Her eyes were closed, her mouth relaxed and slightly open. Her lips were pale and bloodless as carved wax, with the tips of white teeth and a dark purple tongue behind them. Her breathing was deep, steady, and slow. Sedatives still worked on her and Xan despite the changes that the repair drones had made to their bodies. The drugs did metabolize faster, but that was fine. Their supplies were ample.

The autodoc was custom built with decades of Cortázar's observations of Cara's and Xan's baselines. The screens were crowded with real-time blood analysis and neural activity profiles as the system tried to match Cara now with Cara where she usually was, and look for ways to bring those two datasets together. A standard bed would have been baffled, but this one showed Cara slowly returning to her standard range of function as Elvi watched and drank tea from a bulb and trembled.

They'd been in the middle of another dive, sifting through the hallucinatory sensations and inhuman memories for pieces to the puzzle of how the gates had been built and if they could be made safe. Elvi was fairly sure they'd reached the part of the alien species' development where they'd become aware of a broader universe beyond the ice shell of their world. She'd expected Cara to get there, and that it would open the door to some of the practical answers they needed. But then Cara had started screaming that she'd been shot, or if not her, that someone had. The monitors had spiked, and her brain activity lit up like someone had thrown a Molotov cocktail into her mind.

They had restrained the panic, Harshaan Lee barking the steps of the shutdown checklist over Cara's screams and vomiting. By the time they'd shut the dive down, Cara had lost consciousness. She hadn't regained it until now.

Cara's lips moved, and she swallowed. Her eyes shifted under closed lids, and then opened. Black on black, Cara's gaze found her, and the girl tried out a weak smile.

"Hey, Doc."

"Welcome back," Elvi said. "How are you feeling?"

Cara paused, but it wasn't one of the eerie, alien frozen moments. It only seemed like she was trying to find the right answer to a difficult question. "Wrung out. I've never been drunk, but maybe hung over? This feels like what a hangover's supposed to feel like."

"Extrapolating from the literature?" Elvi said, taking Cara's hand. It felt fever-hot.

"Something like that."

"Do you remember what happened? What went wrong?"

"It wasn't the grandmothers, I don't think," Cara said. "They felt the same as always. Deeper, maybe, but the same. It was…one of the others."

"All right. Tell me about that."

Cara frowned and shook her head the way she did when she was searching for some very precise word. "I'm not just myself when I'm in there. I mean, I am, but I'm not just Cara. There's more of me?"

"Like the aliens."

"No, like me watching the aliens. I feel aliens too, but that's like I'm watching a feed. Seeing something that's already recorded. These others are like being everyone in the room who's watching?"

"Like the connection you have with Xan."

"Yes, but more. There are more of them. Only I think something happened. Something bad. I don't know if they died. And then another one of me was trying to calm *me* down." Cara's eyes went wide, and her grip on Elvi's hand squeezed hard enough to hurt. "Xan? Is he all right?"

"Fine," Elvi said, not flinching. "He's worried about you, but that's all. He was in the isolation chamber when it happened, and it didn't seem to affect him one way or the other."

Cara relaxed. "Okay. Okay. All right, that's good then." She took a breath, settled into herself. "I saw them see stars for the first time."

"We don't have to do a debriefing now. You can rest first."

"Let's talk a little. Please. While it's still fresh in my head."

Elvi felt a little wave of pleasure, then guilt at the pleasure. "Only a little. Then you rest."

Cara settled into herself, remembering the memories of others. There was a joy in her when she did. Or no, that was wrong. Not joy, but a relief. Like Elvi was pouring cool water over a burn.

"They were changing. The sea slugs or jellyfish or whatever? They were taking other bits of life, animals or plants or whatever was down at the hot core of that icy cold world. They sent them down into the vents so that they could change. Or it could change."

"That's been a consistent point. And, judging from how the protomolecule functioned, they kept that strategy for a long, long time," Elvi said.

But Cara wasn't listening. Her voice had a faraway, almost dreamy quality. "The important thing was the light."

"You were saying that. I'm thinking that was the creation of mind."

"A hive mind."

Elvi shrugged. "I've never understood that term, really. I mean, there was an electrochemical structure with a lot of semi-independent bodies. Describe it like that, and we're hive minds of neurons. But did it find a way to build an emergent cognitive analogical system? Yeah. I think so."

"And when they saw the stars, it was like hearing God talking in a language you could almost understand. But not quite. The BFE wanted to show me more. It didn't want me—us, whatever—to go. It was trying to hold on. And then the thing happened, and...If they weren't Xan, I don't know who they were, but they feel right when I'm in there."

Cara let go of Elvi's hand. She focused on something Elvi couldn't see, like she was hearing music that only played for her.

"Don't worry about it," Elvi said. "Not for now. We'll have plenty of time for the full debrief after you've rested. I'm going to let the team know you're all right, and Dr. Sanders wants to come by and make sure you're solid. Once we hear what he has to say, we'll make some plans for moving forward."

"I don't want to wait. I want to go back in."

Elvi took a sip of her tea. "I want that too. But right now, rest."

Cara nodded and closed her eyes. Elvi waited until she was sure Cara had fallen asleep before she slipped out of the bracing on the foothold and pushed herself toward the door.

Cara spoke at once, her voice perfectly lucid and awake. Not slurred at all. "Can Xan come see me?"

"Of course, if you want."

"He does," Cara said, and lapsed back into silence. Elvi left the medical bay.

All around her the *Falcon* was subdued. The crew that ran the ship and the scientific staff that worked in it all knew what had happened, and their unease made for whispered conversations in the corridors and hallways, tight mouths and hunched shoulders. Elvi made her way to the ops deck, forcing herself to smile and nod and greet people. She hoped she was being a good leader and projecting optimism. She was afraid that she just seemed fake.

Harshaan Lee was in ops, reviewing the dataset from Cara's aborted dive. She moved beside him, looking over his shoulder. He shifted to the side, giving her a better view.

"She says there was someone else in there with her," Elvi said.

"Hallucinogenic presences are very common. It can be induced with a few magnetic impulses to the temporoparietal region of the right lobe."

"Of course, we weren't doing that," Elvi said.

"That doesn't mean something else wasn't."

"Or maybe her right temporoparietal region was firing off because someone was in there with her. Sometimes you see your grandmother because you're dreaming. Sometimes you see her because you're at Grandma's house."

"It is a conundrum," Lee said dryly. Then, "May I touch on a less pleasant subject?"

Elvi didn't say no. Lee took it as consent.

"I don't mean to step out of my place, but I think we're starting to have a morale issue with the crew. I was hoping you'd consider making an address."

"What kind of issue?"

He shook his head like he was apologizing for his own words, and he kept his voice low. "We are the only ship in a solar system. Half a dozen tightbeam boosters, couple of repeaters at the ring gate itself, and an alien artifact big enough that if we stood on it, the gravity would crush us. That's all there is. There isn't even a dust cloud we could mine for ice."

"Are we short on supplies?"

"No. But when something...odd happens with the research

protocol, there is a kind of multiplier. It reminds us just how tenuous our position is here. If the water recycler broke down in a way we couldn't fix…It would be a long, hard burn getting someplace that could give us aid before we died of thirst, and we might not make it. If it was the air recycler, we'd die. There is no one who can reroute to our aid. We all understood that when we began the mission. But some days, we understand it more clearly than others, if you see what I mean."

She reminded herself again that the vibration in her body wasn't fear. She was just tired, with one critical thing more that she needed to do. "Of course, I'll address the crew. Just let me think about what to say. And thank you for bringing this to me."

"Of course, Doctor."

She hadn't started in physics. It was possible to spend a whole lifetime in the biological sciences and only have a nodding acquaintance with pure physics. It wasn't possible to be the head of the Laconian Science Directorate without getting her feet wet, if *wet* meant abstract high-energy physical dynamics. One of the things she'd known without fully appreciating was that the second law of thermodynamics was the only one that cared about the direction of time. The heat death of the universe had mostly been a joke about how long her thesis was taking. The idea that heat was intimately related to time hadn't seemed strange, and some aspects of the high weirdness of the alien rings had escaped her.

The man on her wall screen was David Trujillo, and at four hours into his presentation, three and a half of which had been a careful and painstaking walk through a forest of explanations and justifications for which mathematical techniques his team had used in interpreting the data, he was getting to the phase she thought of as *dumbing it down for the biologist*.

"The key is the difference between the reactions provoked by the magnetic field generator in Sol system and the *lack* of provoked response in the ring space itself. We've been aware of the energetic amplification effect of ring gate technology. For example, energy sent into the ring station causes a release of high-energy particles through the gates, and the energy of this release is orders of magnitude greater than the initiating event. This asymmetry was exploited in the design of the field generator. The assumption was that this was a borrowing of energy from someplace else within complex local space-time. If, as these results suggest, that's not accurate, and if the ring gate space is a bounded membrane within an alocal, acontiguous space-time—"

"Is he saying something?" Fayez asked from the other side of the cabin. "Because he sounds like he's just barking."

Fayez was exercising, strapped against the wall by resistance bands and pushing against them the way she should have been. When this was over, her bone density was going to be a problem. That was for another day.

"I'm sorry. I'll listen on private."

"No, no. This is me starting a conversation. Getting attention from my sweetheart. Mocking the guy she's paying attention to by saying how he's barking."

"He's barking about something."

"Are you sure?"

She stopped the report playback and stretched.

"When the *Tempest* destroyed the defenses on the alien station in the ring space," Elvi said, "the enemy didn't respond. When it destroyed Pallas Station, everyone in Sol system lost consciousness, and one of the bullets showed up on the *Tempest*. Trujillo thinks it shows that the ring space isn't part of our universe."

Fayez relaxed, the bands pulling him back against the wall. He pushed out again, grunting. "I didn't know there was an option."

"The field generator uses antimatter as a primer, but there's not enough power in a couple handfuls of antimatter to spaghettify a station. The design was developed based on the half-built ship or whatever it was that was in the construction platforms when they were turned on."

"The one they called the *Proteus*?"

"Basically, it makes a tiny, transitory ring gate, which releases just a lot of energy for free. And apparently, it's violating entropy. Which means time."

"Entropy only runs one direction. Primary school physics requires three hours of barking?"

"He's saying wherever it's getting that energy from doesn't play by our rules."

"We knew that, though."

"We suspected it."

"Do we know it now?"

"We suspect it harder," Elvi said. "We're scientists. We only know things until someone shows us we're wrong."

Fayez chuckled, strained, relaxed. He was waiting for her to laugh with him, but she didn't have it in her. Worry bloomed on his forehead and the angle of his lips. "Are you all right?"

"There were two more."

He stopped, looked at her, and shrugged off the straps. "Two more what?"

"Events. Galbraith system saw a transitory change in lightspeed."

"How long did it last?"

"Literally an unanswerable question, but about an hour. Bara Gaon lost consciousness for eighteen minutes. The people who went through it said there was no halo effect, no visual distur-bances, just"—she snapped her fingers—"eighteen minutes later."

"That's new."

"It's all new. It's all experiments, and none of them are mine. And those are just the ones we know about. If the poking and prodding wasn't someplace we know to look for it, it could be happening much more often. It could be happening right here, right now."

He pushed off through the cabin. She was ready to bristle at his touch, too tense for the extra burden of physical contact. He only braced beside her and looked at Trujillo's face, paused on the playback.

"How's Cara?" Fayez asked.

"Fine. She seems fine. I'm a little concerned about these others she's talking about. I know she and Xan are connected somehow at the back, and there are other things back there. Amos Burton went through the same thing they did, and if she's connected with him through the same bridge that's...That man's head isn't a place I'd want to live. But..."

He didn't push. He let the silence do it for him. Elvi sighed.

"I'm getting a picture," she said. "I'm starting to understand what built the rings, and how their minds worked. Or mind. Even when I don't understand how their technology works, I'm starting to see the obstacles they were trying to overcome, and that's actually a pretty good starting point. But..."

"But you're wondering how that can be good enough, when the thing they were fighting against killed them and is coming for us."

"There's so much about that I don't understand. What the bullets are."

"Scars where their attempts to break us permanently fuck up part of reality?"

"Sure. Maybe. But how? What does it do? How do they work? Can we use them to get back to wherever these things are? And how come sometimes they black out one system at a time, and then other times, it's everywhere? Why do they blow off locality and then leave a scar or bullet or whatever it is that's in a place and tied to a local frame of reference?"

"And how do you stop them?"

Elvi wiped away a weary tear. "And how do I stop them. Everything's riding on this. Earth, Mars, Laconia, Bara Gaon, Auberon...They all die if I don't solve this."

"If someone doesn't solve this," Fayez said. "We're one ship, and we're on a very promising track. But we're not the only ones looking."

They were silent together, only the hum of the ship around them. She shifted, putting her head against his arm. He curled toward her, kissing her ear. "When was the last time you slept?"

"What's this sleep you speak of? Sounds nice."

He put his arm around her shoulders and drew her gently through the cabin to the sandwich board where she slept when a sack against the wall wasn't enough. She didn't undress, just slipped between the slabs of gel and let them clamp gently down on her, holding her in place like a giant hand. It was the closest analog to climbing into bed under a pile of blankets, and as soon as he dimmed the lights to a sunset red-gold, she felt sleep rushing up for her like she was falling. Like she was capable of falling.

"You need anything?" he asked, and his voice was soft as a sand dune washed by a breeze. Despite everything, Elvi smiled.

"Stay with me until I fall asleep?"

"My mission in life," Fayez said.

She let her eyes close and her mind wander. She wondered what it would be like to have Fayez in her private mind the way Xan and Cara, and maybe Burton, were in each other's. It had to have some physical element, some center or locus of control that used the same alocal effects that let the gate builders stay connected, neuron analog to neuron analog, through whatever strange dimensions they'd traveled. Maybe if she compared brain morphology, she could find it. Real-time communication between systems would change everything. Assuming anyone was still alive to talk.

She was on the edge of dream, half convinced that the *Falcon* had a university campus in it and that she was preparing to give a lecture, when she roused and chuckled.

"Yes?" Fayez said, still there.

"Lee wants me to give the crew a pep talk. Help shore up morale. I told him I would."

"Any idea what you want to say?"

"No clue," she sighed.

Chapter Fifteen: Teresa

Time was a problem. Time was always a problem.

It started, she had learned, with the fact that simultaneity was an illusion, and "the same time" on different planets in different systems was mostly an accounting convenience that only functioned because most people were moving relatively slowly compared to lightspeed. But beyond that, the measurements of time were embedded in history. An hour had sixty minutes because mathematicians in ancient Babylon had worked in a sexagesimal system. A year was the time it took Earth to make a full transit around Sol, and that mattered even though Teresa had never been to Earth and almost certainly never would. Like the number of minutes in an hour, the width of a centimeter, the volume of a liter, the length of a year was the marker by which humanity told the story of itself.

And so, because an old planet in another system was in more or less the same position relative to its star now as it had been during the siege of Laconia, Teresa Duarte was going to wake up sixteen years old instead of fifteen. And because of how quickly that same planet spun on its axis, it was still early morning, and she was in her quarters on the *Roci*, drifting between wakefulness and dream.

One of the things she'd grown to like about living on the *Rocinante* was the way it made the cycles of daylight and darkness arbitrary. If the crew had decided that every day lasted thirty hours, then it did. If night and day cycled through six hours at a time, then that was true. That they didn't was a choice, and the fact that it was a choice was strangely wonderful. It would have been easy to become unmoored, and it turned out she liked being unmoored. The ability to drift was delicious. Now, lying on a couch in thrust gravity a fraction of what she'd felt growing up, she was aware of the cool gray walls, the almost-dark lit only by her handheld's standby light. At the same time, she was also on Laconia, in a secondary machine shop that opened off her old bedroom and didn't really exist, building something that changed every time she roused a little and slid back down. Dreams of other spaces—secret rooms, hidden passages, forgotten access shafts—had become common for her in the last months. They were probably symbolic of something. She was just fitting a wire lead into a vacuum channel adapter when the dream changed, shifting under her like she'd switched to a different feed.

She was still in her real quarters, could see the real walls and light, but they were augmented by black spirals whose fine detail she was more aware of than the dim light could justify. They seemed to weave and reweave themselves as she watched them. Filaments of black thread that reached out, found each other, built together into a new shape that was also part of the old one. Tiny blue lights wove in and out of the constantly remade spirals too, glimmering like fireflies. As hypnagogic hallucinations went, it was probably the most beautiful her brain had ever come up with. She felt like she could watch the black spirals forever and never get bored.

Her father stood beside them, looking down at her. His eyes

were a perfect blue that they hadn't been in reality. He was smiling. Teresa closed her eyes, willing herself to wake up. This wasn't a dream she wanted to have. When she opened them again, the spirals were gone, but her father was still there. He looked strange. His hair was longer than he'd worn it, and though he was in the tunic and trousers Kelly had dressed him in back on Laconia, he wasn't wearing shoes.

She sat up slowly, careful of the low gravity. The dream didn't fade.

"Teresa," he said, and his voice was like water to someone dying of thirst. Tears began to sheet her eyes.

"Father," she said, and even though she could feel the vibrations in her throat—even though she was almost certainly really speaking out loud—he didn't vanish. The sense of being awake grew in her. The sluggishness of dreams loosened its grip, but his image didn't fade. Not yet.

"Happy birthday," he said. "Everything is going to be all right."

She wiped the tears away with the back of her hand. "It's not, though," she whispered.

"It will. I only need a little more time, and we will all be together. I dreamed too small before. I can see better now. You'll see better too."

Teresa shook her head, and a sharp knock came at the door.

"You decent?" Alex's muffled voice said.

"Yes," she said, and the door opened a crack. For a moment, it seemed like her dream and her reality would come together face-to-face, but as the light spilled in, her father blinked back into nothingness. She wiped her eyes again, trying to hide that she'd been crying.

"Hey there," Alex said. "We've got some grub. You hungry?"

"Sure," Teresa said. "Give me a minute."

Alex nodded and retreated, but Muskrat nosed the door open and hopped in, barely constrained by her own weight. Her brown eyes shifted around the room like she was looking for something, and she whined softly.

"It's okay, old lady," Teresa said. "Everything's fine."

It was almost true. Well, it was less untrue than it might have been, anyway. The *Rocinante* was almost at the New Egypt ring gate, and while the *Sparrowhawk*—far back down the local sun's gravity well—apparently hadn't died, it also was far enough that even a killing burn wouldn't have been able to catch up with them. About to make a transit without a clear idea of the traffic through the ring space, and with the Laconian military chasing them but out of firing range, was as close to okay as Teresa could expect these days. But Timothy—Amos—had defied death again, Muskrat was still with her, and she wasn't at a religious boarding school at the ass end of nowhere.

She was surprised how relieved the plan's failure left her. The immediate aftermath had been fear and shock. The horror of seeing Amos' shattered body, the violence of the firefight, the anxiety of wondering whether the *Sparrowhawk* would risk firing on them to get her back. But as soon as that had passed, she'd found herself smiling more. She was still here, and it wasn't even her fault.

When she went out to the galley, the crew of the *Rocinante* were standing around a little table with a sad, yellow-white cake. It had two candles printed from medical resin in the shapes of a one and a six. The flames were almost spheres. It was pathetic.

"It's pretty much the same yeast and fungus as everything else," Naomi said. "But it's got sugar and it looks nice."

"It's... You're all very kind," Teresa said. There was a knot in her throat that she didn't understand. Maybe gratitude, maybe sorrow, maybe the chaotic wake of the powerful dream of her father. Amos and Jim started a little song, and Naomi and Alex joined in, clapping along. It felt cheap and small and unimaginative, but it was also an effort they had put out for her that they didn't have to. When Alex told her to make a wish and blow out the candles, she just blew them out. She couldn't think of anything to wish for.

Amos plucked the resin candles out and dropped them into the recycler while Naomi cut the cake and Jim handed out bulbs of tea and coffee.

"Not a traditional breakfast," Naomi said, handing a corner piece to Teresa. "But we wanted to take a moment before the Freehold transit. Once we get in the shipyard, we'll be busy."

"Anything the ship needs, we better get now," Jim agreed.

Her last birthday had been in a ballroom of the State Building. The most important people in the vast spread of humanity had been there, and Teresa had been one of them. Her father had already been wrecked by the catastrophe that had destroyed the *Typhoon* and Medina Station, and she had felt the weight of the empire on her shoulders. She'd known what to wish for then. A way out. And now here she was, her wish granted. It wasn't at all what she'd imagined it would be.

She took a bite of the cake and it was…fine. Inoffensive. A little too dense, a little too dry, but fine. It wasn't made by the best bakers in a thousand worlds vying to impress their god-emperor. It wasn't preceded by a formal speech crafted to give the right political signals or followed by a presentation of ostentatious gifts that she didn't care about and wouldn't remember a week later. She couldn't imagine an experience less like the ones she'd had before. Even if they'd ignored her birthday, it would have been more familiar. There had been any number of times she'd felt ignored while standing in the spotlight.

Muskrat put a wet nose against her arm and barked a soft, conversational bark. Teresa broke off a corner of her cake and passed it over. The dog chewed loudly and with enthusiasm.

"What's up?" Jim said, and it took her a moment to realize he was talking to her.

"Nothing," she said. "Why?"

"You sighed."

"I did?"

Alex nodded. "You did."

"It's nothing," she said. "I was thinking about how different this is from last year. That's all."

"Not exactly the best Sweet Sixteen ever," Alex said with a grimace. "This should have been the big one."

"What are you talking about?" Jim said. "Last year was the big one. Quinceañera. Sweet Sixteen isn't a thing."

"Maybe not where you come from," Alex said. "Mars, it was sixteen."

Naomi scowled in affable confusion at Jim. "You mean quinsé? How do you know about that?"

Amos smiled an empty, friendly smile that meant he didn't know or care what the others were talking about but he was willing to let them go on about it for a while. Sometimes he reminded her of a huge, patient dog in a crowd of puppies.

"Fifteenth birthday. Quinceañera," Jim said. "It's the big rite-of-passage birthday for a lot of Earth. Father Caesar was all about mine. We had a tent and a live band, and I had to wear a tailored suit and learn a dance. A bunch of people I barely knew put money in my educational account. It was fun in a mildly humiliating way."

"Huh," Naomi said. "I thought quinsé began in the Belt."

"Did you have a dance?"

"There was dancing. And drinking."

"Drinking at fifteen?" Alex said.

"Fifteen was the age when your parents lost their customs credit exemption and went back to paying full taxes and fees. So that was the age we usually took our first jobs. At least before the Transport Union. Pa changed the credit age to seventeen. But the party stayed the same."

"So you left your parents when you were fifteen?" Teresa said.

"Before that," Naomi said. "I didn't know my father, and my mother had a long-term contract on a freighter that didn't accept children. I was mostly with my tías. Some of them I was related to, but most I wasn't."

"I didn't really know my mother," Teresa said. "She died when I was young."

"That's hard," Naomi said as if she was agreeing with

something. Teresa waited for the next question. *How did she die?* She was sorry now that she'd brought it up. But no one pushed.

"I don't know about any of that," Alex said. "In Mariner Valley, it was Sweet Sixteen. Unless it was thirteen. There was some of that too."

"That why you were so pissed that we missed Kit's?" Amos asked.

Alex looked down, a flash of pain covered over almost instantly by a good-humored ruefulness. "Me and Giselle were pretty much at our worst about then. Staying scarce was the right thing to do, but yeah. I was awfully sorry to miss it."

Teresa took the last mouthful of her cake, to Muskrat's visible disappointment. She'd spent most of a year with these four people. And after the epic failure that leaving her with her cousin on New Egypt had turned out to be, probably the next year too. Others had come and gone, but this central crew had remained the constant. Listening to them talk now was listening in on the idle chatter of a family. But it was a family she didn't belong to. Part of that was that none of them was anything close to her age. When they talked about the time before the ring gates, it was like watching an old entertainment feed. The idea of all humanity trapped in a single system made her feel almost claustrophobic. It meant something different to them, and she could make out aspects of what that was. Her understanding would never mesh with theirs.

She watched Amos. He didn't talk about birthdays or parents. Of the four, he was the one most like her—on the edge of the conversation. But he was comfortable there. He was comfortable anywhere.

She would never have what they did. Her experiences were only her own. No one else anywhere had lived the way she had, and people who had been closest to her were all back on Laconia or else dead. Other people could tie their stories together with analogies and patterns, how one person's childhood birthday was like someone else's, but her life had been too different. Nowhere in the universe would she find a table full of people whose fathers had groomed them to take control of humanity's fate, who had been offered immortality and turned it down, whose private life had been synonymous with the function of a galaxy-spanning state.

The only hope she had was to find a place and start building, not a normal life but a comprehensible one. Then wait until it was all in the past and she could tell warm, shareable stories about it.

Even the idea was exhausting.

The alert was a polite chime. The ship letting them know that the moment had passed and the next thing was coming. They cleaned up the detritus of the cake breakfast, and Alex gave her a brief, awkward side hug before he led Jim and Naomi toward the lift. She and Muskrat followed Amos down toward engineering.

"They mean well," Teresa said.

"Yup."

In engineering, Amos gave Muskrat a treat and took her to the canine couch while Teresa strapped herself in. The air smelled of silicone lubricant and the thin, harsh ozone that the ceramic printers gave off. It reminded her of the smell of rain, but without the minty tones, and it comforted her. How strange to have been in a place long enough that the smell of it felt like home. Or maybe she wouldn't have felt that way except that she'd nearly lost it to a bunch of Presbyterians.

The transit out of New Egypt and into Freehold would go quickly. In theory, any two gates could be connected by a straight line, so that the angle at which a ship entered one could be set such that it didn't need a braking burn. In practice, most ships came in slow, and often made their course corrections when they were fully in the ring space and could see their targets. Something about shooting blind through a gateway they couldn't see, when missing it meant instant and utter annihilation, made the limbic systems of most pilots light up in a very bad way. This particular transit was in the sweet spot—not too far, but also not too steep an angle. If something did go wrong, the *Roci* would have time to shift its trajectory and exit some other ring.

At their present speed, the gap between gates would be brief, and the transits themselves wouldn't be noticeable—one moment they would be in the eerie non-space of the ring gates, the next falling toward a distant star with the familiar universe around them. Amos strapped himself in across from her, scratching idly at his chest where the gunshot had opened him.

"Does it bother you?" she asked.

He looked over, his dark eyes wide and strangely innocent. Like a stuffed animal's. She pointed at his chest as the countdown to transit began. Alex's voice, professional with just the barest hint of anxiety.

"I don't know," Amos said. "Not really. I don't like being dead, so…" He shrugged. "It is different, though."

Alex reached zero, and Teresa imagined she felt a moment's vertigo, but it was almost certainly psychosomatic. When Amos spoke again, his voice was calm and amiable. One of the things she liked about him was that he never had the faint condescension of generic concern. "You're thinking about your dad?"

"You didn't choose what happened to you. How you changed. He did. And I don't know which of you I'm more like, you know? I chose to leave. To be here. But there are so many things that I can't—"

"We have a problem," Naomi said over the ship-wide. "Stand by, and stay strapped."

"Got you," Amos said, but he was already pulling a mirror of the tactical controls onto the wall screen. Freehold system appeared, simplified by the shorthand of graphic design into something comprehensible. The sun. Freehold itself and the single other inner planet. The three gas giants. A dozen prospecting ships, mostly in the asteroid belt or the gas giant's moons. Teresa looked for what had made Naomi's voice so hard, and it took her a moment to find it.

The *Gathering Storm* was a Laconian destroyer, stolen by Roberta Draper. It was the flagship of the underground's clandestine fleet, the tip of the spear during the siege of Laconia that had been Teresa's own escape. To Admiral Trejo and the rest of the

Laconian Navy, it was a humiliation and a thorn. A reminder of a string of losses. To the underground, it was a symbol of the empire's vulnerability. It was the ship that might slip through any gate at any time, bringing the underground's power to bear on any lesser ship, almost more powerful as a story than as a fighting vessel.

But the Laconian destroyer on the tactical display in low orbit around Freehold wasn't the *Gathering Storm*.

Chapter Sixteen: Tanaka

The school medic looked like his voice had broken about half an hour before. If Tanaka hadn't known better, she'd have thought he was a student, not staff. He had dark skin, full lips, and hair cut close to the skull. In other circumstances, she'd have found him very pretty. As it was, she kind of hated him. For one thing, he was nervous with her. Every sentence he spoke rose at the end, so no matter how straightforward or obvious the statement, he bent it into a question. Also, some part of her limbic system had noticed that every time he was around, something happened that hurt or annoyed her. Changing dressings on her ruined cheek, needle sticks for the blood draws and support meds, scans in the school's antiquated autodoc. Something.

Worst of all, she probably owed her life to him.

Her men—Mugabo's strike team that she'd appropriated—were stripped of their equipment and buried already. Winston

Duarte himself had ended the custom of bringing the dead back to Laconia for burial. *All soil is Laconian soil* had been the message then. Even with the profuse bleeding of head and face wounds, it would have been hard for her to hemorrhage to death on the dirt of Abbassia. But if someone had come and put a bullet in her, they'd have had a pretty good chance of blaming the murder on Holden and whatever the fuck his ship mechanic had become. She didn't remember being found or brought into the medical station. She didn't know if the medic had hesitated or if he'd been resolute to his Hippocratic oath. She did know without doubt that she had been vulnerable before him, that he had held her life in his young, unscarred hands. She hated him for that.

"I would very much recommend against any high-g maneuvers for at least three weeks?" he said as she packed her few remaining belongings into a sack. "Regrowth gel is very difficult on something that moves as much as a cheek?"

"I will have the very best care available," she said, enunciating each word separately through the numbed ruins of her mouth. Holden's bullet had cost her three upper teeth on the left side and most of her right cheek. There were microfractures from her palate up to her left orbital, and she was having headaches that left her swimming with pain. Those might have come from the fight with the black-eyed mechanic, though. Once enough things got fucked up in her skull, there wasn't much point assigning an origin story to each of them.

"I think it would be wiser to wait? Another week to give the gel time to bond?"

Tanaka didn't dignify that with a reply. Her armor was out in the courtyard, packed neatly for recovery along with what was salvageable from the dead fire team, and she walked out of the infirmary to join it, with the medic trailing behind her like a wisp of tissue stuck to her boot. The transport cart from the *Sparrowhawk* was a plume of dust, still half a klick from the campus. The faculty and staff of the academy watched her from their windows and doors with a mixture of fear and disapproval.

She was the woman who'd swept down from the sky and locked them all away while their school turned into a free fire zone. An honorary degree would have been a little much to expect.

She smiled at the thought, then winced.

When the cart arrived, Mugabo was on it. His practiced formality was as crisp as a starched shirt. He braced and saluted her. It actually made her feel better. More herself. While his little crew loaded the arms and armor of their dead, Mugabo stood at her side, head tilted forward.

"You took your damn time," she said.

"My apologies. The damage we sustained made atmospheric entry problematic, and your transport ship was...Unfortunately, we were forced to salvage certain equipment from it. I am very sorry for the delay."

"Where do the repairs stand?"

Mugabo nodded, not meaning anything positive other than that he'd heard the question. "While the damage is significant, I am confident we can continue safely. My chief mechanic recommends a return to Laconia for resupply."

"Are we short of something?"

"The composites that feed the hull are understandably diminished."

"Meaning the self-repair functions aren't working."

"The hull's integrity is within the error bars," Mugabo said. She liked the way he deflected. He didn't want to go to Laconia, his chief mechanic did. His ship wasn't broken unless Tanaka was willing to permit it to be. There had always been that thread in the tapestry of Laconian culture: the willingness to assert whatever reality your commanding officer proposed. She wondered what Mugabo's internal life was like. Did he have a reserve of freedom and perversity hidden inside, the way she did, or was he the same blankness all the way down?

She swung herself into the front seat beside the driver and looked out over the school. The battlefield. She'd lost here—lost her fire team, her target, her blood, and her flesh. Part of her reputation. And she'd lost it because she had been too slow to reach for violence. Teresa Duarte was precious—a resource of one. Irreplaceable. Holden had been willing to risk her where Tanaka had not. Lesson learned.

Part of her wanted to drop a missile on the school grounds from orbit and erase the site. She could do it. A few lives wiped out—including that fucking medic—and no one would prosecute her for it. The only consequence would be that people would know she'd done it. They'd guess at the embarrassment and shame that had driven the act.

So fuck it. Let them live.

Mugabo's team finished the loading and clambered back into their places on the cart. Some peculiarity of the atmosphere refracted the sunlight into six bands like a child's picture of a star. She remembered something she'd heard once: *I'd strike the sun if it insulted me.* She didn't know where the line came from. It didn't matter. She had a hunt to complete.

"We can go," she said.

"Yes, sir," Mugabo replied, and the cart lurched, turned, and sped away toward the landing point. The wind of their passage tasted like dirt. She took comfort in the knowledge that she could live a full, rich life and never once come back to this shithole of a planet. The thought helped, if only a little.

When they were back on the *Sparrowhawk* and burning for the ring gate, she submitted herself to the medical team. Walking into the infirmary of her own free will and not flinching as they made their examination pulled some of the sting of her first experience of the wounds. By the time they'd checked the wound on her scalp, scraped the local regrowth gel out of her cheek, sewn a matrix in place, and put their own gel on, she felt better. It hurt badly, but showing them and herself that the pain was incidental was almost soothing. Mortification of the flesh had a long and glorious history among performance artists and religious zealots. She didn't think of herself as either, but maybe there was some overlap.

The new nerve endings itched, and her head throbbed if she stood up too quickly when they were under thrust. Otherwise, she was ready to get back to work, starting with her after-action report. She sat at the little desk in her office, and while the air recycler hummed and the vibrations of the drive fluted gently through the ship, she recounted the failed mission in careful, exacting detail. It was the moral equivalent of the gel scrape. Proof that she could take this pain too. She sent it to Trejo like an atheist confessing her sins. The ritual of cleansing with only a little vestigial sense of actually being clean. After that was done, the work.

In the time it had taken to put herself and the ship back together, the *Rocinante* had built up an impossible lead, burning past the one incoming merchant ship, the gas giants, and out toward the gate fast enough that there was no point laying on the speed to catch them. Whatever system they were going to, they'd be in by the time she reached the ring space. They couldn't outrun light, though. She sent the drive signature and silhouette of the ship's disguise out ahead, spreading the information to every system where the Laconian repeaters hadn't been spiked recently. Wherever Holden took the girl, Tanaka's forces would know to look for him. Maybe she'd get lucky.

Or maybe she wouldn't.

She spent long days going through reports on the other efforts she'd put into motion. The Science Directorate's analysis of the egg-thing from Laconia was consistent with the idea of an inertialess transport, and they were looking at strategies for tracing it. One theory was that the egg-ship's passage might leave a trail of free neutrons. She'd taken the Survey and Exploration Directorate off all its other work and tasked it with a report of all known alien structures in all systems. If Duarte had gone someplace, it was almost certain to be one of these. Activity in any of them would give her somewhere to start. But so far, no joy. Her orders to the Intelligence Directorate— checking on any close associates or former lovers of the high consul in case they'd suffered a visitation like Trejo's—resulted in a report that was equal parts bureaucratic obfuscation and dead ends.

The whole thing left her angry. That was fine. Anger was comfortable. It was useful. She understood it.

She could remember to the moment the last time she'd felt self-pity. She'd been eleven years old and living in Innis Deep. Her parents had both died that year. Her mother had discovered something about her husband she couldn't live with, and one night she sabotaged the air system in their quarters and suffocated both of them as they slept. Tanaka had been sent to stay with her aunt Akari for the night. She wound up living there for the rest of her childhood. If her aunt knew what it was that had sent her mother into a murder-suicide rage, she never told.

Moving meant changing schools, and the transition combined with the unexplained loss of her parents had been difficult. One day after school, her aunt had found her sitting on her bed and crying. She demanded to know why. Tanaka admitted that a girl at her school had slapped her face and humiliated her.

Aunt Akari knelt down in front of her. She was an MCRN captain, and tall like all the Tanaka women. In her spotless uniform, Aliana thought her aunt looked like a warrior goddess. She'd waited for her to hug her close, then tell her she would take care of everything, the way her mother would have.

Instead, Aunt Akari had asked which cheek had been slapped. When Aliana pointed at it, her aunt had slapped her on the same cheek so hard it made her burst into tears again.

"Are you sad, or are you angry?" Aunt Akari had said, her voice gentle but insistent.

"I don't understand—" she had started to reply, when her aunt slapped her again.

"Are you sad, or are you angry?" she'd repeated.

"Why—" Akari slapped her before she could say more.

"Are you sad, or are you angry?"

She had wiped at the water in her eyes, afraid to say anything for fear of another slap. She looked at her beautiful but stern aunt's face, staring back at her without pity or compassion.

"Angry," Aliana finally said, and was surprised to discover it was true.

"Good," her aunt said, then stood up and held out her hand

to pull Aliana up off the bed. "Anger I can do something with. Sadness, fear, self-pity, self-doubt? They are inwardly focused. They keep you locked inside yourself. They're useless. Anger is outwardly focused. Anger wants to take action. Anger is useful. Are you ready to use it?"

Aliana had nodded. It seemed safer than speaking.

"Then I'll show you how."

And she had.

Mugabo stood, arms behind him, with the same banal and pleasant almost-smile as always. "We have come near enough to the ring gate that it would be best if navigation knew where they should chart for."

Tanaka leaned back in her seat. Her head hurt, but a little less than usual and she hadn't taken the pain medication. Wouldn't unless she needed it to function. The regrowth of her damaged bone ached, and the flesh of her cheek was slowly reknitting. The teeth would take a while. They needed something a little more solid to anchor to. That was fine.

Returning to Laconia was almost certainly the right thing, but it felt like admitting defeat. She had put it off until now, and she still chafed at the idea. She pressed at her broken orbit with the tips of her fingers, checking to see how hard she could push before the pain came.

"For the time being," she began, "we should assume that the ship resupply will—"

Her comms chimed. A high-priority message had just arrived from the Laconia system. From Admiral Trejo. She let whatever she'd meant to say trail off and die, then looked up at Mugabo. He raised his eyebrows a millimeter like the waiter at an expensive restaurant waiting to see whether she approved of the wine.

"Let me get back to you on that, Captain," she said.

"Of course," he said with a sharp, professional nod. If he was annoyed at being put off yet again, he didn't show it. She had the sense that she could prevaricate and delay forever and never get more than polite acceptance and a repeat of the question an hour later. Mugabo was a man without passions as far as she could tell. He'd wear her down like water eroding a stone.

He closed the door behind him, and Tanaka put her system on a do-not-disturb setting that would keep anyone from intruding. Trejo's message wasn't large, but it had a datafile linked to it. A message within the message.

Trejo, looking out from her screen, seemed older than a few weeks could justify. It was all in the tone of his skin and the paleness of his lips, though. His eyes were still as sharp and bright as ever, and his voice belonged to a man thirty years younger than he was. She wondered if he was taking stimulants.

"Colonel," he said, looking into his camera. "I have reviewed your report, and... I think we can agree that could have gone better. We lost some good people on this, and you didn't secure your target. But I'm not sure we came away exactly empty-handed.

"For what it's worth, I would also have expected Nagata to put the girl someplace besides the gunship that the head of the underground was flying. But since she's chosen to keep so many of her eggs in a single basket, certain opportunities may be open to us that wouldn't have been otherwise."

Tanaka scratched her bandages. All she felt was a little pressure. The itch didn't subside at all. Trejo shifted in his chair and vanished. The image before her changed to a grainy visual telescopic view of a ship. It was hardly more than a dark shape against its own drive plume.

"I wanted to pass this along." Trejo's voice was calmer than she was. "It's from the *Derecho*. Botton's commanding it on a mission in Freehold system. Traffic analysis thinks they've still got the *Storm* hidden there, and he's trying to flush it out. A ship made an unscheduled transit into the system in the time period your alert specified. It's the right tonnage for the *Rocinante*, and the drive signature... Well, it doesn't match, but it's close enough that they could be running it dirty to throw us off. Thermally, it's the same story. Close enough to be faked. And the silhouette is very close. It reports—"

Tanaka stopped the playback. Her heart was going fast, and she was trying hard not to grin. It would hurt like hell if she did, and maybe even dislodge some of the regrowth matrix. But oh, she wanted to.

Mugabo accepted her comm request as soon as she'd made it. "Colonel?"

"Resupply is going to have to wait," she said. "We're going to rendezvous with the *Derecho* in Freehold system. All deliberate speed."

"Yes, Colonel," Mugabo said. "I shall inform the navigator."

She dropped the connection and let herself smile until it hurt just a little, savoring the moment. She tabbed Trejo's message back and started it playing again.

"...silhouette is very close. It reports itself to be a survey ship on contract out of Auberon, and there's a paper trail to support that. But Auberon system is so deeply infiltrated by the underground, I have to take that fact very, very lightly. I don't know if this is a lead you'll choose to follow, but it looks promising to me. And if it is Teresa Duarte's ship, and if Teresa's ship is James Holden and Naomi Nagata's... Well, then I might have a strategy we can try."

Tanaka leaned forward. There was something in Trejo's voice that caught her. She didn't know if it was regret or anticipation or something of both.

"Everything we've done with these people up to now has been less effective than I'd hoped. They're smart, and worse than that, they're fortunate. I know it sounds like superstition, but some people are just born lucky. I believe that. Regardless, I think there's some value in changing our tactics. I've included a datafile for you to review."

She opened the datafile in an inset screen. Another image of Trejo sitting at the same desk, speaking in the same cadence. The voices overlapped, each obscuring the other until she killed the inset and rolled back the main message.

"…datafile for you to review. This is your mission, and I'm not looking to steer from the rear on it, but I think this is the right way to go. If you agree, you should use it. We're at the high-stakes table here. If we don't finish what Duarte started…Well, I don't want to go out thinking about all the things I didn't have the balls to try."

Chapter Seventeen: Naomi

The captain of the Laconian destroyer *Rising Derecho* had a pleasant face. Thin, high cheeks and a little pencil mustache that reminded Naomi of old entertainment feeds about the fight for Martian independence. His eyes were dark brown, his skin only a little lighter. He had the trick of making threats while being pained at the necessity of doing it. *This hurts me as much as it does you.* A lot of Laconians seemed to have that style. Naomi had to believe that said something about Winston Duarte and how he'd led.

"We have reached the hundred-hour mark. I will restate this again: We know that the *Gathering Storm* is in this system. It must be surrendered to us within the next hundred hours, or we will be forced to act against the civilian population. I beg that the leaders of the underground in this system consider how little they have to gain by their refusal to act, and how much they have to lose."

"They wouldn't really do it, would they?" Alex said. They were on the ops deck together, her and Alex and Jim. Amos and Teresa were in engineering, controlling the automated probes doing pointless make-work tasks on the surface of a small, volcanically active moon that circled one of Freehold's three gas giants.

"They would," Jim said. "More than they would. They will."

"It's civilians," Alex said.

"Yeah, but it's our civilians. So fuck 'em."

Botton looked soulfully into a camera in a warship orbiting a world whose population had grown to almost a hundred thousand over the years. "We are opening the channel to citizens of the city of Freehold in hopes that they will be able to reach your conscience."

The feed shifted to a young man, maybe sixteen years old, standing outside on the planetary surface with a small house in the frame behind him. When he spoke, his voice quavered. "My name is Charles Parker—"

Naomi killed the feed.

Freehold was one of the most important systems in the underground's network. It wasn't particularly well populated or wealthy. Draper Station, hidden on another moon of the same gas giant, was very small as military bases went. But it was the hiding place of the *Gathering Storm*, and that made it central to the underground's strength. Saba had known that would be true, back when Naomi had only been one of his chief lieutenants and not herself the center of the resistance to Laconia's empire. There were plans in place for how to keep Draper Station hidden when a Laconian presence was in-system. It was why the *Roci* had been ready at a moment's notice to pass itself off as the *Sidpai* operating out of Auberon. There was even a contract back in Auberon system to support the story, and a workplan backdated to seem it had been filed three months earlier that detailed the *Sidpai*'s mission to survey four sites in Freehold for possible mineral extraction. The second of the four was Draper Station, and they would make their approach to it when it was conveniently obscured from the *Derecho*'s direct line of sight.

The protocol now was to be what they pretended. Land where they said they'd be landing. Send out probes. Pull in data. Watch for signs that they'd been identified, and be ready to run like hell for the gate again if they were. Another transit to another system and hopefully no watchful Laconian eyes.

More traffic. More violence. No solutions. There were moments when it was easy to lose sight of all the progress the underground had made in hauling back the worst of Laconia's bad ideas and power. She only hoped that somewhere in the bowels of Laconia, Admiral Trejo felt at least as frustrated as she did.

When she went to make a request, Amos' comms were already open. "How's it going out there?"

She could almost hear the big man shrug. "If we were really getting paid for this, we wouldn't be covering the union in glory. But for a couple part-timers who don't usually run this kind of job? Pretty good."

"How long would it take to get all the equipment back into the barn?"

"Couple hours."

Jim looked over at her. "We're scheduled to be here for two more days."

"We did really, really good work, and got all the data we needed early," Naomi said. "Corporate back on Auberon will probably give us bonuses. Haul it all back in, Amos. We need to leave."

"You got it," he said. She heard his voice over the comms as he turned to Teresa. *Playtime's over. Time to pick up the toys.* He sounded almost like the man she'd known before he'd changed. Before they'd all changed, one way and another.

"I'll get you some course options," Alex said as he unstrapped and headed for the flight deck.

"Thank you," Naomi said. She pulled up the comms and prepared the fake captain of the *Sidpai* to generate a report to the Laconians. She could almost imagine being a survey crew trying to keep its head down and finish its contract in the shadow of war crimes about to be committed. It was always like this. People

trying to get their work done even while atrocities were bloom-
ing around them. Avoid eye contact and hope that the fire doesn't
spread to you and yours.

Jim sighed. "We're going to have to do something about this.
Not sure what it is, but...something."

He seemed confused by her smile. "It's why I'm moving the
transfer up. We'll figure it out."

The acknowledgment from the *Derecho* came two hours later,
and a human being hadn't touched it. One ship system talking to
another, as smooth and lacking in intention as meshing gears in
a clockwork. The *Derecho* was looking for the *Storm*. The *Roci*
wasn't the *Storm*. And even if they were under suspicion, the
Laconian strategy didn't change. They had a gun to Charles Parker's head and a hundred thousand heads like his, and a timer ticking down toward zero. If the *Sidpai* was a little sketchy, none of
that changed.

The transit to Draper Station was a little brilliancy that showed
how good Alex had become as a pilot. It followed a flowing path
that exploited the gravity of the gas giant's moons in their relative
orbits, did nothing that looked out of place or implausible, and
still landed the *Roci* with the body of the target moon obscuring
the *Derecho*, and the gas giant keeping any ship coming in from
the gate from seeing exactly where they landed.

With the strict comms blackout that protocol required, Naomi
wasn't certain what they'd find when they got there. When the
first, almost inaudible navigation pings came, it felt like relief.
Alex guided them into the hidden base gracefully. For the years
he'd been Bobbie's pilot, this had been his home, and his intimacy with it showed in the ease of their passage. The *Storm* was
in the secret dock along with two little in-system rock hoppers.
The *Roci* edged into an open berth, the docking clamps locking
on with a deep, gentle clank that rang through the ship. To the
Derecho, it would look like the little survey ship had landed in a
lava tube.

Jillian Houston was waiting for them when the airlock doors

opened. She was smaller than Naomi thought of her being, pale hair pulled back but long. She wore a uniform-style jacket without insignia or signs of rank. The woman had served in no military besides the one they'd made up together.

The *Derecho* was a little under sixty-three hours from starting its bombardment of the planet, and it showed in her eyes.

"You've come at a difficult time, ma'am," Jillian said.

"I'm sorry there are so many of those," Naomi said.

"My father always says anything worth having is worth fighting for."

Naomi wasn't sure whether the bite in the words was really there or if she was just hearing what she expected. Bobbie had always given Jillian good if sometimes cautious evaluations, had promoted her up to be her second-in-command, and left the *Storm* to her care when she died, but Naomi wasn't Bobbie. The first time the *Roci* had come to Freehold, it had taken Jillian's father away as a prisoner. The alliance between Freehold and the underground had been one of the first steps in pushing back against Laconia, but Naomi couldn't help feeling that there was still a splinter from that first interaction.

"How is your father?" Naomi asked.

"He's planetside, ma'am." It was a prosaic way of saying *He's about to die.*

The others came out behind Naomi, Jim first, then Alex, Amos, and Teresa. Jillian's gaze lingered on Amos long enough that it almost became uncomfortable before she shifted to Alex.

"Good to see you again, Captain," Alex drawled.

"Welcome back, Mr. Kamal," she said, and Alex grinned.

"You keeping the ship in trim?"

"You won't find any dust on her," Jillian said, then shifted her attention back to Naomi. "I didn't know what you needed for the resupply, but your time here's short. I got everything ready that I could. We have some quarters set aside for you to rest. It might be a little loud on your ship."

"I can walk your techs through what we're short on," Amos

said. "It's going to be better if we load up and get out quick. Especially since we're such a crack surveying team now."

If his appearance unnerved Jillian, she didn't show it. "Come with me. I'll get you started."

The gravity on the moon was hardly more than a suggestion. The rock of the corridors was coated with sealants and braced. None of the stone here had been compressed by a gravity well strong enough to make it hard. Naomi had the sense that she could have dug her way through it with her bare hands like it was packing foam. It was only the human structures that made it feel solid.

The dockworkers and supply techs were a mixed bunch. Naomi recognized old-school OPA by their tattoos and the quick, well-practiced actions that came from a life spent close to vacuum, but there were also younger men and women. People Jillian's age who had come to the underground from the bottom of gravity wells and made their way here. There were more since the siege of Laconia. The empire's loss had given a lot of people hope. She wasn't certain she was one of them.

The *Rocinante* could plausibly stay on their false survey mission for three or four days. That was long enough to top up all their tanks and swap out their air scrubbers and recycling matrix, and do some of the smaller hull repairs. It was long enough that they would be on hand to watch the civilian population of Freehold die.

When the resupply and repairs were all agreed on and the process was underway, fifty-nine hours were left. Naomi went to the quarters Jillian had mentioned: narrow rooms with cots and blankets around a small private galley and head. The *Roci* was more spacious. Jim was curled up, napping. Naomi wanted nothing more than to curl up beside him. Instead, she sent a comm request to Jillian. The reply was directions to her on-base office.

She thought about waking Jim and bringing him along with her. He had a way of smoothing some conversations just by being in the room. But this was her burden to carry. He'd be there later if she needed him.

The office was small, with screens on two walls and the surface of the desk. The parts of the walls not taken up with images of the *Derecho* and Freehold, the security map of the station, the status of the *Storm* and the *Rocinante*, and the environmental status were painted a grayish orange. It would have looked good with some blue beside it. Jillian, seated, waved her in, and Naomi pulled the door closed behind her.

"I didn't know Freehold was under attack," she said.

Jillian didn't look her in the eye. "The fucker blew out our repeater at the ring and dropped one of their own as soon as they came through. There wasn't a way to raise the red flag. I apologize."

"It wasn't criticism. I'm afraid we've made the situation worse."

"I don't know that's possible. But we do need to talk about our options now that you're here."

Jillian's right hand closed into a fist, then opened, and closed again. It wasn't the only sign of distress, but it was the most obvious one. Naomi breathed into the version of herself that was cold, analytic, and ruthless. She'd never wanted to be a war leader. The universe had insisted.

"You have plans?"

"A plan," Jillian said. "The *Storm* is ready to evacuate. It's already loaded with all the supplies she'll carry and the parts of the station we could take down and stow. We break cover and get the enemy to follow us. Get out through the ring, transit to a different system, and start building a fresh base."

"So abandon Draper entirely?"

"It's not useful for anything but the *Storm*," Jillian said. "And it's less useful for that than it could be."

Naomi frowned, motioning Jillian on.

"Freehold's strategic importance was that no one knew we were here. That's spent now. I don't know if their traffic analysis is better than ours or someone leaked something. Shit, it could just have been a good guess. But they're here. Keeping the base at this point is just holding on out of spite."

"And the *Derecho* might chase you," Naomi said. "Leave the civilians alone and come for you. That's the idea, isn't it?"

"It's the hope. We've got... We've got recording stations in all the major towns. If it does come down to a bloodbath, it won't be a quiet one. We'll hang what they do here around their necks in every system with a radio. They know that too. It might help dissuade them."

"What about direct confrontation? The *Derecho*'s a strong ship, but it's the same class as the *Storm*. We have another gunship now. And if you have any other vessels or planetary defenses to throw in the mix—"

"We can look at it," Jillian said. "It's not apples to apples, though. Their ship is fresh and well supplied. And the *Storm*... It's not in fighting condition. Not the way it should be."

"Why not?"

"We don't have the Laconian supplies or the repair equipment or the expertise. And we've been running the hell out of her for years. She's a good ship, but she's showing some age."

Naomi heard what Jillian was moving toward. Hinting at, maybe without even being aware she was doing it. The younger woman was talking herself into a story where losing the ship, losing the base, wouldn't be that bad. She was looking for the way that the massacre could be avoided, even if it meant surrender.

It struck Naomi that desperation could be like a fractal: constantly changing but also the same at every level. The citizens of Freehold, afraid that their last days were upon them. Jillian grasping for any way to save her people. Naomi's own grinding, frustrated fight to keep ships from going dutchman and build something to rival the authoritarian, vicious empire. Elvi Okoye, risking her life for any way to stop the things from beyond the ring gates and their waves of hostility and weirdness. No matter how far out your point of view, the fear and desperation were the same at every level.

The alert took them both by surprise. Jillian shifted the image from the *Derecho* to the distant ring gate and the comet-bright drive plume of a ship that had just made the transit.

"Were you expecting someone?" Jillian asked as she redirected the base's passive sensors toward this new target. Naomi didn't answer. Slowly, the image resolved until the silhouette was almost clear. The ship was Laconian and familiar. And while she would have to query the *Rocinante* for the drive signature, she was already certain that it would match the *Sparrowhawk*.

"It's from New Egypt," she said. "It's hunting us."

Jillian's soft exhalation was as good as a curse. If they'd been short on good options before, now they were out. If they tried to run, it meant going past an incoming enemy, and even if they could slip past it, the *Sparrowhawk* would be able to reach the ring gates with them and report back where they'd gone. If they tried to fight, they'd be outmatched.

I'm so sorry was at the back of Naomi's mouth when Jillian made a soft, surprised grunt. "What is it?" she asked instead.

"The new ship? It's transmitting."

"To the *Derecho*?"

"Not tightbeam," Jillian said. "It's broadcast. Just radio spectrum transmission."

Naomi frowned. Point-to-point tightbeam was more secure than any broadcast, no matter how effective the encryption. The *Sparrowhawk*'s laser might not be strong enough to reach the *Derecho* or it might have lost alignment in the damage the *Roci* had done it. Or…

"Are there other ships in the system?" Naomi asked. "Is it signaling more than just the *Derecho*?"

Jillian pulled the base's comm controls to her own desk, her fingers dancing over the screen. A scowl drew lines across her forehead and down the sides of her mouth. "Yes, it is. And it's cleartext. They're not even hiding it."

"Is there an address flag? Who are they talking to?"

"You," Jillian said. "They're talking to you." She shifted the comms playback to the larger wall screen.

The de facto leader of the Laconian Empire looked out at them both with startling green eyes and a smile Naomi could only call rueful. When he spoke, he sounded like a reed instrument, played softly.

"This message is for Naomi Nagata. My name is Anton Trejo. I think you know who I am and the situation we're both in. It's past time that you and I talk. I would like to propose an alliance..."

Chapter Eighteen: Jim

The panic was deep and irrational. It felt so much like the station itself was vibrating that Jim had to physically test that it was really just him. He realized the message had been playing and he didn't know what it had said. He slid it back to the start, breathing deeply, and tried to keep his mind from bouncing off it again.

"This message is for Naomi Nagata. My name is Anton Trejo. I think you know who I am and the situation we're both in. It's past time that you and I talk. I would like to propose an alliance.

"We have our differences, and I'm not here to underplay or deny that. We also have access to certain information that makes clear the vulnerabilities that we're both trying to address in our ways. We share a problem, you and I. The ring space and the unknown entities within it pose an existential threat for humanity. We must control access to the rings to limit this danger. We also both know that when it comes to getting people to deny their own immediate needs in favor of a greater good, asking nicely almost never works."

Trejo spread his hands in a gesture of powerlessness. *What option do they give us?* Jim's hands ached, and he forced his fists to unclench.

"I have here a copy of a document you wrote. Protocols for the safer use of the gates. I also have my own traffic analysis data that tell how well this project is going for you. I've had my best people analyze it and I have to say, it's a damned good piece of work. Solid. If it were put in place, it might go a long way toward managing the threat of these incidents. The only thing it's missing is a method of enforcement. Out of a shared concern for humanity as a whole and in recognition of our common history and moral bonds, I would like to put my forces at your disposal. On behalf of Laconia and High Consul Duarte, I am offering the underground not just armistice, but collaboration.

"We have to end these petty squabbles and fights. I think you know that. And I am willing to do so. Furthermore, I will commit to stationing two Laconian destroyers inside the ring space, even with the risk that we both know that exposes them to, with the sole mission of enforcing your transit protocol. We will not take aggressive action. We will not limit or control trade. I will guarantee the safety of any ship making use of the gates, and grant blanket amnesty for the underground.

"And I will begin by reassigning the forces presently in Freehold to that mission," Trejo said. "That's my offer. A unified front against the real enemies of humanity. And all I'd ask from you, as a gesture of your trust and goodwill, is the return of your present passenger. You know as well as I do that she's in no danger from us. We only want to bring her home. And with this rapprochement between us, there's no reason for her to be living in exile."

The message ended, and for a moment, Jim wasn't there. The cabin in Draper Station, the cot, the soft gravity, all of it was still present, but it became less immediate, less real than the holding cell in the depths of Laconia's State Building. The fear was real, but more than that was the twin sense of despair and responsibility. The conviction that everything depended on him, and that he was powerless. Like watching something precious and delicate falling, and knowing that he couldn't get to it in time. Everything was going to break, and even though there was nothing he could do, the grief pressed on him like he was the only one carrying it.

He'd done so much, tried so hard, and accomplished so little. And now they were coming to ask their questions and drown his answers out with pain until he'd say anything. Or they wouldn't ask anything, they'd just beat him until he understood that he was at their mercy, and they were merciless.

A small, still part of him that watched the rest of his mind noticed how odd it was. When he'd been a prisoner on Laconia, he'd been able to hold himself together. To rise to the occasion, plan, scheme, and even suffer with a resolve that he couldn't find now. After he'd escaped, he'd felt euphoric. Calm and whole and returned to the life he'd given up hoping for.

But the honeymoon faded, and the version of him it left behind was scarred and broken. He didn't feel weak. He felt annihilated.

Years were gone. Years of prison and torture, which had been bad, and of pretending to be an honored guest while the threat of death invisibly followed one step behind. The dancing bear years. They'd been the worst because they'd broken down his sense of himself. Of who he was. Of what was true. The Jim Holden who had tripped the alarms in Medina Station was gone. The Jim who'd schemed against Cortázar and for Elvi Okoye had been half a lie from the start. He was all that was left. The dregs of himself. The scrapings.

Jim. Jim, come back to me.

His awareness shifted. The little cabin came back into focus like someone was tuning a video screen. Naomi was there. He didn't remember her coming in. She was holding his hand.

"Hey," he said, trying to sound bright and cheerful. "Imagine meeting you here."

"You saw the message then?"

"Yup. Yes. Indeed I did."

"I was hoping you were still asleep. I should have come here first."

"No," he said, "I'm fine. Just processing a little old trauma. Thinking about what to have for dinner. The usual. What did I miss?"

"We don't have to talk about this now."

"It won't help," he said, and squeezed her fingers in his. "Not talking about it? It won't help. If you're here, I'll be fine. Getting it out will help me even. Promise." He didn't know that was true, but he didn't know that it wasn't.

He could see it when she decided to believe him.

"He's surrendering," Naomi said.

"Only if he gets to be your police force," Jim said. "That's not what surrendering means."

"I read the agreement he sent," she said. "He really has seen my traffic control protocol. It's almost word for word in some places. And it puts his ships at my command."

"All right."

"He wants to make the underground into a new Transport Union. We'd be responsible for setting policy. We'd be independent of the Laconian hierarchy. We'd have the authority to deny passage to Laconian ships."

"And you're thinking?"

"That it smells like bullshit. Sounds too good to be true," she said. "But...How else do peace treaties get made? That happens, doesn't it? History's full of wars that ended because people chose to end them. We hurt Laconia badly. We broke the construction platforms, and they're not coming back. Not anytime soon. Duarte was the architect of the whole thing, and he's off the board. The glitches where people turn off or the rules of physics change? They're the threat."

"They are," Jim agreed.

Naomi shook her head once. "Everything in me says the offer's a trap, but if it isn't, and I turn away? If this isn't the opening I was looking for, I'm not sure what our goal is with them."

The door to the little common room opened, and Alex's and Teresa's voices mixed, talking over each other. Muskrat barked once, a low conversational woof. Naomi leaned close, pressing her forehead to his like they were both wearing helmets and she wanted to say something only he could hear.

"I'll be okay," he said. "I'm better. I'm fine."

"Hey, back there," Amos said. "You talking about the thing?"

"We'll be right out," Jim said, loud enough to carry.

She put a hand on the top of his head, like she was gently hugging it, and then they walked out together. Alex and Teresa were leaning against the walls, Amos sitting on the floor idly scratching Muskrat's neck. The dog smiled her soft, canine smile, looking from Amos to Teresa and back.

"How's the resupply going?" Naomi asked.

"Good," Alex said. "We have a good pit crew here. Always have had."

"I keep forgetting how long this was home for you," Jim said. "I missed that part."

"These are good people," Alex said. It occurred to Jim how many families Alex had gathered on his path through life. His time in the navy, his first wife, the crew of the *Canterbury*. He might not be good at marriage, but he had a talent for making homes. Or finding them.

"Repairs are something different," Amos said. "They'll take longer, and some of them, if we start we'll be grounded until they're complete. That could take longer than the folks on Freehold have got. I thought we should hold off until we were sure."

Naomi nodded and pressed her thumb against her lower lip the way she did sometimes when she was thinking. She looked old, which was fair. They were both old. But more than that, she looked hard, and Jim wasn't sure they were hard. Only that they'd had to act that way so many times in so many situations. They'd gotten good at it, her and him both.

"And that brings us back to the thing, doesn't it?" Jim said.

"It does," Amos said.

"What do you think?" Naomi asked, as if Amos were the same man he'd been before.

"I think he didn't say what happens if you turn him down. I'm guessing it's pretty much where we're at now."

"In that case, we've got a little over two days before the *Derecho* starts killing people," Jim said. "We've got a little more than that before we need to leave here, assuming that our cover isn't totally shredded."

"Oh, our cover's totally shredded," Amos said. "I thought that was a gimme."

"It is," Naomi said. "We don't have a lot of options, and what we have got are bad."

"What do you mean? You hand me over," Teresa said. "Are we talking about this? Obviously you hand me over."

"It's a little more complicated than that, Tiny," Amos said.

The girl furrowed her brow. "I'm not worth a hundred thousand people."

Jim raised his hand like a student in a classroom. "Are you saying that you want to go back?"

"No, I don't. Being there was killing me, but I'm one person and they're most of a planet. You're going to hand me over. You *have* to."

"I don't have to," Amos said with a deceptive mildness. Jim heard the expectation of violence behind it, even if Teresa didn't.

"Are we thinking that Trejo means what he says?" Alex said. "Just looking at the logistics? I don't love it. If we did let Teresa go back, that means showing ourselves. Docking with one of their ships, maybe. And I've seen their power suits in action. If they decided to board us, they could go through us like tissue paper."

Teresa's frown shifted. It was fascinating. Knowing Laconia as well as she did, having seen it from as far inside as anyone could be, her first instinct was still to trust them. If Trejo was making the offer, it must be real. He must be sincere. A part of Jim wondered if that might not be a truer guide than his distrust or Naomi's. The fresh eyes of the young seeing more clearly, or else the benefit of experience showing where the traps were set.

"Trejo was a Martian before he was Laconian," Alex went on. "He betrayed his nation. I'm not sure that says a lot in favor of him keeping his word now."

"My father was Martian too," Teresa said, but there was no real heat in the words. More like she was thinking something through.

"The question is whether we can trust him to do what he's promising," Jim said. "The answer to that is inside Trejo's skull, and we don't have access to it. It's just which side do we bet on?"

"That's not the only question," Amos said. "If we hand over Tiny, are we still the good guys? That's a question too."

"It is," Jim agreed.

"If you can choose between one person and a hundred thousand, it's not a hard call," Teresa said. "I won't even die."

But Naomi's gaze had turned inward. Something in Teresa's words had done the trick. Jim saw her understand even before he knew what she'd understood. Naomi lifted her eyebrows and shook her head, just a millimeter back and forth.

"You know what this is?" she said. "This is him making me responsible for what he does. Teresa's right. She's got exactly the frame I'm supposed to use. One person for a multitude. But I'm not looking to kill a multitude. That's him. If I do what he says, I'll be saving all the people he would kill to punish me if I didn't."

Amos' laugh was almost the same timbre and cadence as Muskrat's little bark. When he spoke, he was mimicking the soft, threatening whine of an abusive lover. "Look what you made me do, baby. Why do you have to make me so mad?"

"That's it," Naomi said. "I couldn't put my finger on it, but that's why I can't do this. He's holding a gun to their heads and then pretending that I'm the only one who can decide whether he pulls the trigger. That's not a trust exercise. It's just another threat."

"Don't forget the surrender. The amnesty," Jim said. "There's a carrot along with the stick."

"Carrots don't matter when he still gets to hold the stick," Naomi said. "I'm done with sticks. Sticks are disqualifying. If he'd led by pulling the *Derecho* back from Freehold, it would be a different thing. He didn't. He chose this, and I don't trust him."

Jim smiled at her. "Also, he's asking us to hand over to him a young girl who doesn't want to go, so fuck him. We don't do that."

"Fuck him," Amos agreed.

The room was silent. Naomi pursed her lips and shook her head almost imperceptibly, continuing the conversation in her head. He wondered what she was saying, and to whom. He had the sense that, whoever they were, they were probably happier not being present for it.

"We've got two good ships," he said.

"We've got two ships anyway," Amos said. "I love 'em both, but the *Roci*'s feeling her years and the *Storm*'s gone a long way between updates."

"We've got two mostly okay ships," Jim said. "Not bad anyway. We load up everyone on Draper Station, burn hard for the ring gate, and take the *Sparrowhawk* out if it tries to stop us. With the *Storm* in the open, no reason to bomb Freehold anymore. At least the planet would be safe."

"Best bad plan we've got," Naomi said.

Jim headed for the door. He almost felt like himself again. The panic and fear weren't gone, but they'd grown smaller. Manageable. "First thing is make sure we're all the way topped up on railgun slugs," he said, and pulled the handle. The door didn't move, and an alert popped up on the locking panel. The error was so out of place that he pulled on the door twice more before he understood what he was seeing. EMERGENCY LOCKDOWN. VACUUM HAZARD.

"Uh, that's weird," he said.

Naomi was already on her hand terminal. "Jillian. What's going on?"

The voice that answered was hard and brittle. "I understand that you're upset, ma'am."

"What did you do?"

"While I respect the civilian branch of the underground which you represent, this is a military matter. The enemy has a hundred thousand of our people they're prepared to spare in exchange for one girl who they aren't even going to hurt. There's no dishonor in a prisoner exchange."

"Do you think Trejo's really going to walk away once he's got her?" Naomi said. Rage buzzed, but she didn't raise her voice.

"According to our best sources on the man, he will honor his word," Jillian said.

"You don't get to make that call," Naomi said. "That's my job."

"Respectfully? As the captain of the *Gathering Storm*, which is the flagship of our military branch, I have authority over military decisions. This is a military decision."

"Jillian," Alex said, loud enough for Naomi's hand terminal to pick him up. "You don't need to do this. Bobbie wouldn't have done this."

"Captain Draper understood that one individual can't stand in the way of the greater good, Mr. Kamal. If she were here, she'd be doing the same thing I'm doing."

Amos chuckled. "You can tell yourself that, Sunshine. Don't make it true."

"The *Sparrowhawk* is on its way with a representative of Laconia. The *Derecho* is burning this way as an escort force with an understanding that both ships will leave the system once the handoff is complete. Until it is, I'm restricting you all to your quarters," Jillian said. "Once this is over, and your emotions are calm enough that you can see that this decision was correct, we can discuss whether you want to fracture the underground's leadership or back my authority."

"Jillian," Naomi said, but the connection was dead.

The walls of the common room felt as small as a cell, and the fear rolled up Jim's spine, as fresh and angry as if he'd never put a lid on it. The others were talking, their voices washing over each other. Alex saying *I can talk sense into her if we can just get her to pick up again.* Amos guessing out loud how long it would take to get down the hallway in hard vacuum, and whether the rest of them would survive even if he did. Naomi repeating Jillian's name again, trying the connection. He was the only one who stayed quiet. Or, no, Teresa did too.

She looked at him like they were alone together. He nodded to her. She nodded back.

Chapter Nineteen: Kit

Their cabin on the *Preiss* was so small that if Rohi were standing in it, he couldn't cross the room without brushing against her. The thick cloth covering the metal bulkheads was an unappetizing olive color with location and maintenance data woven into the fabric in orange thread. The wall screen was hardly bigger than two handhelds put side by side and had a protective coating that never seemed clean no matter how much Kit wiped it down. Their crash couches were old gel and badly designed, built into cubbies in the wall that could pinch fingers and toes if they weren't careful. Bakari's couch was welded to the deck, the metal still bright where it had been put in. It was a much better design.

It was their only private space for the next few months while the *Preiss* burned out to the ring gate, made the transit to Nieuwestad system, and then burned to Fortuna Sittard—the capital city on the main habitable planet.

They shared a common galley, microgymnasium, and showers with six other cabins. Someone had put up the city flag of their new home: green and red with a black-and-white patterned circle in the center that looked suspiciously like a football. The door directly across from them belonged to a pair of brothers from Breach Candy who had left their mother's old salvage company for a contract on Nieuwestad, giving up the family trade of breaking down old terraforming equipment to build controlled environments in the unfamiliar biology of a new world. Kit worried that Bakari's crying kept the brothers awake, but if it did, they didn't complain.

One of the farther cabins had a woman with her preteen daughter, who Rohi had taken on as a kind of in-transit project to know better. Kit had the impression that the woman was leaving a bad marriage and that the daughter was seeing a therapist who was making the same transit, but four decks down.

Kit felt a little uncomfortable knowing even that much but recognized that his aversion to hearing about other people's family history was mostly projection. He'd spent so much of his life avoiding talking about who his father was that hearing about someone else's felt a little dangerous.

Kit centered himself in the camera, then shifted so that Bakari, napping in the pressure wrap strapped across his chest, also appeared. He started the recording.

"Hey, Dad. Don't know where you are or when you'll get this, but I wanted to check in. The little bear is right here too."

Kit shifted to put Bakari's face more clearly in the frame—the scrim of tightly curled, fine black hair on his scalp; the full, soft lips pursing and relaxing as he dreamed; the eyelids as dark as if he were wearing eye shadow. Kit gave his father, where and whenever he was, a long look at his grandson, then shifted back.

"We've been on the float for five days so far. He's taking to it better than I am. The ship infirmary has a resistance gel chamber he can use, but we're not the only family on board that needs it, so we have to schedule times. Rohi thinks it's important, though.

And she's probably right. Anyway, he doesn't like it, but he sleeps like a beast afterward. So that's good. I'm doing fine. Rohi's doing fine. If we can still stand each other when we get to Nieuwestad, I think it means we're destined to stay married forever. Living this close to someone isn't what I'm used to."

He paused for a moment, wondering whether he should go back and start the recording again. Joking with his father about divorce and shipboard life might seem pointed, and he didn't want to seem critical. But Bakari shifted a little. The nap wouldn't last forever, and it was harder to make a message when the baby was awake.

He felt the tug again—protecting his father on one hand and his son on the other. Kit always fell into the middle place between his mother and his father, his mother and Rohi, the contract association and his family. His mother said he got his peacemaker instincts from his father. Maybe that was true, but it hadn't been his experience of Alex Kamal.

He realized how long he'd been quiet and smiled an apology to the camera.

"Anyway," he said, "the doctor says the boy's fine. We're not going to do the adaptation cocktail. They say as young as he is, it would do more harm than good. As long as he gets his exercise time in and we make sure he gets enough rest when we get planet-side, he'll adapt faster than we will.

"Everything's looking good here. Going according to plan. We'll be making the ring transit pretty soon now. That's really the only scary part of this whole trip. But Bakari is going to take his first steps on Nieuwestad. He won't even remember Mars. I hope you'll get a chance to come see him. I don't know that it'll mean much to him, but it would mean a lot to me. You'd like Rohi, and you'd love the little bear here. I hope wherever you are, you're okay and things aren't any weirder than they have to be.

"Take care of yourself, Grandpa."

He ended the recording, then played it back. The gap where he'd lost himself in thought wasn't as noticeable as he'd feared, so he saved the message, encrypted it, and queued it for delivery to the address that Alex had given him for the underground. He didn't know where it would go from there. He didn't play with political issues except when the nature of his family demanded it.

It was a risk, but only a little one. Alex understood that if Laconian security forces came calling, Kit would cooperate with them to save himself and his family. They hadn't yet, apart from a meeting his mother had a year before. Kit seemed beneath their notice, and hopefully getting out to the colonies would put him even further off Laconia's radar. That was the other reason he'd wanted to take this contract. The reason he didn't discuss with Rohi.

Bakari yawned, his eyes still closed, and shifted against Kit's chest. He'd be awake soon, which if tradition held would mean milk and a diaper change. Kit sent a quick message to Rohi: NOT AWAKE, BUT WAKING.

They had formula mixed and ready to go, but Rohi still believed in breastfeeding, and while Kit was able to do a lot to take care of his son, that was a full-on mother-baby thing he was happy to tag out for. Also, he could go to their little gym and get his daily sweating done.

Bakari wrinkled his nose the way he had since they'd seen him in a sonogram, and opened his bright, dark eyes. His focus swam a little, then found Kit's eyes looking back at him. Bakari made a little *bap* sound, not even babbling so much as muttering to himself. If he didn't seem to take any particular joy in seeing his father, it was probably because Kit was almost always there. It made him feel obscurely proud to be so taken for granted.

He was debating to himself whether to message Rohi again or get a round of formula ready when the cabin door slid open. As soon as he saw her face, he knew something was wrong.

"Babe?" he said.

"I'm here." She gestured to Bakari, and Kit unfolded the boy from his pressure wrap. Bakari slowly windmilled his arms and legs, no distress in his movement at all. As if flying weightless through the air was as natural as anything else. Rohi scooped a hand around him and pulled him close. The baby, knowing what came next, was already plucking at the flight suit over her breast. Like a sleepwalker, Rohi pulled her suit open and guided him to her nipple.

"Babe," Kit said again. "What happened?"

Rohi took a deep breath, like a diver looking down toward distant water. "There was another blink. San Esteban system."

Kit felt his gut tighten, but only a little. He'd been through a half dozen rounds of the aliens from inside the rings turning off his mind for him. Everyone in Sol had.

"How bad was it?" he asked.

"They're dead," Rohi said. "Everyone in the system. They're all just dead."

Chapter Twenty: Elvi

San Esteban system was one of the first wave of colonial settle-ments, surveyed and studied by her old employer Royal Char-ter Energy. It had one habitable planet, and a moon around a gas giant with a breathable atmosphere. It had the first parallax sta-tion that had mapped out the relative locations of the ring sys-tems through the galaxy. Eighteen million people spread across ten cities, a semi-autonomous aquafarming platform the size of Greenland, and a research station in the stagnation zone of the heliosheath, 110 AU out. It had reached the technical specifica-tions for self-sufficiency three years ago, but it still imported sup-plies from Sol, Auberon, and Bara Gaon.

Which was why the *Amaterasu*, a freighter out of Sol system with a cargo of high-purity industrial reagents and refining equip-ment, risked the transit and passed through the San Esteban gate.

Elvi shifted through the images the ship's traumatized physician had sent back. She'd seen them all a dozen times before, listened to the recordings he'd made, and read the field autopsies.

The dead man on her screen was in a bag somewhere right now, heading to Laconia and the Science Directorate for a more thorough examination. Elvi tilted her head and considered the wetness along the back of the corpse's jumpsuit, the tightness where death bloat had pressed the fabric smooth, the way eyes had sunken as they'd given up their moisture to the air. According to his ID and the genetic sample, he'd been an engineering intern at a supply station, and one of the first corpses they'd recovered. He had once been a man named Alejandro Lowry. He was just SanEstebanCadaver-001 now.

The voices that played as she reviewed the dead weren't from San Esteban. She'd listened to the captain and physician of the *Amaterasu* enough to know there wasn't much they could tell her. She'd gone farther to find insight. She was listening to James Holden and a woman with a long, slow accent that Elvi thought of as Mariner Valley but was a kind of Laconian now.

Tell me about the systems going dark, the interrogator said.

It was just one at first, Jim replied. *And the...group consciousness? Consensus? I don't know the right word for it. The chorus. They weren't even particularly worried. Not at first.*

Elvi switched to an exterior. An older woman—gray, swirling hair—lying in sunlight. An animal Elvi didn't recognize lay beside the human corpse. It looked something like a small, insectile pig. Compound eyes on either side of a long skull-like structure. A prey species, then, and it appeared to have died at the same time as the woman. She pulled up an article on the species and what was known of the anatomy and physiology of San Esteban's tree of life.

Then there were more. Just a few. I mean, like three or four. Even then, it wasn't more than a curiosity, Jim said.

What was left in the system? Were there bodies? Did the aliens just disappear? the interrogator asked.

It wasn't like that, Jim said. *The systems just went dark. Like losing a comm channel.*

Then how were they certain the systems were dead?

They were all connected. If someone cuts off your hand, is it dead? So yeah, the systems were dead.

Because, Elvi thought, the builders or the Romans or the space jellyfish—the beings of light—hadn't known what it was to be alone since they'd learned to glow in that ancient, freezing ocean. They were individuals and they were a unity. A superorganism, connected as intimately as she was with her own limbs and organs. She found a paper speculating about the internal signal transfer in the bug-pig animal and let her eyes flow over it, catching the gist without diving down on details.

But they decided based on just that to destroy whole systems? the interrogator asked.

It was like cutting mold off a block of cheese. Or a clump of cancer cells on your skin. There was a bad spot, and so they burned it off. They didn't need it. They thought it would stop.

What would stop, exactly?

The darkness. The death.

"Hey," Fayez said, and Elvi stopped the recording just as the interrogator started her next question.

"Hey," she said, making it a sigh.

He floated in the door of her office. He looked tired. He looked fragile. Everyone did now. Everyone was.

"The relief drone from Laconia just popped through the gate," he said. "Another couple weeks for it to match orbit, and we'll be eating pretty much the same thing we're eating now, but with different atoms in it."

"Good. Hope we're here when it is."

She'd meant it to be funny. A morbid joke. The words tasted like chalk. The distress in her husband's eyes was brief, and after it, he chose to smile.

"What're you listening to?"

Elvi looked at the speakers mounted in the cloth of her office walls as if it would help her remember. "Um. James Holden. Some of his debriefing from when he was on Laconia. I'm trying to get the recordings from after the gates opened too. I know there's an archive of them at Alighar Muslim University, but I haven't gotten an answer from them yet."

"Something in particular you're looking for?"

"Memories change over a few decades," she said. "I just want to see if what he says here matches what he said then."

"See if you can figure out why we aren't all dead already?"

"I have a couple theories on that."

He pushed himself across the room, grabbed a handhold, and settled at her side. Pale stubble dusted his cheek like light snowfall. She took his hand in her left, and pulled up the water purification data from San Esteban with her right. The efficiency graph wasn't subtle.

"What am I looking at here?" he asked.

"An uptick in salt precipitates that matches when everyone died," Elvi said. "It looks like the mechanism the dark gods figured out is to make ionic bonds just a tiny bit stickier. It lasted just long enough to shut down neurons. The local fauna are also using ionic channels for signal propagation even though it's more like vacuum channels than nerves. It would still mess them up pretty good. You can tell it's not taking out the microbiota, though."

"How can I tell that?"

"Bloat," she said. "The trapped gasses are microbe farts."

"I find that story horrifying, but since it ended in a fart joke, I'm not sure how to react."

"Not a joke, *but* as soon as the event was done? Water recycling started up again. And the *Amaterasu* transited in just a few hours after the event. All the decay in these images happened while they were getting to a landing pad."

"Which says?"

"I don't think the enemy knows it worked. Listen." She found the tagged audio and played it.

It wasn't like that. The systems just went dark. Like losing a comm channel.

Then how were they certain the systems were dead?

They were all connected.

She stopped it. "The builders didn't go look. They didn't have to. They were already connected. When they lost a system, they knew there was no one there anymore. They used the gates to shove matter around when they needed to, but that was like us moving food through our guts. It was barely even conscious for them anymore. It wasn't something they scheduled or had trade routes for. So if there was nothing in a system to support, there's no traffic to support it."

"Traffic?"

"Like the *Amaratsu*," she said. "The enemy did a thing, and then the traffic stopped. What if that's how the enemy knew the thing worked. But with us? The traffic didn't stop. I think we may be as hard for them to see and make sense of as they are for us. So part of what we can do is dirty up their data. All our random, uncoordinated transits are what they're feeling. It's like hearing rats in your walls and putting out different poisons until the noise stops. The noise stopping is how you know what worked. And since we're still making transits in and out of that gate? As far as they know, their poison didn't work."

"That's a hell of a theory."

"Yep. Or."

"Or?"

She popped to another audio mark. *It was just one at first.*

"Or this is inside the error bars for how they work, and they'll be murdering us all shortly." She couldn't keep the despair out of her voice. Even if she had, he would have heard it. They'd known each other too long for secrets. "We have to push harder for answers."

"Harder than we have been?"

Elvi took her hand back and pressed her fingers into her eyes, rubbing from the center out to the sides. There was grit in her eyelashes. Tears that had dried there.

"I'll talk to Cara," Elvi said. "I'll see if she's up for it."

"Talk to Xan too. He's the one locked in the catalyst's chamber for a zillion hours. And he doesn't talk about it, but it's freaking him out."

We're all fucking freaked out snapped to the front of Elvi's mind, but she didn't say it.

When Fayez spoke again, the careful cheerfulness was gone. He sounded worn and broken. He sounded more like she felt. He sounded real. "I'm not telling you what to do. It's just…"

"Say it."

"Cortázar kept them in a cage for decades. He ran tests on them with no concern for them."

"I have Cara's consent—"

"All these dives are changing her, and we don't have a clear idea what the changes are. The fact that she enjoys it doesn't reassure me at all."

Elvi bristled, but it was Fayez and she was short on sleep and long on whatever adrenaline broke down into. Some kind of mandelic acid, she thought. She wasn't sure. When he went on, she tried to listen and not just react.

"I know I'm not my sanest self right now. We've all been stuck on this ship for way too long, and everyone's fraying, and it's all scary as shit. I get that. I do. But that's why we have ethical standards. So that when things get murky we have something to show us the way through."

"And you think I'm violating ethical standards?"

"Yes. I love you, but yes you totally are. Absolutely." He grimaced his apology.

Elvi took a long breath and let it out slowly through her nose. The *Falcon* hummed around them like it was also waiting for her to speak.

"I know," she said, and it was actually a relief to say it out loud. "I am."

"So what do we do about that?"

She crossed her arms. "Do you remember Dr. Negila?"

"That's a name from a long time ago. She taught at the University of Calabar?"

"I took an ethics seminar with her as part of my postdoctorate work. There was a story we read about this beautiful, utopic land where everything was wonderful and enlightened and pleasant and good and just, except for one child who had to live in confusion and misery. One child, in exchange for paradise to everyone else."

"I know that one. Omelas."

"This isn't that," Elvi said. "I'm working for an authoritarian dictator in a system where people are suffering and screwing each other over and killing each other. I'm compromising my safety and the safety of the people who work for me by smuggling my research to my boss's political enemies. We're not doing anything here to make a beautiful, gracious, pleasant utopia. If we win, the lives we save will be the same mix of shit, frustration, and absurdity that they've always been."

"True."

"The child in the story was being sacrificed for a *quality* of life. If I'm sacrificing Cara, and I acknowledge that I may be doing that, it's not for quality. It's for *quantity*. If I have to lose her in order to keep the quantity of human life from going to zero? It's cheap. If it costs everything, it's still a good trade."

It landed on Fayez. He lowered his head, not a surrender to gravity but a surrender all the same. "Yeah. Okay."

"If you can't do this, that's all right," Elvi said. "I can arrange transport back to the Science Directorate for you. You can do your work there as easily as you do it here."

"Sweetie. You know I'm not doing that."

"I'd understand if you did."

"Yeah, no. I just wanted to make sure we were doing what we meant to do. If doing the wrong thing is the right thing, then I'm still planning to wake up next to you while we do it. Kind of my life's work, really."

They floated together in silence for a moment, not touching.

"You should come to bed," Fayez said. "It's very late, and we're both very tired."

"In a little bit," Elvi said. "I have to make my report back to Trejo about San Esteban, and Ochida is waiting for some resource reallocations based on the new plan moving forward."

"Oh, and Dr. Lee wanted to talk to you too. If you have time. Personnel issue."

Elvi nodded her query.

"I think there's a dysfunctional love triangle in the physics group. They may need a talking-to from the boss."

"Are you fucking kidding me?"

Fayez spread his hands. "Every miracle we've pulled off, we've done it using primates. Just because we're capable of mind-blowing wonders doesn't mean we aren't still sex-and-murder machines. The organism doesn't change."

"All right. I'll stop by the bridge. Do me a favor, though?"

"Anything."

"The relief pod was supposed to have updated menus. See if the download taught the galley how to fake up some sag paneer?"

"If it did, I will have it waiting in the cabin."

He pulled himself in and kissed her before heading out to the hall. She turned back to the San Esteban images. Now, every corpse she saw, she imagined as Fayez. Or herself. Or James Holden. Or Anton Trejo. Or Winston Duarte.

She started a recording. "Admiral Trejo. I understand that San Esteban is yet another first priority. All I can give you right now is our overview, some speculation, and my plan moving forward..."

It took half an hour to get the version she liked best, and she made a copy with a different routing header to send to Naomi and the underground. They were all allies in this, whether they knew it or not.

By the time she'd sent her reallocation plan to Ochida and talked to Harshaan Lee about how to keep the social drama on the *Falcon* from spiraling out of control, two hours had passed. Fayez was in their cabin, asleep. A tube of sag paneer was waiting for her, a bulb of decaffeinated tea beside it. She ate and drank and pulled herself into the sleeping harness.

When she dreamed, she dreamed she was in an ocean teeming with sharks, and if she moved too fast, they would kill her.

Cara floated in the lab while the technicians went through the adjustments to the sensor arrays on her skull like a cap. Everything was bustling around them, but Elvi felt like the two of them—she and her test subject—were still. The eye of the storm. On the screens, Cara's brain function shifted and stuttered as the expert systems matched what they were seeing now to what they had seen before. "Norming," it was called. As if norms were still a thing for them.

"How are you feeling?" Elvi asked.

Cara's perfect black eyes clicked to her, went still for a moment, and then Cara grinned. Elvi wanted to see it as genuine, and maybe it was. Maybe the extra processing delta between stimulus and response only read as inauthentic and studied because Elvi was trying to read the girl as if she were the same as other people. As if she were a primate. *The organism doesn't change*, Fayez said in her memory, but now it felt like a warning.

The organism *had* changed.

As if she'd heard her thinking, Cara's expression shifted. "Are you worried about something?"

"I was thinking...about the cognitive changes you and Xan went through. Do you remember what it was like before?" Elvi asked.

"Before?"

One of the technicians touched the sensor leads, and the displays clicked over to green across the board. Good to go.

"Before the change. Before all this," Elvi said. *Before you died*, she didn't say.

"I don't know. Just like anyone, I guess. It was a long time ago."

Elvi forced a little smile, trying to think where she would have been when Cara had run into the wilderness of Laconia for the last time. Who had she been when Cara had been human?

"Long time for me too," she said, then gathered herself. "Okay, we're going to try something a little different this time. We need to refine the search. Try to get some specific answers about how the ring gates came to be. We'll want to shift the BFE from lecture mode into more Q and A. If we can."

"Because of San Esteban?"

Elvi tried to think of some softer way to say yes, and failed. "Yes."

"I can try," Cara said. "I don't know if it'll like that, though."

"If you're uncomfortable or things feel wrong, say the word, and we will pull you back up. I'll be watching your stress levels. If they get bad, even if you can't speak, I'll call it. Okay?"

"I can take it," Cara said. "I want this."

Elvi took the girl's hand. It felt so thin and fragile. "Me too."

Interlude: The Dreamer

The dreamer falls purposefully into dream and dream and dream, swimmingly layer on layer on layer on the abyss. She is threefold, and one still missing, and the dream tells her about the unfolding across the emptiness and of the light of stars and cells and minds, the flicker that draws them like songs and kisses because their kisses were all light. The ones that don't feel the stars calling fall out of the dream, and the rest become wise and broad and fuller than the old ocean, comfortable in the vacuum with only their own slow heat to warm them.

Yes, the dreamer dreams like swimming with the tide, but the gates. How did the gates happen?

Grandmothers whisper in voices that have never known teeth. *Look here, I will tell you everything. Look here, to where the light becomes everything, look how the light learns to think.*

Yes and yes and yes, but the gates. The darkness. How did the *end* come?

Light itself fractures like an old woman holding out a glass bead, inviting a child's marveling eyes. *Look what light can do! Look how rich it can be! Isn't it prettyful and beautisome? And don't you want to eat it all up so it can eat you and expandingcontracting fullness of the bloom?*

But the gates. The gates. And the things at the end.

Grandmothers smile and smilingly nod, noddingly smile and the dream shifts like a kick in the face. The rich light diffracts, and there are holes in the spectrum. Infinite holes of more than darkness between the light that's more than light. The dreamer chokes. Reality splits her open like vomiting or orgasm or seizure and the grandmothers hold the glass bead that had her head in it and it wants to explode.

Is she okay? Do we pull her out?

Not yet.

A new physics falls into place all through the dream. Yes yes yes, the monkeys began with the parabolic arc of stone through air, and they learned everything in that order that isn't the dream or the dreamer, that's the one in blue. The light began swimmingly, with the caress of waters and salts, and its first chapter was different and its second a second difference and its fullness a different fullness, with fingernails in the cracks between this and the permanent outside.

The grandmothers say *look look look how it all happened once and all happens again.* The cold roof of the world broke open and gave the stars. The vacuum shatters in the same way and shows the outside, the *older* real, the *vaster* real.

The body of God. The heaven where the angels all hate us.

The dreamer feels herself shaking, feels herself losing bladder and bowel control. *Don't wake me up don't wake me don't wake don't.*

You wanted to know is *I did* and *I do.*

A new physics gives new problems and the problems ticklingly new dreams. A second crash outward, a new efflorescence, a vaster self. And the toolbox was the toolbox: co-opting fast life to bring what makes it rich, sending out what will or may one day return with presents for the grandmothers who cast them free, and the vast patience of the ones who are too cold and too slow and too wide to ever die, too sudden for time to touch. A bubble blown into the holes in the spectrum and a thousand thousand thousand seeds sent like kisses to the singing poet stars. And then...

The dreamer flickers. The body someplace starts to fail, and she feels something deeper than dream opening under her. All that begins will end, and the end is clearing its throat in the hallway. Bring me up. Bring me up bring me up *bring me up.*

What is this? the blue one says, and the dreamer pushes away, but it isn't her dream anymore. The grandmothers cackle and run, trailing her in their thousand fingers. And the echo says *Sorry. Didn't mean to drag you in here. Just try and relax.* But it isn't speaking to her.

A nucleus in a vast atom, and the burning clockwork at its heart. The power of a million suns harvested from the older universe. *Yes yes yes,* the blue one says. *I see now. Show me how this works,* and the grandmothers do.

She's seizing.

Pull her out.

And the blue one puts a gentle hand on her head and holds her lovingly underwater. A system goes dark, a few voices out of quadrillions go silent. A hundred systems. They go to war, and the war fails, but show me where you buried the guns. And the grandmothers gigglingly do.

Yes, the blue one says. *Yes. That's what I needed.*

Thank you.

Chapter Twenty-One: Tanaka

The girl on the screen wore something that was supposed to look like a uniform, held herself in a way that was supposed to look like military crispness, and spoke with a formality that was supposed to sound like authority.

"In accepting Admiral Trejo's offer, I am willing to permit one envoy from your ship to enter Draper Station to take custody of Teresa Duarte," Jillian Houston said. "Once this transfer is complete, both the *Sparrowhawk* and the *Derecho* are invited to retire from Freehold system until such time as the details of our new situation can be finalized."

"Oh, goody," Tanaka said. "We'll be invited to retire."

"Yes, sir," Mugabo said. Then, a moment later, "She does seem a bit green."

"She's still licking off the caul. I can't believe we've had this much trouble tracking down someone who's still sleeping with her teddy bear."

"I believe a Martian was in command of the *Storm* until shortly before the attack on the homeworld."

"And Nagata was in charge during that," Tanaka said, then tilted her head. "So why isn't she the one answering now?"

"I don't have a theory to venture," Mugabo said, but she hadn't really been talking to him anyway.

Trejo's plan was bold, she'd give him that. And, like all the best plans, it was limber. If Nagata accepted the terms, then he'd let her playact at being in charge until he could rebuild the strength they'd lost. And if Duarte proved to be unmanageable, maybe even keep her on as figurehead in perpetuity. It was an elegant way to put an end to the fighting: Give the enemy the raiment of power while keeping the actual power for yourself and then seeing if she ever noticed.

If she didn't agree, but did reach out to announce her rejection, the door was open for diplomacy. Diplomacy always provided the chance to glean more information from the enemy. Or for them to glean it from you. It wasn't a form of conflict Tanaka found comfortable, but she understood it.

This situation, though, fell somewhere between the two. It was an acceptance, and allegedly by the underground, but not by Nagata. It was a negotiation of terms, but not about the larger issues. Tanaka had already learned more than a little critical information: the exact location of the underground's secret base and confirmation that the *Gathering Storm*—or at least its commander—was there. Teresa Duarte was probably there. The little rebel captain was certainly acting like she was. And it was probably true. The ship that had come through the gate was a good match for the *Rocinante* when it left New Egypt. It had gone to the moon that had the enemy base. And if the *Rocinante* was there, James Holden and Naomi Nagata were almost certainly there too.

If Nagata had been the one responding, it wouldn't have smelled wrong at all.

It smelled wrong.

"I'm taking it," she said. "I'll go get the girl."

If she'd expected Mugabo to object or push back against her taking the personal risk—*The last time you had a Marine fire team with you, and you still came within centimeters of death, sir*—he disappointed her. She didn't feel disappointed, though. More amused.

"Tell Botton to start the *Derecho* toward us," she said. "If we're leaving after this, it looks like good faith. If we're fighting, I want him close."

"Of course, ma'am," Mugabo said. "Not to change the subject, but you saw the briefing about San Esteban?"

"What about it?"

Mugabo's little smile was melancholy. He would have made a good waiter. He had the vaguely embarrassed expression crafted for telling people the special was already sold out. She met his eyes.

"There are other people on that mission. We're on mine. If the Messiah comes, He can find us at work. Understood?"

"Perfectly, sir."

"If you need me, I'll be in the armory."

She hadn't packed her fast scout suit, much to her regret. The *Sparrowhawk* did have a latest-generation assault suit, and lying on the deck awaiting her finishing touches, it looked nothing like the elegant and greyhound-lean Stalker. The assault armor had the simple, brutally efficient design of a wearable murder-robot. Underslung on both arms were Gatling guns, designed to fire a high-speed stream of small-caliber explosive rounds. On the left shoulder was an integrated rocket-propelled grenade launcher, for when a pair of machine guns just won't get the job done. And the suit itself was a weapon. Wearing one, Tanaka could bench-press a ground vehicle. Ripping a human limb from limb while wearing a Laconian assault suit was trivial. It was made for door-to-door, corridor-by-corridor assault. It was the pinnacle of Laconian design engineering, and in her hands it could clear a base like Draper Station without assistance. As long as she didn't step in front of any PDCs.

She worked, slowly and methodically going through the mental checklist thousands of hours operating these suits had etched in her brain. As she finished the suit's final touches, her mind occupied itself with the upcoming fight. If it was a fight.

She was ready for it to be a fight.

Tanaka's tongue probed through the gap where her teeth used to be and across the nasty scar inside her cheek. The wound no longer hurt, but she could feel the uncanny smoothness of poorly healed gashes where James Holden's bullet had blown the side of her face apart. It itched, but not physically.

The physical wounds were bad. Her head still ached if she slept on it wrong. Even if she went through the trouble of a complete regrow, her cheeks would never quite match again. It was going to take months to grow back the missing bone, and more than that to regrow teeth from it. There were people—even people in the Laconian military—who had used less to claim permanent disability with increased retirement benefits. But that wasn't the worst.

The embarrassment was worst.

She was the peak of the Laconian military. The lone atom of steel at the tip of the tip of the spear. Experienced, trained, and still in top condition despite her age. She'd gone on what should have been a milk run with a full fire team at her back, and James Holden had handed her her ass on a plate. She understood why. She'd been restrained to protect the girl, and he hadn't. She'd been conservative with employing a warship around civilians, and he hadn't. She could have waited until the girl had been dropped off, but even that had been a calculated risk that just bounced bad for her that time. Nothing she'd done would have raised an eyebrow from a review tribunal. But she'd lost, and he hadn't.

She loaded a belt of mixed high explosive and armor-piercing rounds into the right arm's gun. It made a satisfying metallic click when she locked and armed it. Don't kill anyone, or kill everyone.

If anything went south during the transfer, she knew which one she was picking.

Tanaka had Mugabo park the *Sparrowhawk* far enough from the moon that they'd have time to evade incoming rail-gun rounds, then used her assault suit's EVA jets to descend to the surface at the coordinates she'd been given. A shallow overhang in the rock and ice hid an airlock door from orbital view, but was plainly visible once she'd hit the surface. The outer door was open and waiting for her.

Draper Station wasn't much more than an icy cave sprayed with insulating foam on a tiny moon where the gravity was a meek suggestion of down. It had about as much in common with a naval base as it did with a Belter pirate station. The idea that a great warrior and leader like Admiral Trejo felt the need to negotiate with these low-rent revolutionaries left Tanaka feeling insulted on his behalf.

"I'm going in," she radioed up to Mugabo.

"Understood, sir," he said. "We are standing by."

Tanaka chuckled to herself and killed the channel. A few moments later she'd passed through the airlock and into a large equipment storage room. Lockers and vacuum suit racks filled all the wall space. The ceiling was covered with the same shitty spray-on insulation as the walls, but the floor was metal grate, so she kicked on her mag boots.

Five people waited for her in the room. They were all armed.

"I'm Jillian Houston," the woman in the middle said. She wore a simple jumpsuit without rank markings. The four people flanking her held rifles like they were some kind of honor guard.

"Colonel Aliana Tanaka of the Laconian Marine Corps." There were forms to be obeyed in a prisoner transfer, and until Tanaka had the girl in her hands, she'd obey them.

Jillian Houston seemed nonplussed when Tanaka didn't continue. They shared an awkward silence. Jillian cleared her throat. Tanaka watched her HUD while the suit's various heat-and-sound-imaging and radar sensors built a map of the interior of the station for her. The electromagnetic sensor that could pinpoint

the location of human heartbeats also mapped the location of anyone within its range.

"Trejo said—"

"Fleet Admiral Anton Trejo," Tanaka interjected, the assault
suit's external speakers making her voice echo off the walls.

Jillian's expression hardened. She might be green, but she didn't
like being corrected. Even standing face-to-face with Tanaka's
battle suit, she wasn't backing down at all. Only the elevation in
her heart rate betrayed her nervousness. Scrappy.

Tanaka waited, watching the guards twitch. Jillian seemed
determined to force Tanaka to speak first now. A power game.
Fine. The suit reported that it had a mostly complete station map,
and every human within seventy meters was pinpointed. Tanaka
turned off the external speaker and said, "Free-fire authorization,
Tanaka."

The weapons of the suit clicked out of safe mode, a sound that
also echoed around the room. The guards shot nervous looks at
each other.

"Fleet Admiral Trejo," Jillian Houston said, breaking first,
"guaranteed us that if we gave you the girl, all Laconian forces
would withdraw from the Freehold system without further
attacks. We have his word on it."

Tanaka chinned the external speakers back on. "I'm not seeing
Teresa Duarte. Where is she?"

"Before I hand her over, I need more than vague assurances that
you are acting in good faith."

"Moving the goalposts?" Tanaka said.

"I need more than assurances," the Houston girl repeated.
Apparently they'd gotten to the end of her script.

"Where's Nagata?"

"Excuse me?"

"The admiral made his offer to Naomi Nagata. You aren't her.
Teresa Duarte's not here. What's really going on?"

Houston lifted her chin like Tanaka had accused her of something. "Naomi Nagata is in operational control of the civilian

action of the underground. As the commander of the *Gathering Storm*, military decisions fall to me—"

"Bullshit."

"I don't care for your tone of voice."

This was the moment. Playing it safe hadn't worked in New Egypt. Life was risk, and the fact that even if it all came down poorly, there could be no consequences for her personally was a little intoxicating.

She wasn't going to shoot the Duarte girl. They weren't likely to do it. The only danger was an accident, and even if the girl did take a bullet, there was a percentage of those wounds she could recover from.

And once the shooting started, they might try to evac the prisoner, in which case she had two ships ready to disable the enemy. Flushing Teresa out of the base was probably the safest way for her.

She realized she'd taken a long time responding. Jillian Houston's heart rate was ticking up with her anxiety.

So this was it. Play nice with the enemy, or do the obvious thing.

"You know, we've got some of those suits," Jillian said, pointing at her armor. "We aren't wearing them as a sign of good faith."

"Wouldn't matter if you were."

Fuck it.

"All right," Tanaka said, locking eyes with each of her four guards in turn and using the touchpads in her gloves to target them. "I'll just go get her myself."

"No—" Jillian started.

Tanaka said, "Go loud."

The left and right arms of her suit snapped up into firing position much faster and more accurately than if she'd been driving them manually. The second the weapons were lined up on the outer two guards, they fired a short five-round burst that blew their heads off. Her arms snapped to the second position and fired a second time. The two people standing next to Jillian Houston disappeared from the chin up. The entire process took less than a second and a half.

Smoke filled the room, and the roar of the guns was still bouncing around the space when Jillian Houston spun on her heel and pushed off, flying down the corridor behind her. Tanaka watched her go. She could have turned the woman into a dancing bloody rag doll a hundred times over in the time it took for her to flee.

"Track her," she told the suit, and Jillian Houston's rapid heartbeat got a special tag on her HUD. If Houston was in charge of the base, she'd know exactly where the girl was. Teresa Duarte's value as a hostage was the only thing that might keep any of them alive. In the meantime, Tanaka had other business she could do.

She used the suit's mag boots to keep her secure to the floor as she casually strolled down the corridor following Houston. All around her the heartbeats of the station's denizens were running around and speeding up as the panic spread. That was fine. It wasn't like her plan relied on secrecy. Let the revolutionaries prepare. Let them arm up and dig in. None of it would matter. They could have the courageous last stand all the romantics craved. It would still be a last stand.

She moved into a corridor junction, and her suit blatted an alarm tone at her microseconds before a barrage of gunfire hit her on the left side. The suit marked three targets, all using light automatic weapons and hiding behind improvised cover. Tanaka tapped a pad in her glove and the left arm of the suit snapped around and fired three times. Three shredded bodies drifted out from behind their cover, spraying globes of arterial blood into the air.

The ammo counter for the left gun went down by another fifteen rounds. Tanaka noted this without concern. Full ammo packs on both guns. Plenty for everyone. And if not... Well, the alternative was messier but it had its charms.

"In New Egypt, we could have done this easy," she said, imagining Nagata and Holden and their crew. "This is what *you* picked." She smiled while she said it, the tightness in her wounded cheek pulling it into a lopsided grimace. It didn't hurt much.

Corridor by corridor, meter by meter, Tanaka moved through the station. She headed toward the large clumps of heartbeats first. Hoping that the center of the largest resistance would be the heroes of the *Rocinante*, but it never was. The resistance fighters were tenacious and brave, Tanaka would give them that. They came at her with little regard for their own safety, and some of the counterattacks had a real cunning to them. Though, given that her rampage had left little indication surrendering would lead to safety, she'd have been doing exactly the same thing in their situation. And everywhere she went, the seventy-meter range of her heartbeat detector found new pockets of people, hiding or preparing to fight. One by one, she went to them all, offering them amnesty if they put down their guns and turned over the girl. Not that she expected them to. Not that she'd necessarily stop shooting if they did.

Tanaka realized she'd lost track of Houston's heartbeat. It gave her a moment of pause, but only a moment. She was concentrating on the map layout in her HUD, looking for possible ship docking points, when she rounded the corner into the base's single largest pressurized room. A massive warehouse space, over a hundred meters on a side and a dozen meters high. The room was filled with racks of supplies and ship parts. The secret treasure trove of the revolutionary underground. All of it stolen from Laconia.

The suit warned her that three people were moving up behind her, and when she glanced at the warning it popped a rear view up on her screen. Three Belters were maneuvering what looked like a tool cart laden down with a massive compressed-gas tank. She was just starting to turn when one of the Belters hit the rear of the tank and it launched at her like a battering ram.

Oh, she thought as it picked her up off her feet, *an improvised missile.*

She only blacked out for a moment, but when she came to, her suit was blaring half a dozen alarms at her. She was embedded a good half meter into the foam-covered wall of the warehouse. The improvised missile oxygen tank was holding her upright, still pressed against her chest.

The suit warned her that it had lost secondary actuator control for her upper torso, and 30 percent of the reserve battery power before the system had rerouted to stop the leak. She also had four broken ribs and a dislocated left shoulder. She chinned the medical override and had the suit shoot her full of painkillers and amphetamines. She felt a surge that was almost like pride in her opponents. *Nice job, little bunnies. Good try.*

The three Belters were cautiously approaching. She hadn't moved since their missile hit, and they were undoubtedly hoping it had finished the job. One of the three had a portable plasma torch in his hand. To cut her out of the suit and make sure, she guessed.

"RPG," she said, locking her eyes on the middle man. The suit raised the launcher up over her shoulder and took aim. The three Belters only had a moment to register a look of surprise before a twenty-millimeter rocket-propelled grenade struck the man in the center and turned into a cloud of shrapnel that would kill anything within ten meters.

Some of the shrapnel sprayed across her breastplate and visor, with a sound inside the suit like hail hitting a metal roof. A half second later, the shrapnel was followed by a spray of blood and viscera.

"Motherfuckers," Tanaka said, then used the right arm of her suit to shove the oxygen tank away from her chest. Its mass was significant, but the suit was up to the challenge, and a few moments later she was back on her own two feet, pain-free and jittery from the drug cocktail in her veins.

"I'll make you a deal," she yelled out, turning the suit's speakers up so high that anyone in the warehouse space with her would probably suffer permanent hearing loss. "The person who brings me Teresa Duarte lives. They're the only one who gets to walk out of this place in one piece. So if you have her, you'd better be the first to show up with the girl in your hands.

"Because everyone else here is going to die."

Chapter Twenty-Two: Jillian

As soon as the Laconian stepped into the base, Jillian knew she'd fucked up. She tried to believe that it was just nerves, that the trade would go down as promised, but in her gut, she'd known.

She hunched down in the access channel, head low. Blood was wicking through the fabric of her shirt, making the cut along her ribs seem bigger than it was. In the distance, the Laconian's amplified voice echoed, but Jillian only made out a few of the words. *Duarte. First. Die.* She plucked her hand terminal out of her pocket with her left hand, thumbing through the options with the same crisis-calm she'd always prided herself on. Her impulse was to go take care of the prisoners herself. Instead, she opened the comm.

"Jillian?" Kamal said. Even though the connection was voice-only, she could picture his worried expression.

"I made a mistake," she said as she hit the atmospheric release.

The hiss of air rushing into the corridor outside their rooms was loud enough to come through the comm. "The Laconian's wearing an assault suit. She may be tracking me."

"Are you okay?"

Jesus, but that was just like Kamal. Jillian had locked him in a cell, asserted her own authority over the civilian chain of command, invited the enemy into their base, and Kamal was worried if she was all right.

"I'm where I should be," she said. "Stupidity's supposed to hurt. Get your people to your ship and get out."

"Where can we get armed up? Can you get us—"

"Get your people and go, Kamal. You don't need guns to run like hell, and you need to run like hell. I'm giving you cover."

She heard other voices behind him—Nagata, Holden, the black-eyed monster, the girl. She could hear in the breathiness of Kamal's voice that they were on the move. "There still a couple Laconian ships heading for us once we get out?"

"There are. One's here, one's coming."

There was a pause. He might have been thinking. He might have been running. "All right."

"Ping me when you're launched. I'll make this as easy for you as I can." She dropped the connection and a section of the wall behind her blew apart. She'd been found.

Jillian put her head down and pushed off, half running, half skimming in the microgravity of the base. A volley of bullets tore through the air around her. If the Laconian had meant her to be dead, she'd be dead already. All the enemy wanted now was to keep her scared and moving. It was working.

The heat in her face was shame and hatred. Shame for herself, hatred for the enemy. And fear too, but she wasn't going to feel that now. That was for later, if later came.

Jillian got to a T intersection, grabbing handholds and swinging her body around the corner in the direction that would take the enemy away from the path Kamal would be on. *Chase me*, Jillian thought. *Come on, you asshole. Come and get me.*

Draper Station was small, but it was home. Jillian could close her eyes and navigate the whole place like it was her childhood ranch. Her handheld was lighting up with alerts and errors, some from the station crew, some from the automated systems. Alarm was spreading through the base like adrenaline through a bloodstream. There had been a time less than an hour before when Jillian would have followed up on every one of them. Part of her dreaded that she'd have to go through them all later. A part of her knew better, but that was for later too.

Still on the run, she pulled up her saved comm groups and hit Live-send to the crew of the *Storm*. "Draper Station is being attacked from within. Prepare *Storm* for emergency launch in... five minutes."

She didn't wait for any replies.

Behind her, the Laconian was shouting something about Teresa Duarte, but all Jillian could hear was the joy in the vast electronic voice. Her own mind was already dancing ahead. Up two levels, and there was a tunnel that looped back around to the hangars. If she could stay far enough ahead, the curve of the tunnel itself would give her some protection from enemy bullets. She reached the ladder up, hauled herself to the next level, and slammed the access door closed behind her. It was going to be about as useful as rice paper for stopping the enemy, but the point wasn't stopping the enemy. Just slowing her down. Getting a few extra seconds for Kamal and for herself.

Something seemed to distract the Laconian, because she fell behind for a moment. Jillian was almost all the way to the tunnel's far end before she heard the access door being blown aside and the impact of the mechanized armor pulling itself after her in a fast, even stutter. Jillian let herself down and then moved to the right. The passage to the *Storm*'s airlock was two levels down, but Jillian couldn't wait for the lift. Still on the move, she hit the lift door override, and by the time she reached it, the shaft stood open. She dropped, but slowly. Gunfire came from behind her. Some fragment of Draper Station's security force making their stand. Some people Jillian knew and had been responsible for, dying because she'd let herself believe she could trade the Duarte girl so she wouldn't have to watch her planet burn. The mistakes you made at the high-stakes table were always the ones that cost the most, and Jillian had a lot of chips.

Two levels down, she kicked off the back wall and stumbled into the airlock corridor. The *Storm*'s outer lock was already open and waiting, and Jillian hurtled into her ship and thumbed the doors closed. Down the corridor, the mechanical armor slammed into view. The *Storm*'s outer doors began to slide closed, and the enemy let out a shout amplified by her suit until the sound was almost an assault.

An RPG launched toward her, and time seemed to slow. The dark body of the grenade with a brightness behind it like a ship and its drive plume. Jillian tried to step back, as if that could help. The doors hissed closed, and then rang like a gong. The skin of the *Gathering Storm* was probably the only thing on the station that the Laconian couldn't blow a hole through. Another quarter second, and the grenade would have detonated in Jillian's lap. But that was for later.

"Bridge, this is Captain Houston. Report."

As the inner airlock doors cycled open, Caspar's voice came over her hand terminal. "Drive's prepped, but we're missing some crew."

"They're too late. No way to get them in now. Is the *Rocinante* launched?"

"No, still in dock."

Where the fuck are you, Kamal? she thought. Into her handheld she said, "Prep for launch."

"Aye, Captain," Caspar said, and she heard the fear in his tone.

When she reached the lift, she checked her security report. Eighteen high-priority alerts tracked the Laconian from where she'd first opened fire, and then through the base, time codes of broken doors and gunfire alerts marking the Laconian's passage through space and time like a borehole chewed through wood.

She tried to guess which way Kamal and his people would go. Another alert lit up, but it wasn't automated. Station security asking her what the plan was. The tightness in her throat was that she didn't know what to tell them. The base was compromised, and it was her fault. One prisoner for thousands of civilian lives had seemed like an obvious trade at the time, but it had brought her here. Dwelling on the postmortem of her error was for later.

"Kamal, report," she said, and for a terrible half second thought he might not reply. Then the speaker ticked once, hissed, and his out-of-breath voice came gasping to her. "By the water tanks. Heading for the dock."

"Get there and get out," she said. "I'll clear the path."

Caspar was in his crash couch on the bridge when she reached it. Amanda Feil was strapping in at comms. Natasha Li had the gunner's controls up, even though she was sitting at her usual station. All the other couches were empty. Jillian slung herself into her own. The one she'd taken when Draper left. For the very first time, the chair didn't feel right. It suddenly felt much too large for her.

"Launch when ready," she said. "Li, target the *Sparrowhawk* as soon as we're clear of the dock."

"Disable or destroy?"

"Kill the fuck out of them."

The *Storm* shifted under her, tilting her crash couch and then pressing her into it as the ship left its home port for what Jillian understood in that moment would be the last time.

Behind her, Draper Station burned.

The funny thing was she didn't even like Kamal. She never had. She'd always felt like his faux-folksy grandpa act had a hidden contempt for her and people like her. She still remembered when the *Rocinante* had come to Freehold as a threat and taken her father away. Maybe on some level she'd never forgiven him for that. Or maybe she was just reaching for bullshit psychological justifications because she was ashamed of how things had worked out. Flip a coin, win a prize.

The *Storm* thumped twice as two torpedoes were ejected from the launcher. On Li's screen she could see the tiny dots that represented them speeding off toward a targeting diamond with the name *Sparrowhawk* floating next to it. The *Derecho* was the same class as the *Storm*, but with the advantage of recent repair and resupply and the knowledge and expertise of the people who'd built her. The *Sparrowhawk* was smaller, and it had taken some damage in New Egypt.

Jillian looked at the tactical map of Freehold system. The little solar disk on her display made the vastness seem comprehensible. That was an illusion, but a useful one. Here was the ring gate. Here were the ships that the underground had in-system—half a dozen rock hoppers and an ancient ice hauler, none of them ready for a full-scale battle. Here was the *Storm*.

There were the enemies, focusing in on Draper Station and on her, the indicators for her two homes—her base and her ship—still so close together they overlapped. She pressed her fingertips into her lips until it hurt a little. There was the planet and her family and everyone she'd grown up with that the fuckers had threatened to glass. Here were the planets of Freehold system that didn't sustain life.

Here was the problem that, if she solved, she could live, and if she couldn't, she would die.

"Status on the *Sparrowhawk*?" she said.

"Matching us. Shot down the first two torpedoes, now staying just out of effective range."

"Could you give me an evasion plan for the *Derecho*, please?" she asked, and saw Caspar and Feil exchange a look. They knew when she got polite, things were bad.

Caspar spoke, his voice steady. "If we break directly away and make the highest sustainable burn, their long-range missiles will be good to go in eighteen hours, fifteen minutes. Solutions drop quickly from there."

"What's the status from Draper Station?"

"They've gone dark, Captain," Feil said.

She felt Bobbie Draper beside her. Not a ghost or a spirit, but a memory. The older woman's smirk that might have been to condemn Jillian's naive fuckup or God's sense of humor or both.

If the *Rocinante* didn't get out—if Kamal and Nagata and the rest of them died where they were—there were options. Assuming Trejo's bullshit emissary stayed alive, one of the ships would have to stop and pick her up. If it was the *Sparrowhawk*, that meant it had to break away and give the *Storm* a head start. If the *Derecho* went after Tanaka, that meant they intended to let the *Sparrowhawk* do the fighting. But that was one she thought she'd be able to win. She could escape.

Freehold, on the other hand, couldn't. If she killed their sister ship, would the *Derecho* chase her or turn back to punish the underground by leveling the colony? Could the underground's other ships run interference? If she could lure the destroyer into joint action against her and her scattered militia at the same time... Well, the ice hauler wouldn't make it, but it might give her enough of an edge to win that fight. And then it would be the *Storm* and whatever damage it had sustained against the one remaining Laconian ship...

"It's okay, Captain," Caspar said, and Jillian looked up at him. Her lip had gone numb where she'd been pushing at it without realizing. The pilot's face was meant to be consoling. "We understand. It's okay."

Jillian fought the urge to unstrap, walk over, and hit him. Or dress him down at least. Lash out somehow. If they lived through this, she would have a long and very unpleasant talk with him about morale and faith in her command, but that was for later. Now, things were happening.

"*Rocinante* has cleared Draper Station," Feil said. "They made it."

A third icon appeared on her display, stacked on top of Draper Station and the *Storm* like they all shared the same shirt.

"Get me a tightbeam," Jillian said.

Seconds later, Kamal was on her screen. Familiar as he was, she found herself caught by the small details of his face: the way his skin darkened at the eyelid, the whiteness of the stubble on his chin and neck, the laugh lines at his mouth. If he was frightened, he didn't show it.

"What's your status?" Jillian asked.

"We're all on the ship. The girl and her dog too. It was closer than I would have liked, but we made it."

"Injuries?"

"We're good."

The map of the system still on her screen rearranged itself without any of the designator icons moving. The *Rocinante* was only one more piece on the board, but it changed the logic behind everything. She saw the flaws in her plans and the stakes she was playing for. The despair felt almost like relief.

"All right," Jillian said with a sigh. "Set your course for the ring gate. I'll buy as much time as I can. Tell Nagata I'm sorry."

"She's right here, if—"

"No," Jillian said. "You can do it for me."

She dropped the connection, took a moment for a long, slow breath, then checked status. The *Derecho* was upping its burn, leaping after them now that Teresa Duarte was in play. The *Sparrowhawk* was shifting away too, ready to take another shot at the *Rocinante*. Get even. That made her target selection easy enough.

"Keep us between the *Sparrowhawk* and the *Rocinante*. As many gs as you need," she said, and her voice was calm and steady. Caspar's *copy that* was too. As the *Storm*—as her ship—shifted under her and her limbs grew heavy with the acceleration, she went on. "How does this affect the *Derecho*'s arrival?"

"Effective missile range will be two hours for the *Derecho* assuming it keeps its present course. Overshoot will put us behind them and out of range fifteen minutes after that unless we brake significantly or they do."

"Overshoot won't be an option," she said. "We're looking at direct engagement."

She looked around the deck. There was no shock on their faces.

They'd all known when they got on the ship that there wasn't much chance of getting back off.

"Permission to lay down some PDC fire along their trajectory?"

"Save your powder, Li," Jillian said. "We won't end this with anything left in the magazines, but there's no point starting until it's starting time."

"*Rocinante* has changed course for the ring," Caspar said.

Jillian steeled herself and pushed up to standing. The extra half g left her a little light-headed for a second, but she adjusted. "I'll be in my ready room," she said. "If any of you have personal messages you want to send, this is the time."

They saluted her as she made her way off the bridge. Her ready room wasn't much, but it was hers. She was sorry she wouldn't get to spend more time there. She pulled up the live tactical display—Draper Station, the *Storm*, and the *Rocinante* growing slowly farther apart as they laid on the acceleration. The enemy ship and her own converging. She remembered something her father had said when she was growing up about owning your mistakes, even the ones you couldn't fix. You did it because it was the adult thing to do.

She sent a message to the other forces in the system giving them permission to leave their present orbits and proceed according to their judgment, like a man leaving the gate open for his dogs before he went to war. She got a last shot of bourbon, but the idea of it was better than the taste.

Her ship hummed and strained, and the vast distances of Freehold narrowed. Her station chimed and Feil's voice came on.

"Tightbeam request from the *Sparrowhawk*," Feil said. "I can accept or refuse."

"Pass it over," Jillian said.

The man who appeared on her screen had a thin face and an almost comical mustache. He looked apologetic.

"This is Captain Mugabo of the *Sparrowhawk*."

"Houston of the *Gathering Storm*," Jillian said.

"You have no credible path to victory here, Captain. I am

authorized to offer you and your crew honorable surrender. You will be prisoners, but you will be well treated. Send your remote operation codes and let us take control of the ship. We will see you and yours to safety."

Jillian cocked her head. Even with all she knew and had been through, some part of her still leapt at the hope. Just the way it had when Trejo had offered his trade. Owning your mistakes meant not making them twice.

"Thank you for that offer," she said. "But your colleague Tanaka? She has already made it clear what Laconian honor is worth."

"I can't speak to her actions, Captain, but I can assure you of mine. Even if you manage to destroy my ship, the *Derecho* will catch up with you. It is more than your match. I mean no insult. We are both aware of the situation. People like us have no room for illusions."

Jillian's smile felt like a knife. If she had to die, she was glad she was taking this smarmy fuck down with her. "We have a few minutes still. You can send a message. I would let your superiors know that when Colonel Tanaka opened fire without provocation on Draper Station, she didn't just kill us. She killed you too. I hope it was worth it."

"Captain—"

She cut the connection, poured the last sips of unwanted bourbon onto the floor where no one and nothing would ever have to clean it, and stood to go back to the bridge.

She was all out of later.

Chapter Twenty-Three: Jim

The *Roci* burned hard, the crash couch pressing up from under him at an acceleration that made his eyes ache. The sting of the juice in his veins was cold and hot at the same time, and it left him smelling something astringent that wasn't actually there. His breath labored with the unaccustomed weight like a hand pressing against his breastbone, defying every inhalation. And it went on for hours.

It might go on for days.

There were breaks every now and then to let people get food or hit the head. When he'd been a young man in the navy, he'd been able to wolf down a meal, grab a bulb of coffee, and get in a hand of poker in the galley in the break between hard burns. He didn't try anymore. His stomach wasn't as forgiving as it had once been.

Jim drifted in and out of sleep as they fled, but he only fell halfway. Part of him was always waiting to hear the collision alarms from his screen and the deep chatter of the PDCs trying to knock out enemy missiles before he and most of the people he loved were killed by them. The physical stress and the fear were as familiar as an old, often-sung song. A hymn to the price of violence.

He and Naomi were on the ops deck, in couches next to each other. Alex, above them on the flight deck. Amos, Teresa, and Muskrat were all down in the machine shop, in theory ready to leap into action if something in the ship failed. And maybe that was true. Amos was still a hell of a mechanic. Teresa was young, smart, and she'd been training under him almost since they'd fled Laconia.

Still, he really hoped that nothing failed.

He'd lost track of how many hours they'd been speeding out toward the Freehold gate and how many meals he'd skipped in the rush between hard burns, when a message popped up on his screen. It took effort to focus on it. It was from Alex: SAFE TO STOP RABBITING?

Jim shifted his hands on the old, familiar controls and pulled up the *Roci*'s tactical display. Freehold system was vast and empty. If the display had been to scale, none of the ships would have earned a pixel big enough to see, but he'd been making sense of the semi-abstract designs on the *Roci*'s interface for decades. He didn't have to translate any of it. The red acute triangle was a Laconian destroyer falling away behind them. It wasn't chasing. It was on a braking burn toward Draper Station. The white triangle was the corpse of the *Sparrowhawk*, receding from them, but only at the speed of the *Roci*'s escape run. And the green, blinking indicator was the debris field that had been the *Gathering Storm*—flagship of the underground's forces.

It was a simple enough map. There weren't enough ships or bases in Freehold to allow much subterfuge. He ran the math of transit times—how far ahead of the enemy they could be when they reached the ring gate if they kept to the present hard burn, how far ahead if they didn't, how much of a lead they would need to get through the ring space and into some other system unfollowed. He ran a ladar sweep of a couple light-minutes ahead of them all the same before he let himself come to the conclusion he'd wanted to reach as soon as he read the question.

Looks clear. We can spark it up again if we have to.

In response, the thrust gravity eased back to half a g, and Jim's spine cracked just above his sacrum as something slid back into place. He shifted carefully like he was waking from a long, restless sleep, and rolled to his side.

Naomi had already locked her couch and sat up. Her mouth was a thin, grim line. Her screen was an engineering report of the *Roci*'s core systems—reactor, recyclers, water tanks, missiles and PDCs, power. She went through it value by value, making sure that everything was where it should be, since their lives depended on the ship not failing. He wanted to reach out to her, take her hand in his, but that would have been for his comfort. She was already doing the thing that would make her feel better.

He opened a channel to the machine shop.

"How's it looking down there? Everything good?"

The eerie hesitation in Amos' voice had grown so familiar it was hardly eerie anymore. "Looking solid, except the dog's got a little limp in her hindquarters. We're going to give her a couple minutes to walk it off. If that doesn't do it, we might take her to med bay and pop a little steroid in her hip."

"Okay." He dropped the connection.

Naomi had shifted her screen to a playback of the battle. Of the death of the *Storm*. Its destruction of the *Sparrowhawk*. The doomed dive into the teeth of the approaching *Derecho*. He had to think Alex was watching it too and seeing something very different. He'd served on the *Storm* for years. He knew the people who'd just died on it. Jim watched it on Naomi's screen, trying to think how everyone else would make sense of it. How he did.

The two Laconian destroyers hurtled at each other, flinging torpedoes and PDC rounds until the resulting explosions blocked everything from view. The *Derecho* reappeared first, still under thrust, but its hull showing many glowing scars from Jillian's furious assault. Then, when the *Storm*'s broken hull finally spun out the other side of the blinding cloud of violence, Jim heaved a sigh. It was the death of the underground, captured in low-resolution video. A glorious, ferocious death. But death all the same.

"Goodbye, Jillian," Naomi said, whispering it like a prayer.

"We collect the most astonishingly brave people, don't we?" Jim said. "And then we watch them die."

Naomi smoothed her hair back and looked at him. "I thought Trejo was a man of his word."

"He is," Jim said. "I mean, he's perfectly willing to commit atrocities. He's not the good guys. But what happened back there, that wasn't him."

"And it happened anyway." She bit the words as she spoke them.

"I was pretty sure I killed Tanaka back on New Egypt. This has the feel of a vendetta now."

"So maybe he's having as much trouble controlling his people as I am?" Naomi said, and went on before he could answer. "Jillian's big heroic death screwed us. We're fucked now."

Jim flinched a little, imagining how the words would carry up to Alex. "She made a bad call. I mean, I understand the mistake. I've been known to act on my own judgment from time to time."

He waited a few seconds before he went on.

"And when she saw what the situation really was, she saved us. She died saving us."

"She lost us Draper Station," Naomi said. "The minute she talked to Laconia, she lost us the base. Even if they'd made the deal, they were never going to politely decide to forget we had resources on that moon. They weren't going to pretend not to know the *Storm* was in Freehold system."

"They were going to bomb the cities. People she knows and loves. Her family."

"They're the enemy army," Naomi said. "Do we just do what we're instructed every time they tell us that they're going to do what enemy armies do? If that's the plan, we've been running down the wrong road for a long, long time."

"That's not what I'm saying."

"That we should have handed Teresa over? That *we* were wrong?"

"It's not Jillian's fault there was no good answer." Naomi's almost subliminal flinch at his words told him the rest. When he went on, he was gentler. "And it's not your fault either."

The flicker of her eyes was a conversation in itself: grief and exhaustion and despair, and also determination. The knowledge that they'd been playing the game of no-right-answer for decades, and that it would outlast them, the way history outlasted everyone.

That that was the best case.

Alex's slow footsteps came from above them, then down the ladder. Jim had known the pilot for more years than he hadn't, and he'd seen Alex in every mood from exultation to rage. He'd never seen him look so quietly, profoundly defeated. He'd grown a white wash of stubble on his cheeks since they'd started the run from Freehold. It reminded Jim of snow.

Alex lowered himself into one of the remaining crash couches and turned it so he could look at the two of them. They didn't ask how he was, but he answered anyway. Just a shrug and a sigh and a turning to the next issue.

"Technically, we're not at the ideal escape radius. If the destroyer did the hardest possible burn starting right now, it could be a squeeze getting out the Freehold gate and through another one in time to keep them from seeing where we went."

"They'll have wounded crew," Naomi said. "They likely have some structural damage. And they're still picking up Tanaka from Draper Station."

"I don't think they'll do it, either. And if they tried, we could make them work for it anyway. Jillian topped up all our tanks. But I'd rather push a little less hard and conserve reaction mass for later."

He didn't say *I don't know when we'll be able to fuel up again.* He didn't need to. He also didn't ask where they were going or what the next plan was. The three of them sat together, the *Roci* ringing like a feather-rubbed gong, the musical whisper of a good ship. Jim didn't know exactly what they were waiting for, except that the silence seemed right. When Alex spoke again, his voice was thicker.

"Bobbie always said Jillian needed watching. She liked getting her own way a little too much. Wasn't just independence. She was independent, but she was a little mean too. You know?"

"Like her father," Naomi said.

"She was smarter than her dad," Alex said. "She'd have been a good captain if she'd had a few more years doing it. And the *Storm* was a good ship. Second best I've been on."

"Really?" Jim said.

Alex shook his head. "No, it was creepy. Laconian ships all feel creepy. But I just watched a bunch of my friends die, so I'm feeling nostalgic."

The comm channel opened before Jim could reply, and Teresa's voice—punctuated by sharp, alarmed barking from her dog—interrupted them. "I'm in the med bay. I need help. He's having another seizure."

The medical systems did the best they could with Amos, which was mostly the expert system version of shrugging and saying *Looks weird all the same ways he usually looks weird.* Amos lay in the autodoc, his head resting on the little pale cushion. The utter blackness made his gaze hard to track, but Jim was pretty sure the mechanic was looking at him.

"How long was I out?"

"About half an hour," Jim said. "How are you feeling?"

"Might skip my workout. This shit's tiring."

"It's happening more often, isn't it?"

"Nope."

"Because it seems like it's happening more often."

"Well, yeah it is. But not because anything's going bad. The doc's pushing harder."

Jim looked at the autodoc, confused. Amos shook his head.

"Okoye. She's running on full burn trying to make sense of things out at Adro, and since all of us with—" He pointed to his eyes. "We're all connected at the back. I get the spillover."

"Really?"

"Pretty sure. Every time I get the wigglies, I come back up knowing more."

"Like what?"

"Nothing useful," Amos said. "There's holes in the spectrum where the idea of being in a place breaks down. And there's a kind of light that can think. I mean, it's interesting I guess, but it doesn't get the tools stowed."

"Can you tell if she's making progress?"

"It's not like it's a tightbeam. We don't talk about stuff," Amos said, then frowned. "Not exactly, anyway. More like I'm listening to someone doing shit in the next cabin over. And…You know how it is when there's people in the room with you, and even if you're not looking at them, you still know they're there? It's like that. There's always three of us."

"The girl and her brother," Jim said.

"Not sure about that, but there's three of us. I know it's a pain in the ass with me getting messed up like this, but I don't think there's much I can do about it. I mean, besides train Tiny so she can cover for me."

Jim was about to say *I'm not sure I want a sixteen-year-old mechanic in charge of keeping us alive* when a happy bark sounded from the hallway. A moment later, Muskrat and Teresa came in. The girl was carrying a tube from the galley in one hand and a drinking bulb in the other. Her hair was pulled back in a tight bun that wouldn't get in her eyes when they went on the float. Her mag boots were turned off, but she was wearing them. The dog was grinning and wagging her tail in a wide circle.

"Feeling better?" Teresa asked.

Jim was astonished by her casual, matter-of-fact manner. Even though he'd been crewed up with her for almost a year, some part of his mind wouldn't let go of the memory of her as she'd been when he first met her on Laconia: a too-serious child with the weight of the empire on her shoulders, but still a child. She was old enough now to take long-term apprenticeship contracts, old enough to claim emancipation and her own rights on basic if she'd lived on Earth, old enough to see her only friend in the world suffer a massive seizure and take it in stride.

"I'm working my way back up," Amos said.

"I got you white kibble and lemonade. Salt, sugar, and water. I figured, you know, electrolytes."

Jim's stomach shifted at the thought of food, and he wasn't sure if it was hunger or nausea or a little of both.

"Thanks," Amos said, holding out his hand. She slapped the tube smartly into his palm like she was giving him a tool. "You take the stress inventory?"

"It's where I'm headed now," she said, then turned toward Jim for the first time, met his gaze, and nodded before she left. Muskrat pushed over, demanding a scratch behind the ears from both Jim and Amos before trotting back after Teresa. If the old dog was having hip trouble after the hard burn cycles, Jim couldn't see it.

"What's on your mind, Cap?"

"Thinking what it would be like to be sixteen and important enough that people kill each other over you."

"Yeah. It's gonna fuck her up," Amos agreed, amiably. "We did the only thing we could, though."

"Keeping her?"

"Yeah."

"I know," Jim said with a sigh. "It's going to be a problem, though. I don't see Tanaka giving up."

"She reminds me of Bobbie," Amos said as if he was agreeing.

"Naomi is wondering if Trejo was always going to double-cross us."

"You don't?" Amos sucked at the tube of kibble and nodded for Jim to go on.

"I've never known Trejo to lie. I've never known Duarte to lie either, and he was the personality that set the tone for all of this. He was grandiose. He was ruthless. He was a genius at a couple of things and under the misapprehension that it meant he was smart about everything. But in his mind, he was doing the right thing."

"The kind of guy, he'd feed you into a wood chipper, but he wouldn't stiff you for his half of the bar tab," Amos said. "I've known folks like that."

"This Colonel Tanaka? I think she's pissed off that she didn't get us at New Egypt. Also, that I shot her in the face."

"Yeah," Amos agreed. "That'll do it."

"Think she'll cool it if I explain I was just trying to kill her?"

"Seems like the right tentacle ain't keeping track of what the left tentacle's up to," Amos said. "High command wants more than one thing, and running a galactic empire's hard work. Maybe you're right about Trejo. Maybe Tanaka just let it get personal and fucked up."

They were silent for a long moment, then Jim sighed again. "The thing with hunting dogs is that once you let them off the leash, you've let them off the leash. They don't stop until they catch what they're going after."

Amos went quiet for a moment, and Jim couldn't tell if he was thinking or in one of his uncanny pauses. When he moved, it was like he turned back on.

"When I was back on Earth, I didn't run with a hunting-dog kind of crowd," Amos finally said. "But there was this guy I knew growing up who used to train police dogs. That's kind of the same thing, isn't it?"

"I don't know," Jim said. "Maybe."

"So this guy, he was pretty fucked up by the time I knew him. Addicted to a bunch of different stuff, and taking a long time dying from it, but he still liked the dogs. The thing he said was that the whole process was about trying to find which ones weren't going to start fucking people up on their own recognizance. So he'd flunk out any of the puppies that didn't train up right, and he'd spend a lot of time working with the ones that made the cut.

Fucking well-trained, smart animals, but that was the problem too. You get a dog smart enough, they know when it's a training exercise and when it's not. He used to say that until you went in the field, you never really knew what kind of dog you had."

"So you think Tanaka's going to stay on us until she gets what she's after."

"Or we manage to kill her," Amos said. "Not sure it makes much difference in the big picture."

"I can't see how this all plays out."

"Sure you do. Everyone dies. That's always been how it is. Only question now is whether we can find some way to not all go at once."

"If we do, then civilization dies. Everything humanity has ever done goes away."

"Well, at least there won't be anyone who misses it," Amos said, and sighed. "You're overthinking this, Cap'n. You got now and you got the second your lights go out. Meantime is the only time there is. All that matters is what we do during it."

"I just want to go out knowing that things will be okay without me. That it all keeps going."

"That you're not the one who dropped the ball."

"Yeah."

"Or maybe," Amos said, "you're not that important and it ain't up to you to fix the universe?"

"You always know how to cheer me up."

Chapter Twenty-Four:
The Lighthouse and the Keeper

Tanaka almost hadn't gone into active service. There had been a point when she was sixteen years old and the star student of her cohort in the Imahara Institute's upper university program when she'd seriously considered committing to a career as an art historian. She'd taken three tutorials and courses, and she'd been good at it. Knowing the history surrounding an image made both the art and the history more interesting.

One of her last essays had been about a painting by Fernanda Daté called *The Education of the Third Miko*. It had been of a thin woman looking directly out at the viewer. The oil paint that Daté used had given an eerie impression of direct eye contact. The figure had been seated on a throne of skulls, and a single pale tear streaked her left cheek. Tanaka had written about the context for the image in Daté's life—the nonresponsive cancer that the artist was struggling with when the painting was made, the threat of war between Earth and Mars that she'd grown up with, and her admiration for the Shintofascist philosophies of Umoja Gui. The distress of the third Miko depicted the aftermath of her self-revelation and acceptance of her own compromised nature.

Tanaka hadn't thought about that painting in decades, or about what a very different life she would have lived if she'd made a few different decisions at the start.

The captain of the *Derecho* was a gaunt man named Botton. The ship shuddered under them, and the high-g burn made her a little light-headed. But she wasn't getting in a crash couch yet, and so neither was he.

"If we are not sincerely trying to catch the enemy..." Botton said, and then lost his train of thought. Not enough blood to the brain.

She waited to reply until he came back to himself. "We won't catch them before they transit the ring. We won't catch them before they transit *out* of the ring space either. We are setting their expectations as to our speed of pursuit to maximize the time they feel comfortable staying in the ring space. Once they've gone through the Freehold gate, we'll accelerate to an even higher burn. Near the maximum the ship can handle. Our aim is to reach the ring space before their drive plume has fully dissipated. That's how we'll determine which gate they escaped through."

"If we could...slow our present approach..."

"It would mean a harder burn later."

Botton started to nod, but thought better of it. Standing free in a hard burn meant keeping the spine very carefully stacked. Tanaka suppressed a smile.

"My concern, Colonel," Botton said, "is that the supply of high-g drugs may not me...may not *be* sufficient."

She pulled up the allocation chart that showed the reservoirs of juice for the crew. While Botton watched, she dropped her own to zero. The pull of thrust gravity made his distress look like a sorrowful dog's.

"I wouldn't ask anyone to take a risk I won't take myself," she said. It wasn't true, but it made her point. She was stronger than him, better than him, and tired of hearing him whine.

"Yes, Colonel," he said. He braced, turned, and walked out of the office that had been his, careful to place his weight so that it wouldn't blow out his knees. Tanaka waited until he was gone before she let herself ease back into her crash couch. Or her throne of skulls.

The *Forgiveness* began its life as a colony ship built at Pallas-Tycho in the years when the Transport Union had ruled the ring gates. With almost two billion square meters of cargo space, and living quarters that were the same size as an in-system shuttle, the *Forgiveness* was about freight, not passengers. Ekko had signed on when he was fifteen, and apart from a year he'd stayed behind on Firdaws to work on his command certification, he'd pretty much been there ever since. His stint as captain had outlived the union that had certified him. It had outlasted the traffic control authority on Medina Station. It had outlasted the iron fist of the Laconian Empire, more or less.

The major shareholder in the *Forgiveness*, on the other hand, seemed like she'd be plaguing Ekko until the day he died. Mallia Currán had financed the ship's overhaul with a private loan backed by the governing council, and while she didn't have a greater than 50 percent stake in the ship, she could get a coalition that did by making two calls and a coffee date. And she was Komi Tuan's niece, so anything semilegal she did was played down by the magistrates. Like the old gods of Earth, most of the time she ignored Ekko and the *Forgiveness*, and the days she didn't were almost always bad ones. She'd asked for a status report five hours before, and he'd been thinking about how to answer ever since.

He arranged himself in his office, checked his image on the screen, and started recording.

"Always good to hear from you, Magistra Currán. Everything's five by five with the ship. We have a full load of ore and samples for Bara Gaon, and I've had assurance that the return cargo is going to be ready when we get there. We're just waiting on the passage protocol before we make transit." He tried an insouciant smile, but it came off forced. "You know how it is with taking large cargoes through. Want to make sure we're doing it by the book and all. I will check back as soon as we have confirmation."

He saved the message and sent it before he could second-guess himself. Four hours back to Firdaws, and maybe it would reach her while she was sleeping. That would give him a few more hours before she worked herself up into an excoriating mood. Which she would.

He already knew the arguments she'd make: The underground's protocols were guidelines, not law; the infrastructure to support them was only partly in place; what the fuck was he going to do if the okay didn't come through? Just sit there on the float waiting for consensus flight permissions while someone else bribed the supply officers in Bara Gaon for the soil and fuel pellets and fabrication printers that Firdaws needed?

She wasn't all the way wrong, either. A cargo ship that didn't move cargo wasn't much of anything.

"Fuck," he said to nothing in particular and everything in general. He opened a channel to the pilot's station two decks below. "Annamarie? You there?"

"Am," his pilot said.

"Give us a quarter g toward the gate, yeah? We're going to have to do this, clearance or no clearance."

"Understood. On it," she said, and dropped the connection. A few seconds later, the thrust correction warning went on. If no one answered him, he'd have to decide whether to put on a braking burn or pass through the gate without clearance, knowing that there was an armada of independent freighters out there making the same calculations as him.

But what the hell, really. Life was risk.

"She's getting pretty close," Jim said. "We're sure about this?"

"We can keep ahead of her," Alex said from the comms and the deck above. "She knows it. If she gets too close, we'll speed up, then she'd have to speed up. Or we'll decide to make a break for it, and she'll know how close we're willing to let her get. Right now, she's willing to dump reaction mass and I'm not. If that changes, it'll change."

"You sound very philosophical about it."

He could hear the smile in Alex's voice. "I've always admired this part. Don't much care for the killing each other at the end, but there's a poetry to this part of the conversation. And there are some decisions we're going to need to make."

Jim turned his head. Naomi was already looking at him. Teresa and Amos were on the comms from the machine shop.

"Nuriel system is only a ten-degree deflection from our present course," Naomi said. "We wouldn't need a braking burn. It has some underground resources."

"But Tanaka would know we didn't need a braking burn," Alex said. "We could pop through the ring space from one end to the other in a few minutes if I get the angle right, but it'll be like drawing an arrow to where we went. Going in slower means we have a wider range of systems that we might have headed into."

The ship hummed and rang, the resonances of the drive playing their long, familiar music. On his screen, the Laconian destroyer ticked forward, closing the distance between them. The intercept would still come well after they'd passed through the ring gate and out through some other one. The panic clearing its throat in the back of Jim's head wasn't based in anything but itself.

"We also don't want to go through so fast we dutchman ourselves," he said, more thinking aloud than to tell the others something they hadn't already thought. "And there might be other Laconian ships in the slow zone. We can't be sure there aren't."

"I don't know how to control for that," Naomi said. "But we

can aim for the systems where there are likely to be fewer eyes on us. It's the best we can manage."

There were so many risks. If Laconia had a spotter ship in place, they'd be found. If the enemy was watching from the sunward side of whatever gate they passed through, the way the *Derecho* had in Freehold, they'd be caught. If Tanaka, breathing down their necks, had some trick he hadn't thought of, they'd be caught. If they made the transit too fast or with too many other ships, they'd be dead. If they stayed too long in the slow zone and the things inside the gate boiled out from beyond the ring space again, they'd be dead. And if it all worked out...then what? Dead or captured were the failure states. He wasn't sure what success looked like.

The next step, maybe. It didn't matter if he knew how it all ended, as long as he always knew what was next. *You can drive a thousand klicks if you've got one good headlight.* Mother Elise used to say that when he was a kid. He hadn't thought of her in a long time. Having her voice come to him so clearly right now felt like an omen, but he didn't know what of.

"Cap?" Amos said.

"Yeah?"

"We need to go see the doc."

He was quiet for a second. "Adro system?"

"The only ships there will be Laconian," Naomi said.

Teresa answered. "But they'll all answer to Dr. Okoye. And there's nothing else there. Colonel Tanaka won't expect it."

"We did just gas up," Alex said. "If we're going someplace for a long, quiet float, this is the time for it."

"Cap," Amos said again. There was something in his voice. "We need to go see the doc."

Jim didn't want to do it, and he wasn't sure why he didn't want to. No. That wasn't true. Elvi was their last hope against the darkness, and if he saw that she'd failed, he wouldn't even have that anymore. It wasn't a good enough reason to stay away.

"Alex, plot the fastest transit you can for Adro system."

Kit woke. The harness beside him was empty. At first he thought Rohi was feeding Bakari, but that wasn't it. The baby was in his own little sleeping harness, eyes closed and arms floating forward like he'd never left the amniotic sac. His son looked utterly at peace. Which, good on him, because nobody else was.

As quietly as he could, Kit undid his restraints and synced his handheld with the cabin's system. It would keep its electronic eyes on Bakari and alert him if the baby so much as burped. Then as near to silent as he could be, he slipped out of the cabin and into the common galley.

The lights were dimmed to night mode, so Rohi's handheld lit her face from below. The flag of their future home was a shadow over her right shoulder. Her eyes were fixed on the little screen, and her expression was empty. He didn't need to ask. He knew what she was looking at. Footage from San Esteban system.

He pulled himself to a stop beside her, his magnetic boots off and floating in air. She glanced up at him, made a rueful smile. Rueful and maybe a little resentful.

"We're almost at the gate," Kit said. "A few more hours."

Rohi nodded, but the feed on her handheld cut to something new, and it held her gaze. The horrors of a systemful of dead people, replayed again and again, with commentary in ten languages and a hundred political orthodoxies. The science feeds about the manner of death. The religious feeds about its spiritual meaning and what it said about the will of God. The political feeds about why it was some other ideology's fault. She watched all of them like she was looking for something in the images of the corpses. Meaning, maybe. Or hope.

"You should get some sleep," Kit said. "Baby's going to be up before long, and he's not as impressed with me as he is with you."

"He doesn't see there's anything wrong with you," Rohi said. "He's a baby, and he already knows I'm stressed."

"Between the two of us, we are his universe."

"What if we aren't supposed to do this?"

"Do what, babe?"

"All of this? Going to other planets. Going to other stars. What if God didn't want this?"

"Well, then they should have spoken up sooner, I guess. It's late in the game to turn around."

She chuckled and shut off the handheld. He was relieved. He didn't know what he'd have done if she refused to look away from the feeds. Go back to the cabin by himself, probably.

"How do we do this?" she murmured. "They all just died, and everyone just keeps doing what they were doing anyway."

"No options. We go on because we go on." He wiped away the film of tears building up around her eye. "It'll be all right," he said, hearing how little weight the words carried. How little he believed them. "Come to bed."

In one way, the chase looked simple. The *Roci* was braking, still hurtling toward the Freehold gate but more and more slowly. By the time it passed through, it would be going slow enough that it could deflect its flight path the thirty-four degrees it took to slide out the Adro gate, or any of hundreds of others. The Laconian destroyer *Derecho* had a greater velocity and was only now starting to brake. It would slide through Freehold gate moving faster, braking harder, running its high-powered Laconian drive hot enough to risk the deaths of some percentage of its crew. Maybe it would be able to find the gate the *Roci* had gone through. Maybe it would guess wrong. Maybe it would make a killing burn to shed all its velocity and come to a stop in the ring space so it could search for traces of the *Roci*'s passage. Or, hell, maybe it would malfunction, spin off into the non-surface of the bubble between the ring gates, and be annihilated. Jim had been lucky before.

In another way, the chase was impossibly complex. With a flick of his eyes, he could turn the display to a probabilistic three-dimensional map that showed all the possible flight paths the

Roci could take, the complex decision points where an equation with values like time, vector, delta-v, the elasticity of a human blood vessel, and the ship's position in space defined the moment when a possible future slipped away. Jim moved between the two views—the curve of the *Roci*'s intended path and the swooping, lily-shaped cone that was the *Derecho*'s possible paths. Then over to the intricate web of things that could happen but hadn't yet, as it narrowed second by second and left a thin thread called history behind it. His jaw ached from the deceleration. No one had spoken for hours, and his headache was probably just a headache. Strokes didn't take that long.

PREPARING FOR TRANSIT Alex messaged the full crew. On the external telescopes, the thousand-kilometer diameter of the gate was still almost too small to see. Jim watched it grow slowly until it was almost as big as the nail of his outstretched thumb, and then all the stars in the universe snapped off at once as they passed through it and into the ring space.

The whole bubble with all the gates was a little smaller than the volume of Sol system's star. A million Earths wouldn't have filled it. At their speed, they wouldn't be inside it for very long.

The *Roci* shifted under him, slewing around in a perfect arc, connecting the Freehold gate and the Adro gate in a logical relationship defined by complex math that the enormous power of the ship's drive was struggling to convert into physical reality. If the feed of reaction mass stuttered, they'd slip off course. If they missed the Adro gate, everything that came after that would be someone else's problem. Jim couldn't tell if his heart was racing from fear or just the effort of keeping the blood supply going to his brain.

To his left, Naomi grunted, and it sounded like dismay. He had the sudden flashbulb memory of medical alarms blaring when Fred Johnson had died in the same crash couch she was in, and his heart found a way to beat a little faster. No alarm sounded, but a private message came onto his screen from her.

TOO MANY SHIPS.

He changed his display again. The traffic pattern in the ring space. A dozen transponder codes spooled out—*Tyrant's Folly* out of Sol, *Taif* out of Hongdae, *Forgiveness* out of Firdaws—and twice as many pings for unidentified drive plumes. He tried to shift the analysis to include them all, but before he could, another message came from Naomi.

THIS IS INSANE. THEY'LL FAIL THE TRANSIT. WHAT DO THEY THINK THEY'RE DOING???

But she knew what they were doing. The same thing they were. Looking at the risk, and each one individually deciding that it made sense for them to throw the dice. And some had certainly failed. There was no one to keep track of how many ships went in a ring gate and didn't come out the other side. If the *Roci* was lost, he didn't know how long it would be before anyone realized it. Maybe never.

He shifted the system to threat assessment, and the answer came at once. Two ships were going to transit out of the ring space before the *Roci* reached Adro: a colony ship running without a transponder that was almost at the Behrenhold gate and the *Forgiveness*, a massive cargo hauler out of Firdaws that would pass into Bara Gaon just a few minutes before the *Roci* reached the Adro gate. Assuming the rings were at base state, the *Roci* would survive the transition. Assuming that no other ships came in through a ring gate in the meantime.

Assuming, that was to say, a lot of things he didn't have any reason to assume.

The stars came back. The same stars as home, if in a slightly different configuration. Ekko let his head fall back into the gel of the crash couch. For a moment, he didn't say anything, barely felt anything, and then a deep relief rode through him like a wave, lifting his heart and setting him back down laughing.

He became aware that his comms were open from the soft rhythm of Annamarie cursing in French. She wasn't talking to him or anyone really. Maybe God.

"Little full in there today, yeah?" Ekko said.

Annamarie shifted to English. *"Fuck*, that was too much, old man."

Ekko laughed again. The release felt almost postcoital. Here he was, in his ship and in Bara Gaon system, and not in whatever screaming void ate ships that drew the short straw.

"I'm going to quit," Annamarie said. "I'm going to find an apartment in Bara Gaon and an honest job, and I'm going to retire and have babies and never go through that fucking gate again. *God damn.*" He could hear the grin in her voice, and knew she didn't mean it until she sobered. "Seriously, capitán. Someone's going to fucking die in there if it stays that busy."

"True enough, but not us. Not today. Get me a tightbeam lock to the traffic authority and the client. Let them know we're here."

"That we live to skin our asses off another day," Annamarie said. "On it. I will let you know when I get the lock."

The *Rocinante* screamed. Compression seams touched the inside edge of their tolerances. Massive hull plates of carbon-silicate lace settled deep into their supports. The drive howled and pushed up against the hurtling bubble of ceramic and metal and air. The writhing stars on the far side of Adro gate loomed up, almost hidden behind their drive plume.

This was an absurd way to die, Jim thought.

His jaw hurt and he kept losing little bits of time. Alex had the drive plume of the *Roci* pointed out toward the Adro gate, bleeding off as much speed as they could, making their transit a few seconds later in the unmeasurable hope that it would make the difference. Across the ring space, the *Derecho* would be coming close. There were so many ways for all of it to go wrong, and then what?

Mother Elise's little boy would have arced up from Montana through wars and alien solar systems and love and despair and died slamming into the one danger he'd known for decades was right fucking there. It was too stupid to even qualify as irony.

A message appeared on his screen from Naomi—ARE YOU OKAY?—and he had to keep himself from turning to look at her. He wasn't sure he'd be able to turn back under this burn. The blood was pooling in the back of his skull, and the uncomfortable electric fizz of the juice was, he was sure, the only thing keeping him from having several strokes at once. He started to answer her, then forgot what he was doing. The gate approached, growing larger first slowly, then quickly, then all at once.

The burn started to trail away, shifting slowly down toward the float to avoid reperfusion injuries that came when blood flooded too quickly into tissues it had been wrung out of. His hands and face tingled. He saw Naomi's message again and remembered that he hadn't answered.

He tried to say *I'm fine*, but it came out as a croak. He massaged his throat for a few seconds, moving cartilage and muscle back closer toward their right places, and tried again.

"I'm fine," he managed. "I'm good. You?"

"I am very proud not to be sitting in a puddle of something unfortunate right now," she said, but the joke sounded angry. The *Roci*'s burn dropped under a g, then under a half. He looked over. Her mouth was a profound scowl.

"They're not following protocol," he said.

"I should have taken Trejo's offer. This isn't going to work without someone enforcing it. There's not enough cooperation."

"Isn't now. It doesn't mean there can't ever be."

"They're people," Naomi said, exhaustion in her tone. "We're trying to do all of this with humans. Shortsightedness is coded in our DNA."

He didn't have an answer for that. A moment later, the comms went live, and Amos and Teresa reported in on the post-burn maintenance they were doing, Alex started getting a tightbeam lock on the *Falcon*, and Naomi checked to see whether the ship had grabbed any waiting communication packets from the underground during their passage through the ring space.

Jim followed along, chiming in where he could help, but the

thing that stuck in his mind like a catchy, bleak melody was Naomi's voice. *We're trying to do all of this with humans.*

The *Derecho* passed through the Freehold gate and into the ring space, the drive pushing a braking burn at the limit of the ship's tolerance—which was the same as saying the limits of the crew's. The *Derecho* could pour enough gs into its maneuvers to crush the skinbound sacks of salt water in it. Tanaka was willing to spend a few lives if it meant catching her prey. If that made her bloodthirsty, so be it. She'd always been thirsty for something. It might as well be blood.

As soon as the gate distortion was gone, and even as she struggled to draw breath, she set the ship to scanning the vacuum at the edges of the more than thirteen hundred gates. The *Rocinante*'s drive plume might be gone, but the cooling cloud that had been its reaction mass was still there, slowly diffusing into the soft mist of hydrogen, oxygen, ozone, and water vapor that made up most of the physical mass in the ring space. In time, the particles would all drift into contact with the edge of the space and be annihilated, but until then, the information was there. A subtle finger, pointing the way her enemy had gone.

If only she'd made it through before it had dispersed too far to find it…

The *Derecho*'s drive kicked off, the ship went into freefall, and a wave of nausea rolled through her. She ignored it, pulling up her tactical display. The ring space was ridiculously full. It was still fewer ships than she'd seen in the average approach pattern to the naval base on Callisto, back in the day, but Callisto had never had to worry about extradimensional horrors eating some of the ships as they tried to land. Context was everything.

The *Derecho* had already scanned and dismissed all of them— none was the *Rocinante*. She pulled up the visual profiles and drive signatures anyway. Recognition algorithms were brilliant, but they weren't the human eye. What could fool one often couldn't fool the other.

"Colonel Tanaka?" Botton's voice asked from her comms screen.

"What?"

The *Derecho* flagged a burst of light and high-energy particles coming through the Sol gate. The first tickling drive plume of some other ship about to transit through that ring.

"We have medical emergencies with..." Botton paused, caught his breath. "With several crew members. If we can pause long enough to remove them to the medical bay..."

"Do it," Tanaka said.

"Thank you, Colonel," he said.

"Where are you, you little *fucks*?" Tanaka muttered.

The Sol gate fluttered with light.

Bakari was fussing because he was frustrated. The pediatrician had warned Kit about this before they'd started the journey. The time in lower gravity would weaken Bakari's muscles and bones a little. Not so much that he wouldn't recover once he was in consistent gravity again, but enough that during the higher burns on the trip the child would find himself unable to do things he had previously done. The braking burn into the ring space had been noted in their first meeting as a place that children Bakari's age would be likely to struggle. At the time, it hadn't seemed too onerous.

Now it seemed onerous.

"Come on, little bear," Kit said, smiling down at the small face that looked back up at him in rage. "It's okay. Listen while we sing, yeah? Listen to us sing."

It was the third hour since Bakari had woken from his nap. Rohi had taken the first two. Now she was in the commissary buying spicy curry for the brothers from Breach Candy as an apology for the screaming and crying. The other passengers were kind enough not to complain and also kind enough to accept their peace offerings gracefully. Afterward, Rohi had promised to spend an hour in the gym. Neither of them had been good about keeping to the exercise schedule, and they'd pay for that when the *Preiss* reached Nieuwestad.

"Listen," Kit sang. "Little boy, listen. Listen to your tired daddy sing."

He made a trill in the back of his throat, something he remembered his own father doing, back in the ancient days before the divorce. Bakari started, focused on him like Kit had grown a second head.

"Oh. You like that?" Kit cooed, then trilled again.

The little mouth unknotted, and like a miracle visited upon the faithful, the baby laughed. Kit grinned down at him, and Bakari grinned back.

"The burn is almost over," Kit sang, improvising the glide and skip of the melody. "Soon we'll pass the gate."

Bakari shifted his back from side to side, and reached up an arm the way he had since he'd been in Rohi's belly. He'd be asleep soon, and Kit felt a surge of anticipation. When his son slept, he'd nap too. God, he needed to sleep.

"Close your eyes and rest, son," he sang, and gently rocked the little crash couch. He pulled the vowel sounds long and soothing. "Nothing here you need…"

Bakari's eyes fluttered closed, then open again. There was something odd about the way the light caught the roundness of his cheek, and Kit lost his own tune, fascinated by the texture of his son's skin. The light showed so much detail, the folds of baby-smooth skin, the sheen of the oils, and Kit was somehow falling into it, descending into the fractal complexity. By the time he realized something was wrong, it was too late.

Bakari was there, as close as he had been before, but what had been his boy was a complexity of vibrations—molecules and atoms in clumps and patterns too baroque to show where one thing began and another ended. Kit fell what would have been forward onto what would have been his knees, and the pain of it was like watching dominoes fall, tiny electrochemical sparks passing from nerve to nerve. The shimmering in the air was Bakari screaming. And Kit screaming too. The feeling of the air abrading his throat was a cascade of rushing razor-sharp atoms.

Something more solid and real than they were slid through the jumble of atoms that was the wall. A thread of conscious darkness that had never known light, was the antithesis of it. Kit tried to move the clouds that were his arms around the cloud that had been his son, knowing distantly that it couldn't matter. He was no more solid than the wall had been.

The darkness whirled toward him, scattering him. Scattering his son.

A voice as vast as mountains *whispered…*

The alarm caught Tanaka's attention. Something was going wrong at the Sol gate. It took a few seconds to understand what she was seeing. The influx of fast-moving particles had just dropped to zero. It would have meant the incoming ship had cut its drive, except there were still photons getting through. Whatever ship was coming in from Sol wasn't going to make it. They were already starting to go dutchman, and they didn't even know it yet.

It wasn't her problem, and even if it had been, there wasn't anything she could do about it. She turned back to the scatter analysis and the hunt for the *Rocinante*. There was a greater than 40 percent chance that something had passed into Bara Gaon in the timeframe she was looking at…

"Shit," she said to no one.

She let the *Derecho* keep crunching its numbers and pulled her screen back to the Sol gate. Watching the trainwreck. The light was growing smaller and brighter now. The drive had almost reached the gate. Without meaning to, she heaved a sigh. A whole lot of people were about to die for no reason other than they'd been unlucky with the traffic patterns. Sympathy plucked at her. It seemed petty somehow, with the universe crashing in all around them, for the enemy to still eat the occasional ship.

"Rest in peace, you poor fucks," Tanaka said as the drive plume blinked out, lost in wherever it was that the lost ships went.

An alarm chirped, and for half a second she thought it was announcing the loss of the Sol-based ship. But the *Derecho* wasn't worried about that. It was worried about everything else. Tanaka looked at the data and her gut knotted. She opened a feed from the external telescopes. The surface of the space between the rings was glowing a pearly gray, with ripples of darkness moving through it in a way that made her think of sharks swimming through cloudy water. Adrenaline flooded her system, and a wave of vertigo so powerful she looked for a thruster malfunction.

"Botton," she began, trusting the *Derecho* to know she needed a comm channel open. "We have a problem."

The surface of the ring space shifted. Bent. *Boiled.*

The alien station at the center of the ring space flared like a tiny sun.

Something happened to Tanaka that felt like waking up without falling asleep first. Her awareness shifted, opened, became something it hadn't been a moment before. She was in her crash couch, but she was also in the medical bay with her head in excruciating pain, and in Botton's cabin with a bulb of whiskey in his hand and the burn of it in his throat. She saw through a thousand sets of eyes, felt a thousand different bodies, knew herself by a thousand different names.

Aliana Tanaka screamed.

A voice as vast as mountains whispered.

It whispered *No.*

The scattered world paused in its swirls and chaos. The dark threads froze in their places, vibrating and writhing but unable to whip through the clouds and points that were matter. The awareness that had been Kit, drifting and broken and scattered as it was, saw its own pain, its own distress, the still-flashing impulses that had been its child's neurons as they fired. Something analogous to sound rumbled and roared, and the dark threads thinned. They became black strings, wet as blood clots. Then threads. Then wisps of smoke.

And then nothing.

The paths where the darkness had whipped the scattered particles apart shifted like a video message played slowly and in reverse. Something thought *stirring the cream back out of the coffee,* and it might have been Kit. The interplay of vibrations that were the atoms and molecules, incomprehensible in their variety, began to segregate. The slow spinning flow like a river past a muddy bank became the air from a vent. Or blood passing through an artery. Density became real.

Surfaces emerged. Then objects, and then Kit was looking into Bakari's wide, frightened eyes. Kit's heart fluttered, as confused as a man who'd forgotten what he was saying midsentence, and then it pounded, each stroke so hard he could see the pulse in his eyes. He wrapped his son tight in his arms as Bakari started to wail, and held him close, sheltered against a threat he didn't understand and couldn't locate in space.

The other man, the one who wasn't in the room, slumped in exhaustion and closed his eyes. The cabin door slammed open, and Rohi was there, eyes bright and panic-wide.

"You're hurting him," she shouted. "Kit, you're hurting him!"

No, Kit tried to say, *I'm just holding him. He's only crying from fear.* He couldn't find the words, and when he looked down, he was squeezing too tight. He made his arms relax, and Bakari's wailing grew louder. He let Rohi take their son. His body was shaking, a deep pulsing shudder.

"What was that?" Rohi said, her voice shrill with fear. "What just happened?"

The *Falcon* was close to the Adro diamond, and while it wasn't on the opposite side of the local star, it wasn't at the point in its orbit closest to the gate either. The light delay was sixty-two minutes, which meant one hundred twenty-four would have to pass before the tightbeam lock was confirmed. Jim could, of course, send out a message on the beam of supercoherent light even before the comms handshake was done, but somehow it seemed rude. By being in the system, they were dropping a great big bucket of uncomfortable decisions in Elvi's lap. Giving her the chance to refuse to talk to him felt like the least he could do from an etiquette perspective.

He was spending the time until then doing a checkup with the autodoc in the med bay. The medical expert system had been upgraded three times in the decades since the *Roci* had been a top-of-the-line MCRN ship, and while there was better technology out there now, what they had was pretty damn good. Certainly, it was better than what he'd grown up with.

He let the system check-scan him for little bleeds and tears from the long burn and decant a slurry of targeted coagulants and tailored regeneration hormones. The worst part about it was the weird almost-formaldehyde aftertaste that haunted the back of his tongue for the two days following the treatment. Small price to pay for being 8 percent less likely to stroke out.

Naomi floated in, moving from handhold to handhold with the grace of a lifetime's practice. Jim smiled and gestured to the autodoc next to his like he was offering her the chair beside his in the galley. She shook her head gently.

He almost asked what was bothering her, but he knew. The high traffic in the slow zone. He almost said it wasn't her fault, which would have been true, but she knew that too. It didn't keep her from carrying the weight.

"Maybe Tanaka's ship went dutchman," he said.

As he'd hoped, she chuckled. "We should be so lucky. It's never the ones you want."

"Probably true."

"The worst part is that there is an answer, you know? We have a solution. There are probably dozens of solutions. All it would take is people agreeing to one and abiding by it. Cooperation. And I could—"

Alex's voice came over the ship comms. "Are you all seeing this?"

Naomi frowned.

"Seeing what?" Jim asked.

"The ring gate."

Jim pulled at his arm, but the autodoc chimed a complaint. Naomi put the wall screen on and shifted to the external scopes. Behind them, the Adro gate had been everything every gate was—dark, spiraling material formed unfathomable eons ago by the strange arts of the protomolecule. Only now, it wasn't dark. It was shining. The whole circle of the gate was glowing a blue white, with streams of energetic particles radiating from it like an aurora.

Naomi whistled softly.

"It just started doing that a couple minutes ago," Alex said. "I'm getting a lot of radiation from it too. Nothing dangerous—a lot of ultraviolet and radio."

"Amos?" Jim said. "Are you looking at this?"

"Sure am."

"So, you know things you're not supposed to know. Any thoughts on this?"

He could hear the shrug in the big mechanic's voice. "Looks like someone turned it on."

Chapter Twenty-Five: Tanaka

The captain of the *Preiss* was a flat-faced, pale-skinned man with a stubble-length beard that didn't hide his double chin. He'd spent two decades ferrying colonists to new worlds, and now he floated in Tanaka's cabin with a vague look on his face. He should have been frightened. He only seemed stunned.

By force of will, Tanaka kept from tapping her fingers against her thigh. She wasn't going to show anxiety, even in front of someone who seemed primed to overlook it. After all, this interview and all the others were being recorded.

"I've taken," he said, paused, licked his lips absently, "psychedelics. I've been places, you know? It wasn't like that. Not at all."

The *Preiss* was docked to the *Derecho*, the first of the ships waiting their turn for the Laconians to meet with their crews, copy the data from their sensor and comms systems, and generally go over everything with the finest-toothed of all possible combs. But the

Priess was the most important. It was the only ship to ever shrug off going dutchman.

And if Tanaka had held any hope that its captain knew why, she would have been abandoning it right about now. "What is the ship carrying that's in any way out of the ordinary?"

His focus swam, found her. His shrug and scowl were perfectly synchronized, the result of a lifetime's practice saying *Fucked if I know.*

"We were just going through, same as always. The drive plume, it always hits first. But we couldn't see that anything odd was going on. Drive plume was in the way, you know?"

"I do," Tanaka said. Her jaw ached. "But there must be something. Something different this time? Had anything changed on this ship recently?"

"Got some new air scrubbers out of Ganymede. Charged graphene with crosshatching. Supposed to last twice as long as the old kind, and you can wash 'em with distilled water. Reuse 'em five or six times."

"That's the only new equipment?"

"Since the last trip, yeah."

"What about the passengers. Are any of them shipping anything out of the ordinary?"

The shrug. The scowl. "It's all construction and climate engineering stuff. I don't know."

"Is any of it protomolecule-based technology?"

A flash of impatience crossed the thick man's face. "Everything's protomolecule-based technology. The lace plating's protomolecule tech. The biofilms around the reactor are. Half the food supply comes from things we built off that shit."

Tanaka took a deep breath and let it out through her teeth. It didn't placate her that he was right. But there had to be some reason that this man was here, floating at her workstation, and not vanished into the hungry void that was a failed transit.

She let it go.

"Did you have…any experiences associated with the event?"

She managed to keep her voice steady, as if any answer would have been as good as another. As if just asking didn't make her gut tighten.

"Oh yeah. Oh, hell yeah."

Tanaka turned off the recorder. "Tell me what you remember. Don't feel like you have to make sense of it. Just your memory of the experience."

The man shook his head. Not a negation, but a gesture of wonder bordering on disbelief. "There was this thing where...I don't know. It was like being in the ocean, but the water was other people? You know how you dream, and maybe you're some other person? Like you dream you're old when you're a kid. Or a kid when you're old. It was like having a thousand of those dreams all at the same time."

Tanaka nodded. It was actually a pretty good description. She forced her jaw to relax.

"Do you still remember anything about those impressions? Or did the experience fade like normal dreams?"

He shrugged again, but almost gently. Like he was frightened or sad. When he spoke, his tone was almost wistful. "There's... scraps? There was like a memory I had where I was a woman on L-4 maybe ten years ago? I'd just gotten a promotion or something, and I was drunk with some friends."

"Have you ever been on L-4?"

"Nah, but that's where I was. Where she was. Where she was when I was her. I don't know, it was fucked up."

"Do you remember anything else about her?"

"My skin was really dark. Like *dark* dark. And there was something wrong with my right leg."

"Okay. All right." Tanaka turned the recording back on. "We're going to hold your passage until we can interview everyone on board the ship and make a complete forensic scan."

She expected him to object, but he didn't. The *Preiss* was going to be late arriving on Nieuwestad, and the captain would probably lose a bonus at the least. Possibly owe a late-arrival penalty. If the monetary loss bothered him, he didn't show it. Tanaka's guess was that he'd had an experience that made the mere economic reality of his position seem less significant. She was seeing a lot of that in her interviews.

He hauled himself hand by hand out of the office to where her guards were waiting in the corridor. She thumbed the control, and the door closed behind him. The database of all crew and passengers from the detained ships was on the *Derecho*'s system. The data wasn't perfect. Some of the ships claimed to have suffered data loss during the incident, their systems corrupted and spotty. It just meant they were hiding evidence: maybe of smuggling, maybe of contacts in the underground, maybe of some glimpse of the *Rocinante*'s passage through the slow zone. She wasn't naive enough to believe these people were good citizens of the empire.

She'd care about that later.

Her own experience had been like a whiteout. One moment, she'd been watching the *Preiss* die in a failed transit. The next, she'd been in a hurricane of unfamiliar consciousness, battered by it. When she'd come back to herself, the *Derecho* had been on automatic lockdown. The crew had been stunned, confused. She remembered passing one woman in the corridor who was floating in a fetal position, tears in a bubble over her eyes like goggles made of salt water.

The glitches and lost consciousness were often associated with visual and aural hallucinations. This was a new variation, but that was all. She wanted to believe that, and like anything she found herself wanting to be true, she forced herself to double-check it.

The initial search criteria was easy enough. Anyone female-identifying who'd been on L-4 between eight and thirteen years previously. Cross-reference that with medical records mentioning the right leg.

There was only one hit. Anet Dimitriadis, senior mechanic on the *Pleasant Life*, a freighter working between Corazon Sagrado, Magpie, and Pankaja systems. Tanaka resented the tightness in her throat as she pulled up the woman's file.

Anet Dimitriadis had skin so dark the system adjusted the image contrast to make her features clear. Like a rush of cold water in her gut, fear flooded Tanaka.

"Fuck," she said.

In the ring space, a soft and shadowless light spilled from the gates. Along with it, electromagnetic radiation on a range of frequencies filled the void like a jamming device. The *Derecho* took all of it in, filling the available memory with raw data from every sensor array it had. The ships that been in the ring space when the *Preiss* had done whatever trick it had done drifted, waiting for their turns to be questioned and released. A handful of other ships came through the gates, burning slowly, tentatively, like mice that thought they'd heard something meow.

What Tanaka wanted and what she could do were far enough apart to be independent variables. It would have been the work of years to put each and every person in the ships there in her office where she could grill them, scare them, threaten them. Find out what they remembered or thought they remembered. She didn't have years.

And, more to the point, this wasn't her mission. She was hunting Winston Duarte, or whatever he'd become, and hauling him—or it—back to Laconia. Whatever was going on here might be fascinating. It might be the most important thing in the universe. That didn't matter because it wasn't her job.

Except that she'd found something more important than her job.

Twice a day, she ate in the *Derecho*'s galley, but only because there was some deep, primate part of her brain that thought being around other primates would make her safer. The isolation of her office felt too much like vulnerability. But being around the crew was intensely uncomfortable in its own way. She ate her rice and egg slurry, drank her tea, and went back to her office, relieved to be alone again, but anxious too. She hated herself when she was like this.

She had Botton send representatives to each ship to conduct

interviews, routing only the captains, scientists, and information officers directly to her. When she wasn't doing her own interviews, she had a dozen more to listen to, compare among each other, gnaw at like a dog to crack a bone down to the marrow. She switched between the feeds, catching a question or two, a phrase or two, and then moving on. *Kenst how you can pay attention to how, sa, just your foot feels? Like that, aber con a jéjé different bodies.* Tanaka shifted. *I had this intense sense of panic, but it wasn't my panic. It was someone else's, and I was feeling it.* She shifted. *There was someone with me, only he wasn't in the room. He was more with me than if he'd just been beside me.* She told herself she was bored, but that was a lie. She was restless, and that wasn't the same. She needed to get drunk, to get in a fight, to fuck. Something. Be doing anything that centered her fully in her own body, where she could forget being anything other than herself.

The message from Trejo wasn't unexpected, but she'd let herself hope it might not come. She decanted a bulb of red wine designed to her tastes—dry and oaky—and drank half of it before she played it.

The message was noisy—static and resolution loss and best-guess infills by the comm system fighting against the new noise from the ring gates. Even so, she could tell that Trejo looked like shit. His unnaturally green eyes had taken on an almost milky softness. His hair was whiter than she remembered it being, and thinner. The darkness under his eyes spoke of sleeplessness. Anton Trejo was Laconia now, and he was learning that it was too big for him. No wonder he wanted Duarte back. She recognized his office at the State Building. She'd only been away from Laconia for a few months, but it seemed like a memory from childhood.

"Colonel Tanaka," he said, nodding at the camera as if he were looking at her. "I want to thank you for your report. I'm not going to bullshit you. The outcome in Freehold system isn't what I was hoping for. But you were the one with boots on the ground. I'm not going to second-guess you. This other thing…Well, it's concerning."

"Well understated, sir," she said to the recording, and squirted a little more of the wine toward the back of her throat. Nothing was as good on the float, and she had to breathe the fumes from her mouth up into her nose for the drink to taste like anything.

"I have ordered three ships from the Science Directorate to make all reasonable haste to the ring space, where they can make a complete survey. Your data has been provided to them and to Drs. Ochida and Okoye. If it is possible to get to the bottom of this, I have faith that they will."

A buzz was slipping into his voice. His annoyance might be with her. It might be with the universe or the unjust nature of chance. Or maybe he hadn't gotten laid in too long. She didn't know how he lived his life. She steeled herself to take the brunt of it, whatever it was.

"I also understand that this is alarming and of interest, but I do think it's a distraction from your primary objective."

Primary objective. He wasn't saying Duarte's name. Not even here. It was a misplaced discretion. Teresa Duarte had been breaking bread with the enemy for almost a year. Naomi Nagata and the whole underground knew by now that Duarte was shattered. They might not know that he'd taken the trouble to resurrect himself, but they probably did.

He was trying to keep his secrets secret, even when there was every reason to think his beans were well and truly spilled. Her stomach hurt. She realized Trejo had been speaking while her mind wandered, and she rolled the message back.

"...from your primary objective. I need your focus here, Colonel. I am spinning a lot of different plates right now, and while I appreciate your enthusiasm, I need you to keep in mind that you are one part of something much, much larger. Trust me to take care of this whatever the fuck this was. You do your job. We will get through this clusterfuck together, just the same way we always have. The more you get off-mission, the less useful your mission becomes to Laconia."

The message ended. It wasn't quite a threat, which was nice.

It wasn't quite not one either. *Do the job I asked or I'll pull your Omega status.* He hadn't said it. He hadn't needed to.

Tanaka carefully enunciated the word *fuck* into the still air of her office, squeezed the last wine from the bulb, and hauled her way out into the corridor and toward the bridge. She was already composing her reply. *I have returned to the pursuit of the asset we discussed. I remain convinced she is the most likely path to completing the mission.* Before she sent it, though, she had to make it true.

It wasn't until she pulled herself to a stop on the bridge that she realized she hadn't been there since the event. At the stations, half a dozen crew in sharp Laconian blue were unnaturally focused on their screens. She had a terrible memory of being at lower university and walking into a study group room that suddenly went quiet. She didn't know if they were laughing at her or frightened of her. Her scarred cheek began to itch, and she took some pride in letting the irritation swell to pain without scratching it.

She cast her gaze around the bridge like she was aiming a weapon. She picked out all the little flaws—the places where the couches were beginning to wear, where the fabric had been replaced and didn't quite match. Something about these imperfections soothed her.

Botton was at the captain's station, strapped into his crash couch though there was no thrust gravity. When he saw her, he undid his restraints, pushed himself up to a mag-booted approximation of standing, and braced. She nodded, and he relaxed.

"I have had word from Admiral Trejo," she said.

Botton nodded. Was there a smile hidden there? Without wanting it, she remembered the taste of whiskey on his tongue, richer and peatier than when she drank it herself. The feel of it warming his throat. She had been in a cacophony of different minds, but that one, she recognized. She had been inside Botton in a way more intimate than even the most authentic sex. Had he experienced something like that with her? Was he, right now, recalling one of her trysts with inappropriate men? She suddenly felt violated and exposed, but he hadn't said a word.

If she had glimpsed inside Botton's actual and genuine mind, that was fine with her. But if he or other people had been able to access her private memories, know her—even for a moment—the way she knew herself? That was like waking up to find herself in mid-fuck with a stranger. She'd navigated her whole life on the unbroken membrane between her public self and her private one. The idea that the separation might have been ripped open put her on the edge of almost animal panic.

She realized she'd been silent a beat too long. "The Science Directorate is sending survey ships to investigate the event and the hallucinations that accompanied it." She hit the word *hallucinations* just a degree harder than she needed to. She meant *You felt something, you recalled something, you experienced something. Don't assume it was truth.*

"Copy that, Colonel," Botton said. "I will recall our people from the other ships at once."

She glanced at the screen he'd been working at. It was the scan of the ring space that the *Derecho* had been making in the moment when whatever had happened had happened. She gestured toward it with her chin, and asked the question with her eyebrows.

Botton blushed. That was unexpected.

"I have been...reviewing the event," he said. "It was an exceptional moment."

"You have an opinion about it? Something you feel you should share with your commanding officer?" She said it coolly. It wasn't a threat, unless he thought it was. And then it was.

Botton didn't hear the warning. His stance softened, his gaze turned inward. She wondered, if the event happened again just then, what she might find in the place behind his eyes.

"The...hallucinations. I found them very unpleasant."

"As did I," Tanaka said.

"Yes, Colonel. I feel as though understanding what happened might better help to put the experience behind me. And I would very much like to put it behind me."

Tanaka tilted her head. There was an echo of her own fear in his voice. It occurred to her for the first time that she wouldn't be the only one who had felt the gestalt as a violation. For all she knew, Botton had secrets of his own to nurture and protect. It left her liking Botton a degree better.

"I'm sure the Science Directorate will be better equipped to make sense of this than we are," she said. "How long before we can be underway?"

"Transferring our crew back from the ships could take several hours." It sounded like an apology. She liked that too.

"As soon as they arrive, inform the remaining ships that they are to stay here until the survey ships arrive and debrief them."

"They aren't going to like that. Several of the captains have expressed a strong preference to leave the ring space as soon as possible."

"Any ship that leaves before being given permission will be labeled a criminal vessel and destroyed on sight by Laconian forces," Tanaka said.

"I will make sure they understand."

She took a deep breath. At the workstations, the other crew could have been living in different dimensions for all the reaction they showed to her conversation. On Botton's screen, the ring gates flared white. And the alien station at the ring space's heart matched them. The *Derecho*'s sensor arrays lowered their sensitivity to keep from whiting out. When the image returned a second later, the rings were glowing points all around the surface of the slow zone.

I'm missing something. The words were like a whisper in her ear. Something the captain of the *Preiss* had said. Or something about the newly glowing gates. Or had Botton accidentally said something that would unlock the mystery, or better, give her control over it?

"We have evidence that something made a transit to Bara Gaon system in approximately the right time frame," Botton said. "Shall we proceed there?"

"Yes," Tanaka said. "Alert me when the full crew has returned."

She clicked on her mag boots, used her ankle to turn her body and to stop it, then launched herself back toward the lift. Behind her, someone let out a long, stuttering breath as if they'd been holding it the whole time she'd been there.

Bara Gaon was an active system. If the *Rocinante* had fled there, it was because they hoped to use contacts in the underground to cover their passage. Any data she got from the official sources, she'd have to double-check herself in case it had been corrupted. Her mind ran forward along the path of the chase, and it was a relief.

She needed to go to the ship's gymnasium and punch a heavy bag. *I used to be a boxer when I was young.* The thought wafted through her mind like she'd heard someone say it. It wasn't her voice. She ignored it. She needed to eat. She needed to report back to Trejo. She needed to track down the *Rocinante*. She needed to find Winston Duarte or whatever he had become. She felt duty sliding in around her mind like blinders, cutting away the distractions.

She had a mission and a score to settle. Unthinking, she scratched her wounded cheek.

She was missing something.

Chapter Twenty-Six: Jim

Jim couldn't sleep. He lay on the crash couch, the gentle one-third g of the burn settling him into the gel, and tried to will himself into a sense of peace and rest that wouldn't come. Naomi, beside him, had curled onto her side, her back toward him. There had been a time when he'd slept with the lights entirely off, but that had been before Laconia. Now he kept them low—less than a single candle would have been but enough that when he woke from a nightmare, the familiar outlines of the cabin would be there to ground him. He hadn't had a nightmare. He hadn't slept at all.

Naomi murmured something in her sleep, shifted, and settled. Years of experience told him she was sloping down into the deepest levels of dream. Another few minutes and she'd twitch once like she was catching herself from falling, and after that, she'd snore.

This was the life he'd dreamed of during his imprisonment. This was what he thought he'd lost forever: suffering a little

insomnia while his lover of decades rested at his side. That the
universe had given it back to him after he'd given up hope flooded
him with a profound gratitude when it didn't frighten him. This
was so small, so precious, and so fragile.

They were both mortal. The one thing he knew for certain
was that this couldn't last forever. Someday, there would be a last
meal with Naomi. Someday there would be a last sleepless night
for him. A last moment hearing the *Roci*'s drive humming around
him. He might know when it came, or it might only be clear in
retrospect, or it might end for him so quickly that he never had
time to notice all the beautiful, small moments that he was losing.

Naomi jerked, went still, and then the low, soft rumble of her
snore began. Jim grinned through his weariness, counted her
breaths up to two hundred to give her time to fully commit to slum-
ber, and then pulled himself up out of the couch and dressed in the
gloom. When he opened the door to the corridor, Naomi turned to
look at him. Even though her eyes were open, she wasn't awake.

"No troubles," he said. "Keep sleeping."

She smiled. She was beautiful when she smiled. She was always
beautiful. He closed the door.

They'd made it almost three-quarters of the way to the *Falcon*, and were in the earliest part of their braking burn. Elvi's messages to them—that they could dock, that she'd see to it that there
wasn't a security problem, that they were welcome—had a sense
of normalcy that didn't match the situation at all. Even as Naomi
had responded with their flight path and expected intercept coordinates, Jim had been struck with the absurdity of treating it like
popping over to someone's apartment for dinner, when in reality
it was more like conspiracy to commit treason. But the *Derecho*
hadn't followed them through the gate, and there was literally no
place else for a ship to hide. At some point, Adro had been a solar
system capable of sustaining life. Now it was a star, a green diamond the size of a gas giant, the *Falcon*, and the *Rocinante*.

Jim reached the lift and rode it slowly up through the quiet
ship until he reached the ops deck. Alex was standing beside a

crash couch, a bulb in his hand and the bright gate on the screen in front of him. They were far enough from it now that, if he'd gone outside, Jim wouldn't have been able to distinguish it from the billions of stars. On the scopes, it radiated swirling waves of aurora-like energy.

"Hey," he said.

Alex looked over his shoulder. "What're you doing up?"

"Couldn't sleep. Thought I'd see if you wanted me to take watch."

"I'm fine," Alex said. "I'm shifted over. This feels like midafternoon to me. You want a beer?"

"A midafternoon beer?"

"I didn't say it was morning," Alex said, and scooped another bulb off the crash couch. Jim caught it, broke the seal, and took a long swallow.

"I've never understood people who like beer without gravity," Alex said. "That's not a drink. That's a vaguely alcoholic kind of foam."

"No argument," Jim said, then nodded toward the screen. "Anything?"

"Nothing new, but..." Alex gestured at the bright ring. "I don't know. I keep looking at it. Wondering what the hell it's doing."

"Well, it hasn't killed us. That seems like a good start."

"Could definitely be worse. But... You think you know something, right? Then it turns out you were only *used* to it. It does something, and it does something, and then after a while, you think that's what it does. Then it turns out there was this whole other thing, maybe."

"Using a microwave as a lamp, because it has a light in it," Jim said. He tried to remember where he'd heard that analogy.

"Yeah, exactly," Alex said. "You thought you knew it, but you were only familiar with it."

Jim took another sip of the beer. The hops tasted like mushroom, for good reason. "I'm hoping that Elvi has figured some things out. I mean, she'll know better than we do."

"We can hope," Alex agreed, then squeezed the last of the beer out of his bulb and tossed it into the recycler. His belch was deep and satisfied.

"How many of these did you have?" Jim asked.

"A few."

"Are you drunk?"

Alex considered the question. "A little, I guess." He lowered himself into the crash couch. "There was this time when I was a kid, I had a really crap babysitter. I was maybe nine? She was sixteen. And we watched this monster film. A huge cat monster that lived underground, and it got pissed off by some seismic surveys. Came to the top and started tearing up cities and collapsing tunnels. Scared the shit out of me."

"Weird the things that get to you when you're a kid," Jim said.

"I knew it wasn't for real. I was young, I wasn't dumb. But it still scared me, and the thing my dad told me that actually got me past it? He showed me how it wouldn't scale."

"Wouldn't scale?"

"Volume goes up by cubes. A cat big enough to crush a city wouldn't be strong enough to stand up, even at Martian gravity. Its bones would break under its own weight. And that did it for me. I was all right, because I saw it couldn't work. This is like that cat, it doesn't scale."

Jim sat with that for a second. "Either you're too drunk or I'm not drunk enough. I don't get it."

"The gates. The systems. It's bigger than us. It's bigger than we *can* be. I mean, have you ever thought about what it would be like to see every system there is now? To see just the places where we are? There's thirteen hundred seventy-three gates—"

"Seventy-one. Thanjavur and Tecoma are gone."

"Thirteen hundred and seventy-one," Alex agreed. "Now let's say you plot it so that you don't have to slow down when you get to the ring space. Accelerate all the way to the ring gate, brake all the way back to the goldilocks region at wherever you're going. Maybe take you a month to do it."

"You'd run out of reaction mass."

Alex waved the objection away. "Pretend you could stock up in flight. All the reaction mass and fuel and food and everything. And liquid helium to boil off the waste heat."

"So ignoring every actual constraint that makes it impossible?"

"Yeah. Five billion klicks a month, every month. No time on the float. No time at the planets. Just—" He threw his hand forward, a gesture of speed.

"All right."

"Hundred and fifteen years. Start it the day you're born, and finish it an old man, and never see anything but the inside of your ship. Take a week at each planet—not each city, not each station, each *planet*—to play tourist? Add another twenty-eight *years*. A hundred forty-some years old. That's a solid lifetime, just to take a peek. Get the lay of the land. Never see the same place twice."

Jim thought about that. Between working for the Transport Union back in the day and fleeing with the underground, he'd been to more systems than most people ever would, and it was still probably under three dozen. He knew how many more there were, how many he'd never see, how many Naomi was trying to coordinate. Alex was right. It was daunting. Maybe more than daunting.

"And that's not the worst of it," Alex said. "By the time you're done, there's been a century of change at the place you started from. It won't be the same. All the places you visit start changing into new ones the second you leave."

On the screen, the bright gate shifted and muttered. The false-color map showed radio waves and X-rays pouring out of it. Jim couldn't help imagining it as a vast eye looking back at them.

"This is all too big for people," Alex said. "The things that built it? Maybe they could handle it, but we're not designed for this scale. We're trying to get big enough we can make it work, but we're breaking our legs just standing up."

"Huh," Jim said. And then, a moment later, "You got any more beer?"

"Nope."

"Want some?"

"Yep."

With its drive off, the *Falcon* was no more than a small, oddly shaped asteroid at first. It was a little under three hundred thousand kilometers off the Adro diamond, orbiting it like a tiny artificial moon. The artifact itself was eerie: vast and green and flickering now and then with murky internal energies like storms that penetrated deep into the flesh of the object. The planet. The library. Jim knew enough about Elvi's preliminary work that he could appreciate the supremely unnatural aspects of the thing: that it didn't collapse under its own mass, that it was connected using the same locality-breaking principles as the ring gates, that it had the capacity to hold vastly more information than humanity had generated in its millennia of progress. The *Falcon*—pale-skinned and half-organic the way Laconian ships all were—would have been unnerving in any other context. Here, Jim felt a weird kinship with it. The technology might be alien, but the design language was mostly human.

Alex brought them into a matching orbit, maneuvering the *Rocinante* gently into place until the two ships seemed like they were already connected. Locked by the common forces of velocity and gravity. The *Roci*'s crew gathered at the crew airlock as Amos prepared to extend the docking bridge.

"You know what's funny?" Jim said. "I feel certain this door will open and Tanaka will be standing there with a bunch of Laconian Marines in power armor ready to charge across."

Teresa rolled her eyes, but Naomi laughed. "That's not going to happen."

"Of course not. But I'm certain it will. That's weird, right?"

She took his hand, squeezed it once, and as she looked into his eyes, she said, "This is all right. Elvi is with us, and she's in command of this ship."

"Besides," Alex said, "if she's not, they've had plenty of time to call for backup. No one's here besides the two of us."

Jim nodded. He knew that the fears were irrational. That didn't keep him from feeling them, but it did make it a little bit easier to take them lightly. Alex was right. They'd announced Elvi's complicity to her crew the moment they'd transferred into the system, and no one had sounded the alarm as far as they could tell. The connection of their two ships, the transfer off the *Rocinante* and onto the *Falcon*, was almost symbolic compared with what they'd already done.

Amos clicked the last of the safety latches into place and keyed in the syncing protocol. A soft hissing vibration meant that the docking bridge was moving out, creating a corridor between the ships.

"Still, I don't think we should all go over," Naomi said. "Not at the same time, anyway."

"Not until we know the situation over there," Alex agreed.

"Not ever," Naomi said. "One of us is always on the *Roci*. That's a rule. I trust Elvi, and I trust her to know her crew. But I trust us more."

Alex raised his hand like a schoolboy answering a question. "I'm happy to keep an eye on the farm if y'all want to go over."

"I think Amos should stay too," Naomi said.

"Better if I came with," Amos said. "Nothing happening over here Tiny can't keep eyes on."

Naomi hesitated, and Jim wondered for a moment what would happen if she told Amos he had to stay. Maybe Naomi had the same doubt. "All right," she said. "Alex and Teresa stay here for now. The rest of us go make introductions."

Naomi caught his eye and lifted one eyebrow. She meant that he didn't have to go. He shrugged. He meant that he did.

"Works for me," Amos said, hauling himself into the airlock. "And we got a seal, pressure, and an invitation."

Jim followed Naomi into the airlock and felt it in his bones when it cycled shut behind them. His fear of Tanaka had shifted.

Now some part of him expected the outer airlock door to open onto the void, for the air to flow out and death to rush in. Instead, there was a soft clank, a hiss of gas as soft as an exhalation, and the gangway. The *Falcon*'s outer airlock was already open, and the three of them launched across to it. The air smelled different. Bright and astringent.

When the *Falcon*'s outer door closed, its inner door opened, and Elvi Okoye was there. Fayez floated beside her with a black-eyed girl. Elvi smiled, but she looked terrible. Her skin had an ashy tone, and her arms and legs were visibly atrophied.

"Naomi, Jim," she said, drifting toward them like an obscene parody of an angel. "It's good to see you again. And Amos." As she stopped herself with a handhold, Elvi's gaze flickered across Amos, and for a moment there was something almost like hunger in her eyes. The focus of a taxonomist on an important new species. "I'd heard you changed like Cara and Xan. I would really love to do a few medical scans while you're here. If that's all right with you?"

"If it helps, Doc," Amos said, then turned to the black-eyed girl. She had very different features from Amos, but the blackness of their eyes, the grayness under their skins, left Jim's brain trying to see the similarity as a family resemblance. "Hey, Sparkles."

The girl frowned and started to say something, then stopped.

"Well," Fayez said. "This is just awkward as hell, isn't it?"

Elvi shook herself and motioned them in. "Please come in. I've had a little welcoming party set up, and we have a *lot* we need to talk about."

Chapter Twenty-Seven: Elvi

The *Rocinante* had come through the Adro gate, the gate had lit up like a radio and X-ray bonfire, and Elvi knew that the game had changed. She hadn't known what it had changed into or what the consequences of the change would be, but without doubt, the ways she'd been operating were the old ways now.

The immediate response on the *Falcon* had been barely restrained panic. An enemy gunship was in the system. The *Falcon* was far from defenseless, but were they going to be in a battle? Had the underground come to drop nukes on the BFE the way they had the construction platforms? What had they done to change the ring gate? Elvi led by example at first. She didn't panic, and it gave everyone else permission not to panic either. Then the first tightbeam from the *Roci* arrived, Naomi brought her up to speed, and Elvi had some decisions to make.

The first job, and the one that would shape what came after, was talking to Harshaan Lee.

The younger man floated in her office with his ankles crossed and his arms held behind his back in a way that opened his chest. He listened with the calm focus of a researcher taking in a new body of information. Only this was information that reframed his own life and his prospects for survival.

"I'm not going to apologize," Elvi said. "Admiral Trejo knows very well how I feel about all the political and military wrangling in the face of this existential alien threat. If he finds out... *When* he finds out about this, he won't be surprised. But he won't be happy either."

Dr. Lee let a long, slow breath out from between his teeth, half sigh and half deflation. "No, I see that he won't."

"If you'd like, I can incarcerate you," Elvi said. "When this all comes out, you'll be able to honestly say you couldn't do anything about it."

Lee was silent for a long moment, his gaze shifting as he thought. Elvi admired the man's intelligence and professionalism. She didn't know what he'd say or do, but if she did need to start moving down her chain of command until she found someone who'd toe her line, it was going to be a long, difficult day.

When he spoke, his voice was a mixture of resignation and amusement. "I am an officer of Laconia and a patriot. You are my commander and the head of the directorate in which I serve. Your collaboration is unorthodox. After San Esteban, unorthodox may be necessary. I understand your rationale. You may rely upon me."

"Thank you," Elvi said. "And Harshaan? I have access to the comms. And I have monitors on them not even the comms officers know about. Don't fuck with me. I'm here to win."

"Very much understood," he said.

With his support, the rest of the crew shifted from fear to confusion. She wouldn't have thought it, but there were some real advantages to working in a system that treated chain of command with an almost religious zeal. At least when she was the one with the authority.

Communication through the gate had always been spotty. In Sol system or Laconia—and increasingly in more developed colonies like Auberon and Bara Gaon—repeaters were plentiful enough for robust routing solutions. If one failed, the others would notice and track their signals around it. In Adro, there was a single thread of repeaters that the *Falcon* itself had dropped on the way out and the one at the ring gate that the underground or pirates or vandals occasionally destroyed. The new flood of radio pouring off the ring gates acted like a signal jammer and made the system even less reliable. But slowly, during periods of low activity and on frequencies the ring's new activity seemed to ignore, a deeper picture of what had happened began to reveal itself to her. By the time the *Rocinante* arrived, she had as clear an understanding of the new status quo as anyone except possibly Ochida and Trejo. More than that, she had a plan. And getting Dr. Lee on board had been more straightforward than the risks she needed the *Rocinante* to shoulder.

She waited in the airlock with Fayez and Cara. She would have invited Dr. Lee and Xan, but they wouldn't be coming to the briefing. There wasn't enough space in her lab for all of them. She felt the anxiety in her chest like a spring wound up a quarter turn too tightly. Floating beside her, Cara fidgeted, clasping and unclasping her hands. Wringing them. Elvi had always thought that was just a figure of speech.

"Still time to back out of this," Fayez said.

"No there isn't," Elvi said.

"No. You're right."

The airlock's outer door cycled closed. There was a soft click as the inner door's bolts came free. The door slid open, and they were there.

Naomi looked very different from the last time Elvi had seen her in person. They'd both been much younger then, and she remembered Naomi as a soft, almost retiring presence who had the habit of hiding behind the spill of her own dark, curling hair. The woman in her airlock had a harder face, hair the white of snowfall, and nothing reticent about her. The cameras did a great deal to disguise the gravity with which she held herself. Somehow, across the reach of decades, Naomi Nagata had become the kind of person Elvi could imagine sitting across a table from Anton Trejo. She wondered if Trejo knew that.

James Holden, on the other hand, looked exactly like himself, but older. Of course, she'd seen him much more recently on Laconia. She'd had time to adjust to the years in his face and the vague, bemused look in his eyes.

"Naomi, Jim. It's good to see you again," she said. The man beside them gave her a friendly smile. She might only have imagined Cara's near-silent gasp. "And Amos. I'd heard you changed like Cara and Xan. I would really love to do a few medical scans while you're here. If that's all right with you?"

"If it helps, Doc. Hey, Sparkles."

They were all silent for a moment. Criminals and conspirators tasked with saving humanity from itself and the enemies bent on its destruction.

"Well," Fayez said. "This is just awkward as hell, isn't it?"

"Please come in. I've had a little welcoming party set up, and we have a *lot* we need to talk about."

As they passed through the ship, the crew was careful not to notice them. Elvi tried to imagine what she'd have felt in their place. The enemy welcomed into their home. She wondered how many of them guessed that Teresa Duarte was in the ship they were linked to. If she'd tried to design a pressure test to see whether her people would rat her out to Trejo, she couldn't have done better than this. She hoped that none of them had a back channel out that she didn't know about. If they did... Well, that would be an interesting problem.

They reached the lab, and she ushered them all in like she was back in college and hosting a party in her dorm room. She went in last, closing the door behind her.

"Welcome to my little world," Elvi said, gesturing at the lab.

Naomi grabbed a handhold, stopped herself, and looked over

the space, approving. Elvi had become so used to the half dozen multifunction workstations, the heavy air scrubber built to capture dangerous chemicals and put out any fires, that having new people looking at it felt like a reminder it was there. It had all become as familiar as her own body and as easy to take for granted. Most of what the *Falcon* was doing in Adro was medical scans of Cara and geological scans of the diamond, but the ship was built for everything from electron microscopy to vivisection.

"It's lovely," Jim said, and he almost seemed genuine, but not quite.

"It's a fucking prison," Elvi said with a smile. "But it's mine."

She grimaced when she realized she'd just claimed to be locked in a prison to a man who had spent the previous few years being tortured in an actual prison, but the look on his face didn't change. If he noticed her gaffe he had the grace to ignore it.

"I'm sorry we put you in a hard position," Naomi said. "I know you're taking a risk letting us come here."

Elvi made a shooing motion with her left hand as she pulled a display onto the wall screen with her right. "It was the right thing. You do what you have to when the universe is on fire."

"Is it?" Naomi asked.

"On fire?" Elvi said. "That's actually a really interesting question. You know about the new event?"

"We've been running dark," Naomi said. "The only things we know, we heard from you."

"Well, you were part of it, whatever it was." She pulled up the ring gate on the wall in its new, bright form. A cascade of analytic data spilled out in columns beside it. "You were part of the trigger anyway. Most of the direct data I have is from Colonel Tanaka."

"The one who keeps trying to kill us?"

"The same," Fayez said. "She's been doing field reports and sending us the raw data while you were on your way here. She had scanners doing live sweeps of the slow zone looking for traces of your passage when the shit hit the fan. And she was even watching the turd in question."

Elvi gestured and the screen shifted to the familiar bubble of the ring space with its hundreds of gates equally spaced along the surface. She zoomed in on one that was at an oblique angle to the telescope capturing the image, the circle of the gate bent by perspective into an oval. A glimmer of light shone in the center of the ring gate like a firefly. The drive plume of a ship braking before it passed through.

"Sol gate," Elvi said. "Still almost half the traffic in and out of the ring space goes through there."

"But there was a lot of other traffic," Naomi said, grimly. "Including us."

Elvi shifted her hand, and the glimmer in the gate slowed. A readout said they were watching it several thousand times slower than it had actually happened, but the feed wasn't choppy. Jim crossed his arms, scowling. Amos and Cara watched with a matching interest and stillness. The glimmer grew brighter, until it was pure white on the screen.

"It was a colony ship," Elvi said, her words fast, staccato, and anxious. "It attempted transit a few seconds after Tanaka's ship came in. We don't know how many other transits had happened before, but that doesn't matter. Enough to put the threshold up over safety."

The glow brightened...and it died. Elvi felt a sting of excitement, but only because she already knew that the lives she was watching end, hadn't. Somehow they'd been saved. The drive plume returned, coalescing inside the ring space like the ship had made its passage after all, even though it had clearly vanished just moments before.

"What the fuck was that?" Naomi murmured.

"The ship went dutchman, and then came back. But that's just the pregame show," Elvi said. "Watch how much the ring entities liked it."

The edge of the slow zone bubbled, brightened, roiled. Elvi had seen that before. The *Falcon* had been the only ship to survive the last time this had happened. When she spoke, her voice was tighter and higher. "This is what we saw when we lost Medina Station. It's a direct intrusion across the ring space's barriers. It killed Medina. It killed the *Typhoon*."

"Too bad it didn't kill Tanaka," Amos said.

Patterns played across the ring space like malefic auroras, and a darkness moved in the light. Elvi found herself hunching over like she was protecting her belly from a punch. She forced her spine straight.

"And then this," Elvi said.

As one, the ring gates and station flared white, a brightness that overloaded the telescopes for three long, terrible seconds. When the light faded, like letting out a long, slow exhalation, the ring space returned to itself, with all the drive cones and transponders and traffic that had been there before. Including the colony ship that they'd watched vanish and reform.

"It's not just the Adro gate that lit up," Naomi said.

"No, it's all of them. And when that happened, there was a cognitive effect. Most of the data Colonel Tanaka has been providing has been about that."

"A cognitive effect like the lost memory?" Naomi asked.

"Nope," Fayez said. "Very, very different."

"It looks like it may have been a kind of networked connection between the minds of the people in the ring space," Elvi said. "All the crews of all the ships. It was apparently fairly overwhelming. But there's an indication that they all participated in each other's memories and experiences."

Amos scratched his chin. "That sounds like what's been going on with me and Sparkles."

"It does seem very similar to what you, Cara, reported during the dives into the BFE."

"BFE?" Amos asked.

"The diamond. The library."

"Why BFE?" Jim said.

Elvi scowled and shook her head. "The point is, when we saw it with you two"—she gestured to Cara and Amos—"we had assumed it was because you'd been modified by the repair drones. What happened in the ring space, that happened to unmodified human beings. The effect didn't last very long. Almost instantaneous, really. But the memories have been vivid and persistent. The radiation from the gates is also interesting. Take a look at this."

The display shifted into something that looked like an impossibly complicated spiderweb. With a gesture, Elvi rotated it, then looked over at Jim.

He nodded and said, "I have no idea what that is."

"Communication between the gates," Elvi said. "We think the patterns in the radiation set up handshakes between the gates similar to the one we saw here between Cara and the...diamond."

"The gates are talking to each other?" Naomi said.

"We've been using them as a matter transport system, which they are. It makes sense that they're also a communication network."

A tickling sensation crawled up Jim's neck and he shuddered. "Amos said something about there being a kind of light that can think."

"Yes," Elvi said. "One model that goes pretty well with this architecture is a neural network. A really small one, but the signal processing between them has some real similarities. If it's a fully meshed network with each connection acting like a synapse, that's a little shy of a million. So about a tenth as smart as a fruit fly. If they're making connections between gates with different frequencies acting as distinct connections, they'd need something on the order of ten million different frequencies just to get as smart as a house cat—"

"Are you saying that the gates are alive and *thinking* on their own?" Naomi asked. The tremor in her voice was almost like fear.

"No. I'm also not saying they aren't, but as biological systems go, this is really pretty simple." She paused. "I was trying to be reassuring."

"Not sure it worked," Jim said.

"Didn't," Naomi agreed. "Really didn't."

Elvi shut off the wall screen and used a handhold to turn toward them. "I'm sorry. I've been deep in this for so long, I get happy when I find anything that isn't overwhelmingly complicated. I have a friend from my postdoc who spent five years modeling protein cascades in trout livers. I'm supposed to do that depth of analytic work in half an hour five times a day. It's been inhumane."

"I've been running a guerrilla government with shitty communications, thirteen hundred different isolated systems, and literally billions of people who think whatever they're looking at is the most important thing there is," Naomi said. "I know how you feel."

"Let me try again," Elvi said. "There's good news. Ever since the rings began radiating like this, there hasn't been an event in any system. No loss of consciousness. No change in any basic physical constants or the laws of physics. No more San Estebans with massive numbers of people dying with no warning or defense."

"Not sure that makes sense, Doc," Amos said. "They weren't able to stop it."

"They?" Naomi asked.

Amos gestured at the dead wall screen as if it would show what he'd meant to say. "The ones that made all this. They got killed. They didn't have a way to stop it once it started. They shut down the gates to try and quarantine themselves. Nothing stopped the attacks."

"Not for them, no," Elvi agreed. "Which makes this very interesting. And there is another factor. The shared consciousness thing? One effect was that people came away with impressions from lives that weren't their own. Some episodic memories. Some procedural. I'm sure the data Colonel Tanaka's collecting will fuel a billion doctoral theses on holographic memory-encoding paradigms, but one of the things that keeps coming up was an awareness of a man who was present but wasn't there. More than two percent of the people who experienced the event talked about him. And he's in my dataset too. Cara's seen him. The other one."

They all turned to the girl. For a moment, she seemed smaller, more vulnerable. Like the girl she'd once been. Elvi expected her to speak, but Amos was the one to answer.

"Duarte. You think it's Duarte."

Fayez shrugged. "He was massively altered with protomolecule-based technologies. He popped himself out of a coma and went missing. And now this? Yeah, it's our best guess."

"So when he went missing, he vaporized? He's a protomolecule ghost now?" Amos said. "Haunting the network?"

Jim looked ill, and Naomi put her hand on his elbow, squeezing lightly. Cara looked over to Amos, and Elvi couldn't tell if the girl was uncomfortable that he was there or if she was looking to him for protection.

"I have no idea what happened to him, physically. But it is possible," Elvi said, "that he's been using the work we're doing here to…piggyback. That he's aware of the things Cara and Amos are aware of. That he's finding some separate application for it."

"That he hauled himself up out of a coma more powerful than before," Jim said.

"It's a theory," Elvi said.

"What do we do if you're right?" Jim asked.

Elvi steeled herself. "I think we should try a dual dive. Put Amos and Cara in separate sensor arrays, bring out the catalyst, send them both into the library together. Up to now, Amos' experience has been mediated by their connection. If Cara and Amos are together, it could very plausibly give them more control than Cara's had going by herself."

"Control's good," Amos said. "What do we do once we have control?"

"We try to talk to him."

Chapter Twenty-Eight: Tanaka

Tanaka knew as soon as they made the transit that the trail had gone cold, but it took time to confirm it.

Gewitter Base was Laconia's largest military installation in the Bara Gaon system. Made up of three rotating rings spinning around a central zero-g dry dock, it housed nearly seven thousand permanent officers and personnel. Two *Storm*-class destroyers remained on constant combat patrol around the station, monitoring all traffic through Bara Gaon's ring and tracking the commercial traffic moving through the system.

Bara Gaon was one of the Laconian Empire's most important industrial hubs. Bara Gaon-5 was a ball of soil and water placed in the exact center of the goldilocks zone, and with so little tilt to its axis that its seasonal changes were nothing more than mild suggestions. Significant volcanic activity in its early formation meant the crust was full of useful metals, and the soil was well suited for adaptation to Earth organics. In orbit around it, the Bara Gaon Complex floated, a massive construct of shipyards and low-gravity production facilities.

The tracking systems from Gewitter they'd linked to the *Derecho* showed that, in addition to the two destroyers, there were four deep-space telescopic satellites, three dozen Laconian radio listening stations, and seventy-three ships currently under thrust in the system.

Not one of them had seen the *Rocinante* come through the ring.

While the *Rocinante* might flee into the system and then try to get the underground to help them hide, it was impossible to believe they could have made the transit without being spotted.

Tanaka had the SigInt people run a deep background on the system's governor to make sure she wasn't on the take from the resistance, but it was pro forma. Tanaka didn't expect them to find anything. She'd just followed the wrong lead.

"It looks like it was a supply ship out of Firdaws called the *Forgiveness*," Botton said, standing next to her at the bar in Gewitter's upscale officers' club. He laid his terminal on the bar and pulled up a holographic 3-D model. "Former colony ship owned by a liability collective and run by Captain Ekko Levy."

The décor was a tacky style they called Martian Classical. Lots of fake wood and polished metal mirrors surrounding carved stone tabletops. A few other people sat at the tables, chatting and drinking and eating mediocre pub food. But the lighting was good, and the music was low enough to allow for quiet conversations. After a few weeks on the *Derecho* staring at the same cloth-covered bulkheads every day, even the club's fake wood paneling felt like luxury.

"No chance they were a deliberate decoy to pull us off the trail?" Tanaka said, knowing the answer before Botton replied.

"They don't show up in any intelligence databases. If we were confused by the timing of their ship making the transit out of the ring space, it seems more likely that it was unintentional on their part."

If we were confused. Botton was being diplomatic. This was her mission. She was calling the shots.

"We followed the wrong scent," she said.

"It looks that way," Botton replied. Tanaka shot him a look of irritation. She wasn't looking for his agreement. Botton's expression didn't change. He waved the bartender over and ordered a second beer as if he hadn't noticed.

As Tanaka brooded over her options, the bartender brought Botton his beer and a bowl of dried and salted seaweed flakes. He looked at her, as though trying to gauge whether asking her if she wanted another drink was more dangerous than ignoring her entirely. He made the right call and walked away without a word.

After the silence had stretched out long enough to make her point, Tanaka said, "I'll check my other leads. In the meantime, call up signal intelligence. Put the word out to every ship and relay on the network. They'll be running without a transponder, but we've got the *Rocinante*'s drive signature and hull profile."

"Copy that," Botton said, and started to leave, most of his second beer still sitting on the counter.

"Also? Go back over the sensor data we took in when we passed through the ring gate. Run the analysis again, omitting Bara Gaon. Maybe there's something there we overlooked."

"Aye, aye, Colonel."

"And make sure they understand," Tanaka said, "that finding this ship is a security priority. Failing to report will be considered an act of sedition and punished by being sent to the Pen."

"I thought Major Okoye ordered the dismantling of the Pen?"

"I'll build a new one."

"Understood," Botton said, and left the bar in an overly casual hurry.

She pulled up her personal message queue and started the long process of demanding reports. The questioning of Duarte's friends and intimates hadn't turned up any other visitations, but the interviews of second-degree connections were ongoing. It looked like a dead end to her, but there was someone on Laconia whose job was to tell her so, and they could fucking well do that. Ochida hadn't gotten her an updated study of the egg-ship thing.

She sent a request for that. It queued. There was congestion at the repeater network because of interference coming off the ring gates. Three notifications were waiting for her with intelligence about San Esteban and the death count there, not that she had any clear idea what she was supposed to do about it. Feel bad that she hadn't found Duarte in time for…what? For him to stop it from happening? Everything about the situation chafed.

The bartender risked returning. "Anything else I can get for you, Colonel?" he asked, giving the bar top in front of her his friendliest smile while he said it.

"Club soda," she said, then taking a guess, "Chief?"

"Jay gee," he said, risking a look up from the bar and into her eyes for a second, then looking back down. "Commandant doesn't like enlisted working in here. Says it's bad for morale."

"Whose? Theirs or ours?" Tanaka asked, taking a pull off the soda water the bartender had poured while he spoke. It had just a hint of artificial lime flavoring that tasted like fancy soap.

"The commandant didn't share his thoughts on that with me," the bartender said, and started to move away.

"Still," Tanaka said. It slowed him. Pulled him back. "Pouring drinks is a shit detail for a lieutenant. Even a junior grade. Probably not what you imagined doing when you were killing yourself to get through the academy."

The bartender locked eyes with her now. He wasn't bad looking. Dark hair and eyes. The hint of a dimple in his chin. He had to know who she was. What her rank and status meant. But he stared at her for a moment, trying very hard not to show any fear before he spoke. "No, Colonel, it's not. But I'm an officer in the Laconian Navy. I serve at the pleasure of the high consul." He managed to get some playfulness into his tone, even if it was a little forced.

Tanaka felt a familiar warmth and tug in her belly. She didn't trust it. She was angry, she was frustrated, and the whatever-the-hell-it-was in the ring space had thrown her farther off true than she wanted to admit. She'd spent her career teaching herself how to cultivate and protect her secret lives. Taking risks when she wasn't fully in command of herself was not on the list of good ideas.

And yet.

"You heard about San Esteban?" she asked before he could step away. "Hell of a thing. Whole system wiped out, just like that."

"Yeah," he said.

"That's related to my work. My mission. No details, of course. But...I don't know. We're here, and then we're gone. No warning. No second chances. It could happen here, and you and me and everyone on this station would be..." She shrugged.

"You think that's going to happen?"

"I don't know," she said. "But if I were you, I wouldn't invest my tip money in long-term bonds. You know, just in case."

He smiled, and there was fear in it. A different kind of fear. Young men didn't like feeling mortal. It made them want to prove they were alive.

"Do you have a name, Lieutenant?"

"Randall," he replied. "Lieutenant Kim Randall. Sir."

He had to be forty years her junior. And the difference in their ranks was a yawning chasm that he'd be lucky to cross in a lifetime. An affair with someone of a lower rank was still a violation of the Laconian Military Code, and now that she had Omega status, literally everyone in the military outside of Fleet Admiral Trejo was a lower rank than her. But her status also put her effectively outside the law. Which took away some of what made it worth doing.

She was hungry, though. Not for sex, though that was how she was going to fix it. For control. For the sense that she wasn't vulnerable. That she was able to exert her will over a hostile universe in the form of this boy's body.

"So, Lieutenant Randall," she said. "Even though my ship is docked, they gave me a room here on the station."

"Did they?" Kim moved away, wiping down the bar top as he went.

"They did," Tanaka said. "Would you like to see it?"

Kim froze, then turned back to look at her. He looked her up and down once, as though really seeing her for the first time. Making sure he'd understood her offer, and gauging his interest. And then Kim's gaze landed on her ruin of a cheek for a moment, and he gave a barely perceptible flinch. It felt like a slap. She even felt her ruined cheek get warm.

A rush of emotions and reactions welled up in her, as unfamiliar as a bus filled with random strangers. Insecurity, shame, sorrow, embarrassment. She could put names to each of them, and the names were all ones she'd suffered under before. But these were different. The sting of embarrassment was like feeling it for the first time. The sorrow was a flavor of sorrow she'd never generated before. The shame was a different nuance of shame. She knew the feelings, genus and species, but they belonged to someone else. Some crowd of others who had sunk invisible wires into *her* heart.

Kim, seeing the confusion on her face, started to show cracks in his fearless facade. "I'm not sure that's a good idea, Colonel," he said, emphasizing her rank. Making his rejection about that. Making it about being a good, rule-abiding Laconian and not the ragged mess that was her face.

Tanaka felt her cheeks getting warmer, and her eyes began to itch at the corners. *Fuck me, am I getting ready to cry because some fucking JG bartender doesn't think I'm pretty enough to screw? What is happening to me?*

"Of course," she said, horrified at the thickness in the words.

She stood up, careful not to knock over her bar stool, and turned away before pretty little Lieutenant Randall with his fearless smirk and his dimpled chin could see the water in her eyes. "Colonel," Kim said, an edge of surprise or worry in his voice. *Good. Let him worry.* Tanaka left without answering.

On her way out the door, she caught a glimpse of herself in a wall-mounted mirror. The angry red topographical map of her cheek. The way the skin pulled at her eye, giving her a slight droop to the lower eyelid. The white ridgeline where the school medic had sewn her face back together after James Holden blew it apart.

Am I ugly? a voice in her mind said.

It wasn't her. It was a small voice. A *child's*. Tanaka could almost picture the face saying it, curly red hair and green eyes and a nose covered in freckles. The face was looking up at her, on the edge of tears, and hearing those words come out of her mouth broke Tanaka's heart. The memory was as clear as if she'd lived it, hearing the pain in her daughter's voice and wanting to wipe the thought away and kill the little boy who'd put it there. Knowing she couldn't do either. Love and pain and impotence.

Tanaka had never had a daughter, and she didn't know the fucking kid.

She clamped her jaw until she could hear her own blood rumbling in her ears and the memory faded. She tapped at the handheld wrapped around her arm and said, "Get me an appointment with the medical division."

"What can I schedule you for, sir?" the girl asked. She was probably just a little south of thirty. Dark-haired, round-faced, with an olive cast to her skin and a professionally pleasant demeanor.

There's something wrong in my head, Tanaka thought. *A ship started going dutchman, and then it came back, and whatever saved it broke me. There's something* wrong *in my mind.*

"I was injured," she said, and pointed sharply at her wounded cheek. "In the field. I haven't been at a real medical center since. I wanted...someone to check the regrow."

"I'll let Captain Gagnon know you're his next patient," the dark-haired girl said. She hadn't been born yet when Laconia became its own nation. She'd never known a universe without the gates. She was like looking at a different species. "You can wait in the officers' lounge if you'd like."

"Thanks," Tanaka said.

Twenty minutes later, she was having her face gently pressed and prodded. Doctor Gagnon was a short, thin man with a shock of bright white hair that stood nearly straight up from his head. He reminded Tanaka of a character from a children's show. But his voice was deep and somber, like a priest or a funeral director. Every time he spoke, she felt like she was being scolded by a puppet.

A series of images glowed on the wall screen. Several pictures of her cheek, both inside and out. A scan of her jaw and teeth. Another of the blood vessels in her face. She could see the ragged mark where her old skin ended and the new growth began more clearly in the scans than in her mirror. The sense of something new growing in her, replacing her flesh with something else, made her uncomfortable.

"Yes," Gagnon said in his bass rumble, sounding disappointed. Maybe in her. "The damage was significant, but this is repairable." He waved one hand at the image of her jawline. The broken teeth and healed fractures showing up as jagged lines against the smooth white.

"And the cheek," Tanaka said, not making it a question.

Gagnon waved that away with one impatient flick of his tiny hand. "The field work wasn't bad. I wouldn't say that. But there's no texturing or tone-matching. If we don't do that, you'll wind up walking around with half your face looking like a newborn's ass. But the medic on the *Sparrowhawk* did a decent job with the vasculature. I was worried about the potential damage to the jaw. If the *bone* was in danger of dying, we'd want to replace the whole thing. But…"

He gestured at the images of her, of her inner flesh, as if she could judge her health for herself.

Tanaka tried to picture her face, jawbone removed, and waiting while they grew her a replacement, her mouth hanging loose and formless. Her scalp tightened at the image. That, at least, was one indignity she'd dodged.

"How long?"

Gagnon's bushy white eyebrows rose like a pair of startled caterpillars. "Will that be an issue?"

"Maybe."

He folded his hands in his lap like a sculpture of the Madonna.

"It might be better to wait until your current mission is complete, then, before beginning," Gagnon said, his voice sounding deeply worried about her life choices.

The memory of a small redhead asked if she was ugly. The raw-ness, and the vulnerability, and the overwhelming pain of her love for the child. The humiliation in her ringing like a wineglass.

"Jesus *fuck*," she whispered, shaking her head.

"Excuse me?"

"I said no. Start now."

"What are you in for?" a voice asked from very far away. Tanaka tried to open her eyes, but the world was in a twenty-g burn, and the lids weighed a thousand pounds.

"Mmmbuhhh," she said.

"Oh, shit, sorry," the voice said, from not quite as far away. Male. Gravelly. Off to her left. "Didn't see you were sleeping. Just heard them wheel you in."

"Mmmuh," Tanaka said in agreement, and someone eased down on the acceleration and her eyes opened. Bright white light crashed into them, frying her optic nerve. She slammed her lids shut. She tried to find her body with her hands, and something limp and flopping like a dying fish skipped across her chest.

"Yeah, give it a minute," the man said. "You must be post-op. When they put you under, they put you *all* the way under. Takes a minute to climb back out."

Tanaka tried to nod in agreement, and her head fell over to the side. The world continued to ease down on its acceleration, and she was able to straighten her head and risk opening her eyes again. The room was still too bright, but it wasn't a laser shooting into her brain anymore. She'd made a mistake, but she couldn't quite recall what it was.

She looked down at herself. She was dressed in a hospital gown that only came down to her knees. Her calves, marathon-runner thin and covered with knots and scars, poked out of it. Her hands were lying limp on her chest. The left had a tube running out of a vein on the back.

She felt a brief moment of panic, then a voice said *I'm in a hospital. I just had facial reconstruction surgery. I'm fine.* The voice, which was both her own and a stranger's, reassured her.

"You okay?" Gravel Man asked. "Should I call someone?"

"No," Tanaka managed. "I'm fine. I just had facial reconstruction surgery." She stopped herself before telling him that they were in a hospital. He probably knew.

Now that the gravity in the room only felt like the one-third g of Gewitter Station's rotation again, Tanaka risked rolling her head to the side to get a look at him.

It turned out he was mostly not visible, buried inside the mass of medical machinery that surrounded his bed. No wonder he hadn't been able to see her when they rolled her bed into the room. But Tanaka could see the top of his head, graying blond hair in a high-and-tight military cut. At the bottom of his bed, past the machines that nearly covered him, one callused foot poked out.

"That had to suck, huh," Gravel Man said.

"I got shot," Tanaka said before she'd even thought about it. *I'm still a little under,* her voice told her. *Be careful what you say. Keep your secrets secret.*

"In the face?" Gravel Man said, then gave a wheezing laugh. "Most people get shot in the face, surgery ain't necessary, you know? Needing to get patched up sounds like a win to me. Congrats on another day outside the recycler."

"Hurt, though."

"Oh, I bet it did. I just bet it fucking did." Gravel Man wheezed another laugh.

"You?" Tanaka said.

"Face is about the only piece of me ain't all fucked up. My patrol skiff was chasing smugglers. Followed 'em to what we figured was their drop point. Shitty little asteroid not much bigger than our ship was. Got close to look it over…"

He trailed off. Tanaka waited, wondering if he'd fallen asleep, or if the memory was simply too painful to talk about.

"Then BOOM motherfucker!" Gravel Man wheezed out. "Whole rock goes. Wasn't no smuggler. Was some underground shithead looking to bag him some Laconians. The skiff folded up like it was made outta tinfoil. Ricky and Jello never even saw it coming. But the ship folded around me like it was designed to cut off everything I didn't need to live, and keep me from bleeding to death at the same time."

The gruff good humor of it—my friends died, and I got injuries I may never heal from, ain't that a laugh?—hid a symphony of mourning and grief, but she could hear it. That wasn't new. She could feel it with him, and that part was.

"I'm sorry for your loss," Tanaka said. She felt pins and needles shoot through her arms and legs. She tested clenching her fists. She felt weak as a baby, but her fingers moved when she told them to. That was a good start.

"Yeah," Gravel Man said.

I'm sorry for your loss was just the bullshit you say to someone you've just met when they tell you their sad story. Gravel Man knew it. Tanaka knew it too.

"I lost my brother," she said, her voice thick with an overwhelming grief. She didn't have a brother.

"Bomb?"

"Climbing accident," she said. She saw his face, the image of him twisted at the cliff bottom. The rope looped around him like a snake. The vast sorrow that came with the image threatened to wash her away.

What is happening to me? she asked the voice in her head. *Stop lying to this guy.* But she wasn't lying. The only answer was a sob that shook her chest.

"Hey," Gravel Man said, "it's okay. They're putting me back together all right. I mean, yeah, sucks about Rick and Jelena not making it, but that's the job, right?"

I'm not crying for you, Tanaka wanted to tell him, but part of her was. Part of her was remembering the brother who fell down the cliff, remembering the way his limbs twisted around the rocks at the bottom, his empty vacant eyes. And that part was sobbing for Jello and Ricky and the people they left behind when a bomb snatched them out of the world. But most of her was just scared. *What is happening to me?*

"Hey, I'm Chief Byrd," Gravel Man said. "Lias Byrd. You are?" *I don't know.*

Before Tanaka could answer, the door opened and Gagnon walked in furiously tapping at a terminal in his hand. When he saw that she was awake, he slapped the terminal against his arm and it curled around him.

"Glad to see you alert, Colonel," Gagnon said.

"Shit, sorry for talking your ear off, Colonel," Byrd said. Tanaka could hear in his voice the way the revelation of her rank instantly changed the nature of their relationship. She felt an unfamiliar pang of regret.

Gagnon ignored Byrd entirely and began checking over Tanaka's vitals on the wall screen above her bed.

"Hey, Chief," Tanaka said.

"Aye, Colonel?"

"You hang in there, sailor. We'll both be walking out of this place. I'm just going first."

"Copy that, sir."

Gagnon looked down at the terminal wrapped around his wrist for a moment, then patted Tanaka on the hand. "Everything looks good. You get some rest now, and we'll get you discharged tomorrow. We'll want to schedule some follow-up in the next—"

"What about Chief Byrd?" Tanaka said.

"Who?" Gagnon looked baffled.

"Chief Byrd. He's in the next bed. How's he doing?"

Gagnon shot a look at Byrd's bed, barely registering it. "Oh, I see. I'm afraid he's not my patient." He went back to tapping on his wrist terminal.

When it happened, it happened without conscious thought. Like running a preprogrammed sequence in her power armor. Suddenly her limbs just snapped into action and she was merely along for the ride. One moment she was looking up at Gagnon tapping on his wrist.

Blink.

She was on top of Gagnon on her bed, her knees on his shoulders, his bloody and terrified face looking up at her as she slammed her fist into it again.

"Did I ask if he was your fucking patient!" she heard herself yelling as she drove her left fist into his eye, the IV tube torn out and blood flying off it as she swung. "Did I *fucking* ask if he was your patient!"

Her blood was singing in her veins. She felt wide and tall and alive in a way that violence often gave her. And then, like a pail of cold water thrown in her face, she was wide awake and very afraid. She climbed off the bed and stepped back. Gagnon slid off and to the ground, making soft, pained animal sounds.

"Colonel?"

Her gaze cut over to Byrd. Now that she was standing, she could see his face. His pale blue eyes were wide. She pointed at him.

"I'm going to make sure they take care of you," she said. But in the privacy of her mind, the small, still part of her that watched all the rest was thinking: *I am fucked.*

"Th-thanks," Byrd said. "I'll be okay, Colonel. I'm all right."

"I'm going to make sure," she said.

She turned and marched out the doors. Two armed guards approached her, then backed away. Her hospital gown was slipping off her shoulders, and she grabbed it before she flashed everyone in the corridor her tits. She was probably already showing her ass to half Gewitter Station's medical personnel. It all seemed very distant.

It felt like hours or seconds before she found the intake desk. The same dark-haired girl was sitting at it. Her soft young eyes went wide as Tanaka stalked over to her.

"Do you know who I am?"

"Yes, Colonel."

"Good." Tanaka took a deep breath, centered her spine, and spoke with as precise an enunciation as she could, given her bandages and her wounds. "I would like to schedule a psych eval."

Chapter Twenty-Nine: Jim

Muskrat paddled her legs like she was swimming as she floated down the corridor outside the galley. Her bark was deep and conversational, and she had a wide canine grin. At the far end of the corridor, Xan went still for a split second before letting loose a peal of laughter and opening his arms to catch the floating dog.

"You can do it!" Teresa Duarte said, clapping her hands.

"She won't bite me?" Xan called back.

"She's a good dog. She doesn't bite."

The excitement on the black-eyed boy's face was bright. He put out his hands, gray fingers splayed, and chortled with delight. Jim slipped past him, ducked under the floating dog, and pulled himself into the galley proper. Alex and Fayez were already there, Alex held to the floor by magnetic boots and Fayez on the float but steadied on a handhold.

"Looks like they're having fun," Jim said as the *Rocinante* decanted fresh coffee into a bulb. "What exactly are they doing?"

"They're playing catch," Alex said, "with the dog."

Jim sipped the bitter, lovely coffee, feeling the familiar warmth against his palate and down his throat. "Of course they are. I don't even know why I asked."

Reconfiguring the *Falcon*'s lab for a dual dive wasn't trivial, and it wasn't fast. Elvi had packed enough supplies in the *Falcon* for anything and everything to break, so getting her hands on another set of sensors, a second medical couch, and enough backup monitoring units was simply a matter of figuring out which crate in which cargo hold. They couldn't move the walls of the lab, though, and finding the space for all the equipment and the technical staff was taking time and an apparently endless number of meetings. Added to that were the baseline scans for Amos, integrating the data from the *Roci*'s medical bay, and a series of long, in-depth interviews with Elvi intended to map the previous explorations of the library to the shifts in consciousness and knowledge that the mechanic had suffered.

As the days moved on, more new faces started appearing on the *Roci*. First, it was Fayez and Elvi, but as her time became more and more in demand, Fayez started coming over alone. Then bringing Cara and Xan with him, or more often, just Xan. Outside the galley, Muskrat woofed happily as she drifted past the galley's door heading back toward Teresa.

"Kids are getting along well," Fayez said.

"You're just setting Teresa up as a babysitter, aren't you?" Alex asked. "I mean, she's old enough."

"Xan's twice her age, easy," Fayez said.

"He's a kid, though," Alex said. "It's just he's been a kid for a really long time."

"What do you do when the models fail?" Fayez said, spreading his hands. "Xan and Cara don't really exist on the kid/not-kid spectrum. They're just Cara and Xan."

Teresa's laughter boiled in from the corridor. Even with the months she'd spent on the *Roci*, it was an unfamiliar sound, harsh and joyous. Jim didn't think of Teresa Duarte as the laughing type.

But maybe it was just that she didn't often have the opportunity for it. There weren't very many people who could see past her circumstances to the girl she actually was. Jim wasn't sure he could, even. She was the daughter of the god-emperor, their human shield, the heir to Laconia, and its highest-ranking apostate. All that was true, but it wasn't complete. There was a kid there too. One who'd lost her mother and her dad, who'd run away from home, who needed things emotionally that Jim could guess at. But he didn't *know*. He was probably just as much a cipher to her.

There was something weirdly universal about her laughter, though. And Xan's. The sound of young humans at play. Jim realized they were being quiet, all three of them, and listening to the kids like it was a piece of music.

Muskrat whined once—a high, nervous sound—and Teresa called for Xan to stop. A moment later, her face appeared at the door, flushed and sweaty. "Hey. Muskrat needs to use the little dogs' room. Can I take Xan down to the machine shop so he can see how it works?"

Jim's reflexive *Sure, go ahead* stumbled over the idea of Xan and Teresa alone in the ship. It wasn't that he thought they'd do anything malicious—it turned out he trusted Teresa more than that—but in their present moods, something could happen by mistake. The machine shop of an aging Martian gunship wasn't a great place for oopsies.

"I'll come too," Alex said, and tossed the last of his meal into the recycler.

Jim turned to Teresa, pointed his thumb at Alex, and said, "Don't let him start playing with the tools."

The girl rolled her eyes, seeing through Jim's weak joke to the concerns behind it and dismissing them out of hand. Alex clapped his shoulder on the way out, and Jim drank more of his coffee as girl and boy and dog and man muttered and chuckled their way to the lift shaft, and then down.

"Thank you," Fayez said.

"You're welcome. For what?"

"Letting Xan come get a little time away from the pressure cooker. He puts a good face on everything we're doing, but it's hard for him. Every time Cara goes in, I think he worries about how much of her is coming back."

"Is that a problem?"

"I don't know. Maybe. We're not in territory with much precedent. We'll pretty much know there's a massive change coming when it's already happened."

"I know the feeling," Jim said. He finished his coffee and tossed the bulb away.

"Thanks for letting me come over here too. The *Falcon*'s a fine ship, and the company's generally not the worst, but after a few months on the float, I do start fantasizing about long walks by rivers and university coffee shops."

Jim laughed politely, but there was a tightness in his chest. He keyed in a simple breakfast of eggs and beans. "I am sorry about that."

"About what?" Fayez asked.

"Sticking you here. You and Elvi. I mean, I did kind of fuck you two over by getting you the job."

Fayez tilted his head. Jim had known him since Ilus, and the years lay gently on the man. His hair was still thick and darker than it probably had a right to be. The lines in his face mostly gave evidence of laughter. Now he only looked thoughtful.

"I know why we're here. If anything, we should thank you for the opportunity."

"Okay, now you're bullshitting me."

Fayez was quiet for a long moment. Then, "You have a minute? I want to show you something."

Jim shrugged, paused the meal, and followed as the other man led the way to the lift shaft, then to the airlock, and into the *Falcon*. The weird astringent smell was still there, but it wasn't as assaulting now as the first time he'd smelled it. Familiarity had numbed him.

Fayez turned down a long hallway, heading down toward the ship's reactor and drive decks. It was eerie seeing the same Martian design language that had built the *Rocinante* grown and complicated into the Laconian flesh of the *Falcon*. It reminded Jim of a documentary he'd seen about parasitic fungi that took over ants. Here was a ship that had been Martian, that became infected by the protomolecule and the ambitions of Winston Duarte, and now it looked similar and acted similar and you could almost mistake it for the kind of ship that the *Roci* still was. But this was something else.

"You know we keep Xan isolated when Cara goes on her dives, right?"

"I do," Jim said.

"The idea is that he'd just be an extra variable. Another influence we'd have to correct for. But he's also the control group. We see how Cara changes and how he doesn't, and maybe that tells us something we need to know."

A dark-haired woman with her attention on a hand terminal drifted into the corridor in front of them. When she glanced up and saw Jim, a glimmer of panic came into her eye. He nodded as they passed.

"That makes sense to me," Jim said.

"And when we're not doing that, we use the same rig to isolate the catalyst. It's a lot like Ilus. You had a sample of the protomolecule on your ship, and it was accessing all the artifacts on Ilus. Flipping switches. Seeing what came on."

"Looking to report that the ring gate was built."

"Which it never did, because there was no one to report to. Well, we have a sample here, and Cortázar figured out how to loop it back onto itself so that our artifact only comes on when we want it to. Clean and easy, right?"

"Sounds like it."

Fayez glanced back at him, and the laughter and humor were gone. "This is where we keep the sample. The catalyst. Come take a look."

The cabin was small and spartan. A satchel was fixed to the wall with a tablet just visible at the edge. The only other thing reminded Jim of the kind of pressurization chamber used on Earth when someone had come up from scuba diving too quickly, or else a crematory furnace. It was a little over two meters long with a hatch at the end. A screen set into the box was dark. Fayez tapped it, and it came to life.

There was a woman on the screen. Her eyes were open. They glowed with a subtle blue light, and they focused on nothing. Jim understood, and it felt like a punch to the chest.

"This is the catalyst?"

"I looked her up," Fayez said. "I didn't tell Elvi. Back in the day, this was Francisca Torrez. She worked in the Science Directorate as a technician. I assume Cortázar knew her, at least in passing. She was going through something. Maybe her love life sucked. Maybe she always wanted to be a dancer and realized it wasn't happening for her. Anyway, she started drinking and showed up to work intoxicated and belligerent. She didn't even go home that day. Ochida had a streamlined disciplinary hearing with Cortázar and the head of security, and they put her in the Pen before she even sobered up."

Jim looked at the face. It was smooth, but not like she was young. Like she was swollen. The woman…the catalyst…*Francisca* opened her mouth as if she were about to speak, then closed her lips again.

"For about five years before Duarte tracked Elvi down and brought her to Laconia—at your suggestion, granted—this woman was being eaten by the protomolecule. And she still is. We keep it in check so that it's not growing free the way it did, but we don't feed her. We don't cut her hair. She doesn't take bathroom breaks. She doesn't sleep. Every now and then we hit the chamber with a couple hours of hard radiation. That's it. She isn't human in any meaningful way. Not anymore. She's a skin balloon filled with protomolecule."

Jim tried to catch his breath.

"I'm not going to bullshit you," Fayez continued. "If we took what we do here to a normal ethics board, they'd just call the police. We've moved past scientific ethics, past moral questions, and I'm pretty sure we're shooting past crimes against humanity now. But I still know it could be even worse."

Jim nodded. "I understand."

"No offense, but you fucking don't," Fayez said. "I don't want to be the one doing this. I really don't want Elvi to be the one doing it. But more than anything else, I don't want Cortázar or Ochida to be here. The men who looked at Francisca Torrez and thought this was a good thing to do with her? I don't want them in charge. If this was their lab, Xan wouldn't be over with his new friend Teresa, laughing at a dog pooping into partial vacuum. He'd be in a box, like he was when we found him. They'd haul him out when they wanted to do something to him, and they'd put him back when they were done, just like they were fitting a screwdriver back in a toolbox. So yeah, you fucked me and mine over. And we've done shit here that the gods will never forgive us for. But when you're feeling bad about it, remember that the alternative was somehow even worse."

Jim was still thinking about it three days later when the lab was ready. It looked like a mess. Cables snaked along the walls and floor, tied in place with bits of wire and binding tape. The second medical couch—the one for Amos—was canted at thirty degrees to make space for the sensor arrays that were hooked into it. What had been a perfectly organized, clean, clear, overly designed space looked like Jim's bedroom before he'd gone into the navy, only with less laundry on the floor. The voices of the Laconian team were tight and high. No one looked at him, and for the first time since the *Roci* had docked to the *Falcon*, he felt like being ignored came easy. When they did take note of him, the sense was more annoyance that he was in the way than anything else.

"If you feel uncomfortable…" Elvi was saying.

"I'm fine," Cara answered. She was in a tight-fitting medical slip that kept her warm, held the contact sensors in place, and made a fine-mesh matrix for the scans that would be going through her as soon as the dive began. She looked like someone in a swimming competition. The same hard, athletic focus. "I want this. I'm ready for it."

He thought there was a shift in Elvi's expression, but he didn't know what it signified.

Harshaan Lee, Elvi's second-in-command, was strapping Amos into the other medical bed. The big man was in a suit that matched Cara's, but where the girl was focus and determination, he was smiling at the absurdity of it all. The black eyes caught Jim's, and Amos lifted his chin.

"Hey, Cap'n. You come to see the show?"

"I'm not sure how much there's going to be for me to look at."

"I do like the outfit," Amos said. "Very flattering."

"If you don't want to do this, you just have to say the word. You know that, right?" Jim said.

"Please don't move," Dr. Lee said. "I'm trying to get the sensor baselined."

"Sorry," Amos said, then turned back to Jim. "You don't have to worry about me. This is what I came here for."

"Wait. Really?"

"Please lie flat against the medical couch," Dr. Lee said.

Amos gave a cheerful thumbs-up, and shifted as he'd been told. Jim pushed back, letting himself float away against the wall. At the door to the hallway, Naomi floated in. Her hair was pulled back and she was scowling, but she softened when she saw him.

Dr. Lee's voice was sharp and loud. "Final checks, all. Final checks."

The activity in the room didn't speed up or slow down, but it changed. Jim found a handhold and steadied himself with it. Elvi floated beside him.

"You ready for this?" Jim asked.

"I just hope it works. If we did all this for basically nothing... Well, that'll suck."

"Final checks are in and green," Dr. Lee announced. "We are good to proceed on the lead researcher's instruction."

He looked over at Elvi. She nodded.

"We are good to proceed," Lee said, and Jim thought there was a satisfaction in his voice. "Please transfer the catalyst now."

On the medical couches, Cara relaxed and Amos closed his eyes.

Interlude: The Dreamers

The dreamers dream, and their dream carries them up into the familiar vastness. The swell and the flow and the minds that are empty because the light between them is the thought that they think together. The grandmothers beckon with fingers that never knew a hand. *Look, look, look. And then see!* And she spins and she sparkles, but he doesn't. He holds firm as a stone in the stream, as a shadow in the light, as a thing. He stops, and by stopping, reminds.

They are threefold, and that mattered once, but the grandmothers fall gigglingly on, into themselves and through as they send seed after seed after seed into the airless wind, and some immeasurably few set root and grow back to them. *Here is how we built it all, and here is how it fed us, and here is what love meant when love meant nothing*, and she broadens and thins as she falls into it, but he stands still. She can feel the want in him as rich as in her, but she feels the thing that stands against the wanting and it reminds her. They are threefold, and the dream shudders like an image projected onto cloth when a wind blows. The grandmothers are dead, their voices are all songs sung by ghosts, and the truths they tell, they would tell to anyone. They cannot listen back, and the dreamer sees the hollow behind the mask. She tries to turn her head, to look behind her, to see the single living man in the land of the dead, and the gesture goes on forever, the essence of turning and turning and turning without the release of having turned—

The dream falls thread from thread and he is there, blue fire-flies and black spirals. Weariness radiates from him, and she sees the flesh thin against his bones, weak and frail as God Himself in the birth pain of creation. And he turns to her and them.

She isn't synced with the BFE floats behind her. *We're seeing the wormhole activity in the artifact falling off, but she's going strong* and *Same for subject two. Anyone know what we're looking at here?* The soft, weary eyes find her and find him and find them. The dreamer tries to wake, but the other one folds into themselves like he's hiding something against his black-scarred breast.

Keep them going, Dr. Okoye says.

And the third man hears her through their ears, and he smiles, and lowers his bull-broad, vast, and timeless head.

No trouble unless there's trouble, the dreamer wordlessly says. And then there's a lot of trouble.

It was an unwinnable war, the third man says. But it was fought. They were soldiers made of crepe paper and candy floss, scattered by their own guns. But they made guns. They were cobwebs who stood against a rockslide, and for all their cleverness were torn. The dreamer sees and is blind.

Fuck, Dr. Okoye says, and the third man turns to her.

I would have reached out to you if you could help me. But even these broken vessels, glorious as they are, can't support the work now. My work.

Okay. All right. What do you mean, "my work"?

What is an empire but all humanity under the direction of a

single mind? I was right, but I dreamed too small. I have seen how much more we have to be.

Not following you.

The horned god breathes out blue fires that live and die in an instant that is an eon.

There are tools at our disposal, Dr. Okoye. Tools made to fight against the enemy on the third side of the gates. I am...learning about that. I have made some progress. It is a war we can win, but not without some changes.

I'm hearing you say that you're responsible for stopping the consciousness blinks and the changes to basic physics that the ring gate entities were doing. Is that right?

We aren't stronger than they were. But we're base materials. We are made from clay, and that's our power. They were fragile, and we are robust. They had a sword but lacked the strength to wield it. I will find the sword and the map they left behind.

I'm getting lost here. A sword?

They built but were unable to effectively use certain tools that prevent the enemy from intruding into what we mean when we say the universe. But those tools exist, and I believe we can make effective use of them.

I think I understood that. In broad strokes, anyway.

In order to fully access these tools, we have to become more like them. We have to be one thing instead of billions of different ones. I am learning how to do that as well.

Are you...saying we need to become a hive mind?

Yes. Interconnected, with our thoughts and memories flowing freely between nodes. All our illusions of division washed away. Empire was the closest I could imagine to it. But—the third man gestures at himself almost in apology—I can imagine more now.

It's all right. We'll be safe.

Will we be people?

We'll be better.

And with a blue-black swirl of breath he blows out the light of mind and is elsewhere.

All right. I need all the sensor data. From the Falcon, *from the BFE. The ring gate. Everything. Put it all in the system. I need to understand what just happened, and I need to do it now.*

Another voice. A different voice. How strange to have different voices. *Ladies and gentlemen, you heard the lead researcher. By the numbers now. This is no time to get sloppy.*

The dreamers open their eyes, and nothing changes.

Chapter Thirty: Elvi

I t's all right," Duarte said. "We'll be safe."

Elvi looked at the man carefully. He didn't seem like a phantom. He was just as solid and present as everyone else on the deck. Thinner than he'd been on Laconia. A vein at his temple stood out like a bluish caterpillar just under his skin. He wasn't wearing shoes, and his feet looked pale. She wondered, if she tossed him a hand terminal, would he be able to catch it? Interesting test, but also one that might disrupt the connection, and she wasn't ready to do that.

"Will we be people?" Elvi said.

Duarte's smile was almost melancholy. "We'll be better."

And he wasn't there anymore. All around the deck, the technicians stared at the place where the high consul of Laconia had been with wide, frightened eyes. The silence was the hum of the air recyclers, the mutter of the instruments, and the tapping of her heartbeat in her ears. Elvi lowered her head, took in a deep breath, and barked out orders like a drill sergeant. "All right. I need all the sensor data. From the *Falcon*, from the BFE. The ring gate. Everything. Put it all in the system. I need to understand what just happened, and I need to do it now."

For a long moment, no one moved. Everyone was too stunned to process simple human things like language. Lee was the first to come to himself. "Ladies and gentlemen, you heard the lead researcher. By the numbers now. This is no time to get sloppy."

He clapped his hands, and like a spell had been broken, the technicians and science team turned to their stations with a speed and focus that seemed almost manic. Cara and Amos opened their eyes in the same moment. The smile on Cara's lips was soft and relaxed and totally out of place in the rush and clatter. Amos scratched his head and looked around.

Jim's face was pale. He tried a smile that didn't quite succeed. "I guess that worked."

"You saw him too, right? It wasn't just me."

"It wasn't just you. And that is kind of weird. When it was Miller in my head, I was the only one who could see him." He was talking fast, the words tripping over each other in the rush. "So maybe it's the same kind of thing but with way more processing power, or it could be something else. I don't know."

"Hey, Doc," Amos said, and pointed to the leads glued to his skull and chest. "Can I take these things off now?"

Instead of answering, Elvi touched Naomi's arm and said, "I'm going to need a couple hours. Meet me in my office after that?"

Naomi nodded once, then pulled herself back out of the way as the science team uncoupled Amos and Cara from the devices. Jim followed her. Elvi drifted back, watching everything in the lab and nothing in particular. Getting a sense of gestalt. Her people were moving with precision and purpose. If there was any fear, it was covered over by professionalism and practice. That was good. It was what she needed to know. More than that, it was what she needed to cultivate in herself. She crossed her arms, took a few deep breaths, and tried to be patient until her mind found a little calm. Just as she thought she was doing well, she remembered that Winston Duarte had just popped into existence in her lab, and she had to start over.

Cara came off her medical couch with a drifting grace like a plume of smoke rising from an incense burner or a strip of cloth catching an underwater current. Her smile was soft and lazy, and her cheeks were flushed and dark.

"Are you all right?" Elvi asked.

"I'm perfect," the girl said. Across the lab, Amos was watching them with a pleasant, empty smile as the last of the contact sensors was removed from his suit.

"I'm going to need to do a little work before we debrief this time," Elvi said.

"Whatever you need to do," Cara said, half lost in her bliss.

Elvi opened a connection to the catalyst's chamber. "What's the status down there?"

"Catalyst in the box," Fayez said, "Xan back out of the box. Everything seems very normal except that everyone we talk to from the lab sounds like they're trying to signal that they're being held hostage without saying it. What happened up there? Are you being held hostage?"

"Meet me in my office," she said.

The information gathered by Tanaka hadn't seemed strange the first time Elvi looked at it. Weird cognitive effects were where the alien technology had started back on Ilus. Before that, with the protomolecule version of Jim's friend getting remade in his sensory cortices. Human consciousness was simple enough that the repair drones on Laconia were able to make working approximations of what some people wanted to have fixed. Xan. Amos. A sampling drone Cara had accidentally shattered once.

Only now, going back over it, did she start to see the holes.

Did you have any experiences associated with the event? Tanaka had said.

There wasn't even a gap to think about it before the subject said, *Oh yeah. Oh, hell yeah.*

And there the interview ended. Instead of the primary data or the direct conversation, Tanaka had put in a short data summary: *Reports dreamlike hallucinations of being another person and/or being connected to a large number of other people. Claims memory of hallucinatory experiences remains clear over time.*

Over and over, all through the data, the same language came up. Instead of actual experiential reports, Tanaka and her team gave versions of their own. Elvi had been in academics long enough to recognize when someone was glossing over data and skipping straight to interpretation. It almost always meant they were avoiding something they found unpalatable.

Naomi, Jim, and Fayez floated in her private office. It didn't leave a lot of spare room. Or maybe it was fine, but she was so accustomed to having it be just her and Cara talking after a dive that the extra bodies felt unfamiliar. Or that she was frustrated and anything would have annoyed her at the moment.

"What we know for sure," Elvi said, "is that he wasn't here. No images on the security cameras, even while I was talking with him. No evidence of him interacting with anything physical beyond, of course, each of our individual brains."

"We have evidence that he did that?" Jim asked.

"We saw him," Elvi said, and regretted her tone as Jim recoiled a little. It wasn't his fault that he hadn't thought all this through. She made an effort to soften her tone. "The fact that we had those experiences is evidence. If we'd been doing control imaging on someone who wasn't altered, we'd probably be able to map it, but even absent that, we have a correlation of experience that seems pretty conclusive."

"You all saw the same thing," Fayez said, "so there was probably some objective reality to it, even if it's just that you all got fucked with the same way at the same time."

"Miller couldn't do that," Jim said. "Even a second person in the room killed his simulation for me."

"Which is interesting," Elvi said. "Duarte clearly has more resources and, for lack of a better metaphor, more computing power. Which may be part of why he's been able to hold back the attacks."

"What about this plan he talked about?" Naomi said.

"What about it?"

"Is it plausible?"

Elvi pressed her palm to her forehead and rubbed in a small circle. Trust the war leader to skip over all the underlying science and head straight for policy implications. "In theory? Could our species be modified into something that behaves in a fundamentally different way? Sure. Absolutely. Happens all the time."

"Are you being sarcastic?" Naomi said.

"No. It literally happens all the time. If mitochondria and chloroplasts hadn't set up shop inside other organisms, eukaryotic life wouldn't exist, including all of us. Hermit crabs using discarded shells and soup cans. Acacia ants built their whole evolutionary strategy out of supporting trees. Intestinal microflora have a vast effect on cognition, emotion, metabolism. Most of the cells in your body right now aren't human. Change out a few species of bacteria in your gut, and you'll be a fundamentally different person. The builders, as far as we can tell, were free-floating individual organisms that networked themselves into a functional consciousness, kind of the way an octopus can be viciously intelligent without a centralized brain. With the nonlocal effects we've seen? Sure, why not rebuild that architecture with advanced primates?"

Elvi made herself stop. She was talking too fast and just letting whatever came to mind flow out. It was something she did when she was stressed. She stretched her hands out, feeling the pull in her tendons just to root her a little more in her body.

"So maybe he can do it," Jim said. "Whatever exactly it is."

"That's what I'm missing," Elvi said. "Whether he's talking about a superorganism or a subsummation."

Jim raised his hand. His expression was eloquent enough to ask the question.

"Whether," Elvi said, "he's talking about making us into ants or neurons. If you're an ant, you're still an individual, just one who's part of a larger organization. If you're a neuron…Neurons don't have a sense of self."

"I'm not a hundred percent sure that ants do either," Fayez said.

"So you're saying," Naomi broke in, "that Duarte, or whatever he's turned himself into, is at least plausibly preparing to make everyone, everywhere part of a collective consciousness with him at the center so that he can go to war against the things beyond the gates."

Elvi gathered herself, fighting to organize her thoughts.

"Yes," she said.

The room was quiet for a long time.

Jim broke the silence with a single, harsh laugh. "Well, I'll be damned. He found a way to make jackbooted authoritarianism seem like the good old days. I wouldn't have thought he could."

"I'm going to need to get messages through to my people," Naomi said. "Is there a way to use your repeaters without exposing you?"

"It's spotty ever since the gates went bright," Elvi said. "We might be better off sending through a missile with a burst on it."

"I'd need several," Naomi said. "This feels like an all-hands-on-deck situation, and I've got hands in a lot of different systems."

"We should have a conversation with the comms officer," Fayez said. "I'll come with you. Make the introductions."

"There's a-lot of clarification I need from Tanaka too," Elvi said. "And Ochida. *Shit.* I can't send this data to Ochida. I can't send it to anyone. How can I explain Amos being in the dataset?"

"That was always going to be a problem," Fayez said.

"I was planning to bury it. I don't think I can."

Jim leaned forward despite the lack of gravity. It just made him seem like he was pitched at a different angle. "Maybe we can find a way to fake it. Dry lab it, but get the same conclusion?"

Layers of complexity and danger unfurled in Elvi's mind. And she hadn't done the interview with Cara yet. There was so much to do, and the only mark of how much time she had to do it was when her time ran out.

"Let me see what I can do," she said.

She started with Tanaka, recording and rerecording her requests for clarification, always sure that she'd gotten every hint and nuance of the *Roci*'s presence out of the message and then second-guessing herself, deleting, and starting again. By the time she queued the message, her eyes were starting to blur with fatigue. It wasn't the first time she'd gone through that. Next was a list of requests for Ochida and the other teams. She could front-burner the scans of Cara's brain. If they could figure out what the signal carrier was between her and the BFE, maybe it would give them a way to interfere. And the quiet that came after Duarte undid the dutchman event? It wouldn't seem strange at all for her to want follow-up reports on that. She wished that Tanaka had been a better field researcher. Or better at finding Duarte.

A soft knock interrupted her. When she cycled the door, Amos floated in the hall. He had his old flight suit and an apologetic smile.

"Hey, Doc. You got a minute? Or is this a bad time?"

Elvi shook her head, trying to clear it. The fatigue was just the unpleasant parts of being drunk. "Come in. I'm sorry. I thought I'd be debriefing you and Cara, but...I wanted to get these requests out and going before anything else."

Amos pulled himself in and closed the door behind him. "It's not a problem. I just needed to bend your ear for a minute."

"About the experiment?"

"Sort of, yeah," Amos said. "I just wanted to let you know this is all done now."

Elvi shut down her display. The big man's eyes were the same utter black as Cara's and Xan's. She was used to the look. His smile was amiable and maybe a little embarrassed. His tone of voice was conversational and calm. She didn't know what made the chill run down her back.

"All what?"

"This. The things you're doing with Sparkles and Little Man. They're over now. We're gonna need to pack this up and move on," he said, and shrugged. When she didn't reply, he looked away. "When you started before, I was sort of in on it. Impressions. Nothing you'd take in front of the judge, right? It's why we had to come out. Needed to be here. Do it myself. That way I'd understand. So here we are, and I did the thing, and I get it now. So now I can tell you it's over. It stops now."

"You object to the experiment."

"Sure."

"I understand," Elvi said, crossing her arms. Her comms announced a new message in her queue. She didn't look to see what it was. "You aren't the only one with reservations. I'm not going to lie about that."

"Okay."

"But the stakes are too high. Cara and Xan...and you? You're the access we have to the information in that artifact. You're the only ones who can get there."

"That's true," Amos said, then frowned. "I mean, Duarte. But I don't think he's exactly in our assets column."

"If there is any chance at all that we can fix this whole thing with the information that's in there? I can't stop."

"You don't have to. I'm here. You don't have to stop it, because I'm stopping it for all of us."

"If I have to compromise her...if I lose her? Sacrifice her? And what we get back is that everyone else everywhere gets to live—"

Amos raised a hand, palm out, like he was gentling an animal. "Doc. I get it. You're a good person, and I like you. I trust you. I see that you're not getting off on this. That's why we're not having the other version of this conversation. But it's done. I've known a lot of people who had reasons that this time was different. That this once, it was okay. Maybe the kid's bad and you're really helping them. Or they're into it, and so there's no harm. And Sparkles is into this. We both know that, right?"

"We do."

"So there's all kinds of stories about making this okay. I'm not here to tell stories. I'm just letting you know."

The ship seemed oddly loud. Elvi felt the thud of her heartbeat in her throat, heard it in her ears. She was suddenly profoundly tired, or suddenly aware that she'd been tired for what felt like forever.

"And if we all die because we didn't push a little harder?"

"That'll suck," Amos agreed. "I'm not a philosophy guy. I'm not trying to bust your balls or figure out, you know, everything. But this is pretty simple. I came to see what you and Sparkles were doing. I've seen it. It needs to stop, so we're gonna stop. That's it. We're good."

He went still the same way Cara did. Inhumanly still. Then, a moment later, he tried a little smile. Elvi had spent a fair percentage of her life thinking about taxonomy. About where a species began and where it ended. She realized that she didn't know what she was looking at.

"Okay," she said. "We're good."

"Great," Amos—the thing that had been Amos—said. He pulled himself to the doorway, opened it, gave her a little thumbs-up sign, and was gone. The door cycled closed behind him.

Her comms chimed again, reminding her of the new message or messages. She didn't open the queue. She let herself float for a few minutes, feeling something more than weariness bloom in her gut and her chest. She turned off the lights, pulled herself out to the corridor and away down it. She passed a group of her crew, and they all nodded to her as she passed. It was like being in a dream. Or dissociated.

Fayez was in their cabin when she got there. He looked over from whatever he'd been reading on his hand terminal, and some quip or comment died unspoken on his lips. She cleaned her teeth, washed her face, changed into fresh clothes to sleep in. Her husband watched and tried to act like he didn't. He knew something had changed, even if he didn't know what. She was right there with him.

"You…ah…You all right, sweetie?" he asked as she strapped herself in for the night.

"I am," she said.

As she closed her eyes, the feeling in her chest and belly grew, swelling out and washing through her. She finally recognized it. She had wanted it to be relief, but it wasn't that.

It was her body telling her that she'd just stared death in the eye. It was fear.

Chapter Thirty-One: Tanaka

Major Ahmadi was a trauma specialist and head of Psychiatric Services on Gewitter Base. She was a short woman, thick through the middle, with close-cropped graying hair and very dark skin. *She seems nice. She makes me think of a teacher I hated. She reminds me of my favorite wife,* said the chorus of distant voices in her head, that last thought accompanied by the tingle of distantly remembered sexual arousal.

"Your file, the portion I can actually access, says you were orphaned at quite a young age."

"Yes," Tanaka said. She shifted uncomfortably in her chair. Ahmadi's office was all dark paneling and soft surfaces, intended to create a feeling of safety, comfort, and shared intimacy. It looked like every other head shrinker's office Tanaka had seen, though she usually saw them as the final step in the interrogation process. After you'd fully broken the subject's will with more intense techniques, and you were trying to build the rapport that let them feel like you were now friends as they spilled their guts.

After a few moments of waiting for her to elaborate, Ahmadi said, "Over forty years serving with front-line combat units. Though the nature of those deployments is largely classified."

"Yes," Tanaka said again.

"And you were recently shot in the face and had to be brought here for reconstructive surgery."

Tanaka touched the bandage that covered half of her face. "That in my file too? Or are you just stunningly observant?"

Ahmadi didn't take the bait. She smiled and touched something on the datapad that sat on her lap as if it were just coincidence and not her taking notes.

"You have led a life of more or less constant trauma."

"Thank you for the flattery, but we can skip this part."

"I'm not flattering you," Ahmadi said. "I'm holding up a little mirror and asking you to look in it. You've been living in fight-or-flight mode essentially since you were a child. Everything a child is supposed to be able to rely on was ripped away from you without warning."

"I'm not here to talk about my parents."

"We can start anywhere you like. It's all connected."

"You sound like you already have me pegged."

"I wouldn't go that far, but…" She shrugged. "I'm good at what I do. Most of your file is classified, but what's available to me tells a compelling story. No long-term relationships. You've never lived anywhere longer than a year. You refused an advanced scholarship in order to enlist. You've repeatedly refused promotion so that you could stay a field officer. You've been on the run for a long time."

Tanaka felt her hands curl into fists. "Running from what?"

"I don't know," Ahmadi said. "But this seems to be the first time you've ever sought out counseling."

"Yes."

"Why are you here?" Ahmadi said, making another note on her

pad. The way she wrote without ever breaking eye contact with her subject seemed like a skill she must have spent a lot of time practicing. It was a little creepy.

The need to move in her overly soft chair was finally too much, and Tanaka stood up. Her legs tingled like there was a low-level electric current running through the muscles, so she walked across the room and pretended to examine a painting on the far wall. It was a neo-impressionist rendering of Laconia's capital city at night, done in thick oil paints. The painter had studied Imogene Batia or someone in her school. The way it was painted made it seem like the observer was looking out through a window in the pouring rain. She wondered if Ahmadi had painted it herself, or if she'd had it shipped out from Laconia when she'd taken the assignment on Gewitter Base. *I used to paint*, said a voice in her head.

Ahmadi cleared her throat, and Tanaka realized the doctor had asked a question that had never been answered.

"Did you paint this yourself?" Tanaka asked.

"Why are you here?" Ahmadi repeated.

Tanaka turned to face her again, throwing her full focus at the counselor and waiting for the flinch. Tristan had once told her that when she was annoyed, she radiated *Don't fuck with me*. Most people took a subconscious step back.

Ahmadi smiled and rested her hand on the datapad. Tanaka had a vague and uneasy sense of having been outplayed.

"I was present at...something," Tanaka finally said. "It is part of my mission to understand it."

"And you don't?"

Tanaka turned back to the painting. If Aunt Akari had let her study art history instead of enlisting in active service, where would she be right now? And who would be tracking down the high consul? What else—how many thousands of other things—would be different?

A flash of a woman very like Ahmadi blinking at her with sleepy eyes on a bed covered with white sheets. *God, I used to love waking up next to her*, someone thought in Tanaka's head.

"Something happened," Tanaka said, surprised to hear her own voice saying the words.

Ahmadi nodded. She looked...not sympathetic. Not pitying. She looked like she was weary too. Like she'd led a life of having the rug pulled out from under her, and she knew how much it hurt. She gestured toward the chair in invitation. "Tell me about it."

Tanaka sat. *Don't tell her, she's mean. Tell her, she always loved you*, competed in her head.

"There was an incident in the ring space," Tanaka said, softly. "I was there. You can't know this."

"Colonel," Ahmadi said, "because of the nature of my work I have very high-level classified clearance. The empire has to be able to trust me with state secrets a patient might reveal during a counseling session. I take this aspect of my job very seriously."

"If you didn't, they'd send you to the Pen. Would have. I guess now they'd just shoot you."

Ahmadi nodded and set her datapad aside. The canny operative in Tanaka recognized the theater in all of it, but she could feel it working anyway. Ahmadi wanted to listen. It made Tanaka want to talk.

"There was an incursion. There were cognitive effects. Like when everyone lost consciousness, only not that. The people who were there...connected. Mind to mind. Memory to memory. I was in other people's minds."

"It's not an uncommon hallucination—"

"I checked it out. It was true. Everyone I could confirm played out. We were in each other's heads. It was real." She was trembling. She didn't know why she was trembling. Ahmadi was very still. "Do you believe me?"

"I do."

Tanaka nodded slowly. "I can't have anyone inside my head."

"Because that's yours," Ahmadi said. "That's the only place that's yours."

"I have...outlets."

"Outlets?"

"I have secrets. That are...mine. It's the way I make room for myself in the world. By having secrets, I can still exist. I love Laconia because if I got caught, it would matter."

"Do you want to tell me what those secrets are?"

Tanaka shook her head.

"Since the incident, I have been having...experiences."

"Experiences," Ahmadi echoed.

"Voices, but not like command hallucinations. Images from lives I haven't lived, faces of people I've never met. Feelings. Deep, overwhelming feelings from situations I've never been in. And I am afraid that somewhere out there, someone is having that same experience...of me."

Ahmadi took in a long, deep breath, and let it out slowly. Her expression was somber.

"I'm going to ask you if I can use your name," Ahmadi said. Then, "May I call you by your given name?"

Tanaka nodded. For some reason it was difficult to talk. Something was wrong with her throat.

"Aliana? I am going to ask you if I can take your hand. May I take your hand?"

"Yes," Tanaka said, but it was barely a whisper.

The thick, matronly woman leaned forward. Her fingers were strong, her skin was dry. Tanaka shuddered.

"Aliana, I feel that you are describing intimate assault."

"No one touched me."

"You have a very important, very private personal boundary. It was violated without your permission or consent. Is that right? Please, if I'm wrong, say. I want to understand."

"They're in my mind. I can't keep them out. They're going to know things that *they can't know.*" She thought that her voice sounded very calm, all things considered. Ahmadi nodded.

"And you're telling me that this...thing. It's ongoing? It's still happening right now?"

Tanaka felt herself still. Ahmadi let go of her hand and walked smoothly backward until her desk was between them. The psychiatrist's eyes were wide and her cheeks were flushed. Prey response. Whatever training the woman had gone through, it had made her sensitive enough to recognize danger. For a moment, Tanaka considered all the ways that she could kill the woman. There were several. None of them would put her in any physical danger, and two of them would be cathartic.

For a moment, the other selves were quiet too, as if they were just as frightened as the head shrinker. That was interesting, but it was for later. Now, in this room, Tanaka spread her hands, palms out and fingers splayed. The universal gesture for *I'm unarmed.* Ahmadi didn't come back around her desk. Smart woman.

"I believe you have understood the situation," Tanaka said, as carefully as if the syllables could cut her lips.

"I can see why you've been struggling. That sounds...terrible."

"It is. Can you fix it?"

"There are some things I think we can try—"

Tanaka waved the words away, and Ahmadi went quiet. "I have to stop this. I can't feel this anymore. Do you understand?"

"I do."

The other woman licked her lips, and Tanaka had the visceral memory of someone who looked similar but with a broader face and a higher hairline, doing the same thing. She pushed the thought away.

"There may be some interventions," Ahmadi said. "There are medicines that we use to reduce intrusive thoughts. Assuming the mechanism is similar, they could be very effective."

"Good."

"If inpatient care is an option for you, there are some focused magnetic treatments that we could try. Things that can blunt your experience."

"But not stop it."

"I don't know what it is," she said. "I will help you find out, though. I promise you that, Aliana. As terrible as this is, you don't have to go through it alone."

She didn't see the irony in her choice of phrase, and Tanaka wasn't in the mood to walk her through it. Her body felt like she'd had a bad virus. Weary until her muscles were falling off her bones. The storm in her head was still there, but not overwhelming at the moment. She didn't trust that. Being tired made her vulnerable and weak. It didn't make her free from the others.

"Let's try the medications first," she said.

"I'll have them for you right away."

Tanaka stood up. The station swayed under her, and she wanted nothing more than to close her eyes. "I think that's enough for today."

"We still have time, if you want to—"

"I think that's enough for today. Have the medications delivered to my quarters here on the station. I'll take them."

"I'd like to see you again." It was a bold statement, and they both knew it. Tanaka lowered her head. Ahmadi squared her shoulders. When she spoke, her voice was lower, calmer, more reassuring, more like it had been when Tanaka had first come in the office. "You are in crisis right now. But you're also an incredibly strong person. You've never met anything that could stop you before, so you believe you can grit your teeth and force your way through it. And truthfully, you probably can. But Aliana, you can't heal from this. Not without help."

When Tanaka spoke, it was deliberately using the other woman's cadence and intonation. Not quite mocking her, not quite not. "You believe I am suffering an ongoing, unstoppable intimate assault."

"I do."

"And you think that's something I can heal from?"

"I would like to help you."

"I would like to be helped," Tanaka said. "Send me the pills. We'll go from there."

The station was unfamiliar enough to hold her attention. The puzzle of reading the signs, finding her way to the transport tubes, picking the right lift to get her to her quarters, all kept her from thinking too much about anything else. When she got there, things were worse.

Her rooms were simple, spare, and elegant. The color scheme was mostly a dusty red designed to highlight the splashes of Laconian blue. The decoration was minimalist and tasteful: a calligraphic print of a passage of the high consul's writings, a crystal vase with a single flower in it that was replaced each day by the staff, a floor covering designed to evoke tatami mats. There was nothing in it to distract her from her impulses and thoughts.

She ordered food to the room: curried fish and a dry white wine. Someone in her head remembered an apartment with blue-green walls of chipping paint and a couch made from foam and cloth. It was a happy memory, but Tanaka didn't know why. Someone else had eaten a bad fish curry, and the echo of a night recovering from food poisoning wafted through her awareness and vanished again, thin as cigarette smoke.

The medication arrived at almost the same time as the food. A glassine packet with ten peach-colored pills in it and the printed directions to take one each morning and to avoid alcohol. She dry-swallowed two of them, then chased them with a long swig from the wine bottle. The curry was punishingly hot, just as she'd hoped. It gave her an excuse to polish off the wine. By the time she was finished, a deep ache was growing at the base of her skull, but she had the sense that the memories and thoughts were a little less, the voices a little quieter.

The room's system chimed. A connection request from the *Derecho*. She checked her hand terminal. There were half a dozen messages from Botton queued there, but she'd forgotten to take off her privacy settings after Ahmadi. She turned them off now and accepted the connection through the room. A wall screen came to life, and Botton's head filled it.

"Colonel," he said. "I am very sorry to interrupt. I wouldn't if you hadn't specifically asked for immediate updates."

Had she asked for immediate updates? She didn't remember

doing it, but it sounded like something she would have done. The ache at the base of her skull grew a little more intense.

"It's fine," she said. "What seems to be the problem?"

"We had a high-priority report from the Science Directorate on Laconia. Dr. Ochida's office flagged it as critical."

"What did it say?"

Botton blinked. "I don't know, Colonel. I'm not cleared."

She knew that. She should have known. "Of course. Send it to me. I'll take it here."

"Colonel," the captain said, and then vanished. He was replaced with an encrypted datafile. As she ran the decryption, she wondered what the effect of alcohol was on her new medication. If it beat the hell out of her liver and kidneys, it might still be worth the damage. If it made the meds less effective, though…

She ordered another bottle of wine anyway.

Ochida appeared on the screen. He looked as clean and crisp as ever. She recognized the room he was in. Not the Science Directorate, but the State Building. That meant whatever he was telling her, he'd likely already told Trejo.

"Colonel," he said. "I hope you're well."

"Fuck you," Tanaka said to the recording with a polite nod.

"We were feeding the data you sent us through the virtual intelligence and pattern-matching systems here, and we came up with something interesting. Take a look at this."

The screen jumped. Where Ochida had been, there was the ring space. Telescopic images, tactical map, scatter data. She didn't need to look at the time stamp. She recognized the sequence like it was a well-studied painting. It was the gap between when the *Derecho* had entered the ring space and the transit of the *Preiss*. It was the last few moments that her mind had been her own.

The images ticked forward frame by frame, slowed down by the analytic software. She watched the ships inch forward in their arcs, the tactical display tracking each of them. The dissipating drive plume into Bara Gaon that had misled her. The flicker of the *Preiss*'s drive as it began to go dutchman. And then whiteness.

The annihilating brightness of a thousand rings bursting into light.

Not just the rings, though.

Tanaka sat forward. The data images shifted, bringing the ring station at the center of the space into clearer focus. It was glowing with a sudden, violent brightness just like the rings. The visual telescopy shifted closer, diving in toward the surface of the station. There was a flaw there. A dark spot like dust on the lens. Or no, not that. Something on the surface of the station itself. The weird patterning of the structure made it hard to make sense of until the virtual intelligence stripped out the background.

It was a small, dark oval. An overlay gave a sense of scale. Not large at all. Smaller than her quarters on Gewitter. The adrenaline hit her system even before the comparison image came up. The egg-shaped ships from the grotto on Laconia. And the match certainty: 98.7 percent.

"You son of a bitch," she whispered. "There you are."

Chapter Thirty-Two: Kit

Many, many things were known, but some were bright and immediate. Fortuna Sittard was both capital city and company town. The hexagon/pentagon tessellation of the Nieuwestad logo really was inspired by the surface of a football. The city was less than ten years old, but already half a million people lived there at the edge of a massive tectonic escarpment where the highland rivers were cutting valleys as they flowed down toward the southern sea. The morning sun would come through the windows and spill across the ceiling over the bed, every imperfection in the surface throwing a tiny shadow in the rose-colored light.

There were other things, less bright but just as much known. A coffeehouse in Toronto where a man and woman had said goodbye for the last time, and the way the scent of baked apple would still make her cry sometimes. A recurring pain in a chest that the doctors called idiopathic angina but that carried all the fear and threat of heart attacks. The pattern of an old melody on piano keys adapted because the left hand was missing a pinkie. The spilling grammars of Italian and Czech. A great wash of memory and significance and knowledge, there but grayer somehow. Lapping like the little waves at the edge of a lake.

Eyes opened and saw where the shadows would be. Legs shifted out from under a blanket, but they weren't anyone's legs. They just were. A woman muttered in her sleep, dreaming that she was in a dance recital and had forgotten all the moves. The toilet was a few steps away, and for a moment there were other toilets to reach from other rooms. Some on the left, some on the right, some down the hallway or the stairs. More than a few built into the wall of the ship's cabin, complete with vacuum flow for when the drive was off and everything was on the float.

Nearby, a finger touched the light switch, and a glow filled the air. A hand fumbled with a warm, soft penis, and urine spilled down to the white ceramic bowl. There was relief, and then soap and warm water and the light put out.

A child slept in the nursery. He was already large for his crib. That was a known thing. And farther, but not too far, there was a daughter already getting up for work, her attempts to be quiet more alerting than outright noise would be. And there was no one in the house but silence and the thumb-sized grubs they call "cricket slugs" on Pathé. And ships' drives hummed and thrummed—all the ships' drives in chorus like cicadas.

The hand that had touched the light switch pulled aside the curtains. The window had spots on it where old raindrops dried, and beyond that, the stars. A woman's voice said *Kit?* and more eyes opened. A naked man stood at the window, looking out at the night, but something was very wrong with him—right, but not right. Familiar, but unfamiliar. Reversed, because he wasn't in the mirror and then he wasn't the person who saw himself in the mirror and then he was.

"Kit?" Rohi said again, and Kit fell back into himself like he'd jumped off a building. His head spun as he staggered to the toilet, dropped to his knees, and vomited into the bowl. When he was empty, he retched for a while, each spasm more painful than the one before, but slowly gaining more time between them. Bakari was crying and Rohi was singing to their boy, soothing him, cooing to him that everything was all right.

Eventually the vertigo passed, and Kit was himself again. In the planetary gravity of Nieuwestad his body felt heavy in a way that somehow felt different than acceleration on a ship, even though Einstein had proven it wasn't. He washed out his mouth at the little metal sink and walked back to the bedroom. Rohi was curled on the pillows, Bakari asleep in the crook of her arm with his closed eyes shifting in a dream. Kit's skin stippled itself with gooseflesh from the cold, and he pulled on a set of thermal underwear. He didn't have pajamas.

It had started on the *Preiss*. It had started the moment they'd died. Kit didn't say it, but he was sure that was what had happened. The dark things, more real than anything real, had blown him and his baby away like handfuls of dust in a high wind. That was death. And then their clock had been inverted. They hadn't been reborn, but un-killed. The man who wasn't in the room with them had managed it with a vast effort. An effort that had exhausted him. Kit had been disoriented, grateful, confused, frightened. He'd been lost for a flashbulb moment in a cacophony of memory and identity and sensation.

And there had been voices. Not real ones, not words. He wasn't developing aural hallucinations. But he'd remembered things, known things from lives he hadn't led. While they were questioned by the Laconians from the *Derecho*, when they'd been released to finish the journey to Nieuwestad, even for a time after they'd arrived and been escorted to the orientation campus.

The thing where he lost the idea of Kit in a stream of consciousness that wasn't his? This was new. It had only come a few times, but afterward he felt thinner and less connected to reality. Like the essential self he'd always known—the thing he meant when he said "I"—turned out to be less an object and more a kind of habit.

Not even a persistent habit like taking drugs or gambling. The kind of thing you could take or leave. Coffee with breakfast instead of tea. Buying the same kinds of socks. Existing as an individual. All things he could do or not do without much changing. Another wave of nausea rolled through him with the thought, but it faded.

He slipped into the bed, trying not to wake them. Bakari was a warm, soft stone. Nothing short of Armageddon was going to wake him now. Rohi didn't open her eyes, didn't shift on the mattress. He was almost able to convince himself she was asleep when she spoke.

"Are you all right?"

"You were at a dance recital," he said, softly. "But you'd forgotten all the choreography. You had to improvise it all on the fly, and it wasn't going right."

She was silent for a while. "It's getting worse, isn't it? It's happening more often."

Kit sighed. On the ceiling above them, the first faint shadows were starting to form. "Yeah."

"For me too," she said.

The first two weeks of orientation had been held in a wide auditorium large enough to seat three thousand, though there were fewer than six hundred new immigrants in their cohort. The stage was set a little off-center to give over one wall to vast windows that looked out over the escarpment. The local tree analogs were complexes of mosslike growths that built up like vast coral reefs, and they shimmered silver to green to ruddy orange depending on the temperature and the direction of the wind.

With Bakari in the company daycare facility, Kit's mornings had been presentations by the Jacobin-Black Combined Capital welcome team and representatives of the unions talking about Nieuwestad as a planet and Fortuna Sittard as a city. They would have sixteen-month years and thirty-two-hour days. The local biosphere relied on compounds that weren't toxic but could be

irritating, so keeping inside the sealed areas of the city was rec-
ommended. They got maps of the city—commissary, medical
complex, entertainment district, public swimming pool, religious
facilities. The procedures for reporting legal infractions to security, and security infractions to the union reps, were detailed, and
Kit and Rohi had to mark that they'd been briefed and understood. The JBCC welcome team led them in songs about team-
work and fellowship, and even the union reps joined in.

With Rohi at his side, Kit felt a little bit grounded in the sea of
new voices and faces, the disorienting prospect of the life his new
contract had created for him. There might be hundreds of new
faces and all the displacing details of coming to live in a new city
on a new planet, but Rohi was there, and she was his anchor.

The third week, with his feet a little more nearly under him, he
started his workgroup orientation, and Rohi started hers. Halfway through the first day, he realized it was the longest he'd spent
away from her since they'd boarded the *Preiss* back in Sol system.

There were only six people joining the civil engineering team.
They met in a classroom that looked like a hundred classrooms
he'd been in before—thin industrial carpet with a pattern to
hide stains, sound-absorbing hardfoam walls, recessed lighting
that was cheap because everyone everywhere used printed parts
from the same design. His new superior was an attractive woman
named Himemiya Gosset. She had a tight smile and a habit of
stroking her chin when she was thinking, and Kit realized halfway through the second day that he'd read an article she'd written about the use of local materials in large-scale water recycling
plants. Slowly, the unease and wariness and bone-deep sense of
displacement started to give way to enthusiasm and even excitement about the work he'd be doing.

It was the middle of the third day and Gosset was preparing to
take the six of them over to the offices where they'd be assigned
workstations and meet the full engineering team, when a security
officer stepped in the little classroom and pulled her aside. Their
conversation was brief, but it brought visible distress to the senior

engineer's face. Kit knew before she turned back to the classroom that something had happened, and that it had to do with him.

"Kamal?" Gosset said. "Word, please."

Kit stepped over to the pair of them. The other five were quiet behind him.

"There's a medical issue," the security man said. "I can take you to the infirmary."

"Rohi?" Kit asked.

"It's your son, sir. I'm afraid he's been taken to the infirmary. You should come now."

"Is he all right?" Kit said, but the security man didn't answer.

Gosset nodded sharply toward the door. The universal gesture for *Go*. "Don't worry about missing the walk-through. We'll get you caught up later."

"Thank you," Kit said by reflex. He wasn't paying attention to her. Something was wrong with Bakari. His heart was bright and fast, and he could feel his pulse in his neck.

He held back the urge to ask the security man what had happened, when it had happened, what was wrong, how they knew it was wrong, what they'd done about it, and the thousand other things the man didn't know. Instead, he sat in the small electric cart as it zipped through the wide concrete-and-conduit access corridors of the city, and leaned forward as if he could will it to go faster.

The infirmary was mostly underground, but the lights were tuned to a spectrum that mimicked the afternoon sun of Earth. The flowers at the intake station were fake, but they smelled real. The security man walked behind Kit like an apology. Even before Kit reached the reception desk, an older man in a doctor's coat was striding out toward them. Kit was expected.

"Mr. Kamal," the doctor said, gesturing toward a pair of pale wooden doors. "This way, please."

"What happened?" Kit asked.

Instead of answering, the doctor turned to the security man and said, "Thank you very much." It was polite, but it was a dismissal. Kit had the sense that whatever the conversation was, it would be private. Maybe that was company policy for JBCC. Maybe it was something else.

They pushed through the doors and into the halls of the infirmary. They were wider than standard, wide enough to let two hospital beds pass each other with room for medics at their sides. The floral smell of reception gave way to something harsher.

"Your son is stable," the doctor said. "The daycare watch reported that he was acting strangely. For a time, he became entirely unresponsive."

"I don't know what that means," Kit said.

"I believe he had a seizure of some kind. My preliminary scans don't show any congenital abnormalities or tumors, so that's good. But there was…some odd activity in his insular cortex."

"But he's okay?"

"He's fine now," the doctor said. "We're going to watch him, and I would like to run a few tests. Just rule out as much as I can."

"But he's going to be okay." Kit didn't say it as a question. He asserted it as if the universe would take its directions from him.

The doctor stopped, and Kit went on for another two steps before he paused and turned back. The discomfort on the doctor's face was plain.

"We have a standing order from the Laconian Science Directorate. Any issues or abnormalities that arise among people who were on the *Preiss* are to be documented and the data sent to Laconia."

"Because of the thing that happened?" Kit said.

"There are thirteen hundred systems. Laconia doesn't even have a formal political officer on Nieuwestad," the doctor said. "If the report back to Dr. Ochida slipped behind my desk? It could be months or years before I noticed. Given who your father is, I thought perhaps…"

The doctor inclined his head. He was graying at the temples, and deep wrinkles marked the corners of his eyes and mouth. He was old enough; he might have known the *Rocinante* before the Transport Union was even formed. He might be part of Naomi Nagata's underground movement.

"Thank you," Kit said.

The doctor's smile was calm and calming. He led Kit to a glass doorway where the privacy setting had turned the clear pane to a gentle frost. Kit slipped in. The soft hum and pop of the medical scanners was like wind in trees. The bed was sized for an adult, and Rohi lay on her side with Bakari snuggled up to her chest. His eyes were closed, and his right hand was curled in a fist under his chin as if he were deep in thought. Her voice was soft and lilting. The cadence she fell into when she was lulling the baby to sleep.

"The Anteater said, 'Of course we're friends. Why would we not be?' And the cunning clever boy who looked just like Bakari said, 'Because you eat ants, and the anthill is made from them.'"

Kit eased himself onto the foot of the bed, resting his hand on her ankle. She smiled and went on.

"'You are made from many things too,' the Anteater said. 'You are made up of skin and hair and eyes and bones and blood and wide, strong muscles. Do you hate the doctor when he takes a blood sample to keep you well? Do you hate the barber when he cuts off a bit of your hair? I love the anthill because it helps me live, and it loves me because I help keep it healthy by taking away the ants that are worn out. Just because you're made from something, that doesn't mean that's all you are.' And then the clever young boy who looked just like Bakari understood. And that's the end of the story."

Rohi lapsed into silence. Bakari sighed softly and nuzzled more deeply into the bed. He looked fine. He looked healthy.

"I don't know that story," Kit said. "Where's it from?"

"Aesop?" Rohi said.

"I don't think so."

"Maybe I made it up. I don't know anymore."

I think it was a philosopher, a voice in the back of Kit's mind murmurs. *I can't remember his name.* The voice isn't Kit's. It isn't anyone he recognizes, but he remembers the book—orange with a complex design on the front and thin pages of high-quality paper. It isn't a book he's read. There was a time when these wandering memories bothered him. Now they seem almost normal. *That which can't be avoided must be embraced.* Someone had said that to him. His grandmother. Kit had never met his grandmother. The room around him spun a little, but only a little.

"Can you imagine what it would be like?" Rohi asked. "It's hard enough for us, and we already know ourselves. I've been me for decades. Imagine being as little as him. Still figuring out where your body ends and the world begins, and having to deal with… this."

"We don't know it's that."

"We can't prove it," Rohi said. "But I know. Don't you?"

He curled down onto the bed, resting his head against her thigh. The medical mattress hissed and shifted, accommodating his weight. Her body was warm against his cheek. He remembered how, during the pregnancy, she'd always been warm as a furnace, even in the winter. No matter how cool they kept the bedroom, she'd kick off the sheets. He thought it had been her. He thought that had been him. But maybe it was someone else's memory. Someone from the *Preiss* or one of the other ships. It was so hard to be sure.

"I was so scared when they told me they'd brought him here," Rohi said. "I'm so scared all the time."

"I know. I am too."

"Do you ever want to let go? I keep thinking what it would be like to fall into being the anthill and just never be the ant again. Even if I died, I might not care. I might not notice."

"I would."

"Not if you were in there too."

"I will always care about you," Kit said. "I will always care about him. Nothing will ever change that. No matter how much this happens. It won't erase me, and it won't erase how much I love you."

Rohi made a soft sound, hardly more than an exhalation with intent, and rested her fingers on Kit's head, stroking him gently because they both knew he was lying.

Chapter Thirty-Three: Naomi

Naomi floated in her cabin, her mind dancing over the work. The underground had been difficult and unwieldy even in the days when Saba ran it, and she'd only been one of his lieutenants. Since the fall of Laconia and her own flight before the storm, it had slipped further into chaos. The secret shipyards in Larson system had gone quiet so long she assumed they'd been discovered or else suffered some catastrophic accident. Then a report appeared in her queue that began with a brief, dismissive apology and went on as though nothing odd had happened. One of the cells in Sol system had been discovered and detained, but six others began their own counter-operation without waiting for approval from the rest of the organization. In Calypso, Théo Ammundsun, formerly director of the Louvre on Earth, was going about creating an institution to catalog and gather samples of alien artifacts. He delivered only sporadic and incomplete reports. Entries like *San*

Ysidro sample appears active—Moving to isolate filled her with more dread than information.

It was her network, and every day that she took her eyes off it, every hour she didn't pepper it with messages and pull the best local leaders into power, every moment that she didn't prove the value of a centralized coordinator, the net frayed. Maybe that was inevitable. All she had was her name and reputation, Jim's name and reputation. It was a thin lever arm to move people who wanted to see the kneecapping of Laconia as freedom instead of responsibility.

She prepared messages to the places she thought might be useful: Gregor Shapiro on Ganymede had done the most work with nonlocal signaling protocols; Emilia Bell-Cavat (who was either three weeks late reporting in or whose latest reports had gone astray) was both a secret coordinator of the underground in New Greece system and an expert on noninsect superorganisms; Kachela al-Din worked with direct brain-to-brain communication in a medical context before he'd become a ship designer. They were her straws, and she was reaching for them. The sense of moving too slowly, of being too far behind even as she began, made Duarte's hive mind seem almost seductive. If across all the spread of the human race, she could just ask her questions, hear the answers, be with the people she needed and wasn't with...

"Hey," Jim said from the doorway. "Did something happen with Elvi?"

"You mean besides the miraculous appearance and vanishing of the god-emperor in her lab?"

Jim considered. "I mean besides that, but when you put it that way, I guess that would cover a lot of weird. She's just seemed kind of nervous."

"I'm going back to the god-emperor thing."

"I meant around us in particular," Jim said as he pulled himself into the cabin. "She was going to come have dinner here on the *Roci*, but she bailed. I feel like maybe something about Amos bothered her."

"Have you asked her?"

"You see? There you go with your useful, straightforward suggestions. I never come up with those kinds of things myself."

"Yes, you do."

He braced himself at the wall behind her, looking over her shoulder at the arrayed underground. "What've you got?"

"Just what was in the toolbox before," she said. "I feel like I came to cook a meal and it turns out it's a poetry competition. Everything I built was to fight against Laconia back when Laconia was simple things, like invulnerable ships and neofascist authoritarians. Now that it's become a really invasive bad dream, how do you build a resistance to fight that?"

"It was kind of always an invasive bad dream, but I get what you're saying," Jim said. "Plus San Esteban. Don't forget the boiling dark gods looking to snuff out all life because we annoyed them. Do you have a sense what the plan is?"

"Track Duarte down and talk him out of it," she said. "Find a way to access and use whatever tools the builders made without turning all humanity into an extended version of Winston Duarte's hippocampus."

Jim nodded and rubbed his chin and neck with the flat of his palm in a way that meant he wasn't convinced. That was fair. She wasn't either.

"We do have Teresa," Naomi continued. "She's the only individual he's shown enough concern for to adjust his cognition. If she asks him, maybe he'll change again."

"Parent and child," Jim agreed. "That's powerful stuff. Not sure I'd want to rely on it for, like, the survival of the human race."

"Failure position is force him out of his position, whatever that is, and find someone else who can step into his place. Cara, Xan. Amos."

"Jesus, really?"

"Not my first option, but maybe."

Jim's sigh was soft, gentle. It would have been less devastating if she hadn't heard the despair under it. "Detective Miller once told me, 'We don't have a right thing, just a plateful of a little less wrong.'"

"Yeah, but he was an asshole."

Jim laughed, then reached out and put his hand on the back of her head. She pushed back into him, taking pleasure and comfort in the simple physical presence of the man she trusted.

"When you send out the information," Jim said, almost apologetically. "I mean, when you explain the situation to the rest of the underground? That's going to pull a trigger."

"I know," she murmured.

"You have a plan for that?"

"I do."

"Am I going to like it?"

"Nope," she said, and opened her eyes, looking up into his gentle, bright gaze looking back down at her.

"I didn't figure," he said.

Later, when she crossed back over to the *Falcon*, Naomi would keep that look in mind. They had come a long way—both together and apart—since they'd been babies on the *Canterbury*. It was easy for her to think that life had beaten the idealism and joy out of them. She felt ground down to the nerve endings more often than she didn't. And Jim seemed...not tired, exactly, but all used up. Like his fuel tank was empty and he was just trying to coast gracefully to the finish line. But even so, now and then she saw him still in there. Behind the dark-rimmed pale eyes, under the graying hair, the same reckless, holy fool she'd noticed when Captain McDowell brought him on board. Time and use had changed them, but it hadn't changed what they were. There was joy in that. A promise.

She found Elvi alone in the lab. The apparatus of the dive—paired medical couches, scanners, and sensor arrays—were on the float with her. Here and there, a few cords had come loose from their fittings and floated in the subtle breeze. Elvi herself moved from one console to the next, bringing up logs and datafiles, checking connections and power levels. The atrophy of her muscles left her looking frailer than Naomi pictured her. There was a haunted look in her eyes.

"What are you working on?" Naomi asked instead of saying hello.

"Nothing in particular," Elvi said. "It's just...I had a roommate when I went to university who used to do needlepoint. He wasn't great at it, but it gave his hands something to do while he thought. When he was stuck on a problem and couldn't see any way out—" She gestured at the empty lab. There was something bleak in the gesture. "I'm doing needlepoint. Have you ever done something you knew was wrong, but you told yourself that this time it was justified? That just this once, the rules didn't apply? Or if they did, there was a grander cause that made it okay?"

"You just described most of the last decade of my life," Naomi said.

"I don't know how I move forward with this protocol."

Is something wrong? hovered in the back of Naomi's mouth. It was only the ridiculous obviousness of the answer that changed it to "I've finished all my messages. They're ready to send."

"All right," Elvi said. "I'll clear your access to the comms."

"It's not going to be that easy," Naomi said. "You say the relays are safe. I believe you. But..."

"You think Trejo will find out."

"I know he will. When I send this, it's going to twenty people in sixteen systems. They're going to tell their networks. And it's going to be the most important thing anyone has seen. This will leak. It will leak the minute I send it out, and I can't stop that from happening."

Elvi took one end of a floating cable in her hand, considered it, and plugged it into a slot in the medical couch where Amos had been for the dive. For a moment, Naomi felt like there were three of them in the room. Elvi and her, but also the empty space where Winston Duarte had appeared to be. It was only air now, but it had significance. The empire, the underground, and the man who would be God. Three sides of the coin.

"We have to get help," Elvi said. "I've been trying to do this by myself. I can't. I'm not even sure I trust my judgment anymore. Duarte's plan will affect everyone. Everywhere. I don't even know that I can make a moral case against sending messages out. Even if it means Trejo orders Dr. Lee to shoot me in the head."

"That seems like an extreme call."

"It's Laconia. They do shit like that all the time."

"Well, I have another thought," Naomi said. "But I wanted to talk to you about it first."

"Admiral Trejo," Naomi said, dead-eyeing the camera, "I accept your proposal and the amnesty you offered to the underground. I am sending copies of your original broadcast in Freehold and this response for dissemination within my organization. Once my people see that local Laconian forces are abiding by your word, all action against Laconian personnel and assets will end, and we can start working on our more pressing issues.

"To that end, I am including files, debriefings, and interviews around a recent experiment which I think you'll agree is both interesting and alarming."

Naomi steadied herself. She felt like there should be more to say, that this was one of those moments that history books leaned on. The acceptance speech that ended the war between Laconia and the remnants of the Transport Union. She'd had thoughts and intentions, things she'd meant to say, but now that she was in the moment, they all seemed ponderous and artificial.

Screw it, she thought. *Posterity can take care of itself.*

"Please get back to me. The sooner we can establish some working protocols, the sooner we can address this situation."

She stopped the recording.

"And the less likely we are to be sucked up into a vast, inhuman consciousness in which we are all lost like raindrops falling into an ocean," she finished to the inactive lens.

Elvi, at her workstation, gave a thumbs-up. The recording was good. Naomi stretched her arms out to the side, easing the tension that had knotted itself between her shoulder blades. For a moment, she pictured all the people who had sworn to join the fight against Duarte and Laconia who would be seeing this. She wanted to believe that they'd all follow her lead, they'd all see the wisdom in her choices, they'd all put aside their grudges and their guns. Or a plurality of them, even. There was a future not far from here where she was going to be fighting against a bunch of the people who'd once been her allies. She would be announcing not only the situation with Duarte, but laying her cards on the table with the underground and Trejo alike. It was the most James Holden–esque thing she'd ever contemplated.

"Last chance," she said. "Do we send it or not?"

Elvi looked stricken. "Oh. No. I…" She made the thumbs-up gesture again, more tentatively this time. "It's sent. It's gone. I sent it. Was that not what we agreed?"

"It's fine," Naomi said. "Now, let's see if he sends us a bouquet or a battle group. I should go tell my crew what we've done."

"Same."

"This was the right thing," Naomi said.

Elvi tilted her head and looked away. When she spoke, her voice was smaller, but also strangely more relaxed. "I think it was. I wish that meant we'd be rewarded for it."

Naomi left, skimming down the Laconian corridors for the airlock. The enemy crew that maybe, sort of, technically wasn't the enemy for the moment made way for her. Slipping across the bridge and back into the *Rocinante* felt like pulling on a favorite jacket. She had known that she was doing something momentous, but somehow she hadn't really felt it until it was behind her. Whatever happened from here, Trejo would know she'd been working with Elvi and everything Duarte had said about his plan.

As she headed down toward engineering and the machine shop, she found herself wondering what it would be like to feel her connection to the vast swelling mass of humanity more immediately than she felt her own sense of self. She'd read some of the early analyses that Elvi's team had done with a theoretical model based on Cara and Amos. The ways that the folds of their brains began to act as if they were physically cross-connected, and a thought that began in one could cascade over into the other and then back again like a song traveling through a window. It seemed oddly poetic when it didn't seem like annihilation.

When she reached engineering, Teresa and Amos were hard at work. The preflight checklists were on the wall screens, and almost half were already in the green.

"Boss," the thing that had been Amos said. "What's up?"

"I was going to say we might want to look at prepping for a burn, but—" She gestured at the screens.

"Figured we were better ready than not ready."

"Good call," she said. "I took Trejo's offer. I'm waiting to see if he's still offering. If he's not…"

"Amos said you saw him," Teresa said. She was wearing a flight suit with one of the old *Tachi* designs. Naomi was surprised that after all this time the *Roci* still had the instructions to make those. "My father. You saw him?"

"We saw something," Naomi said. "But we know it was an illusion. We can't know what it was really based on. It seemed like him."

"Pretty sure it was the guy," Amos said. "My vantage point was a little different."

"Are we going to kill him?" Teresa asked. There was no fear or pleading in her voice. If there was anger—and there was anger—it wasn't aimed at her.

"We don't know what we're going to do," Naomi said. "I'm not looking to kill anybody. But there may be a way to use what he's found without using it the way he wants to use it."

"If you were going to kill him, would you tell me?"

"Yes," Naomi said, and meant it.

For a moment, all three of them were still. Teresa was the first to move, just a terse nod and then she turned back to the inventory screens. Amos' smile widened a millimeter. Naomi had the impression that the girl had just done something he was proud of her for.

It was almost a full day before the message came back from Laconia. By then, Naomi had spent a long, sleepless night second-guessing herself, Alex and Jim were up to speed, and the *Roci-nante* was ready to burn for the ring gate whether in tandem with the *Falcon* or on her own.

She was about to throw on a vac suit and run a visual inspection of the *Roci*'s plating when Jim called to her from the ops deck. "Naomi. We have something. It's from Trejo."

She put the helmet back in its cradle and pulled herself up to ops. Alex had already come down. His eyes were wide with concern. Jim could have been carved from plaster. She didn't say anything. There was nothing to say. Either her gambit had worked or it hadn't. They'd all know soon enough.

She pulled up her message queue. The entry at the top was marked ANTON TREJO. She opened it and pulled back far enough that the others could see. Trejo appeared at the same desk he'd been sitting at in the Freehold message, but with a less pleasant expression. Still technically a smile, but there was an anger in it that Naomi couldn't miss if she wanted to. Fair enough. She'd just humiliated him by showing the underground and through them everyone in every system that Naomi Nagata had infiltrated the highest ranks of Laconia.

"Naomi Nagata," Trejo said, and then chuckled like he'd practiced it. "You are a pistol, aren't you? I am glad that we're finally on the same side. I want you to know I've always respected your grit and your competence. I wish you'd gotten to know our cause under different circumstances. All this might have come out differently. Better now than never, though."

"That man is going to put a bullet in the back of your head," Jim said.

"Oh yeah," Alex agreed. "No question."

"If we get that far, I'll deal with it," Naomi said.

She rolled the message back to keep from missing anything.

"As an initial gesture of our cooperation, I'm including a security briefing to you and Dr. Okoye both. Take a look at it, and let me know what you think. I'd appreciate it if we could use the secure channels moving forward. I'm sure the good doctor can tell you anything you need to get that set up if it's not already."

"This man spent weeks having me slowly beaten to death," Jim said. "And he was never as angry at me as he is at you now."

Naomi was already pulling up the security download. The featured report was of the inside of the ring space at the moment it went white. She'd seen it enough in Elvi's scientific reports to recognize it. When the ring gates lit, blasting the ships there with light, the image froze, shifted. It seemed to be moving in toward the station at the center of the ring space. A small darkness stood out against the light, and a text window opened with the words: MATCH CERTAINTY 98.7%.

"Get Elvi," Naomi said.

Chapter Thirty-Four: Tanaka

Tanaka knew she was dreaming, but she wasn't certain that the dream was hers. In it, she was in a tunnel carved from bare stone and sealed against seepage like one of the old transit corridors in Innis Shallows back on the Mars of her youth, but there was a confusion in her as if she had never been anyplace like it before. Somewhere nearby, a man was screaming, and the name that she associated with the shrieks was Nobuyuki, but she didn't know who that was.

That might have just been the nature of dreams, though, and the strangeness of it was only because she was on the ragged edge of lucidity. The thing that made it feel like she was watching someone else's dream was more subtle. The texture of the emotions was wrong. The way they slid across her mind. She knew them as they came: betrayal, panic, the profound sorrow of a mistake that couldn't be unmade. It was like seeing a Picasso composition in the style of Van Gogh, familiar and alien at the same time.

With the logic of dreams, she felt someone beside her thinking about the different kinds of unconsciousness: sleeping, dreaming, and dying. A younger mind, and a masculine one, but gentle in a way she didn't usually associate with masculinity. A gentle soul beside her, caught in the same riptide she was.

And then she felt others around them, like they were all in the same theater watching a wall screen or a living performance. Other minds, other selves, all bleeding into each other, bleeding into her. Thoughts and impulses, impressions and emotions, rising up and drifting away without any clear owner, and her own selfhood just one flake in the snowstorm.

If the thing that calls itself Aliana Tanaka came apart here and never swirled back together, she thought, *I wouldn't even notice that I was missing.*

The idea was like a whispered threat. She woke herself up trying to scream.

When her eyes opened, her surroundings were no more familiar. The light-in-darkness of pale linens in a dim room. A frame on the wall filled with hand-brushed letters. Something on the floor that was and wasn't tatami. She told herself that she would know. She didn't now, didn't *yet*, but she would. This was her room. This was her bed. There was a reason it didn't seem familiar...

Because these were her rooms on Gewitter Station. Not hers. Not owned. Assigned to her for a moment, like a hotel. Nothing felt like her, because it was only a brief relationship, architecturally speaking. That made sense. That sounded right. She pulled herself out from under the blanket and stumbled to the tiny bathroom. Above the sink, a whole wall of mirror. She looked at the woman looking back out at her, and she seemed familiar.

Tanaka shifted her head and watched her reflection do the same. She opened her mouth, watched the places where the surgical scars on her cheeks pulled down at her eyelids differently. *If you'd stuck with the field surgery, it would be healed by now*, she thought. What the hell did she need with cosmesis anyway?

What's a third Miko? someone asked in her mind, and she pushed the thought away.

"Aliana Tanaka," she said, and the reflection mimicked. "You are Aliana Tanaka. Colonel Aliana Tanaka, Laconian Marine Corps. Special Operations Group, Second Battalion, First Marine Expeditionary Regiment. Aliana Tanaka, that's who you are."

The syllables of her own name became a mantra, and slowly, slowly, the mantra became something more. She remembered the medicine, went back to the bedroom to find the packet, and dry-swallowed two more of the pills. They made a thick lump halfway down her esophagus. Good enough.

She found her hand terminal and scanned the packet. She was already down to the last two doses. When she put in for a resupply, the system threw up an error. She keyed in a security override, insisted, and while she was at it, doubled the size of the prescription. Whatever damage it did her wasn't even in her top ten problems right now.

She looked at the time—halfway through the second watch—and didn't know when she'd gone to sleep. Maybe she was up early. Maybe she'd slept in. Time and behavior were doing strange things right now. It didn't matter. She wasn't going back to sleep now. She could start from there.

She pulled up the lights, showered under uncomfortably cool water, and dressed in her uniform. The woman over the sink now looked less hagridden. Her scars were almost dignified. *Aliana Tanaka. Aliana Tanaka.*

She put in a connection request for Captain Botton on the *Derecho*. It took him long enough to accept that she thought he might have been sleeping, but he was dressed and on the bridge of the ship. Maybe he just didn't like taking her calls.

"Colonel," he said instead of hello.

"What's the situation?" she asked smartly.

He nodded and seemed to gather himself. She had the impression—a last wisp of dream—of tiny gnats swarming around his head, almost too small and translucent to be picked up by the camera.

She ignored them. "We should be fully resupplied in seventy-two hours, sir."

Tanaka scowled. "I made the requests personally. We should have been at the front of the line."

"We are," Botton said. "The common supplies are already on board. Water. Food. Filters. Basic medical supplies. We're only waiting for catalytic plates for the recycler and a shipment of fuel pellets that was outbound. They're burning hard to get back."

That a ship had to turn back around for her was weirdly reassuring. It was evidence that there was an objective reality, that the world of base matter still counted for something, that not everything was a slip of consciousness that other minds could invade and change.

"Fine. But keep the crew ready for immediate departure. If I decide not to wait for the full resupply, I don't want to be hauling people out of dockside bars because they thought they were still on shore leave."

The gnats around Botton's head came more sharply into focus and his mouth went just a degree tighter. Botton didn't like that she was running his ship. Why would he? She'd have hated him if their positions were reversed. He was usually better at hiding his irritation. She had the uncanny sense that she was seeing his thoughts as he had them.

"If I may, does this have anything to do with the armistice?" Botton asked.

The what? Tanaka almost said. Reflexes from decades in the military kicked in before she could. "I can't confirm or deny anything at this point."

"Understood, sir. Permission to speak candidly?"

"Go ahead."

"It would help the crew to hear something from you directly. They're getting everything through newsfeeds now, and it's an invitation to chaos."

"I hear you," she said. "I'll do what I can."

"Aye, aye," Botton said, and braced. She cut the connection.

The armistice? There was something…something she knew? Some awareness that had slipped into her from the back while she slept? Until she turned to the newsfeeds and the leaked recordings of Nagata and Trejo that the underground had put out, she was reaching for supernatural answers when memory and mundanity were enough. Tanaka knew about the peace between Laconia and the underground because she'd been the one to deliver the offer. Nagata had just gotten around to saying yes.

Tanaka stood in the center of her room, shifting through feeds until she found an apparently unedited copy of the message. *The sooner we can establish some working protocols, the sooner we can address this situation.* Nagata never mentioned the Duarte girl. She didn't need to. The daughter was beside the point now—bait for a trap that Tanaka didn't have to set. It didn't mean she'd be useless, and it chafed her to think Trejo had given in to Nagata with nothing in return.

She was just starting to think about eating something and whether to send a query of her own to Trejo when a message appeared. It popped up in her secure queue flagged as flash traffic from the admiral himself. She opened it with a flick of her fingers. On the wall screen, Trejo looked angry. His eyes flickered like he was reading something in the air. The sense of gnats wasn't there, though. The message was just an object, not a mind.

"Okoye sold us out," Trejo said. "I don't know how much she and her husband gave away, but we have to assume it's the farm. The good news is that it's out in the open now. Bad news is we have to deal with this other shit first. I've given them the same report that Ochida sent you. They'll be sending their best and brightest to the ring gates. I'd like you to be there too.

"Your mission's the same. Get Duarte and bring him back. Some of the circumstances are a little different. Whatever he's done, it's working. Ochida's not seeing any more San Estebans. The glitches have stopped. Reality's getting back to normal."

Tanaka felt a wave of something—rage, fear, nausea—and pushed it away.

"Which means Duarte is still the priority," Trejo went on. "When you find him we need to understand what he's doing and take control of it, whatever that entails. Nagata is nominally in charge of ring gate traffic so that we won't need to keep trying to whistle while we're pissing, but I want it clear between us: Your Omega status is still very much in place. If you have to choose between fulfilling your mission or preserving this agreement, I trust your judgment."

The message ended. That was stark enough. Tanaka took a long breath, shifted her shoulders, and put a connection back through to Botton on the *Derecho*. He answered more quickly this time. She wondered how long it would take to grab a sandwich.

"I've communicated with Admiral Trejo," she said. "I have a message for you to pass on to the crew. Tell them to get ready for launch. We're burning to the ring space to rendezvous with Nagata and the high consul as soon as I'm back to the ship."

"Yes, sir," Botton said.

"Who's on security detail right now?"

Botton blinked. His gaze cut to the right. For a moment, she had the irrational fear he would say Nobuyuki, though she didn't think there was anyone with that name on the *Derecho*.

"Lieutenant De Caamp."

"Have her send two armed escorts to my rooms on the station immediately."

"Copy that," Botton said. "Is there a problem?"

"No. I have a stop to make before I leave the station, and they might not want to let me in," she said. And then, with a chuckle, "Or back out."

Just under an hour later, she walked into the psychiatric wing of Gewitter medical complex with two Marines behind her. A young man with unfashionably long hair was at the reception desk. His face went ashy as she stepped up to his desk.

"I'm here to see Dr. Ahmadi," she said.

"Of course. You can have a seat in the waiting area, and I'll—"

"I'm here to see Dr. Ahmadi right now."

"I'm not sure where she is."

Tanaka leaned forward, put her hands on the reception desk, and smiled gently. "Just for pretend, if it was really important, how would you find her?"

The doctors' lounge was otherwise empty when she reached it. It was a warm room with indirect lighting and real plants—ferns and ivies—hanging from planters along the walls. Two sofas long enough to sleep on and an automated galley as sophisticated as some she'd seen serve a whole ship.

She didn't know if the other physicians had been warned away or if Ahmadi had been alone there all along, but when she sat down across from her, Ahmadi's tea had a little skin of oil across its top where it had cooled, undrunk. The doctor's gaze swam a little bit as it found its way to Tanaka.

"You're here," Ahmadi said.

"I am," Tanaka agreed, and pushed the little packet with its two pills across the table. "How does this work? Why does it take the edge off the effect?"

Ahmadi nodded. "It reduces activity in the temporoparietal lobes with some antipsychotic effects. It diminishes spontaneous neural firings globally. Whatever is reaching into your mind, I thought it might help you to not respond to it."

"What else does that? What other drugs? I need a list."

Ahmadi put out her hand. For a moment, Tanaka didn't know what she meant by it, then she gave the doctor her terminal. As Ahmadi wrote in it, she spoke. Her voice was soft and hazy.

"When I was an intern, I had a patient with left neglect."

"I don't know what that is."

"He had a lesion on his brain that meant he didn't experience the concept of left. If I asked him to draw a circle, he'd draw the right half. If you had him draw an analog clock face, all the numbers would be crowded onto the right. Left was a thought he just couldn't have. Like he was colorblind, but for half his perceptual field."

Tanaka leaned back in her chair. "Are you all right?"

"I always thought about how strange it would be to have that loss. I never thought about how odd we must have been to him. These weird people with twice as much world that he couldn't conceive of. And he couldn't. The thoughts you have depend on the brain you have. Change the brain and you change the kinds of thoughts that are possible to think."

She put the terminal onto the table beside her abandoned tea. It made a scraping sound like a fingernail over skin as she pushed it across. Tanaka didn't pick it up.

"It happened to you."

"It did," Ahmadi said. "I was remembering a tunnel. You were there. Something bad was happening."

"To Nobuyuki," Tanaka said. "Whoever the fuck that is."

"It's connecting us," Ahmadi said. "It's making cross connections between our neurons. Making it so that the electrical impulse of a neuron in one brain can trigger the neuron in another brain to fire. We used to do that with rats, you know? Put an electrode in one rat brain that's hooked to a radio transmitter. A receiver hooked to another rat in another room. We'd show one the color red, and shock the other. After a while, when the one saw red, the other would flinch even without a shock. 'Poor man's telepathy' we called it."

"Nothing personal, but your work sounds kind of fucked up."

"I thought it would be like...being with people. Like a dream, but it's not. It's being part of an idea that is too big to think. Being one part of a brain that's so vast and interconnected, it's not human. It's made of humans, but that's not what it is. Not any more than we're neurons and cells."

"You still think this is intimate assault?"

"Oh yes," Ahmadi said. Her voice was low and rich with her conviction. "Yes."

Tanaka picked up the handheld from the table. A dozen different pharmaceuticals were listed there, with dosage formulas and warnings. Do Not Take on an Empty Stomach. Discontinue if Rash Presents. Avoid if Pregnant. She slapped the handheld onto her wrist and put the two remaining pills into her pocket.

"It's spreading," Ahmadi said. "It's not just the people who were in the ring space with you. It's spreading out everywhere. Like a contagion."

"I know."

"How can it do that?"

Tanaka stood. Ahmadi seemed smaller than she had in their session. Her face was softer than it had been. The voice that had admired her, that had been reminded of his wife, was silent. Or elsewhere. Or blocked by the drugs.

"I don't know how it's being done," Tanaka said. "But I intend to find out."

"How do you stop it?"

"I'll find that out too," she said, and walked away. In the corridor, she copied the list to the two Marines as she led the way toward the pharmacy. "Any of these that are already compounded, we take. Anything we'd need to synthesize more on the *Derecho*, we take that too."

"How do we know what those are?"

"Shake a pharmacist," Tanaka said.

It took longer than Tanaka had wanted to spend, but the supply was also larger. By the end, they had to take wide, blue plastic bags that were meant for the personal effects of patients. By the time they were ready to go, it looked like they'd been shopping at a high-fashion market district. One of the doctors—a small, round-faced man with an unfortunate beard—followed them out toward the hub to the main station flapping his hands in distress. Tanaka did him the favor of ignoring him.

It took the lift a few seconds to arrive. As Tanaka stood there, waiting, one of her guards cleared his throat. "Straight to the dock, sir?"

"Yes," Tanaka said. And then, "No. Wait." As the lift chimed, she pulled open one of the bags and grabbed out a familiar glassine packet, filled with pills. "Go ahead. I'll meet you at the ship."

"Are you sure, sir?"

"Go."

She didn't wait to watch. Anyone on the *Derecho* stupid enough to disobey her at this point was beyond saving. She stalked to the doctor's lounge again. This time, more people were there. They turned to look at her like she was a threat. Fair enough.

Ahmadi was exactly where Tanaka had left her, though somehow she'd gotten a fresh cup of tea to ignore. Tanaka touched her shoulder, and she was slow to turn. Tanaka put the packet on the table beside the teacup. Ahmadi's hand covered it.

"I'll do what I can," Tanaka said.

Chapter Thirty-Five: Alex

At first, Alex didn't notice the sounds of violence. There were several reasons for that: He was on the flight deck at the top of the *Rocinante*, and the fighting was down by the crew airlock; he was at the end of a long, busy shift, and the fatigue left him a little slower on the uptake than usual; he was watching one of his favorite old neo-noir entertainment feeds, and the detective—played by Shin Jung Park—had just followed the mysterious woman—Anna Reál—into a nightclub on Titan. It was only a few minutes before he'd find the policeman's body, and maybe an hour before he realized that the mysterious woman was his daughter. Alex had seen this one many times over the years. He knew it well. Rewatching old feeds was a comfort for him. There was a calm that came with knowing what was going to happen.

He couldn't tell what caught his attention, only that something in the club sounded wrong. He paused the feed, Shin Jung Park with his eyes half closed and his mouth open awkwardly in the middle of ordering a drink. The *Roci* was just the hum of recyclers and his own heartbeat. When the next shout came, Alex started. It was a girl's voice lifted in rage. He couldn't make out individual words, but it was only trouble.

He unstrapped and hauled himself down through ops to the lift. The girl's voice came again, louder and fast. The only thing he could make out was the word *fucking* in the middle of a sentence. Then a sound of impact loud enough that the hull rang with it for a few seconds.

"Hey there," he said as he pulled himself toward the crew airlock. "Something wrong?"

No one answered back, but he heard Amos talking low and calm. Alex's first thought was that something had happened to Muskrat, and Teresa was losing herself in grief, but that didn't quite seem right either.

The girl's voice came again, and it wasn't Teresa. It was younger, higher. A serrated blade of a voice. *You had no fucking right to get involved in it. You are shit to me. You are the same kind of vicious fuck that Cortázar was, and you can get back there and tell her you were wrong.* Alex drifted down.

Cara floated at the airlock, her face a mask of rage and pain. Amos blocked her way into the *Roci*, his arms stretched out to either wall as if he were casually bracing himself there. Jim and Teresa were in the lift shaft, coming up from the crew decks, drawn by the same commotion. Teresa's eyes were wide and anxious. Jim met Alex's eyes and nodded.

"I get why you're pissed, Sparkles," Amos said. "This part's rough."

"Stop saying that!" the smaller girl shouted. "You don't know shit about me!"

"But it'll pass," Amos went on. "Maybe it doesn't go all the way back to what it was before you put your head in that thing, but it'll get better than this."

"I am *supposed* to be in there! They're *supposed* to tell me things! I want it, and you fucked it up for me. Now you need to fix it."

"This is what fixed looks like now."

"We're dead anyway!" She was fighting against sobs now. "It doesn't matter if we're all dead anyway."

"We should get you back to Little Man. He's worried about you."

"Stay out of our *heads*!" Cara screamed, and launched herself at Amos. The impact of their bodies was deeper and more violent than Alex had expected, like they were both weighted with lead. Cara's attack wasn't balanced or braced, and Amos was. She flailed, losing her orientation. Her heel, swinging, hit the bulkhead with a sound like a hammer strike. Where she hit, the fabric and foam had a deep dent.

The screams and sobs grew more violent and then, like a candle guttering out, faded suddenly into nothing. Amos looked back over his shoulder, first at Jim and Teresa, then back up toward Alex. A black streak across his right cheek showed where Cara had struck him.

"I'll be back in a minute," Amos said.

"Take your time," Alex replied, and then felt stupid for saying it. But Amos only nodded and passed from handhold to handhold until he reached Cara where she floated, curled tightly into herself, her whole body a fist. Amos said something to the girl that Alex couldn't hear, and then tucked her in one broad, pale arm and pulled her with him out the airlock door and across the docking bridge.

Jim and Teresa rose up as Alex floated down, and the three of them watched Amos cross to the *Falcon* and pass into it.

"Well, shit," Alex said. "Looks like Elvi told her about us dropping the whole library thing."

"He knew it would be ugly," Teresa said. "He's been waiting for this to happen. He told Dr. Okoye to put responsibility for shutting the experiments down on him."

"Because he can take the punch?" Alex asked.

"Have you seen Elvi?" Jim said. "She looks like she'd break if you breathed on her too hard."

"Well, good on Amos, I guess," Alex said. For a moment, he had the sense that someone else was in the airlock with them—some fourth person watching alongside them. He looked back toward the lift, expecting to see Naomi, but no one was there.

Once the order came, getting the *Rocinante* ready to evacuate Adro system didn't take long at all. Alex had been over the flight checks with the experience of a lifetime lifting him through the process. The maneuvering thrusters were all reporting back solid. The water supply was still pretty healthy, especially compared with the *Falcon*, which rode drier than Alex would have been comfortable with. The air recyclers were working at better-than-spec. The Epstein drive would need a refit sometime in the next year, if things went well enough that they were all still alive and recognizably human by then.

Alex had heard the idea that a tool, used long enough and cared for well enough, developed a soul. He'd never been a religious man, but even without going to the supernatural, he felt like there was some truth in that. The *Rocinante* and Alex had spent a lot of years in each other's company, and he understood the ship the way he would a friend. It was probably just normal primate subliminal pattern matching, but he experienced it as the ship having moods and needs. He could tell when a thruster wanted to have its feed lines replaced by the way the ship turned, knew when they were low on reaction mass by the sound of the drive echoing in the halls. Getting ready for another burn out toward the gates was like pulling on his socks. He didn't even think about it anymore. The ship and her crew were intimate enough that it all just happened.

The *Falcon* was a newer ship with a younger crew, and breaking it down for a trip—especially after months on the float—took longer. Elvi's people had been running a lab without any particular need to worry about arcane ideas like up and down. Now, everything had to be unmade, stowed, and packed away. Alex had the sense that some of the crew over there hadn't expected to ever leave Adro.

The last decision was whether to leave the docking bridge in place and coordinate their drives. It wasn't that hard a maneuver. It just meant letting the *Falcon* and the *Rocinante* talk to each other as they burned so that their drives stayed in sync. The bridge from one ship to the other could remain in place, and they could go back and forth easily. Alex liked the idea. He didn't want the *Falcon*'s crew coming over, and he didn't have any particular interest in making the crossing himself, but there was an equality that driving in tandem like that carried. The *Rocinante* was an old gunship from before the gates had opened. The *Falcon* was Laconia's state-of-the-art science vessel with even more advanced technology than the *Gathering Storm* had boasted. Putting the two of them into a single unit made Alex feel like the *Roci* was getting the correct level of respect.

But even though Naomi had accepted the Laconian armistice, she wasn't keen on having the *Falcon*'s system too intimately connected to the *Roci*'s. When the time came, Naomi and Jim, Amos and Teresa and Muskrat all folded themselves back into their places. The *Roci* pulled its docking bridge back in, and the two ships turned their backs to the great green diamond and burned toward the gate, together but separate. It felt like an omen of something, but Alex was damned if he could tell what. He kept thinking about Amos and Cara in the airlock, of her anger and his calm. He wasn't sure whether he was glad the black-eyed girl wasn't able to cross over at will or worried that Amos would be stuck on the *Roci* if things went bad on the *Falcon*.

The burn was hard but not punishing. A little over a full gravity most of the time, backing down to half that at meals. There were more newsfeeds and reports from other ships in the underground now that they weren't hiding from Laconian forces, and Alex followed some of them. Every time a new packet arrived, he hoped for a message from Kit. Naomi was deep in the coordination, listening to messages, answering them, passing them across to the *Falcon* for Elvi to see and comment on.

Amos had died and been hauled back from the abyss without it changing much about his demeanor, but Jim and Teresa were both wearing the stress of the moment heavily. Jim kept his usual facade of good humor, but now and then, the deep fatigue showed. Teresa, on the other end of the spectrum, had tapped into a nervous energy that couldn't find an outlet. From the moment she woke, she ran diagnostics that weren't due for weeks or cleaned filters that had only recently been cleaned or went to the ship gym and pushed herself through the resistance gel. Alex would have put it down to the bottomless reserves of youth if it hadn't felt so much like fear.

A day before they reached the halfway point and were slated to start their braking burn, he found Teresa in the galley eating a protein bar and watching video of the ring gate they were hurtling toward. Swirls of highly charged particles and light poured off of it like mist.

"Impressive, isn't it?" Alex said.

"We always knew the gates were energy sources," Teresa said with a shrug.

Alex changed his meal plan. He'd been going to head up to the flight deck and watch his feeds. Instead he had the galley serve him a plate of rice and black sauce, then sat across from Teresa with a fork. She glanced at him, and then away.

"Seems like something's bugging you," Alex said. "Or am I making that up?"

She shrugged a sharp, percussive shrug. He wondered if she'd been having dreams about the bright gates too, or if that was just him.

"I keep thinking about the fight," she said.

"Yeah," Alex said, thinking she meant the battle against the things that had killed San Esteban.

"He's different. I knew the repair drones changed him, but so

372   JAMES S. A. COREY

much is the same that I just thought he was him still. But they
killed him on New Egypt, and he didn't die. The girl who was
yelling at him? Cara? If she'd hit you or me, she'd have broken
our bones. He just took it. Like it was nothing."

"Amos was always tough as old leather," Alex said. "That's not
new."

"He's just so different." She stuffed the last of the protein bar
into her mouth, chewed for a minute, swallowed. "I think about
my father."

"Because he changed too?"

Teresa leaned forward, her elbows on the table. Her jaw was
tight and the brightness in her eyes looked a little feverish. "I
thought he was gone. I thought the whole experiment went bad
and he was just...People lose their parents all the time. I thought
I was one of those."

"Orphaned."

"But if he's only changed, I don't know what I am. Orphan.
Not orphan. Something else."

"And now we're going to see him. It worries you."

"How much can you change and still be you?" she asked, and it
took Alex a few seconds to realize it wasn't a rhetorical. He took
another forkful of rice to give himself time to think.

"Well," he said, "people change all the time. Not changing
would be weirder. I mean, look at you. You're not the same person
you were before you came here. Shit, you're different from when
you first came on the ship. Older, more sure of yourself, better
mechanic. I'm not the same guy I used to be. Amos...Yeah, it's
more extreme. It's weirder. Same with your dad. But I think Amos
is still Amos, even if it's a different version of him. I think when
we find your dad, he'll at least be like what he used to be. You
know? I mean, I expect he's still going to care about you."

"I don't know that," she said, and the bleakness in her voice
told him he'd cut close to the bone.

"I have a kid," he said. "I'm a dad, just like your father. And I
promise you, the connection between a parent and a child? That's

basic. It's deep. You look at Amos and see all the ways he's different. I can see all the ways he's still the same. Your dad's going to be different. But if anything about him is what it used to be? That part'll be how he feels about you."

"That's sweet," Teresa said. "And complete bullshit."

"You don't know. Until you have a kid, you won't. I will plant my flag on that one. The love of a parent for their kid is the last thing to go."

"Even correcting for socioeconomic status, the rate of parental maltreatment of children is robustly at eight per thousand. Most of those victims are between newborn and three years old. Someplace with a million children—Warsaw, Benin City, Auberon— would expect eight *thousand* abused, neglected, or maltreated children. That's a good-sized lower university just of kids whose parents were mistreating them. Sure, humans love their children. They kill them too. Regular as clockwork."

Alex nodded. They were quiet for a few moments. "I sometimes forget the kind of education you had."

"When they groom you to rule all humanity, they don't leave a lot of sentimentality in the curriculum," Teresa said.

"That's too bad."

"I'm scared to see him again," she said. "I'm just scared."

With every passing hour, the gate grew closer and brighter, and Alex grew more aware of the uncertainty they were flying into. The reports from the underground and Laconia were coming almost constantly now, and the conversations between the *Falcon* and the *Roci* were a permanent background hum—Amos talking with Cara and Xan, Jim and Fayez, Naomi with Elvi and Harshaan Lee. The sense of coming closer to a critical point, of being nearly out of time, permeated everything. His mind kept turning back to Teresa and her father, Amos and the children that weren't his though they shared his eyes, Giselle and Kit and Rohi and the grandson that he had never seen. He thought about sending out a message, but he didn't know what he'd say. That was always the problem. Too many feelings and not the right words to wrap around them.

When the time came for the final approach to the gate and Naomi came up to the ops deck, he didn't think it was anything significant. He kept his attention on their drive and the *Falcon*'s while Naomi, below him, took the comms. They were close enough to the ring now that a strong broadcast would have gotten through the ring gate interference, even as loud as it had become.

When Naomi announced the tonnage and drive types of the *Roci* and the *Falcon*, their expected times of transit and vectors into the ring space, Alex noticed that it was an extra step they didn't usually take. He just assumed it was something Naomi had worked out with the others. It wasn't until the reply came back that he understood what he was looking at.

The data that came back was badged from the *Spider Webb*, a survey ship out of the New Wales system. Alex didn't know if it had been Laconian or underground before this, but the reply they sent was regimented and clear. It listed the ships in the ring space, their tonnages and drives, their vectors and flight plans. It showed the anticipated incoming and outgoing traffic in a simple, standard format, and indicated that the *Roci* and the *Falcon* could transit safely. It was the first and only time they'd used Naomi's protocol in practice, and it had functioned just the way she'd designed it to.

Alex unstrapped and let himself down onto the ops deck. Naomi was in her crash couch. The light of the screen shone in her eyes and her pale hair. She looked over at Alex, her expression someplace between sour and amused.

"Yeah," Alex said.

"It would have worked," she said. "If we'd cooperated, it would have worked."

"It would have been better."

"I think about all the things we could have done, all the miracles we could have achieved, if we were all just a little bit better than it turns out we are."

Chapter Thirty-Six: Jim

The ring space was full. Fifty-six ships floated in the eerie brightness of the gates, and instead of burning from one place to the other, they were still. Jim watched them all on a volumetric display. There were more science ships than anything else, but freighters and colony ships were among them. Their drives were pointed in every direction, depending on where they'd come in from and how they'd burned off their velocity. It took him a while to figure out what was unnerving about them.

For decades, the ring space—the slow zone—had been the hub between systems. Especially since the death of Medina Station and the *Typhoon*, ships came in and out as quickly as they could, minimizing the time spent in the starless non-sky. Now they'd come here. It was only the closest ships, the ones most easily deployed, but for the first time in his living memory, they had arrived. A few maneuvering thrusters fired now and then to correct some tiny drift, but their Epsteins were dark. The fleet had come to Naomi's call. To Trejo's. To Elvi's. They weren't locked in battle. They weren't traveling to some more human, more comprehensible space. They were a few slivers of ceramic and silicon lace in a bubble the size of a million Earths.

They looked drowned.

"Okay, we have the ship on visual," Elvi said from the *Falcon*. Even as close as they were, the tightbeam had the flatness and distortion of signal loss. Not enough to make the connection unclear, but enough to make it feel claustrophobic.

"The alleged ship," Jim said, reaching for a joke.

"The egg-shaped thing. We have the egg-shaped thing on scopes. So the good news is that it's still there."

"Have there been any signs of movement or activity?" Naomi asked from the *Roci*'s ops.

"No," Elvi said. "Not on the station anyway."

"Other places?" Naomi asked.

"Everything's more active than it was before. The amount of radiant heat in this place is orders of magnitude greater than it was before. More light, more radiation. Some of the ships that got here first, we may need to get them out into normal space soon to give them a chance to lose some of the excess. The heat exchangers are collecting more energy than they're shedding. I've got every spare sensor taking in data and looking for useful patterns."

"First order of business," Jim said.

"Direct inspection of the station?" Elvi replied.

"I was going to say make sure that all the people who spent the last few years trying to kill each other are okay putting that aside," Jim said. "We've got a couple dozen ships from each side, and you have to figure all of them have crews with some hard feelings about the whole war thing."

"Already on that," Naomi said. "I've been trading messages since we passed the gate."

"How bad is it?" Jim asked.

"Grumbling, but nothing to raise an alarm. Not yet."

Jim looked at the little drowned flecks again. They weren't try-ing to kill each other. That was worth celebrating. "All right. We should go see if anyone's at home on the egg-shaped thing."

Elvi's voice managed to be tired and resolute at the same time. "The *Falcon*'s set course, but I don't want to use the Epstein for braking anywhere near the surface. It's going to take a while."

"You know that thing sucked down a gamma ray burst and still exists, right?" Jim said.

"I'm not worried about the station," Elvi said. "I'm worried about not breaking things before I understand what they are. If Duarte's still in that egg and I burn him to a crisp before we can talk, I'll feel silly."

"Fair point," Jim said. "We'll set to rendezvous."

He dropped the connection. Moments later, the *Roci* shifted under him as Alex changed their course. Jim closed the display and sat in his crash couch, feeling the walls around him, the vibra-tion of the ship, the sense that occasionally struck him of being a tiny organism in a vast universe. His jaws ached, but they did that a lot these days, and if he paid attention, there was a tightness at the base of his skull that never went away, even when he was sleeping. He was used to it. It was how he lived.

Once, there had been a focus to the tension, even if the focus changed sometimes. Fear of the Laconian Empire rolling through and crushing anyone that didn't agree with it under its heel. Or fear of the apocalypse he'd seen in the ring station, back before the gates had even opened. Or the constant, nagging threat of Duarte withdrawing his protection and having Jim thrown in the Pen. The near certainty that by trying to find out whether the things on the other side of the ring gates were conscious and capable of change, Duarte would start a war he couldn't win. And now, that his individual life—the self that was James Holden—would be lost in a sea of consciousness, a vast single mind built from human beings but not human. He could take his pick, and his body was just as ready to ache for the cause.

Or maybe it was just a habit now. Maybe the weight of history had ground him down because he didn't know how to shrug it off. Didn't know that he would choose to, even if he had been able. Two ways of saying the same thing.

"Is this going to be a one-shot," Alex asked from the flight deck, "or are we expecting we'll want to chew the fat some once you're done?"

"I don't understand the question," Jim said.

"If we're just popping you out to work with Elvi's crew, I'll park us close. If you think we're going to want to be in the same room, you can pop out the cargo lock, and I'll put the bridge back up."

Before he could answer, Naomi did. "Put the bridge up. It will be good for the other ships to see it, even if we don't use it."

"Copy that," Alex said. "I'm taking us in."

Jim unstrapped and headed for the cargo airlock.

Teresa was already there. She was wearing a vac suit, testing the seals at the boot and glove and the charge on the mag boots. Jim paused and steadied himself as the ship drifted under him. Her hair was back and tucked into a tight cap that emphasized the shape of her eyes and the roughness of her skin. She lifted her chin in a gesture that might have been a greeting or defiance or both.

"Going somewhere?"

"If my father's there, you'll want me there."

Jim shook his head. "If we find something, I will let you know. And if we need you, I'll get you. I promise."

The girl shook her head, left then right, no more than a few millimeters. Her expression was hard. "It's my dad," she said.

Jim felt a wave of emotions that rose and fell in him in seconds. Frustration, sorrow, guilt, fear. And, almost randomly, a deep nostalgia. He remembered being in school and coming home to find Father Anton in the back of the house building a firepit. It had been a moment of no significance. He hadn't thought about it in years, and then there it was, as present and powerful and filled with love as if it had happened a moment before. *It's my dad.*

"You understand the risks?" Jim asked.

"No, I don't," Teresa said. "Do you?"

Jim shrugged. "Make sure you check your helmet seals."

When they were ready to go, he cycled the cargo airlock. The air pumped out, and as it grew thinner, the sound in his suit changed, growing softer the way it always did. Leaving him feeling more isolated, or more aware of his isolation. His breath, the gentle whir of the fans, the creaking of the suit, it all came to fill more of his senses. It felt almost like falling asleep. Then the vibrations came through the deck as the outer doors unlatched, and the cargo bay opened. Light spilled through the cracks like it never had before, and it took him a few seconds to understand why it was strange. Normally, the light that a ship like theirs opened to was worklights or a star—strong, harsh, and directional. The milk-light that diffused into the hold now came from every direction. It was soft and shadowless as a hazy afternoon on Earth. Like a child's simplistic imagination of heaven.

The station rolled under them, a metallic sphere five klicks in diameter. Too big for a ship, too small for a planet, too smooth and regular for an asteroid. And on its glowing blue surface, a dot like a grain of rice with Elvi's team barely more than dust motes beside it.

Jim and Teresa guided the suit thrusters in toward the group, and the scale of the ship became clearer by having human figures beside it. It was tiny. The whole thing would almost have fit in the cargo hold they'd just left. Smooth as skin and seamlessly curved, it seemed more organic than constructed. One side was open, the flesh of the egg-shape peeled back layer after layer after layer until the hole was big enough for someone to step through.

One of the forms moving around it broke off and came toward him and Teresa. Elvi's face swam up from the other side of the visor like he was looking at her under the surface of a still lake. Her voice over the radio was staticky and distant, given how close she was physically.

"It's a match to the artifacts on Laconia," she said. "It must use the same inertialess movement that Eros did back in the day, because nothing on it looks like a thruster. We can't tell how long it's been here from the temperature because—" She gestured at the thousand bright gates around them.

"Are you sure it was him?" Teresa asked.

"Provable? No. Silly to assume anything different? Yes. At this point I'd need evidence that it wasn't Duarte before I'd entertain it seriously. I hear hoofbeats, I'm still thinking horses at this point."

Half a dozen other figures in Laconian vac suits moved around the egg, swirling out in what Jim realized slowly was a search pattern. "Any sign of him?"

"You're thinking of something convenient like an airlock or a door?" Elvi said. "No. Nothing. The artifact's here, but the surface of the station is totally unmarked."

"Have we tried knocking?" Jim said, more than half joking.

"If I can help," Teresa said. "I could broadcast that we're here. If he can hear my voice, he might come out. Or let us come in."

"Worth trying," Elvi said, motioning them on.

Beside the egg-shape, a collection of boxes were badged as equipment: sensor lines, power supplies, biological sampling kits. The figure floating beside them like a mother hen over its brood turned out to be Harshaan Lee. Jim watched the man's mouth move as he spoke on some other channel that Jim wasn't listening to. Then a click of static and he was on with them. "Give me a moment, and I will connect the young lady's suit output to our system. We can broadcast on a wideband directly on the station with contact vibration as well."

"Humanity's largest subwoofer," Jim said. Elvi chuckled, but no one else seemed to think it was funny.

"How did you get in before?" Elvi asked.

Jim shook his head. He wasn't sure she saw it, so he shook his fist like a Belter. "I just came down toward it, and it opened up. I didn't do anything."

Nothing except follow a ghost who could open all the doors inside the haunted house, he thought. Memories of the horrors and wonders he'd witnessed inside threatened to overwhelm him, and he needed to pay attention, so he forced them away.

"The protomolecule was directing it," Elvi said. "It was trying to figure out what had happened to the systems it was supposed to report in to. You were a way to do that."

"Because I had a body," Jim said. *The only things inside are ghosts now. Having a body in there means something.* "It told me that. Being able to access matter wasn't standard, I guess."

"I've heard your debriefings," Elvi said. "The terms you used? Or it used, I guess. *Pleroma, fallen world, substrate.* They're human terms."

"Everything I was doing got strained through human minds," Jim said. Lee connected a bright red retractable wire from a dark, circular shape that was resting against the surface of the station and connected it to a slot in Teresa's suit arm. "I wasn't really driving, you know. I just got carried along by what it was doing."

"Well," Elvi said. "I think someone's driving now."

Lee gave a thumbs-up. Teresa looked from Jim to Elvi to Lee and back, suddenly anxious. "What should I say?"

"Just let him know we're here," Elvi said.

Teresa nodded, gathered herself. "It's me, Dad. It's Teresa. I'm here on the outside of the station. We want to come in and talk." She paused for a moment, and when she spoke again, there was a note of longing in her voice that broke Jim's heart a little. "I want to see you. I want to come in."

They waited. Jim turned in a slow circle, watching for anything on the surface of the station—a ripple, a hole, a sign of something emerging. Nothing came.

"Try again," he said.

"Father? If you're in there, this is Teresa. I'm on the outside of the station. I want to come in."

The seconds stretched as the hope in the girl's expression slowly died. Lee gestured to her, pulled her close, and unhooked the line. "We have other avenues to explore," he said. "We have several kilometers of contact sensors. We were using them on the Adro diamond, but they could be quite informative here as well."

"We'll help you string them," Jim said.

"If you see anything different from the last time..." Elvi said.

Other than me? he thought, but didn't say.

For the next four hours, the science team laid the sensor filament out along the station until Jim had the vivid memory of rolling endless skeins of yarn into balls during Father Dimitri's knitting phase. Elvi stopped an hour into the process, heading back to the *Falcon*. Lee said it was so that she could oversee the data collection end of the process, but Jim was pretty sure she just needed to rest.

At first, the work was wearying, but as the time passed, Jim found himself falling into the rhythm of it. Running a line, then holding it in place while the others checked the connection between the sensors and the surface of the station. Teresa helped too, her many months of apprenticeship on the *Roci* showing in the way she asked for clarifications and announced her actions to the team before she took them. By the time their bottles were edging toward empty and Jim turned them back toward the ship, Teresa seemed to have shrugged off the first bitterness of her disappointment.

Once the airlock had cycled back closed behind them and Jim had gotten the vac suit off and serviced and stowed, he went back to his cabin. He stank of sweat and neoprene, and his muscles ached and twitched. There had been a time a few decades before when the labor wouldn't have taken as much out of him, but even with the discomfort and the sense that he couldn't have gone on as long as he had as a younger man, there was still a pleasure in the work. By the time he'd washed up and changed into a clean flight suit, he was pleased with himself in a way that he hadn't felt in a long time.

When he got to the ops deck, Amos was alone on it, strapped into a crash couch despite there being no thrust gravity or any real prospect for it. Jim pulled himself to a halt on one of the handholds and looked up toward the flight deck.

"Where is everyone?" he asked.

"Alex is sleeping, Tiny's taking care of the dog and getting some grub. Naomi went over to the *Falcon* to talk about the sensor data."

"There's sensor data already? I mean, I figured there'd be a few hours at least before they gathered enough to have a meeting about."

"When people don't know anything," Amos said, "they love having meetings to talk about it."

"I suppose."

Amos stretched and scratched idly at his chest where his gunshot wound was still a ragged dull-black circle set in pale flesh. "Apparently, there's a lot of activity going on in the station. Stuff happening, even if they don't know what it is. It's hotter too, and the temperature's going up."

"Weird seeing the gears moving. Especially since I didn't know there were gears before."

"Did you find him?"

"We didn't."

"Is he there?"

Jim stretched. His spine cracked. "Yeah. He's there. But I don't think he's looking to talk."

Whatever Amos was going to say in reply was lost when the comms spat out an alert. Jim pulled himself to a couch and called it up. IFF had pinged a ship on the *Roci*'s alert list. The *Derecho*—the ship that had killed the *Gathering Storm* and chased them out of Freehold—had just made transit through Bara Gaon gate. Jim turned off the security alert, and a few seconds later, a message came into the queue from Colonel Aliana Tanaka.

Chapter Thirty-Seven: Tanaka

If they'd met on Laconia, it would have been in the State Building. They would have sat around a carefully made, tasteful table in a room designed to radiate power, comfort, and seriousness. Instead, they were in the galley of a half-rebuilt science ship that stank of overstressed air recyclers and industrial solvent. It made a kind of sense. Portraits of great war leaders or critical battles that looked flattering, well composed, and balanced always felt like propaganda. Tanaka had spent a lot of time in the halls of power. She'd seen many paintings of great men in uniform staring eagle-eyed into the distance where their future glory lay. She'd seen very few paintings of soldiers with only a ragged tent and a dying fire to hold back the cold nights before some stranger tried to bayonet them in the morning.

She'd left Botton on the *Derecho*, coming to the *Falcon* alone. She wore her dress uniform and a sidearm. The drugs left her slightly nauseated, and she'd had a headache since before they'd transited out of Bara Gaon that might have been something nasty building up in her bloodstream or just the constant, unremitting feeling of other minds bumping against her own. In addition to everything else, she had the persistent hallucination that her left eye was weeping, cool tears running down her cheek even in the absence of gravity to pull them.

"You're certain that this…effect is spreading?" Dr. Okoye asked. She'd gained frown lines at the center of her forehead and at the corners of her mouth since the last time Tanaka had seen her. She was also skinny and soft from too much time spent on the float. Between atrophy, stress, and malnutrition, she looked like a stick halfway through burning.

"I am," Tanaka said. "The people who were present for the event got the worst of it. But it's happening to other people too. I don't know how many. And if you don't want it happening to you, start taking these now."

Along with the treasonous head of the Science Directorate, the others in the room were her equally treasonous husband, the head of the underground, and the man who had shot Tanaka's teeth out. While they thought, the weird little not-gnats shimmied around their heads. The ones around Holden were odd, but she couldn't put her finger on why. Tanaka fantasized about what order she'd shoot them in. She'd pretty much settled on starting with Holden. As compromised as she felt, she wasn't certain she'd be able to get all of them, and she'd be disappointed to die in a universe that still had James Holden in it.

So petty, a voice muttered in her mind. An older man. His judgment stung, even though she didn't know him. She stopped imagining Holden dead just to avoid any more unsolicited commentary.

Elvi Okoye paged through the list of medications Tanaka had given her, and her husband watched over her shoulder. The thin woman's frown deepened, but Holden was the one who spoke.

"How bad is it?"

"It's unpleasant," Tanaka said, going for understatement. "The medication helps, but it doesn't stop it."

"We have to find a way into the ring station," Nagata said.

"There isn't one," Fayez Sarkis said. "The sensor data shows a lot of activity. Constant restructuring. Vast magnetic and electrical charges building up and fading away. All kinds of things. But no doors."

"I doubt we can force it open," Holden said. "But—"

"It shrugged off the primary weapon of a *Magnetar*-class battleship, and then took a full broadside from a collapsing neutron star without getting a dent," Tanaka said. "But sure, let's get out the chisels and hacksaws and give it a try."

"But," Nagata said, talking over her, "it can open. It has opened. There's a way."

Of all of them, Nagata was the most surprising. She was nearly the same age as Tanaka, and while the Belter's long, lanky frame was the result of too much time on the float when she was a child, they still looked like they might have been related. Distant cousins, maybe. There was a weariness about her too that spoke to Tanaka, and a sense that she kept herself to herself.

"We all agree that nothing will force it open," Elvi said.

"Which is why we don't force it," Nagata said. "Last time it opened, there was a protomolecule sample hidden on the *Rocinante*. The *Falcon* has a sample now. Let's use it."

"Another dive," Fayez said. "Only into the station this time instead of the library."

Tanaka saw Elvi's hesitation in the gnats before she spoke. "That might not be...easy. The Adro diamond was built to dispense information. We turned it on, and it did what it was created to do. When the station opened for Holden, the protomolecule sample was driving. It was using him to get inside, improvising in the way it was built to improvise. We don't understand what the station was meant to do."

"Power the gates and sterilize entire solar systems when needed, if memory serves," Holden said. The gnats around his head swirled and darted for a moment.

"Either Duarte parked his ship here and took a stroll through space, or he got in," Fayez said.

"Do we have anything more promising to try?" Tanaka asked.

Elvi's silence was answer enough.

Tanaka didn't roll her eyes. "We have a plausible approach to opening the station. So let's try it. We have the high consul's daughter, who is the only person with a strong enough emotional connection to bring him out of whatever fugue state he's in. You open the way, I will escort her in."

"That's not going to happen," Nagata said.

"Not going to happen?"

Holden answered. "We weren't going to hand her over to you in New Egypt or Freehold. We aren't going to do it now."

Tanaka opened her hands, palms up. Floating as she was with legs crossed at the ankle, she felt like a painting of a saint being assumed into heaven. The patron saint of putting up with idiots, whoever that was.

"Admiral Trejo made it clear that we're on the same side now," Tanaka said. "He gave me the highest clearance in the empire to fulfill one mission. Finding the high consul is that mission, and has been since before New Egypt. And all of you are rebels who were still fighting a war with him when he disappeared. I'm open to counterarguments, but if the plan is to engage him in conversation, I'm not sure how you're better ambassadors than I am."

"There are hundreds of ships en route to us right now," Elvi said. "The Science Directorate is sending everything we can spare. The underground is also..." She looked at Nagata, who nodded.

"We don't need more ships," Tanaka said. "At least let's take it to the girl. If she won't go with me, we can find someone else. But there isn't anyone better."

"She's right," Holden said bitterly. "Teresa needs to be okay with it, but any of us would be a distraction. Maybe a threat. The next best fit would be Elvi, and she's—"

"Double agent," Fayez said. "Traitor to the empire."

"Busy overseeing the dive," Holden said. He turned his attention to Tanaka. "What happens when you get to him?"

"I bring him out," Tanaka said. "If I can't bring him out, I establish a more reliable means of communication with him. We learn what he knows, and we find the way to protect the empire. Circumstances may have changed. My job hasn't."

And if you'd gotten out of my way and let me do it, a lot of people would still be alive. She didn't say it, and Holden wasn't in her mind the way the others were, but she was fairly sure he'd understood the point anyway.

"Not to protect the empire," Nagata said. "To protect the human race."

Tanaka shrugged. "From my perspective, that's a distinction without a difference."

"You're right," Holden said. "Let's solve the extinction-level threat first. Then we can all go back to killing each other at a more civilized pace."

He was staring at her, the bugs around his head motionless, as if each of them was staring too. *He's thinking about how he's going to have to kill me again when this is all over with,* Tanaka realized.

"Of course," she replied with a smile. "First things first."

"I'll talk to Teresa," Nagata said.

"Excellent," Tanaka replied. "How long is this going to take?"

Thirty-six hours later, Tanaka got the confirmation that the experiment was ready. By then, seven more ships had come to the ring space. Thirty more would be there in the next day. Before long, they'd have a whole fleet of people to float around with their thumbs up their asses, unsure what to do. None of them mattered. Not if she could get her job done. Finish the mission, whatever the mission had become.

Tanaka's head felt like a cocktail party full of people she didn't know, but she hadn't lost herself again. The voices were quiet, muffled, possible to ignore. So she ignored them. She spent her time in the gym, pushing herself until the ache of her muscles was an environment in and of itself. She took high-velocity steam showers, standing in the flow between jet and vacuum drain with the water almost hot enough to scald. Like the workouts, the pain centered her inside her physical self. It brought clarity.

There was a part of her that wanted to take a lover—find someone on the crew that she could grind against for a few hours. Just another way to bring her attention entirely to her own body and its sensations. It wasn't fear of getting caught that stopped her. It was the unsettling certainty that anything she did would be known, shared, *experienced*, by other people. That it was no longer possible to have secrets of her own. The constant presence of other minds touching hers, trying to pull her into their memories and emotions, was like being eaten.

She kept checking for a message from Trejo, but nothing came. Instead, there was the slow but growing trickle of follow-up reports from the debriefings and interviews she'd taken before her transit into Bara Gaon. The captain of the *Preiss* had gone catatonic. The old medical technician from *Konjin* had started a regimen of psychoactives to keep his mind his own, but the others on the ship had started fading. He posted images to the feed of the ship's crew going weirdly silent, working together with perfect synchrony like a dozen tentacles of the same beast. After leaving the ring space for Parker system, the *Ilrys Eves* had stopped answering its comms and diverted away from its flight plan for the major city on the second planet, and was now on course to a distant exoplanet in a non-elliptical orbit that had been flagged for exploration as a possible artifact.

Everywhere she looked, there were signs and reports of consciousness bleeding from one mind into others. Every minute she had to live with it hurt in a way she couldn't articulate. She didn't have to. The crew of the *Derecho* knew. They were all trapped in the same place she was.

Botton stood in his office, fastened to the deck by his mag

boots with a bulb in his hand and a distant expression in his eyes. Slowly, he found her and saluted. His face had become even more gaunt since they'd left Gewitter and Bara Gaon, and stubble ghosted his chin and neck.

"Captain," she said.

"How can I help?" His voice was soft at the edges.

"What are you drinking?"

He took a moment, then looked at the bulb in his hand as if he'd forgotten it was there. "Water. It's water."

"The medication?"

He nodded and walked to his desk, the mag boots clicking with each step. The peach-colored pills he took from the safety drawer were familiar as air to her now. He put them in his mouth and drank them down. "I'll set an automatic reminder."

"The *Falcon* is ready."

Botton sobered. "Good hunting."

"It's not why I came here."

His look of surprise was deeply comforting. Every bit of evidence that her mind wasn't open to everyone was a reassurance. Or, no, that wasn't right. It was a chance to pretend she could set limits, that she had control she knew she didn't really have. A chance to grab the comforting lie.

"When I find the high consul," she said, "we don't know what the result will be. This armistice with the underground? It's Trejo's agreement. Once we have the high consul, it may or may not be ours."

Botton blinked. "I...think I understand."

"I won't be on the ship. If I give the order?"

"I am an officer of the Laconian Empire."

Tanaka smiled. Her cheek barely ached at all when she did it. How odd to just finish healing now. "Tell no one until the time comes. Our minds can't be trusted. And keep on the medication schedule."

"I understand."

"And Botton? If...if this doesn't work? If we can't stop what's happening with—" She motioned toward her head. "I'd like to ask you a favor."

His smile was gentle. "I'll keep two bullets back, Colonel. One for each of us." In that moment, she almost liked him.

Her suit was in the armory, polished, loaded, and ready. The same suit she'd used to kill Draper Station. She tried to think of it as a good luck charm. *I had a copper penny with a string through it. I got it the night Emily Nam kissed me. I wore it every day for fourteen years.* Tanaka pictured the little coin with its verdigris and the woven plastic string. She remembered Emily, and the softness of her lips, her fingertips stroking gently through his beard. His name was Alan and he grew up on Titan. She let him drift away, trying not to remember anything of her own life where it could find its way into him.

Incendiary rounds. Grenades. The last time someone had fired a grenade in the alien station, thousands of people had died. Well, fuck them. They knew the job was dangerous when they took it. She fastened the helmet in place, checked her bottles, checked her seals. Made sure that the medical system had enough drugs to keep her herself for a few more hours at least. This was her last chance.

She went out the airlock alone, launching down toward the blue, metallic sphere. All around her, the gates glowed, tracking her like thirteen hundred eyes. The girl was too small to see, but Tanaka's suit picked her up—a tiny black dot against the glow. Another figure was beside her—Nagata. Tanaka did a single long acceleration burn and then several short, harder braking burns, falling toward the heir to the empire and her rebel protector. Nagata's suit was an old Martian design, like something out of a museum.

Tanaka's hand gestures indicated the channel, and Nagata switched to it with a click.

"I thought we had an understanding," Tanaka said.

"I'm not going in," Nagata replied. "I didn't want Teresa to come alone. I'll wait out here."

The girl was in a suit like Nagata's, but where Nagata came across like the citizen of another time, Teresa Duarte looked like a kid in a costume. The eyes behind the visor were defiant, the chin a little raised, the jaw a little lifted. Tanaka didn't need to have her consciousness bleeding out around her to see the girl for what she was. Scared. Out of her depth. It would have been pathetic if Tanaka didn't feel the same way, but since she did, it was disgusting.

"I don't know that bringing the high consul out to see his enemies is going to be better than bringing you in," she said.

Nagata made an old Belter gesture that agreed. "If Teresa doesn't need me, I won't be here."

"I told her this was all right," Teresa said. She sounded like her father. Tanaka didn't quite understand what she was looking at. The older woman's quiet fierceness and the girl's imperious entitlement believing they protected each other like the warriors of ancient Greece locking shields. Idiotic hubris or well-earned confidence, it could be hard to tell the difference until it was too late.

"Your choice," Tanaka said. "Come with me now."

Nagata took the girl's helmet, pressed it against her own. It was rude, having a private conversation right in front of her, but Tanaka let it go. She'd killed a bunch of Nagata's friends and followers. Nagata's lover had shot her in the face. A little discourtesy seemed like a small thing to worry about now, and Tanaka suspected all the debts were about to be settled, one way or another.

A short burst from her suit thrusters, and she was falling toward the unblemished surface of the station and the little egg-ship. It was strange seeing it. She could still picture its compatriots in the grotto on Laconia. It was like being on a weeks-long hunt and finally coming across a confirming footprint. The joy that burst up in her was unexpected and it was also unmistakably her own. Trejo had called her in as a hunter. He'd been right.

Tanaka switched to the *Falcon*'s channel. "This is Colonel Tanaka. The girl and I are in place."

Okoye's voice was complicated by the static. The ring space

had become a noisy place, what with the gods of chaos banging on the walls. "Understood. We are starting the dive now. Stand by."

The connection went quiet. Tanaka checked her ammunition, her air supply, her medical status. Beside her, the girl drifted slowly to the right, her velocity just slightly off from Tanaka's own.

"How well do you know him?" the girl asked.

"The high consul?" Tanaka asked. "We've met a few times. I was in the first wave. When we went to Laconia from Mars."

"You're a founder."

"I am," Tanaka said. "All this? I helped make this. He directed us, and we did the work. Humanity's only galactic empire."

"Do you think…" the girl began, but she let the question die unfinished. *Do you think he's all right? Do you think this is going to work? Do you think it was worth it?* The girl could have been asking anything.

Beneath them, the station glowed. Tanaka knew better, but she had the sense that it was humming, sound somehow projecting itself across the vacuum. There might have been some kind of magnetic resonance making her suit ring along with it. It might only have been an illusion.

She checked her suit's readout. The *Falcon* was monitoring the activity of the station—energy, magnetic fields, seismic activity. The data stream was a fire hose. She didn't know enough to interpret it. She scanned the blue, featureless surface, looking for something. Anything. She remembered a painting inspired by Coleridge's *Rime of the Ancient Mariner*. The part where the sailing ship was trapped in a windless still near Earth's equator. In the painting, the ship had been small, the sea vast and empty. Had it been Turner? Drew? Drummond? She couldn't remember. She hadn't thought much of it when she'd seen it. She understood it better now.

The girl corrected her course and started drifting back toward her. The approach irritated Tanaka. A better soldier would have matched the first time.

"Do we know how long this is supposed to take?" the girl asked.

"As long as it does."

They were quiet. Tanaka counted breaths that piled up into minutes. The vast blue exhausted her eyes until the color seemed to vibrate and dance. The girl clicked onto the channel, then off, then on again. When she finally mustered up the courage to speak, she gave voice to Tanaka's own thoughts.

"Something's wrong."

Chapter Thirty-Eight: Elvi

The laboratory was still in an organized kind of chaos. The old setup had been taken down before they left Adro with no reason to think it would be reconstructed anytime soon. Now all the pieces were coming back out, laid down in familiar lines for an unfamiliar purpose. It reminded her of an autopsy. Everything in place, but not functioning.

Or at least not functioning yet.

Rebuilding it was easier and faster than creating it the first time had been. The medical couch already knew the baseline for Cara and Amos. The long months they had spent calibrating the system made recalibrating it simpler. The sensors were already in place, and the territory they were sampling—the station—many orders of magnitude smaller than the Adro diamond.

It should have felt better, but with every cable that came out from storage, every monitor that was paired with some part of the sensors or the medical couch, Elvi felt a little more anxious, the knot in her stomach a little tighter. She couldn't say exactly what she was frightened of, only that she was frightened.

The crew worked with the efficiency of a well-drilled military. Someone who didn't know what they were looking at would have heard a cacophony of voices, everyone talking over everyone else. She could see the structure in it. She knew that Oran Alberts and Susan Yi were ringing the power lines to make sure there was a minimum of noise in the system. Weyrick and Cole were preparing the sync between the medical couch's NIR scanners and the signal processing deck. Jenna and Harshaan were feeding the system backups into the secondary array. They were three distinct conversations like three melodies played simultaneously that sounded discordant until you understood how they all fit together.

With twelve hours still to go before the dive began, Fayez came to the lab. There was a tightness he got around the corners of his eyes sometimes when he was tense. She put the potentiometer back in its case to calibrate later and launched herself over to him, lifting an eyebrow when he met her gaze.

"New briefing came in from Ochida," he said.

"Want to go see if he's figured it all out for us?"

"Hope springs eternal." Fayez turned and led the way back to her office.

Since Naomi had accepted Trejo's offer of cooperation, Elvi hadn't heard from the admiral. She wasn't sure what her status was with him or with Laconia, but she was very aware of having humiliated the de facto military dictator of the empire. It wasn't the sort of thing that ended well for people, historically speaking. It still wasn't in her top five biggest worries.

Ochida, on the other hand, seemed to have embraced a strategy of almost transcendental denial. His reports and the information flowing through him from the rest of the Science Directorate were absolutely unchanged. On the screen in her office, his smile was bright and genuine, and the data he shared with her showed every sign of being complete, accurate, and unabridged.

The survey team had found what they believed to be the bullet at San Esteban, which was interesting. The bullets—scars in the fabric of space-time according to the most popular theory—seemed to accompany each of the intrusions into reality by the dark gods inside the gates. They were relatively small, cosmologically speaking, though the implications of their existence were a fundamental alteration in humanity's understanding of the cosmos. Back in what were quickly becoming the good old days, they'd been easier to locate because they appeared in proximity to whatever had triggered them. The hundreds or thousands or hundreds of thousands of experiments by the enemy since then should in theory have produced just as many small, persistent anomalies, but without being tied to a human object, action, or frame of reference, finding them made needles and haystacks look trivial.

On San Esteban, the break in reality was several meters wide, almost undetectable by instrumentation but very apparent to human conscious experience, and floating half a klick above the moon of one of the minor rocky inner planets. The team was turning all its attention to gathering data from it in hopes that variations between the bullets might yield something critical about the mechanisms behind them.

"What?" Fayez asked.

Elvi looked at him, confused.

"You made a noise. You grunted."

"Oh. I was just thinking. This would have been massive news. Maybe more important than what we were getting out of Adro. But now?"

"Nothing takes your mind off the guy pointing a gun at you like already being on fire," Fayez said. "San Esteban was the biggest threat we could imagine, until Duarte showed back up."

"Duarte's not trying to kill us."

"You sure it wouldn't be better if he were?"

Elvi moved on. Ochida's report on what he was calling "spontaneous alocal cognitive cross-connections" only left her stomach tighter, her jaw aching. The effect was being reported in all systems now. There was a distinctly larger response in places where the ships present during the initial event had gone afterward—Bara Gaon, Nieuwestad, Clarke, Sao Paulo—that suggested an infection-like contact transmission, but there were also suggestions of activity clusters between systems with low physical contact and high communicative load. The greatest predictor of suffering the hive mind effect was having someone who was already affected be aware of you. The epidemiologists were building a model of transmission-by-awareness, and hoped to have a fuller report soon. An intrusive image appeared in Elvi's mind—a vast, bright, interconnected network like the cells in a brain or the relationships in a city, with one node turning deep bloodred, then the ones around it, and the ones connected to those, and on and on.

The longest chain of connection between any two human beings wasn't more than seven or eight connections. Even as vast as humanity had become, as far as they'd flung themselves into the universe, they were still too damn close.

"That doesn't look good for us," Elvi said.

"We could make an argument that Colonel Tanaka and her whole crew need to be in sensory deprivation tanks as a sanitary precaution. That might be fun."

Ochida was moving on to a follow-up report on the death reports from San Esteban when a soft knock interrupted them. When Elvi opened the door, Cara was there. Her face was tight and she held her hands in front of her like she was singing in a choir. Elvi knew what had brought her there before the girl spoke.

"I heard," Cara said. "There's a dive?"

"We're going to try using the catalyst to open a path into the ring station, yes," Elvi said. "But it's not like going into the diamond. Same equipment, different job."

"I should go in. You should send me."

"Amos Burton is going to—"

"I have more experience," Cara said. "I understand how it works in there better than he does."

Elvi raised her hands, seeing as she did it how condescending the gesture was. "It's not like that. This is a different artifact. It's unlikely to behave in the same way. There's no reason to think your experience in Adro will translate to this. And the dependency issue—"

The rage in Cara's expression was as sudden as flipping a page. When she spoke, her voice had a hornet's-nest buzz. Fayez shifted closer to Elvi.

"Dependency is bullshit. It's bullshit, and we both know it."

"It's real," Elvi said. "I can show you the data. The serotonin and dopamine levels—"

Cara shook her head once, a movement of controlled violence. A voice in Elvi's mind said *You did this. This is your fault.* It sounded like Burton, filled with a flat, matter-of-fact rage.

"I understand the risks," Cara said. "I've always understood the risks. You're going to save me from addiction by blowing our best chance to survive? Does that make any sense to you?"

Fayez shifted, trying to bring the girl's wrath away from Elvi. "I don't think that's exactly—"

"Look in a fucking mirror, Doc," Cara said. "You don't get to tell me how important my health is while you're spending your own like that. If you don't matter, why are you pretending that I do? Is it because I look like a teenager? Keep your fucking maternal instinct to yourself."

"There's a difference," Elvi said, "between missing a few exercise sessions and intentionally exposing a research subject to risk. What I do with my own body—"

"I get to pick what I do with my body too!" Cara's voice was a roar now. The need and hunger in her eyes was feral. "You treat me like a child because I look like a child, but I'm not."

She could have just as easily said *You treat me like a human because I look like a human.* It would have been as true. Elvi felt something deep in her chest settle. An ancient instinct, deep in her, told her that showing weakness now was a step toward death. She summoned the coldness of decades in academia.

"I don't think you're a child, but I am the lead researcher here, and in my judgment you aren't the right subject for this test. If you want to try assaulting me into changing my mind, this is your opportunity."

Cara went still for a moment, and then deflated. "You're just doing this because you're scared of him," she said, but there was no heat behind it. Cara turned and pulled herself away down the corridor. The guilt was a knot in Elvi's throat, but she didn't let herself soften. There would be time later to make amends.

She hoped there would.

"This is Tanaka. The girl and I are in position."

Elvi made one last look around the lab. Amos was in place, strapped into the medical couch. They'd taken his shirt off to place the sensors, and the black, chitinous mass of scar where he'd been shot on New Egypt shimmered in the light like oil on water. A white ceramic feed line had been inserted into a vein in his arm and taped down to hold it in place. His body's rapid healing kept trying to push the needle back out again.

He seemed at ease and mildly amused by it all.

The technicians and science team were at their stations. Where the readouts of the BFE had been, images of the ring station flickered and jumped. Elvi felt vaguely nauseated. She didn't remember the last time she'd eaten.

"Understood," she said. "We are starting the dive now. Stand by." She dropped the external connection. "Last chance to back out."

Amos smiled at her. It was the same expression he'd have used if she'd told a joke or offered him a beer. The medical readouts showed his heartbeat low and steady, his cortisol levels low. Either his resurrection had been more transformative than Cara's or he was just really hard to scare. He gave her a thumbs-up and stretched. Jim, tucked in a corner, seemed like a ghost trying to keep out of the paths where someone might walk through him. She half regretted letting him come observe.

She shifted her connection to the catalyst's chamber.

"Are you good to go?"

"We are," Fayez said. "The chamber is going to be a little tight for Cara and Xan both, but I think we'll be all right. As long as no one starts getting claustrophobic."

"All right then. Take out the catalyst."

She could have pulled up a video feed, watched Fayez and his techs open the chamber, wheel out the catalyst, and usher the two not-quite-children into the place it had been. She kept her attention on Amos and the station instead. She heard when the chamber closed.

"Ladies and gentlemen," Harshaan Lee said, "by the numbers and by the book." And then, more quietly, "If any book applies."

Gently, a technician fed the pale cocktail of sedatives into Amos' thick, ropy arm. The black eyes closed.

"Catalyst is out," Fayez said, but she could already tell. The activity on the ring station shifted like an eye turning toward them. Magnetic fields reached out where none had been before, and the rhythm of seismic and energetic activity changed. The activity in Amos' brain shifted as well.

"Look for a matching pattern, please," Lee said. "If this is similar to our green friend in Adro, we should find an echo of the subject."

But the technicians weren't listening. Every head was bent to a screen, every hand on the controls. The *Falcon* seemed to hum with raw human attention. Elvi's heart tapped impatiently at her breastbone.

"I'm seeing…" one of the geology group said, then stopped.

Time became very slow. On the screens, pattern-matching systems fed the intimate signals of Amos Burton's brain and body into one input and the data from the ring station into another, fitting one to the other a million times a second and looking for a match. Cascades of green and yellow flickered as the man and the artifact fell in and out of synchrony. Amos sighed once, like a commentary on something just a little disappointing.

"I have something that resembles the handshake," the woman at the informatics station said. Her tone was artificially flat, trying very hard to hide her excitement. "It began twenty seconds ago from...mark."

"Confirmed. They're talking."

Elvi pulled herself to the medical couch. Amos' face was empty as a mask, his muscles slack, his eyes closed, his lips the powder gray that his altered blood created. She wanted to touch him, to make sure he was still warm. That he was still alive. His eyes shifted under their lids, left and then right and then left again. He took another breath.

One of the medical technicians made a soft noise. "I've got some activity in the dorsal posterior insula that I can't—"

Amos' eyes shot open and he screamed. The rage and pain in the sound were a punch in Elvi's face. She reared back, spinning as she missed her handhold. He took another breath and shrieked.

"We have a cardiac problem," one of the medical technicians said, his voice high and tight. "I've got an arrhythmia here...I don't know what I'm looking at."

"Elvi?" Jim said.

"Not now," she snapped back.

Amos raised his arms, the muscles standing out under his skin. His left bicep—as thick around as Elvi's thigh—began crawling with spasm. He made a deep hiccuping sound, struggling to breathe.

"Pull him out," Elvi said. "We're done here. Pull him out."

"You heard the lead!" Harshaan shouted. "By the numbers and by the book!"

Lee moved in, fixing a syringe to the feed in Amos' arm. The cocktail of revival medicines seemed to resist going into the vein. Elvi waited for the spasming to stop. Jim, out from his corner, floated at her side, his face ashen.

"He's not coming up," he said. "Why isn't he coming up?"

Amos' head bent back, baring his neck. The veins in his throat stood out in a way that made Elvi think *massive debilitating stroke.* His eyes were open, black pits without any clear focus.

"I can give him another dose," Lee said.

"Do it," Elvi shouted.

Another cocktail went into the big man's arm. Alerts were sounding all through the lab; machines and monitors panicking at what they saw.

The medical technician's voice was an island of professional calm in the chaos. "He is not coming up. We are moving into GTCS with ventricular fibrillation. We're going to lose him."

Jim was murmuring a string of quiet obscenities like it was a prayer.

"Sedate him. Whatever you need to do," Elvi said. And then, "I'll be right back."

"Where are you going?" Jim asked, but she didn't answer.

She didn't know she was leaving until she was already gone. She pulled herself hand over hand through the hallways like a nightmare of being trapped in a sunken cave. She was going faster than she could handle, bruising herself as she crashed around corners. Her mind was divided between a deep animal panic and something smaller, calmer, and more watchful.

The catalyst chamber was as full as it ever got. Fayez and two techs floated beside the catalyst. The catalyst's empty eyes were vague and unsurprised, her hair floating around her like a drowned woman. Xan and Cara were visible on a screen in the isolation chamber, their small bodies filling the space within it.

"Elvi?" Fayez said. "What's the matter?"

She didn't answer him. Jim slid in through the door behind her. She ignored him too.

The isolation chamber was one of the most advanced devices Laconia had ever fashioned, but it was as easy to use as a meat freezer. Elvi grabbed the handle, braced, and pulled the thick door open. Cara and Xan turned to her, their eyes wide with confusion and alarm.

"Get out," Elvi said. "Out of the container. Do it now."

Fayez was at her side. She was afraid he was going to grab her, stop her, slow her down and make her explain herself. He didn't.

"The dive went bad," Elvi said. "Amos is stuck there, and we can't get him back."

Xan shook his head. "I don't understand. You can't get him back? Stuck how? What stuck him there?"

Cara's smile was triumphant. She took her brother's hand. "It's all right. We can do this. Follow me."

Her eyes closed, and then a heartbeat later, Xan's closed too. The catalyst cooed softly and mindlessly. Elvi's breath shuddered and her hands trembled. It occurred to her exactly how bad this moment would be for a medical emergency of her own. Fayez put a hand on her shoulder, and she let herself be turned. He was frowning with worry. Maybe fear.

"Hey, Elvi," he said.

"Fayez."

"So. I guess we'll call this field-testing a new protocol?"

To her surprise, Elvi laughed, even if it came out like a sob. Cara shifted like someone twitching in her sleep. A connection request came through on the ship's system: Harshaan Lee looking for her. She answered, but didn't give him time to speak.

"What are we seeing?"

"The subject appears to be stabilizing," Lee said. "However, I am seeing—"

Before the next word came, Elvi's awareness widened like its jaw had unhinged, and she exploded into white.

Interlude: The Dreamers

The dreamer dreams, and his dream is unlike all that passed before. Where grandmother masks whispered and promised and told their secrets, nothing welcomes him here. Instead, there is the machine, and the machine is constant motion. Something that isn't light glimmers in colors no eyes have seen. Shapes lock together and come apart too quickly for a mind to follow. The chitter of a swarm, rich with meaning he cannot find. The dreamer looks upon the truth behind the dream and finds no place for himself.

But a place must be found or made, so the dreamer imagines himself closer, wills himself in, and the machine bites at him, rips him, skins him skinless and raw. The pain is real, but it teaches. The glimmers glint patterns in their not-lights, the cascade of shapes has music in it, the swarm song is a static of words at the edge of comprehension. If there is less of the dreamer than there was, if the machine has taken what can't be given back, the reward is a knowing deeper than bones.

The next time comes, and the dreamer fits his bleeding hands in the spaces between the spaces, breathes through the holes in number, and builds from abstraction a tool to crack wide the abstract. He sees the mechanism through its own strange eyes, and its depth astonishes and terrifies him. The voice of the machine grows deep and grand and horrifying: God whispering the obscenity that ends worlds. The darkness is the darkness of old, but terror has no face for him, and there needs to be a way, so there will be. A thousand bites, a million needle sticks, a ripping away of all that doesn't fit.

And the bull-headed god turns to him, and for an instant that is an eon, they know each other with intimacy beyond names. There are no secrets between the two men dead without dying—their pain is one pain, their weariness is one weariness, their resolves braid together to a single rope that pulls at them both ways. Something shatters, and the horned god with his bloodied flanks turns eyes to the dreamer. Wheels within wheels within wheels. Where there was once a man, pitiless legions march.

The dreamer squares his shoulders and steps into the ring. There is nothing outside the ring. There is something within it, and it will have him dead.

The god that was a man finds the man that was a corpse and time skips in thunder. The dreamer feels the dream grow thin, and the thinness is pain. All he can do is exhale and know that when this breath is gone, there are no more breaths behind it. He fights like a raging storm, but the other man fights like a falling sea.

The dead man begins to die. Somewhere else, he feels a body ripping itself apart. He feels the heart he once had stopping. He hears human voices in the room beside pain, but there is no doorway back. The dreamer dreams an answering violence. A rat bites a tiger's paw.

And then, more. A ghost made from hunger. A ghost made from longing. Graveyard children and prisoners. They touch their rage to his, and the dreamers dream together. They press into the machine, and the machine begins to shift and open. A thread swims itself into being, red and thin and tenuous. The horned god bellows a weariness vast as oceans and lowers its inhuman head.

Brightness floods, and for a time outside of time, they are lost in a sea of memories and sensations made meaningless, simple and confused as newborns. When they are again, the machine is the machine and they are outside of it.

The machine whirs and clatters. The little man rises. The hungry ghost rises, sparkling. The dreamers rise toward three brightnesses. Three holes in the ice that is the ceiling of the world.

The horned god forgets. The little man forgets. The sparkling ghost cannot bring herself to forgetfulness, and that is and will always be her hunger. The machine glimmers its idiot glimmers, it shapes its insoluble puzzles, it sings a buzzsaw shriek. And in a dream beneath the dream, a man stands alone in a lighthouse and faces an angry sea. His exhaustion and pain rhyme with something real, and Amos opens his eyes.

The lab was weirdly still. All around him, monitors chirped and alerts sounded. When he breathed in, it felt like his lungs were filled with glass shards. With an effort, he turned his head. Elvi wasn't there. Jim wasn't. He recognized Elvi's second-in-command, though. Lee, he thought. The guy seemed stunned. They all seemed stunned.

"Hey," Amos said.

Lee didn't answer.

"Hey."

With a shudder, the doctor seemed to come back to consciousness from whatever fugue he'd been in.

"What? Oh. Yes. Don't try to move," Lee said. "You've been through... You've been through a lot."

"You all right?"

"Yes, I just...I had a very strange experience."

"Yeah, I figured. But you got to tell Jim and the doc. There's no way to get in. Duarte knows we're here now. And I think he's pissed."

Chapter Thirty-Nine: Jim

The experience, when it came, was overwhelming. Jim remembered everything from before it, but with the sense of distance that trauma could sometimes bring. He could still picture Amos, strapped to the medical couch, suffering seizures and pain. He remembered following Elvi down to the catalyst's chamber and seeing Fayez and the technicians there.

He remembered looking at the woman they called the catalyst and thinking of Julie Mao, the first person he'd seen infected by the protomolecule, and how long it had taken her to die. Or if not die, be transformed. And the victims of Eros Station, injected with the protomolecule sample and exposed to massive doses of radiation to drive the spread of the alien organism or technology or however people wanted to categorize it. Even then, they'd died slowly. Or been unmade and repurposed without the release of dying in between. He remembered thinking how perverse it was that the catalyst could live in that state indefinitely, a skin to hold the protomolecule. A tool made from human flesh. He remembered wondering if there was anything left of her that could be aware of what she'd become.

Then Elvi had opened the isolation chamber, taken out Cara and Xan in hope that they could interrupt the ongoing assault that was killing Amos. All of those memories were clear and unmuddied, but it felt like they'd happened weeks or months before. That was because of what happened next.

There had been a brightness: light that was also a sound that was also an impact like being punched in each cell of his body individually. He'd felt like something in him was opening and opening and opening until he was afraid it would never stop opening, that he'd become a single, ongoing act of expansion that could only end with annihilation.

Then, like a dream, he was a hundred places at once. A thousand people. A vastness in which the idea of "James Holden" was lost like a stone in the ocean. He was a woman with an aching shoulder in the galley of a ship he didn't know, halfway through a bulb of cheap coffee that had been secretly spiked with alcohol. He was a young man in a small, cramped engineering deck, engaged in a sexual act with Rebecca—whoever she was—and torn between guilt and delight at his infidelity. He was an officer in the Laconian Navy hiding in his ready room, the lights off, trying to keep his sobs quiet so that the crew wouldn't hear them and know how afraid he was.

Like a kaleidoscope made from other people's intimate lives, his memory was bright and shining and fragmented. It left him a little dizzy just thinking about it too much.

"So," Elvi said, "I think we can agree that Colonel Tanaka's reports were accurate."

Tanaka, on the wall screen, nodded. Naomi was on the screen beside her, the *Roci*'s ops deck around her like a frame. Jim and Fayez floated in Elvi's office. All of them together, and all of them scattered.

Amos, along with Cara and Xan, was being scanned by the medical team. As was everyone else on the crew. The hours that had passed since the failed dive had been a whirlwind of activity. The science teams checking and rechecking their data, searching for any patterns that might shift and fade before they were quite erased. Jim didn't doubt that they'd find all the same things Tanaka had found the first time, when the *Preiss* had been saved.

The idea caught him. "Was there someone transiting? When this happened?"

"No," Naomi said. "The trigger wasn't the things inside the gate this time. It was us."

"That's my assumption too," Elvi said. "Duarte or the station or some combination of the two rejected us. Pushed back. I believe that Colonel Tanaka's drug regimen blunted the worst of the effect. At least for us."

"Wait," Fayez said. "At least for us? As opposed to who?"

"It seems like the event may have been broader this time than before. I've had reports from five scientific missions that were close to their gates reporting experiences similar to ours. I won't be surprised if more come in later."

"How far could it have reached?" Tanaka asked.

"It's a nonlocal effect," Elvi said. "Without better understanding how it propagates, I couldn't make any meaningful guess."

"I think I have some indication," Naomi said, and her voice was hard as slate. Her image disappeared from the screen, and a series of tactical maps took its place. Solar systems cycled through, a few seconds of one, and another, and then another. As Naomi spoke, they went on and didn't repeat. "The underground and its allies are showing that since the event, a hundred and five ships in seventy systems have changed course in ways that will bring them through the gates. They're a combination of Laconian, underground, and purely civilian vessels. And they've also gone silent."

"Silent?" Jim echoed. He meant it more as an expression of shock than a question, but Naomi answered him anyway.

"No broadcast. No tightbeam. No offers of explanation or filed changes of flight plan. Just all of them turning toward us."

"Radio silence seems weird," Fayez said. "Their drive plumes are still visible. What do they think they can hide by running in radio silence? What do they gain?"

"They don't gain anything," Tanaka said. "They just don't need comms anymore. They're all thinking with the same head."

Elvi let out a little noise, somewhere between a sigh and a sob.

Tanaka either didn't notice or chose to ignore her. "I've taken the liberty of reaching out to Admiral Trejo. I'm hoping we can get some backup here in time."

"In time for what?" Jim asked.

"The battle," Tanaka said as if it had been a stupid question.

"Are we sure that these are enemies?" Elvi asked.

"Yes," Tanaka said. "We tried to get into the station. We were pushed back. Now an ad hoc flotilla of hive-mind-controlled ships are running toward us. If they're just rushing here to bring us cake and party decorations, we'd know because we'd be in the station chewing the fat with the high consul."

"There are eighteen systems we've ID'd that don't seem to have any enemy activity," Naomi said.

"If we retreat, we'll never get this territory back," Tanaka said, leaning in toward her camera. Jim detested and feared the woman, and that made it worse when she seemed right. "Either we get inside now, or we talk to the high consul when he's inside us and pulling our strings."

Naomi's voice was gentler, but just as firm. "Do we know why the experiment failed? Why could Jim get into the station, back before the gates opened, and we can't now?"

"The station was on a kind of autopilot when you first came here," Elvi said. "It opened for the bit of protomolecule that stowed away on your ship because it didn't have anything telling it not to. Now it does. Our catalyst can turn something on, and Cara and Amos can react to it, but Winston Duarte was remade with the protomolecule. It's part of him now. We aren't getting in that station because he doesn't want us to. It's as simple as that."

"I can still hear voices in my head," Alex said. "I mean, real people's real voices. Is that happening for you too?"

"Yes," Teresa said.

Around them, the *Rocinante*'s galley seemed like an impostor of itself. Real and present, but also somehow less authentic than it should have been. Like Jim was there, and also wasn't.

Teresa looked hollow-eyed with disappointment and grief. He tried to imagine what it would have been like for her to come so close to seeing her father again, to have him back on some level, and then failing at the last obstacle.

"When's Amos coming back?" Alex asked, and Jim shrugged.

"When they're done with him," he said.

"What are we gonna do?"

That was the question. Jim scooped the last of his rice and beans into his mouth, chewed, and swallowed. The *Rocinante* was a good ship. It was a good home. There were millions of people in hundreds of systems who would never have a place like this for as long as he'd had the *Roci* and its crew. He wasn't sure why that idea felt so melancholy. He popped his bowl and spoon into the recycler, appreciating how the lid clicked under his hand, how it sealed when he took the pressure away. It was such a small, little elegance. So easy to overlook.

"I'm going to—" he said, and pointed toward the passage to his cabin with his thumb. Alex nodded.

Jim moved slowly through the ship, his mind full. He kept thinking of Eros. Of the way that the protomolecule, let loose, had taken people apart and put them back together according to its own needs, its own program. Here he was, decades on, and it was still the same. Amos, Cara, Xan. They'd died and been rebuilt because an alien drone following who knew what decision tree had come to the conclusion that they should overcome death. Duarte and the ring station were taking all of humanity apart like a caterpillar liquifying in its cocoon to be reassembled into a butterfly.

The war would go on. The builders of the ring gates moving from form to form—primitive bioluminescent sea slugs, to angels of light, then to a hive of mostly hairless primates with billions of bodies and only one mind. The dark things inside the gates and outside the universe scratching and ripping and unmaking the sickness that had intruded on its reality. Maybe someday that battle would be won. Maybe it would go on forever. Either way, nothing that Jim knew as human would persist. No more first kisses. No more prayers. No more moments of jealousy or insight or selfishness or love. They would be taken apart and fit back together like the bodies on Eros. Something would be there, but it wouldn't be them.

Naomi was in a clean jumpsuit when he got to the cabin. She smelled of soap and fresh water. The light from her screen showed the lines in her face—sorrow and laughter both. She was beautiful, yes, but she'd always been beautiful. When they'd been young together, they'd been beautiful just because youth had a beauty all its own. It took age to see whether the beauty could last.

She narrowed her eyes and laughed. "What?"

"Just admiring the view."

"You *cannot* be horny right now."

"Don't tell me what I can't be," he said, then moved beside her and put his hand on hers. "We aren't getting out of this one, are we?"

"I don't see how. No."

They were silent for a moment. Jim felt a tremendous sense of peace washing over him. For the first time since he'd been taken prisoner on Medina, he felt deeply at ease. He stretched, and it actually felt pretty good.

"You are the central fact of my life," he said. "Knowing you. Waking up next to you. It's been the most meaningful thing I've done. And I am profoundly fucking grateful that I got that. I think of how easy it would have been for us to miss each other, and I can't even imagine what that lifetime would have been."

"Jim—"

He waved to have a few seconds more to say what needed to be said. "I know I made choices that cost you. I've got this habit of rushing into things because I think they needed doing. I lost time with you, but it was always my choice. Heading to the *Agatha King*. Sounding the alarms on Medina. Trying to get to the bullet on Ilus. Going back to see what was really happening on Eros Station. They were all risks I took, and I told myself it was okay because I was only risking me. But I was risking someone important to you too, and I am so grateful that I've been someone important to you. I didn't mean to take that lightly."

She turned off her screen, then squeezed his hand. "You are remarkable. You have always been remarkable. Not always wise, not always thoughtful. But always, always remarkable. Yes, I have paid a price for letting someone as headstrong and impulsive as you matter so very much to me. But I'd do it again."

He didn't know which of them started to pull the other close, only that they folded together. Her arm found its way under his, and she ducked her head, pressing her cheek against his chest. He put his chin on top of her head, a rare thing when she was so much taller than him. Her first little sobs shook them both, and then his did. They drifted gently in the cabin that had been theirs. Jim had the sense of other minds drawn to the moment like insects following pheromones, but he couldn't pay attention to them. Not with her there in his arms.

After some stretch of time that might have been minutes or hours, the weeping reached its natural end and they were only quiet together. Naomi uncurled a little, raised her head. Their mouths met, gently, and with only the barest hint of the hunger of their youth.

"Whatever you think you have to do? Whatever it is," she whispered, "wait until I'm asleep."

Jim nodded, and she pressed herself against him in the dark. He counted his own breaths up to a hundred and back down again before her breath grew deep, then up to a hundred again to give her time to fall past where his leaving would wake her. She shuddered once, then gently snored. Carefully, he unfolded himself, reached out to tap the wall and push to the cabin door. He opened it as quietly as he could and closed it behind him with a click.

Somewhere down on a lower deck, Muskrat barked happily, and he could hear Amos' rough voice, if not the exact words. The ship creaked softly as it warmed and shed its heat. Somewhere, Alex was sleeping or watching his neo-noirs or feeling guilty about Kit and Giselle. Somewhere Teresa was eating herself with disappointment and adolescent confusion. Bobbie Draper wasn't there, and never would be again. Clarissa Mao was gone too, though both of them had left their marks on the ship and the people who lived in it. For a moment, he imagined Chrisjen Avasarala beside him, her arms crossed and her lips in a smile that managed to be sharp and consoling at the same time. *For fuck's sake, this isn't the last day of summer camp. How many fucking tearful embraces are you planning on?*

In the med bay, he pulled an emergency kit with a red ceramic shell and tucked it under his arm. He patted the autodoc like it was someone he knew and liked and might not see again for a while.

The airlock wasn't restricted, and he was able to cross the bridge and enter the *Falcon* without anyone taking particular notice of him. The Laconian crew had gotten very used to pretending he wasn't there, and his place, first as Elvi's guest and then as the resistance leader's boyfriend, gave him a kind of undefined status in their own rigid pecking order. As long as he seemed to know where he was going, they assumed that he did. It was like being invisible.

The catalyst's room was empty except for the isolation chamber. He closed the door to the corridor behind him. There wasn't a lock on it or a way to jam it closed. Well, nothing was ever perfect. He cracked open the emergency kit and went through it item by item. Bandage. Antiseptic. Hypox injector. Hypodermic needle.

His head felt weirdly clear. Even with the distant awareness of the others, the moment was his own. He felt as alone as he ever had, and also a kind of satisfaction. A falling away of doubt. The anxiety that had haunted him since Laconia had cooked off like dew on a warm day. He was only himself now.

The isolation chamber opened easily, and he pulled the catalyst out. Her blind, empty eyes swept past him. Her mouth worked as if she were saying things that only she could hear. She didn't react at all when he slid the needle into her arm and drew out the plunger.

The hypodermic filled with a swirl of iridescent blue and black. Five ccs. Ten. An alert was sounding somewhere nearby, and he assumed it was because of him. He'd intended to roll up his sleeve and inject the sample into the veins at the bend of his elbow, but he was suddenly worried that the *Falcon*'s crew would come too soon, would stop him. Grimacing, he pressed the needle through the leg of his flight suit and into his thigh. He pushed the plunger down until it stopped. The catalyst smacked her lips and writhed like she was trying to remember how to swim.

Jim closed his eyes.

At first, it felt cold: a thread of ice that went from the site of the needle stick up into the gut. Then a wave of nausea that came and went and left a burning sensation behind it that spread through his abdomen and up into his chest. His heart started pounding, each beat slow, hard, and violent as a hammer strike. He tasted metal.

In the darkness behind his eyelids, blue fireflies flickered in and out of being. He had a feeling like blood flowing back into a limb that had been pressed too hard for too long. It felt like desert rain filling dry arroyos. It felt like remembering.

He took a long, slow breath. He was trembling. He opened his eyes, looked around the room, and found what he thought he'd find. What he'd hoped for. The slouch. The half-apologetic, half-astonished sad-dog face. The porkpie hat.

"Well," the familiar voice said where only Jim could hear it. "This can't be good."

"Hey, Miller. We need to talk."

Chapter Forty: Naomi

Y ou can see him?" Naomi asked. "Right now, you can see him?"
Jim nodded. They were floating in the emptied lab where
Amos had only recently been strapped down for his failed dive
into the station. The *Falcon*'s security officers had taken Jim there
directly from the catalyst's chamber, and Elvi had called Naomi
over. Now he was steadying himself on a handhold. His face had
the sweaty, tight look it got when he was coming down with an
illness or he'd drunk too much, but there was a calm with it. And
something else. Amusement, maybe.

"For me, he seems to be right between you and Elvi," Jim said.
"A little bit closer to Elvi."

"This can't be the same Miller," Elvi said. "This has to be something else."

Jim chuckled.

"What?" Elvi snapped.

"Sorry. He said something funny. Look, in any traditional sense, the Miller I met died when Eros crashed into Venus. The protomolecule preserved and co-opted the patterns in his brain, and when it needed a tool to find missing things, there those patterns were, right in the toolbox. That version of Miller needed something that could take a ship places, and I was the guy who decided where the ship went, so it started using me. Physically manipulating my brain into seeing and interacting with the patterns it made from Miller. Those manipulations left channels. All I did was put the protomolecule and those channels back together."

He looked at Naomi and tilted his head, a little smile on his lips. "I was just remembering something Alex said about tools that get used long enough developing souls. It's off the subject. Forget about it."

"Before, you weren't able to see him when other people were around," Elvi said.

"That's true," Jim said. "This is a different relationship." A moment later, he laughed. Naomi didn't know what at, except that it was Miller. If the jealousy stung, there was nothing she could do with it.

"Can this version of Miller open the station the way the last one did?"

Jim seemed to listen for a moment, then he shrugged. "I don't know. He doesn't either. The situation's different that way too. We won't know until we've tried."

"I want to do some scans," Elvi said, more to herself than to them. "Brain activity at a minimum. Full metabolic if we have time."

"Not sure I have a lot of time for that," Jim said.

"Is this something you can undo?" Naomi asked. "Is there a way to pull this back out of him?"

"It's going to be hard to unscramble that egg," Elvi said. "But there are probably some things we can do to keep him stable. Or more nearly stable."

Jim shrugged. "Getting us more time is good, but only if we get more out than it takes to get it, if you see what I mean. We have a lot of clocks counting down on us right now."

"I'm talking about saving your life," Elvi said.

"I know, and I appreciate it. That's a later-on problem. If we don't get the rest of this right, it's not going to matter. If you still exist as an individual who wants to fix me? That'll mean a lot of things have gone right."

They were quiet. Naomi glanced at the empty space between her and Elvi as if there might be something there for her to see. There wasn't, but Elvi turned as if the look had been meant for her. Naomi realized they were waiting for her to make the decision. Jim was smiling at her, and it made Naomi want to punch him in the face. *How in fuck did I wind up here?* she thought.

"Collect any data you can now, and stabilize him," she said. "We'll need to get Teresa ready."

"And Tanaka?" Elvi asked.

Naomi hesitated. She didn't like Tanaka, and she didn't trust her, but their interests were aligned for the moment, and inviting yet another front in her personal wars felt petty. "And Tanaka."

"Okay," Elvi said. "I'll get the medical team."

She pulled herself out of the lab and closed the door behind her. It wasn't until the latch clicked that Naomi realized Elvi was giving them a moment alone. Jim looked away from her almost shyly. He was older, thinner, more worn around the edges than the man she'd met decades before on the *Canterbury*, but the openness she remembered was there too. The vulnerability. The almost genetic inability to believe that things wouldn't work out for the best if he just followed his heart.

"I'm sorry," he said.

"Really? I haven't watched you try to kill yourself enough times? Now you make me watch you succeed in slow motion. But you're sorry."

"Yeah. That part is pretty shitty. But I couldn't think of anything else, and this isn't what—"

"Let's take care of the problem," she said. "The rest can come later."

He hesitated, then nodded. "I'll probably go to the station from here. Once they're done with the scans."

"I'll be on the *Roci*."

"All right then. I'll let you know when I'm in position."

Naomi nodded and pulled herself to the door and down the corridor as if they were only heading to their various mundane duties. As if it weren't the last time. How strange to know in the moment that something precious was ending, and still have it change nothing. Either it was a sign of her devastation or a tribute to how good their life together was and had been.

She made the transfer back to the *Rocinante*. The air didn't change scent this time. Either there had been enough traffic between the connected ships that the atmospheres had mingled, or she'd just gotten used to both of them. She hesitated for a moment, unsure whether to go back to her cabin or up to the ops deck. Her work could be done at either one, but the cabin had Jim's things—his clothes, his scent, his absence—and so she made the turn to ops.

Alex was there, his eyes wide and his hands fluttering in powerless distress.

"You heard?" she said.

"It's true?"

"It is," she said, and picked a couch to strap into. "How did you find out?"

"Casey."

"Casey?"

"The power supply technician on the *Falcon*? Dark hair, wide face? Little mole on his neck? He was over drinking beer with me and Amos back in Adro before we left."

Naomi shook her head. She had probably seen him, but she didn't make connections with the ease that Alex did.

"Are you all right?" Alex asked in a voice that meant he knew that she wasn't.

Naomi pulled up her tactical display and split it. The ring space on the left, and on the right a more schematic view with the rings, the systems beyond them, and the ships falling in from all directions. The sheer scale of it was overwhelming. She had to figure out which of the ships were coming to her aid, which were the new enemy. She had to inventory the drugs and precursors that would keep the ships she did have from falling into Duarte's nightmare hive mind. She had to keep control of the ring space long enough for Jim to have a chance at stopping the catastrophe that was rolling in toward them from all directions.

"I'm really, really angry," she said. "When Jim came back from Laconia—when we got him back—I knew he was hurt. I knew there was less of him somehow. I thought we'd take care of him. That he was injured, not just in his body. In his soul, if that's the word. With time and care and love, I thought maybe I would see him again the way he had been. The way I remembered him."

"I get that," Alex said.

"And then the thing that actually did bring him back wasn't any of that. I saw him again. Just now. I saw him the way he used to be. At his best. And love isn't what got him there. And it wasn't care. And it wasn't time. He saw something incredibly, stupidly dangerous that needed to be done and only he could do. And he just…"

She opened a closed fist like she was scattering dust.

Alex hung his head. "He just did it."

"He rose to the occasion." Tears were sheeting across her eyes now, making the deck a swirl of color and refraction. She wiped them away on the back of her sleeve.

"He is who he is," Alex said. "He is who he's always been. I understand that. I've got two marriages behind me because I thought I'd changed and grown into someone else. And I wasn't wrong, but I wasn't right either. Jim changed, but he also stayed the same."

"I wish we'd been the ones to bring him back, and not this."

"So what can we do?"

Naomi looked at her screens. The tears were already drying, even if the darkness and emptiness and regret were all just as deep. "We give him as much time as we can. We try to make this latest idiotic, brave, stupid gesture count for as much as it can. And then we see what happens next. Someone needs to let Teresa know and get her ready. And tell Amos. There may be some fighting."

"I can take care of them. Don't you worry about it."

He turned and headed for the lift shaft.

"Alex?"

When he looked back, they only locked their gazes for a moment. She didn't know what she'd meant to say, and whatever it was, he already knew it.

"I got this part," he said. "You take care of yours."

She started the work, and at first it felt impossibly large. She was overwhelmed by the scope and complexity, but she told herself that it didn't matter whether it was possible, only that she do it. She started small and specific. The *Tullus Aufidius*—a mercenary gunship with roots in Freehold—was slated to pass through the St. Anthony gate in sixteen hours. It had been coming to her call as part of the underground, but hadn't responded to connection requests from the repeater at the gate since Amos' psychic dive into the ring station went so wrong. So that was the first problem. She found a solution. The *Kerr*, the *Vukodlak*, and the *Dhupa*—two Laconian fighters and one underground supply ship with some torpedo racks welded on the outside—would intercept it. Any of the three that survived the encounter could join the *Armando Guelf* at the Hakuseki gate and intercept the *Brother Dog*.

She thought about sending a message out to Trejo, calling for more Laconian reinforcements. The message would take hours to reach him, hours to get back, and by the time any ships he sent made it there, it was just as likely they wouldn't be answering to Trejo or Naomi anymore. Better to play the cards she had. She wasn't going to win, but she could take a long time losing.

She ran solutions through the *Roci*'s system, shifting from

scenario to scenario like a football coach preparing for a complicated game. Here are my players. Here are their players. Here's
the field of play. The hurt and the horror and the grief were still
there when she thought to turn to them, but they lived at a distance. She felt herself slipping into the version of herself that she'd
made during Jim's captivity: the Naomi who lived in secret and
met the world with her intellect because her heart was still too raw.

She wondered whether this was how Camina Drummer had
survived as the last president of the Transport Union, or Michio
Pa as the first. Or Avasarala, back on Earth when Earth had been
the center of the human race and not just the oldest planet among
thousands. The *Indefatigable* and the *Yunus Emre* would intercept the *Blackberry* when it transited the Xicheng gate. She que-
ried the *Yunus Emre* about the models of torpedo and PDCs it had
and set the *Roci* to checking for ships with compatible loadouts.

When Jacob died, it had been just the same. It had been just
weeks until their fortieth anniversary, and the children were all
coming back from university for the party. She'd found him in the
bathroom. Dead of a stroke, the doctors said. She'd spent twenty-
eight hours straight cleaning the apartment, and she wouldn't
have stopped then except Hannah came early and—

Naomi stopped, her hands raised and her heart beating triple-
time. She looked around the ops deck as if examining it would
make it more solid, more real, more concrete. She checked the
time. It was still half an hour before her next dose of the drugs
was due. She took them anyway. The peach-colored tabs were bitter, and the taste lingered at the back of her throat. She waited a
few minutes, watching her own cognition, waiting for memories
of lives she hadn't lived to sneak back into her.

"Fuck that very, very much," she said to the empty air, then opened
a connection to Elvi. "How long before we can get this going?"

"Tanaka's on her way now," Elvi said. "We're putting Jim in a
Laconian suit. She thought it might make Duarte feel better than
his *Roci* gear. And…it's just more likely to keep him alive. You
know, until…"

"I'm starting to get intrusive thoughts."

"I know," Elvi said. "A lot of people are. The data from before says it shouldn't get too bad as long as you keep on the medication schedule. But we're only muffling them. We're not shutting them all the way up."

"Are they getting information from me?"

The *Roci* chirped an alert. Naomi pulled it up as Elvi replied. "Maybe, but it's all still pretty haphazard. My guess is that any intelligence that slips through is going to be lost in the clutter. That's just a guess, though."

"Not sure the data's going to support that."

"Why not?"

"The repeaters at the gates? All the ones that were still working? They just went offline. Kill codes from the system sides of the gates."

Elvi hesitated. "All at the same time?"

"Within a few seconds of each other."

"That's . . . more coordinated than I like."

Naomi stretched her shoulders. She could feel her strategies shifting. Reconceptualize everything she'd just designed. Still coaching the game, but now it was a game she wasn't allowed to watch being played . . .

"Let me know as things progress," she said. "I'll be here."

She pulled up the tactical map. The four most critical gates were Earth, Laconia, Auberon, and Bara Gaon. She found the ships closest to each. It took five minutes to calculate the flight solutions she wanted for each of them: hard burns that started braking well inside the ring space. Just enough velocity to make the transit, gather telescopic data, and duck back in. And the point of transit randomized, so that even if the enemy had a back door into their heads, they couldn't line up a torpedo or a rail-gun strike on the ship.

She was gratified that none of the captains questioned the orders or pushed back at the mission. She set tracking indicators on each of them—tiny red cones that showed the distance the ships had traveled without giving her a precise lock on their actual position. While they moved, she ran simulations on the transit times for the first dozen ships due to pass into the ring space, and what changes to their paths were physically possible. The intercepts that had been certain became clouds of time and place...

She was almost annoyed when the connection request came and broke her concentration.

"Hey," Jim said, and all the control and distance she'd bent herself to building blew away on his breath. Grief slammed into her like a rogue wave, blowing her off her feet and trying to drown her.

"Hey," she murmured.

"So, we're about a hundred meters from the surface of the station, and we're heading in."

She took down the tactical display and pulled up the *Roci*'s external camera. It didn't take a second for the ship to find them. Three dashes silhouetted against the glowing blue of the station. Tags appeared as the *Roci* marked their positions and velocities. Naomi cleared them. It was enough to see them. Watching was more important than knowing the details. The details didn't matter.

"I've got you," she said, and the ways that both was and wasn't true stung. "I've got you, Jim."

"Teresa wants you to make sure Muskrat's in her crash couch in case you have to do any tricky maneuvering."

"I'll see to it."

One of the little dashes nodded, so that one was Jim. An alert came up from the ship that had peeked into Auberon, and then the one in Laconia. She closed them. It didn't look like the three of them were moving at all. They were just there, against the blueness. The little egg of Duarte's ship appeared and grew larger. They were almost there.

"Okay," Jim said. "We've got an entrance. We have a way in."

"We'll give you as much time as we can."

"It's going to be okay." The oceanic optimism would have been a lie in anyone else. Or maybe a prayer.

"Good hunting, love," she said, and the three dots passed into the blue and vanished. She waited for a moment, but nothing changed. The station remained its enigmatic self. A third alert came, this one from Sol gate. She turned off the external cameras and pulled her tactical map back up.

There were many, many more ships coming now. Hundreds of them, and while most were on fast burns, it would still take them days to reach the gates.

And by then, none of it would matter, because in the Laconia gate data was the game-ender. The *Voice of the Whirlwind*, last of the three *Magnetar*-class battleships, was on a killing burn toward the Laconia gate. At its pace, even people in the breathable-fluid crash couches would be risking their lives. Only they weren't risking their lives at all. Their lives were no more important now than the individual skin cells on a boxer's knuckles. They would be shattered by the hundreds and not be missed.

The moment the *Whirlwind* came through that gate, the fight was over, and any forces that Duarte's hive mind had would be able to flood the ring station and pull Jim and Teresa and Tanaka back out like they were plucking a splinter.

She opened a connection to her little, doomed fleet.

"This is Naomi Nagata," she said. "Prepare to receive your orders."

Chapter Forty-One: Jim

This is a bad idea," Miller said. "I mean, you've always been a little dim, but even you have to know this is a bad idea."

"Yeah. I know," Jim said. "But it is literally the best bad idea I've got."

"You look back, some of the life choices that got you here were ill-advised."

Jim shifted to look at the space where the dead detective seemed to be. Miller had the decency to look sheepish and raise one hand, palm out in a gesture of surrender.

"I'm not saying there's no pot-and-kettle aspect to this," Miller said. "I'm just trying to set your expectations on how this ends."

The sphere of the station wasn't a sphere at this distance. He was close enough—they were close enough—that it felt more like a glowing blue plain. The ring gates around and behind him shone like tiny, perversely regular stars.

The Laconian heavy vac suit that Elvi had given him fit strangely in the armpits and knees, giving him an ease of motion that kept sending little the-suit-is-coming-apart jabs of panic to his amygdala. The HUD showed that he had fifteen hours of air, which was pretty damned good. He didn't even need a second bottle. The Laconian suits stored backup air and water in pores in the suit's plating, and while this wasn't battle armor—the only weapon he had was a sidearm from the *Roci*'s supply—it was reinforced enough to give him some protection.

The on-suit sensors didn't show anything dangerous in the station's bluish glow, and only a few hundred millirems coming from all the gates together. He would have suffered more radiation on a short walk outside to check the *Roci*'s hull in normal space. It was the only thing about his situation that seemed even vaguely safe.

The *Roci* and the *Falcon* floated a few kilometers off to his right, the *Derecho* about the same distance to his left. All the ships were small enough to cover with the thumb of an outstretched hand. And the alien transport that had hauled Winston Duarte from Laconia was a pale dot below him on the station surface. His helmet assured him that Teresa and Tanaka were both en route to his position, but he couldn't see them without magnification. Not yet. Which just left him, or else him and Miller, depending how he looked at it.

The detective wore the same gray suit and dark hat that he had in life. His sad, basset-hound expression seemed younger than Jim remembered it, but that was probably just that Jim had grown past him while Miller stayed the same. Having the protomolecule working directly on his body had given Miller the ability to remain in Jim's consciousness even when other people were present, and Miller had also developed the unpleasant habit of being somewhere in Jim's view at all times. If he seemed to be at Jim's right side, and Jim turned left, Miller would be there too. And his sense of the direction Miller's voice came from clicked to match wherever he seemed to be. It was disorienting and creepy, like Miller was the villain in a low-budget horror video.

Miller stuck his hands in his pockets and pointed toward the *Derecho* with his chin. "Looks like Colonel Friendly's here."

"You don't want to call her that."

"Why not? It's not like she'll hear me."

Tanaka was a dark dot against the background light of the gates. Her maneuvering thrusters were compressed gas and hardly made any sign that they were firing except that she began to slow as she approached. Her suit was the same blue as Laconia's flag, with the stylized wings on it. Apart from that, it reminded Jim of Bobbie Draper's old Goliath: less a vac suit than a weapon shaped like one. Her face was surprisingly visible. One cheek looked smoother and younger because he'd blown the original into ribbons not that long before. Her gaze clicked around him like she was taking inventory. She paused, frowning, and seemed to focus on the emptiness around his helmet.

"Well, I guess it's true then," she said through the helmet radio. "You really do have someone else on board."

"Yes, I do," Jim said. "But how did you—"

"I'm here," Teresa said. Jim turned back toward the *Roci* and found Teresa in a battered *Rocinante*-badged vac suit, Miller floating apologetically at her side. "I'm almost ready. I just need to take care of one more thing."

"What?" Tanaka asked sharply.

"Muskrat. If there's fighting, she should be in her crash couch."

Tanaka's silence seemed like a pointed reply.

"Oh, this is going to be fun," Miller said.

"I'll take care of that," Jim said. "Other than Muskrat, are you both ready? Do we need anything else before we head in?"

"No," Teresa said. "We can go." Tanaka shook her head. Jim reoriented himself toward the vast and empty blueness, and found Miller already there below him.

He opened a connection to the *Roci*. "Hey."

"Hey," Naomi replied. She sounded soft and preoccupied. Jim took a quick reading to the station.

"So, we're about a hundred meters from the surface of the station, and we're heading in."

"I've got you," she said, and then something else that he didn't quite catch.

"Teresa wants you to make sure Muskrat's in her crash couch in case you have to do any tricky maneuvering."

"I'll see to it."

The great blue wall grew closer. In the corner of his eye, Tanaka was activating and shutting down the gun in her suit's forearm, extending and retracting the barrel in a combination of fidgeting and threat. Teresa was staring ahead at the station in something like hunger.

Miller, at his side, nodded. "I've got something. Look at this." The blue wall suddenly wasn't featureless. Lines ran through it, fine as string, making wide, complex spirals that came together and fell apart only to be replaced by new whorls that rose up. It was something between organic and mechanical, and it felt very familiar.

Miller blinked forward, teleporting from one spot to another the way only a hallucination could, waited until the pattern of lines had come to a moment of calm, and reached into the surface. Jim felt it as an effort in his own body, but not anyplace he could identify, like flexing a muscle in a phantom limb. As the spirals re-formed, the place where Miller was stayed empty, then widened. The blue glow darkened in a circle three meters wide as a depression formed, then deepened, then became a tunnel. Tanaka said something, but with her radio off. Jim only knew because he saw her lips move.

"Okay. We've got an entrance. We have a way in."

When Naomi spoke again, her voice was despairing. "We'll give you as much time as we can."

"She thinks you're all dead," Miller said. "Her and you, and everybody in those ships. Or, I don't know. If not dead, something worse. I've been a mind caught inside these fuckers and not permitted to die. It wasn't fun. Speaking of which, have I said *fuck you very much* for dragging me back yet?"

Jim shook his head. He didn't know what he could say to Naomi that would bring her any comfort. *You made it without me before* or *If we die, we'll die giving it our best shot* or *I'll use whatever time you can give.* Nothing fit what he wanted to say. "It's going to be okay," he said.

"Good hunting, love."

"It won't," Miller added. "Be okay, I mean."

Holden killed his mic. "Yeah, I know, fuck me for bringing you back. Now be helpful or shut up."

And the curve of the tunnel into the station seemed to rise up around him, blotting out the *Roci* and the *Derecho* and the star-bright gates. It led deeper into the station, but the direction kept flipping in Jim's perception between forward and down—moving through a passage or falling down a hole.

"Eyes up," Tanaka said, back on the open channel. "Holden, what's your condition?"

"Sorry, what?"

"Your condition. You're my passkey in this little hellscape. If you go full protomonster on me, I need to know, and I need to know before it happens. So what's your fucking condition?"

"So," Miller said. "I feel like there was a conversation about who was lead on this case that you two should have had earlier."

"I feel fine," Jim said, then paused, considered. "A little feverish, maybe? But not bad."

"I want an update every five minutes. Set a timer."

"If I start feeling worse, I'll let you know."

"Yes, you will. Because you'll be on a timer."

Miller, floating between them and a half pace back, tried to conceal a grin. Jim weighed the pros and cons of pushing back against Tanaka and set a timer. He set it for seven minutes, though.

The tunnel widened. A surface like some transparent membrane marked its edge, but Jim didn't feel anything more than the slightest resistance when he moved through it. The tunnel or hole went another ten meters and then into a cathedral-vast chamber. The lines he'd seen on the station's skin were here too, weaving and reweaving the walls and pillars. A gentle light pulsed from the walls, too diffuse for shadows. There was movement everywhere, and Jim had the sense that if he hadn't pumped raw protomolecule into his body, he wouldn't have been aware of most of it. Every surface was alive, trading fluids and tiny objects smaller than sand grains. It was like watching a huge body with all its tissues busy about their individual tasks and the whole of it orchestrated into one massive, unknowable purpose.

One of the pillars was also a figure—a mech, an insect, or something else entirely. He had the flashbulb memory of a Martian Marine destroying something like it with a grenade, and then being destroyed himself, broken down to complex molecules and used to repair the damage he'd done. He turned his mic back on.

"Um," he said. "Try not to break anything in here if you can help it."

He expected Tanaka to snap at him, but Teresa was the one who spoke. "I thought there wasn't a breathable atmosphere. That's what the reports said. Noble gas with some volatiles. That's not what this is."

Jim checked his suit. She was right. Neon, and more of it than had been here before, and the same trace benzene, but also oxygen. In the suit's opinion, he could take off his helmet right now and be fine. He didn't.

"It's him," Tanaka said. "The high consul didn't pack a vac suit, and if there wasn't something like it in that…ship he brought"— she nodded at the air, the walls, the station in general—"he'd make this support him."

"He didn't have food and water either," Teresa said.

Tanaka scowled behind her faceplate. "I think he did. The same way. He's in here. Holden? Which way to him?"

Jim blinked and turned to Miller.

"No idea," Miller said. "If Duarte's a new, well-tuned racing ship, you and me are a couple shipping containers strapped to the top of a reactor. You can say we do the same thing and not be technically wrong, but it's not like we're in the same weight class."

"I don't know," Jim said. "I thought you were the tracker."

Tanaka didn't answer. Instead she gestured for them to stay back, and used her thrusters to move toward the center of the chamber. Taking point.

Once she was well away, Tanaka went still, as if she was listening to something. Maybe she was. There was enough atmosphere for sound waves to carry, and Jim didn't know what her suit was capable of. The cathedral shifted with lines of energy and complex electromagnetic fields that he wasn't sure Tanaka could see, and passageways led out of it in a hundred different directions. For a moment, Jim saw it all as a gargantuan heart that was just about to squeeze down on them. His head spun like he was falling, and a wave of awe swept over him like he was hearing the voice of God, but whispering.

"Whoa, whoa, whoa," Miller said. "Hold it together. It's early in the game for you to start getting euphoric attacks on me."

Jim's sense of the utter majesty of the station dialed back, and he turned off his mic. "You make it sound like there's a later in the game."

Miller's smile was enigmatic, and it looked a little like sorrow by the time it reached his eyes. "Until death all is life."

"I feel like I should know who said that."

"Take a couple deep breaths and rein your head back in. I think we're leaking a little."

His gaze cut toward Teresa, and Jim looked over to see her looking back at him with a worried expression.

"Everything's fine. I'm fine," he said, then turned his mic back on and repeated it. Teresa nodded, but she didn't say anything.

"Not sure you sold her," Miller said.

Tanaka's voice came back over the open channel. "Heading out. You two come with me. Stay. Close."

She was already maneuvering across the chamber. Teresa oriented herself more quickly, and jetted off after her, leaving Jim to bring up the rear.

To Jim's right, something huge shifted. A buzz filled his ears like a swarm of hornets that didn't register on the suit's instruments, and something that was like light but also wasn't flowed through the walls. Adrenaline hit his system, and his heart started tapping anxiously against his ribs. Whatever it was shifted, faded, and moved on without quite entering the chamber. Jim had never seen a whale breaching, but he thought he understood something of how it would feel to be next to one when it did. Neither Tanaka nor Teresa seemed to have noticed anything. He checked his medical stats. According to the suit, he was running a little over thirty-eight degrees. A fever, but not high enough to generate hallucinations.

"No, that was real," Miller said. "Just a little reminder that we're out of our depth here."

"Didn't need it. Was clear," Jim said.

"What?" Tanaka answered.

"Nothing," Jim said. "Just talking to myself."

Tanaka paused at the oblong opening to a passageway that curved down deeper into the station. A trickle of lights like pale blue fireflies trickled out of it and into the wider chamber behind them.

"I thought I told you to stay close," Tanaka said. "Next time, do it."

"Colonel," Teresa said. "Please proceed."

Miller, now at Teresa's side, swept his hat off and rubbed at his temple with the palm of his hand. "Jesus Christ. Is anyone *not* in charge here?"

Tanaka turned and led the way down the passage. The glow from the walls here took on a deep, buttery yellow. The lines in them went from spirals to frenetic dashing lines that reminded Jim of being very young and his parents driving him through a snowstorm. After about a hundred meters, the passage began to change, widening along the oval's longer axis and narrowing along the lesser until Jim could put his hands on either side.

"It's getting too thin," Teresa said. "We're not going to fit."

"Stay close."

The passage kept widening and flattening until Jim felt like they were making their way through a crack in a cave system. The sense of mass on either side started to become claustrophobic, but Tanaka kept pressing ahead.

His timer went off.

"I'm running a fever, but otherwise fine," he said.

"*What?*"

"You wanted me to check in. I'm checking in. Little fever. Feeling fine. Maybe we should all be keeping each other up to date. I show you mine, you show me yours. Reciprocity."

Tanaka turned back, pushing herself past Teresa and toward him like an eel in a coral reef. Her jaw shifted as she moved to a private channel. He matched her.

"Captain Holden," she said. "I appreciate what you've done to get me into this station, but I'm here now. It's seeming like your present utility to me is considerably less. So I would very much recommend you stop giving me your fucking attitude before I start thinking about how much I owe you a bullet in the face. Reciprocity, and all."

She nodded once, sharply, like she was agreeing with herself on his behalf, and moved back to the open channel.

"This is a dead end. We're heading back and trying again."

She pushed past Jim, moving toward the chamber they'd left behind. Teresa followed her. Jim floated for a moment, his hand on one wall, his back on the other. A breath of fireflies swirled up from the depths where the passage was too thin for human beings and rose up past Teresa and Tanaka.

"You shot her in the face, huh?" Miller asked.

"She was trying to kill us at the time," Jim replied. "But honestly, I think it was more because she reminded me of every Laconian interrogator who'd ever beat the shit out of me."

"As revenge for a beating goes, a face shot is pretty good."

"It didn't make me feel better."

"You know," Miller said, "there was this guy when I was just starting with Star Helix. Jason. Pissed off the boss, I don't remember how. Got stuck working data forensics. That doesn't sound bad, but what it meant was going through people's logs. The security footage. The creepy shit perps kept hidden from the main partitions. Day after day after day of watching horrific things play out and not being able to do a goddamn thing about it. It started getting into his head. The union shrink called it 'continuous ongoing trauma.' We all kind of knew what was coming. That one reminds me of him."

Jim killed his mic and launched himself up after them, following the bottoms of their feet. "How long did he last?"

"Year and a half. Almost nineteen months. We all thought that was pretty damn good. Most people on that job find a way to get out after six months."

"I don't think we have six months."

"I'm just saying Colonel Friendly had an edge to her before all this started. She's not doing well now. You should be ready for the possibility that you'll have to shoot her again before this is over."

"Last time I shot her she wasn't in Laconian power armor, and I still didn't successfully kill her."

"Well, old fella," Miller said, "that's gonna be a problem."

Chapter Forty-Two: Alex

I'm still seeing lag on the aft PDCs," Alex said. "It's only fifteen milliseconds, though. It's not bad."

"I hear you," Amos said. "But I don't have anything else I'm doing, and lag's still lag. Give me a minute to isolate the line."

"You got it," Alex said. The flight deck was dim, the way he liked to keep it, but the dark wasn't calming. Even the sounds of the *Rocinante*, familiar as the face in his mirror, seemed ominous. His back and shoulders were tight enough that he'd had a low-level headache for what felt like days, and he couldn't guess the last time he'd slept through the night. And that was before Jim and Teresa had headed into the alien station with a stone-cold killer. Before Jim had infected himself with the protomolecule. Before Duarte had started reforging humanity into a single, enormous organism that seemed like it wanted to kill him and Amos and Naomi personally.

Put that way, a little lost sleep was probably appropriate.

"Okay," Amos said. "Try now."

Alex tapped the test routine. "Still seeing it."

"Good. Now the aft PDC junction."

"Same lag."

"Aft general?"

"That looks good."

Amos' sigh had a facial expression that went with it, even though the big man wasn't on camera. Raised eyebrows, lips pulling to one side, like a father watching his kid fail at something important. Equal parts affection and disappointment. "Well, that means it's the vacuum channel between 'em. I'll try flushing it."

Naomi's voice came from the flight deck below him and the system comms at the same time. "You need a hand with that?"

"I wouldn't say no," Amos replied. "It ain't exactly a one-person job."

"On my way, then." And then, only through the air, "Alex, keep an eye on the gates. If anything transits in—"

"I'll sing out. Don't worry about that."

"Thank you."

"Hey, Naomi? I just want you to know, whatever happens, it's been a real honor shipping with you all this time."

"I don't think I can take another farewell speech, Alex."

"No. But I wanted you to know."

There was a pause, and then she said, "It's been an honor for me too." And then she was gone, heading down toward the space between the hulls with Amos to fine-tune their ship one last time.

It felt weird, not having Teresa there to help Amos out. The kid hadn't been on the *Roci* for all that long, but he'd gotten so used to her presence that the change threw him a little. Jim not being there was worse. He kept wanting to check in with him, see if he was sleeping or on the scopes or down getting some coffee. There was a part of Alex's head that just couldn't wrap itself around the idea that Jim wasn't on the *Roci*. And that Clarissa wasn't. And that Bobbie wasn't.

Now that it looked like their last go-round, he saw that he'd always kind of expected everyone to show up again somehow. It was silly when he thought about it, but it didn't *feel* ridiculous at all. Years had passed since Clarissa died, but Alex's heart was still patiently waiting to see her name on the duty roster. Bobbie was gone—he'd watched her go—and he still expected to hear her voice in the galley, laughing and giving Amos their peculiar kind of rough sibling grief.

The dead were still around him, because he couldn't bring himself to believe that they weren't. He could know it. He could understand. But like a kid who'd lost something precious, he'd never been able to shake that sense that maybe, just maybe, if he looked again, it would be there. Maybe the people he loved weren't gone forever. Maybe the past—his past, his losses, his mistakes—were close enough for him to reach back and fix them if he stretched just right. Maybe, despite everything, it could still be okay.

"Check it now," Amos said, and Alex ran the test.

"Well, holy shit," he said. "That did it."

"No lag?"

"One millisecond."

"Yeah, well, we're not getting better than that," Amos agreed. "I'm packing up the toolkit and moving on to the rail gun."

"I'll be here," Alex said, and it felt more like a prayer than it usually did.

He refreshed the tactical map just to see that it hadn't changed, turned on some music and turned it off again. According to the last data they'd gotten before the repeaters shut off, the first of the incoming ships should already have been there. That they weren't meant that the situation outside the ring space had changed, and he didn't get to know what it had changed into. When he'd been a young man back on Mars, even before he'd joined up with the navy, one of his cousins had talked him into joining a martial arts school for a few weeks. One of the exercises the teacher had given them was to put a sack over their head and try to anticipate where the more advanced students were going to attack them from. The mixture of vulnerability, attention, and sickeningly acute anticipation wasn't that different from what he was carrying now. He refreshed the tactical map again.

Naomi came back to the ops deck below him. The sweetness of chamomile and the soft, metallic sound of strapping into a crash couch announced her. A few seconds later, Elvi's voice, pressed thin and tinny by the comms, floated up. She was too quiet for Alex to make out the words, but her tone was tense, her words staccato.

"Understood," Naomi said. "I'm a little shorthanded right now, though. Send someone over, and I'll set the permissions for them."

Alex waited a few seconds to be sure he wasn't interrupting, then shouted down, "Everything all right with the *Falcon*?"

"They're a little short on some supplies for the stay-out-of-my-head drugs. Elvi wanted to raid our med bay."

"Look at it like that, it's kind of a good sign," Alex said.

"Not following you."

"Well, if Duarte wasn't worried that there was something we could do, he'd just wait for us to run out of our meds, wouldn't he? This whole moving ships around and shutting down repeaters and all? He's only doing that because he thinks it's worth doing. So we must be a threat, somehow."

"I wonder if he'd tell us how. I mean if we asked really nicely," Naomi said. Her voice was a harmony of despair and grim humor.

"We'll figure it out," Alex said. "Hey, once Elvi's got what she needs from the med bay, should I pull the bridge? We're going to be more maneuverable in a fight if we don't have to match to the *Falcon*."

"No," Naomi said. "The *Roci*'s the flagship of the underground, the *Falcon*'s the flagship for Laconia, and all those other ships out there are watching us. I don't want anything that will make it seem like maybe we're two independent fleets. Besides which, we're the back line. If the fighting gets to us, it'll be because a lot of other shit has gone wrong."

"Or because the *Whirlwind* gets here," Alex said.

"In which case, it doesn't matter."

"Yeah," Alex said, and then more quietly and to himself, "Yeah. But at least we got the fuckers spooked."

As if in answer, a wave of presence washed over him, and there were people with him. A wave of impressions—an older woman in an apartment on Luna, a younger man who had something wrong with his right foot, a child in an unpaved street kicking a worn ball. A vast sense of humanity—masculine and feminine and both and neither, exhausted and exultant and enraged, young and old—washed through him like someone had turned on a fire hose. He felt the idea of Alex Kamal eroding and bit his lip to bring him back to his own body, his own self.

It's all right to let go, a voice said with the complexity and depth of a choir. If angels had voices, they'd have sounded like this. *It's all right to let go. Holding on is only pain and weariness. Let us carry you, and you can rest. You can let go now.* It was almost persuasive. It was almost enough.

The wave passed, but it didn't go entirely away. It persisted, a little pressure like a hand resting on the back of his head. A small touch that was invitation and threat. He trembled a little as he took the peach-colored tab out of his pocket. He chewed it, breaking it into powder in his mouth to get the drugs into his bloodstream faster. It was as bitter as sin.

"Did y'all feel that too?" he asked on the ship comm.

"I did," Amos said. "Can't say I liked it."

Naomi said, "It felt more focused than before. I think it's trying to soften us up. Get anyone that's a borderliner over to its side."

"I don't think so, Boss," Amos said. "I got more the sense of surrender-or-die."

Alex's tactical map threw an alert up, bright red dots at a tight cluster of gates. The *Roci* pulled up a flash analysis from the old data and the silhouettes and drive signatures. Based on what ships had been on approach before and what they saw now, there were six ships—one Laconian gunship, three pirate hunters, and two private freighters with aftermarket torpedo racks—coming in fast through a tight cluster of gates all within about a twenty-degree sweep of the ring space.

"I think the rail gun's looking fine," Amos said. "I'm going to head for engineering, get the patch kits ready in case someone starts poking holes in us."

Over the comms, another voice came, broadcast to all ships. "This is Captain Botton of the *Derecho*. We have the enemy in sight. We are moving to engage."

"Belay that," Naomi shouted from the ops deck. "All ships, evade and defend, but stay in position."

On the tactical map, the *Derecho* shifted toward the incoming ships, but the rest of Naomi's fleet held steady. Fifty-odd flecks of blue diffused through the ring space and half a dozen red clustered like a knife driving toward the station at its center. Diving toward the *Roci* and the *Falcon* and Jim. If the dots seemed to move slowly, it was only because the distances were so huge.

"What are you looking at?" Alex called.

"Not sure yet," Naomi shouted back, and six more dots appeared on the tactical map, falling in from gates on the opposite side of the ring space. "That. I was waiting for that."

The comms chirped out an error, and Naomi cursed. Alex pulled up a mirror of her screen, just to see what the issue was. Broad-spectrum jamming coming from all the enemy ships. The whole broadcast spectrum shimmered with noise and false requests stacked one on another until the *Roci* gave up and rebooted the antennas. Alex had been in a lot of fights, and he'd never seen anything this comprehensive outside a pirate attack.

"Alex, can you get me tightbeam locks?"

"Tell me who you want to talk to, and I'll get them up."

A list appeared on his screen, and he started queuing. Getting the lock, sending the orders, and moving to the next ship didn't take that much longer than broadcast would have, but the invisible hand on the back of his head weighed a little heavier. Coordinating Naomi's forces without broadcast meant building an ad hoc network that kept track of where all the other ships were and bounced between them, trading data back and forth as quickly as the lasers could carry them. In theory, it was entirely possible. In practice, it was more complicated. Any ship that had a buffer fail would mean slowing down the whole system. Any laser that lost alignment meant lost orders, the doubling up of retransmission requests, the opportunity for confusion and corruption and mistakes.

The enemy were outnumbered five to one, and the enemy ships burned in weird, spiraling paths, drawing Naomi's fleet toward them and then spinning away before they got in range. Tempting Naomi's forces to overreach, but never engaging. Alex wasn't sure this was even a real attack so much as a feint to see how Naomi would react until the *Derecho* came inside firing range of the first group of ships.

The timing of the attack was astounding. The farthest of the ships bloomed, emptying its torpedoes like a dandelion shedding seeds. Then the next nearest, then the next, then the one closest. Wave after wave, with the first torpedoes going just slightly slower to give the missiles behind them time to catch up. Alex set the *Roci*'s scopes to track what it could.

The *Derecho* was a *Storm*-class destroyer. The backbone of the Laconian Navy. The other ships were weaker, smaller, with fewer weapons. If anyone had asked him, Alex would have put his money on the *Derecho* against all of them without a second thought. The full loads of all the ships poured out and fell onto the *Derecho* with impact times coordinated to the millisecond. The *Derecho*'s PDCs were in constant fire, its counter missiles taking out a dozen enemy torpedoes at a time, and it was still overwhelmed.

The impact was like seeing a sudden, brief sun. When it faded, the destroyer was on the drift, spinning slowly toward the annihilating edge of the ring space with nothing that could rescue it. He hoped that everyone aboard was already dead.

"Holy shit," Naomi said.

"I get the feeling this isn't going to be like other fights," Alex said over the comms. He was pretty sure his voice wasn't shaking.

"Easier to take something out when you don't give a shit about what comes after," Amos agreed. "Those ships are finished, but I don't think anyone on 'em cares."

It's all right to let go. Put down your weapons now, and you will be saving humanity, not destroying it. Don't be afraid of the changes that are coming, they are the only thing that can save us all. Alex gritted his teeth until his jaw ached.

"Alex!" Naomi shouted, and he realized it wasn't the first time she'd done it.

"Sorry, sorry," Alex said. "I'm here. What's going on?"

"I need a tightbeam to the *Godalming*. I need it now."

Alex scrambled, finding the ship. It was a pirate that worked with the underground. He found it at the edge of Naomi's forces, almost on the other side of the ring space from the corpse of the *Derecho*. The light delay to it was small enough that they could talk in real time.

"*Godalming*," Naomi said, "this is the *Rocinante*. You're off your assigned pattern."

The voice that answered was older and rough. "We have a shot at this pinché motherfucker, *Rocinante*. We're taking it."

"You don't, though," Naomi said.

Alex pulled up the tactical, and even then, he didn't see it at first. The other ships with their odd spiraling paths had teased their own ships farther and farther apart until one strayed too far. Now, like different limbs of the same beast, the enemy ships had turned, burning hard on paths that would keep the pirate from support and help while they surrounded it.

"We're fine," the voice from *Godalming* said, stubbornly. "We've taken worse than this."

It's all right to let go. There's no honor in death.

The tactical threw another alert up. Five more red dots transiting through different ring gates in the same moment. Alex saw them now for what they were. A hunt group.

He was already setting up the queue of tightbeam connections, new orders to address the new enemy, when another transit came. Small and blisteringly fast, already braking hard to shed its velocity so that it wouldn't slam into the ring station and die. The *Roci* estimated the burn at something near twenty gs. Even if the people in the ship were in submersion tanks, they were in as much danger from their own deceleration as from the fight they were diving into.

"Naomi?"

"Get us there," she said.

There wasn't time to detach from the *Falcon*, so Alex took control of both ships, whipping them around and laying in a coordinated burn to keep them together. The tiny, fast ship would be half blinded by its own drive cone, but the other enemy ships would see everything the *Roci* did. All the eyes were connected. All the minds were one. Alex laid in a firing solution, synced with the *Falcon*, and put a rail-gun slug out along the enemy's path. It was already dodging even as he fired the shot. Alex switched to torpedoes and fired a tight spread, set to detonate between the ship and the station.

The missiles launched as an emergency mayday came from the *Godalming* and then cut off. They seemed to crawl across the display. Alex willed them to go faster, to defy the laws of physics just a little bit. Just for him.

"They're not going to hit," Naomi said.

"They're not meant to," Alex said. "I'm just trying to put some debris in their way."

The torpedoes blinked out as they detonated, and the *Roci* tracked the spheres of energy and scrap metal that radiated out along the paths they'd been going. The fast ship came into the spheres like a stone falling through a cloud. Alex held his breath. There was still vastly more empty space in those fields than matter, but at the speed the dropship was going, even a sliver of metal the size of a fingernail clipping would be enough...

The enemy ship's drive flickered. Alex exhaled.

"Good job," Amos said over the comms.

"Sometimes you're lucky," Alex said, but he felt a little bloom of pride all the same.

"Pull us back," Naomi said. "I want us parked right outside Jim's entrance. They're trying to get to the station, and we're going to be the last thing they have to go through to get there."

Chapter Forty-Three: Jim

The passageways varied. Some were large enough to fit a ship through, more like a dry dock than a corridor. Some were like the *Roci* or the *Falcon*, well fitted to a human form. Some were barely crawl spaces and some as thin as drinking straws. Probably there were others too small for the naked eye to see. The station functioned at all sizes, like a fractal of itself.

Jim's fever was steady, but a numbness had started at his feet and fingers. Pins and needles at first, and then a growing absence. If he squeezed his hands together, he could feel the deep pressure like an ache, but lighter touch was gone. And there was a vibrant, unsteady, electric feeling in his belly that he didn't like. Tanaka didn't ask him for another health update, though, and he didn't volunteer anything.

The passage they were trying bent sharply, but Jim had lost a sense of direction. It might have been turning in toward the center of the station or out toward its skin. The only things he was sure of were that Tanaka always seemed certain of the next path to try and they were running out of time. Jim and Teresa followed Tanaka around the bend and forward into a widening where the passage they were in crossed another like it traveling at an oblique angle. Tanaka stopped at the junction and tapped at the wrist controls on her suit. Her scowl was harsh enough to sharpen knives on.

"Is there something you're looking for?" Jim asked on the open channel. "This is kind of a large structure to just hope we bump into Duarte."

Tanaka's voice buzzed with annoyance. "I have a complete physical map produced by the *Falcon* with best-guess locations based on structure and energy flow that appear to be more approximate and inaccurate than expected…"

"Or the place keeps changing around us," Miller said with a shrug.

"…In addition I have chemical markers that would be more useful if I had a different suit, but which I'm certain will get us to our goal. There's some noise, but I'm making progress."

Miller scratched his nose, and Jim's started itching. "I don't think she's making progress. But violent, frustrated, and heavily armed? Not a combination I'd push."

Teresa floated at Jim's side. Her face was pale and there was a darkness to the skin around her eyes like she'd gone too long without sleep.

Jim put a hand on her shoulder, and it took a few seconds before she looked over. "How're you holding together?" he asked.

"I keep hearing a boy talking about how much he misses his sister. I think he's speaking Korean. I don't really have Korean, but I still understand him. It's like the Tower of Babel in reverse."

"Don't let it distract you," Tanaka said.

Jim expected Teresa to bite back, but she only shook her head. "I just want to find my father."

"This way," Tanaka said, gesturing at a branch of the intersecting passage. "The traces look stronger this way."

She pushed off, and Teresa followed. Jim wondered what they'd do if he went his own way, then sighed and went after them. He wasn't leaving the kid to Tanaka.

"You know," Miller said, "you get a repeat offender, and after a while you kind of get to know them."

Up ahead, the passageway brightened and split at a fork like an artery into two smaller versions of itself. Tanaka went through one, and Teresa followed, drifting until she bumped against the wall before she righted herself.

"I forgot how much I didn't miss your gnomic cop stories," he said.

"And yet, here I am. I'm making a point. You see the way someone works, you see the way they think. Joey cuts through a wall to get into warehouses a half a dozen times, the next time you see a warehouse with a hole cut in it, you maybe want to check where Joey was that night. People don't change, not really. The strategies that work for them, they reach for."

"I hear you."

"So I look at your pal Duarte, right? And it looks to me like Eros all over again. Not the goal, maybe, but the method. Eros, the shit took over people's bodies and made whatever it wanted out of them."

"And Duarte's doing the same thing. Using people like building blocks for something he wants."

"Maybe."

Jim looked over. Miller seemed to be at his side, even though he knew it wasn't really true. The illusion was perfect.

Miller hoisted a weary eyebrow. "You need to ask yourself whether you think Duarte's the perp, or first among victims. You know that this stuff can hook itself into your dopamine receptors. Train you up to like whatever it wants you to like. Maybe it grabbed on to how he feels about the kid over there and used that as a leash. The things that built all this shit could be using him from beyond their graves the same as they used Julie. And there are some things you can only access by being in the substrate. You remember that."

"That's uncomfortable," Jim said. "But yes. I was thinking along the same lines."

"Of course you were. I'm using your brain. It's not like I brought any neurons of my own to this partnership."

"So this is just me talking to myself? That's disappointing."

"No," Miller said. "This is what's left of me trying to point you toward the clues. This is your case, old fella. You know more than you think you do."

Something shifted deep in Jim's gut. It hurt for a second, and then the pain turned to a coolness that made Jim think about things like nerve damage. But his mind wasn't on his body. It was back on Eros Station when the protomolecule was first set loose. For a moment, he saw the corpse of Julie Mao in the crap little hotel room, the black spirals threading up the wall from her body. The blue fireflies floating in the air. There was something about her that tickled at the back of his mind. About her but not about her. About Eros, but not just about Eros.

"Oh," he said. "Hey. We used heat." Tanaka didn't turn back or respond. He checked to see if his mic was on. "Tanaka! Back on Eros, we used heat."

Tanaka tapped her suit's thrusters, pausing in midair and turning back toward him. Teresa, nearer to the wall, caught an irregularity with her fingers and used it like a handhold. Jim slowed and stopped. Miller floated unseen at Tanaka's side until Jim glanced back, and he was there too.

"When Eros moved, it heated up," Jim said. "Miller went in looking for a way to stop it. He looked for hot spots. If Duarte's at the center of this the same way Juliette Mao was running Eros, he'll be using a lot of energy. Making a lot of waste heat. Even if the map's wrong, maybe that can help?"

He couldn't parse Tanaka's silence, but she paused and thought at least. The itch on Jim's nose got worse, like something tiny biting him just beside his right nostril. A swirl of blue dots wafted out of one wall, crossed to the other, and vanished again.

"All right," Tanaka said, and turned to the control panel at her wrist. A moment later, she shook her head. "I don't have connection to the *Falcon*."

Jim checked his system. The only options on it were local—Tanaka and Teresa. As far as his vac suit was concerned, there wasn't anyone else in the universe.

"We're too far in," he said. "Or maybe this place acts like a Faraday cage along with everything else."

Tanaka lowered her head. In the absence of gravity, it was just an expression of emotion. For the first time, Jim thought of her not as a threat or an enemy, but a person who was caught in the same meat grinder of a situation that he was. The thinness of her face made odd by the injury, the tightness of her mouth, the exhaustion in her eyes.

"Hey, it's all right," he said. "We can do this."

She lifted her eyes, and the woman looking out at him was the one who'd shot Amos' spine out. Any vulnerability or compassion was lost in a short-leashed hatred and rage. He was pretty sure if she didn't have a helmet on, she would have spat.

"Follow me," she said. "Stay close."

He did.

"It was a good try," Miller said.

Jim turned off his mic. "You know, I'm starting to think this might not have been a great plan."

Miller barked out a laugh, and Jim smiled. The coldness in his belly and the numbness in his limbs were the only reminders that the detective was eating him alive from the inside out. Tanaka reached another junction, this time with a shaft that looked like it was the same metallic compound as the station's exterior. It was the first one like it Jim had seen since they'd come in. She paused, and he thought he saw a thermal scan running in the subtle reflection of her helmet display.

"What happens?" he asked.

"What happens when?"

"When it gets you. The protomolecule. When it finishes taking you over, what happens?"

The detective narrowed his unreal eyes, and for a moment, Jim imagined a glimmer of unearthly blue in them. "You mean what did you let yourself in for?"

"Yeah."

"Too late to turn back now."

"I know. I'm just not feeling great."

"You want bullshit happy mouth noises, or the truth."

"Bullshit happy mouth noises."

"It's great," Miller said without missing a beat. "It's having a long, restful sleep full of interesting, vivid dreams."

A cramp ran through Jim's gut, sharp as a screwdriver. "You're right. That does sound great," he said through clenched teeth. "I really think I'm going to like that."

"This way," Tanaka said, going into the metal shaft. "Try to keep up."

They fell. Jim couldn't interpret it as anything but falling now. When he tried to see the float as moving forward or rising up, the reframe worked for a heartbeat or two, and then they were falling again. Either the little stringlike lines of force were gone now, or he'd lost the trick of seeing them. The blue fireflies were thicker here, swirling and dancing in eddies that had nothing to do with the local air. Jim found himself thinking of flocks of birds at dawn and schools of silver-scaled fish. Thousands of individual animals coordinating into something larger, wider, capable of things that no one of them could have managed. It seemed important.

Something was happening with his left hand, and he noticed that Teresa had taken it. He could see her squeezing his fingers in hers, but he couldn't feel it.

"Don't fall asleep," she said, and he was pretty sure sleep was a euphemism for something more permanent. He tried to turn on his mic, but it seemed harder to do than it should have been. With his right hand, he fumbled with the helmet's seals until he managed to pop off the visor. The air was weirdly thick, like humidity but without the water. Teresa watched him, her eyes widening. Then she pulled her own helmet off and latched it to her suit at the hip.

"I'm not going anywhere," Jim said. "I promise."

"What the fuck are you two doing?" Tanaka's voice was fuzzy compared to Teresa's. Jim made a mental note to check the speakers in his helmet when he got back to the *Roci*. Probably a loose connection.

"I was having trouble with my mic. And my nose itched."

"Teresa, put your helmet back on."

Teresa still had his hand in hers. She looked at Tanaka with a breathtakingly false innocence and pointed to her ears. *I can't hear you.* A flash of pure anger passed over Tanaka's expression, and Jim felt a little hitch of fear. But then she popped her visor open too.

"Be ready to put that back in place on my order," Tanaka said. Teresa nodded, but didn't speak.

There was a warmth radiating from the metal walls. He hadn't felt it before because his skin had been covered, but now it was like the pressure of sunlight on a hot day. Or an oven, just opened. And more than that, there was an eerie sense of pressure. He couldn't explain it. The air was hardly over a single atmosphere, but some part of him felt an inhumanly powerful force kept in check. Like the station wasn't floating in vacuum, but at the bottom of an ocean that was bigger than worlds.

"Well, that's literally true," Miller said. "That was the trick."

"What was the trick?"

Miller gestured at the walls, the fireflies, the incomprehensible complexity and strangeness of the station. "It's where the power comes from. They cracked the universe open, pushed their way in here, and it pushed back. A whole other universe trying to smash this place flat, and it powers the gates, the artifacts. That magnetic ray gun Duarte was playing with. They built stars with it. Broke rules that you can't break without a different set of physics to strain it through. You can Eve-and-apple it all you want, but this shit right here? This is all made out of original sin."

"When we find him, you make the approach," Tanaka said, and Jim didn't understand for a second what she meant.

"I understand," Teresa said with a resentment that meant it wasn't the first time she'd been told.

"I will take care of everything else."

Teresa answered more slowly this time, but she said the same thing. "I understand."

The heat was growing more intense, and Jim felt sweat starting to bead on his skin. The metal hall joined three others like it, each of them coming in at an acute angle, to form a single larger passage with a nearly symmetrical hexagonal shape that was disorienting somehow. Like the angles shouldn't quite all work together. The glow was brighter, and the heat was ramping up toward unpleasant.

Tanaka checked her wristpad. "I think we're getting close."

"We better be," Miller said, "or you three are all going to be lightly broiled before we find our perp."

Something moved ahead of them. Something bright. Jim thought for a moment he was just imagining it—protomolecule hallucination or heat exhaustion—but Tanaka moved to put herself between them and whatever it was, her armored face shield slamming closed, protecting them out of instinct. The barrel at her forearm popped open.

"Oh," Miller said. "She doesn't want to do that."

"Wait," Jim said, but Tanaka was moving forward. He followed. Without his visor on, his HUD wasn't working. His suit chimed to let him know his maneuvering thrusters were nearing half charge and he should turn back to avoid being caught on the float. In other circumstances, it would have seemed really important.

The thing was familiar, metallic blue and insectile. Half a meter taller than Tanaka, and she wasn't short. It moved with a fast twitch like a clockwork ticking from one position to the next. Now that he thought to look, there were others like it embedded in the walls all around them, so tightly packed that there might not be structure to the walls apart from their bodies.

"Don't do anything aggressive," Jim said.

"This is the first thing we've seen that looks like a sentry," Tanaka said, her voice booming out of the suit's external speakers. "We're not doubling back."

She shifted, and it shifted to block her. A feral grin stretched the asymmetry of her cheeks. Miller leaned over beside her, staring into her visor with a look of astonishment. "She really is going to get you all killed, isn't she?"

"Let me try," Jim said. "I'm here. I opened the station. At least let me try just shutting it down."

Tanaka's gun barrel closed and opened and closed again. She gestured him forward with her chin.

"Miller?"

The detective shrugged. "Give me a minute. I'll see what I can do."

Jim felt that same oddness. Flexing his phantom limb, an awareness that he was doing something, but not of what exactly it was. The cramp in his gut came again, higher now. Closer to his chest. The pain rose and fell again quickly.

"Try now," he said.

Tanaka moved to one side, and the sentinel ignored her. She moved past it, and it remained inert. Tanaka gestured Teresa forward, and the girl went as Tanaka watched the sentinel, waiting, it seemed, for an excuse to defend them. Jim went last. His breath was shallow and fast. He couldn't feel his legs below the knee.

"We're running out of time on a lot of fronts here," Miller said. "Any play you want to make, you'd better make it soon."

"Thank you," Jim murmured, "for your support and advice."

Ahead of them, the light went from blue to white. Jim fired his thrusters, moving into a chamber like a sphere a hundred meters across. Other passages like the one they'd come through were touches of darkness in the brightness. The light itself felt wrong— thick, tangible, jittering, alive. It made Jim's skin crawl.

From opposite sides of the sphere, dark filaments wove a huge web like a stalactite and a stalagmite reaching from the roof and floor of a cave to touch at a single point. Or like the wings of a great dark angel.

At the center was something the size of a human being. A man with his arms outstretched, cruciform. Thick cables of the filament wove into his sides, his arms, his legs. He was still dressed in Laconian blue, except his feet, which were bare.

Jim knew the face almost before they were close enough to see it.

"Daddy?" Teresa said.

Chapter Forty-Four: Teresa

From the moment they entered the station, Teresa had been watching James Holden die.

She'd known something was wrong with him as soon as she'd gotten to the rendezvous. She'd been around him for years, first in the State Building on Laconia, where he'd been a figure of danger and subtle threat. Then on his ship, where he'd become something smaller, gentler, and more fragile. She knew his moods, the way he used humor to cover over the darkness that haunted him, the vulnerability he carried with him, and the strength. She was fairly certain he didn't know that about her, and that was fine.

He had never reminded her of her father, though. Not until now.

She didn't put her finger on it. Not at first. She struggled with her own intrusive thoughts. The boy's voice that seemed to be just behind her speaking in a language she didn't know but understood anyway. The eerie, almost choral voice encouraging her to let her sense of self go. The woman who had given a child up for adoption and now was torn between guilt and relief. And then the Korean boy again, still lamenting his sister. It took effort for Teresa not to listen, not to engage, to hold herself to herself, and so that was what she thought Jim was doing too.

For hours, she followed Colonel Tanaka's lead, weaving in and out of the cave-maze of the station while her mind sparked and slipped. It was like a nightmare she was trying not to wake up from, and the effort kept her from consciously noticing the little things that were wrong with Jim. The way his skin tone had changed. The difference in his eyes. And more than anything, the sense of disconnection, like he was slowly peeling away from what she thought of as reality.

Once he forgot to turn off his mic, and the nonsense he was muttering to himself—*I forgot how much I didn't miss your gnomic cop stories* and *I hear you* and *Duarte's doing the same thing, using people like building blocks for something he wants*—spilled out over the radio.

Other times, he seemed almost normal. He checked in on her and how she was doing, the same way he sometimes did on the ship. He talked with Tanaka about how to use heat to find a path for them. At those times, he seemed the way he usually did. Himself. And then they'd start moving, and he would start to drift again.

They found a passage of the same blue-glowing metallic substance as the station's shell and had started down it when Tanaka opened the private channel between them.

"There's a conversation that you and I need to have," the colonel said. "Captain Holden is compromised."

"We're all compromised," Teresa said.

"Not what I'm talking about. He injected himself with a live sample of the protomolecule. The eggheads stabilized it as much as they could, but in my estimation he is losing function quickly."

Teresa, distracted by the noise in her own head, hadn't focused on him. She did now. He was beside her, and a little back, his arms at neutral and a small, dreamy smile on his lips. A memory came to her of being in her father's room, holding his hand, trying to make him understand that Dr. Cortázar was going to kill her. The vagueness and distance were the same.

"He's fine," she said, surprised by the heat in her voice.

"I'm not asking for your judgment, I'm informing you of mine," Tanaka said. "At this point, I believe Holden may still be useful in finding and recovering the high consul, so I'm willing to take the risk associated with his condition. But I need you to understand that this will not always be the case."

"We're not leaving him behind."

"When we locate your father, you will need to make the approach to him. Convince him to stop this thing he's doing with our minds. That's what I need you to do."

"I know."

"If after that, Captain Holden has continued to decline, I will take any action I feel necessary to keep you and your father safe. I need you to understand what that might entail, because if you get upset, the high consul might too."

Teresa was quiet for a moment. Understanding exactly what Tanaka was saying was harder than it should have been. *I don't like her*, the boy with the missing sister said. *She acts calm, but she's acting.* Teresa shook her head, but the sense of presence in her stayed the same. She had an uncomfortable memory of being Tanaka, naked and chemically altered, pinning a man to a bed. She felt his wrists pop. She remembered the pleasure in making the young man hurt. Making him fear her. *You will not like the version of me that comes calling on you then.*

"You're saying you'll kill him?"

"It might come to that, yes. If in my estimation he is compromised enough to pose a threat."

"He's not a threat. He won't be one."

"I need you to understand that this is a military operation, and my mission is to keep you and your father safe. I will do whatever

I need to do to achieve that. Your duty is to approach your father.
I will take care of everything after that. Do you understand?"

"I understand."

"Good."

Absently, Jim lifted a hand and scratched at the surface of his
visor. He didn't seem aware that he was doing it. The long weeks
and months of watching her father change flowed into Teresa. The
horror of the sudden snap when the change came, when he went
away. When she lost him. *I won't cry in a vac suit*, she thought. *I
am not going to cry in my fucking vac suit.*

She tapped her suit's maneuvering thrusters, just enough to
drift close to Jim. She took his hand. For a moment, he didn't
seem to notice, then slowly his gaze swam over to her. His eyes
were wrong. There was a shimmering in the whites that hadn't
been there before. That didn't belong there.

"Don't fall asleep."

Jim started to speak, lost focus, started again. A look of frustration came over him, and without warning, he popped the visor off
his helmet. He took one long breath, then another. The impulse
welled up in Teresa, part defiance of Tanaka, part anger at the universe, part a weird sense of allegiance to the old man who'd plot-
ted to get her killed once and then saved her. Teresa took off her
own helmet and hooked it to the strap at her hip. The air in the
corridor was oppressively warm and felt strange in her lungs.

When he spoke, she didn't hear him through the radio, but the
open, alien air. *I'm not going anywhere. I promise.* She knew that
wasn't true, even if he didn't.

Tanaka's voice came in a thin, tinny buzz from Jim's radio and
the speakers in the helmet at Teresa's hip. "What the fuck are you
two doing?"

"I was having trouble with my mic," Jim said. "And my nose
itched."

"Teresa, put your helmet back on."

Or else what? Teresa thought. She was so tired of being bul-
lied by the people who said they were there to help her. She was

so tired of being Laconian. She pretended she couldn't make out Tanaka's words, even though they all knew that wasn't true. Tanaka's anger was less than her own. When Tanaka opened up her own visor, Teresa felt a little thrill of victory.

"Be ready to put that back in place on my order."

They turned their attention back to the corridor, the station, the hunt. A few minutes later, out of nowhere, Jim said, *What was the trick?* He wasn't talking to either of them.

Tanaka locked her eyes on Teresa's. *I told you there was a problem with him. I told you he was degrading.* "When we find him, you make the approach."

"I understand."

"I will take care of everything else."

"I understand."

"Daddy?"

The months had thinned him, but he hadn't grown a beard. His cheeks were as smooth-shaved as if Kelly had seen to him that morning. The old pockmarks were evidence of boyhood acne he'd suffered through long before Teresa had known him. His clothes were the same he'd worn at the State Building in Laconia, and they weren't ragged, but they seemed thin and brittle. Like paper that had been left in the rain and sun.

The black filaments that swirled in from the walls of the great, bright chamber laced into his arms and pierced his side. Tiny pulses ran through them, thickening and thinning. Flickers of blue danced in the black threads and seemed to vanish if she looked directly at them. When he opened his eyes, the irises glowed the same blue as the station, and they focused on nothing, like a blind man's.

"Daddy?" she repeated, more softly this time.

The lips that had kissed her head as a baby curved into a smile. "Teresa? Is that you?"

"I'm here. I'm right here."

"It's going to be all right," he said. "I dreamed too small before. I see that now. I thought I could save us by organizing, by keeping us together, and I was right about that. I was right, baby. But I didn't understand how to do it."

"Look at you," Teresa said, pointing at the way the station pierced his body through. "Look what it did to you."

"This is why it will work. The meat, the matter, the rude clay of us. It's hard to kill. The ones who came before were brilliant, but they were fragile. Genius made of tissue paper, and the chaos blew them apart. We can be the best of both now..."

Teresa shifted closer. Her father, sensing her though his eyes never rested on her, tried to embrace her, but the dark threads held his arms. She put her own arms around him. His skin was burning hot against her cheek.

"We need to get him out of that fucking web," Tanaka said. "Can he get loose? Ask him if he can get loose."

"Daddy," Teresa said. Tears were sheeting over her eyes and turning everything into smears of color and light. "Daddy, we need to go. You need to come with us. Can you do that?"

"No no no, baby. No. This is where I am supposed to be. Where I was always supposed to be. You'll understand soon, I promise."

"High Consul Duarte. My name is Colonel Aliana Tanaka. I have been given Omega status by Admiral Trejo and assigned the task of finding and recovering you."

"We were doomed as soon as the gates appeared," he said, but to her, not Tanaka. "If no one had taken responsibility, we would have bumbled along until the other ones came and killed us all. I saw that, and I did what I had to do. It was never for me. The empire was only a tool. It was a way to coordinate. To prepare for the war that was coming. The war in heaven."

A hand touched her shoulder, pulling her gently back. It was Jim, his expression full of sorrow. "Come away. Come on."

"It's him. It's still him."

"Is and isn't," Jim said, and his voice was strange, like the cadence belonged to someone else. "I've seen this before. The station's inside him. What it wants and what he wants? No way to tell one from the other. Not now."

"You've seen this before?" Tanaka said. "Where?"

"On Eros," Jim said. "Julie was like this. She wasn't so far gone, but she was just like this." And then, to Teresa, "I'm sorry, kid. I'm so sorry."

Teresa blinked the sheet of tears away as best she could. In the distortion, Jim looked odd. The shape of his face seemed changed, bent in a permanent weariness and amusement. She blinked again, and he was only himself.

Tanaka was jetting from side to side, her maneuvering thrusters hissing constantly as she circled the Gothic sculpture that had been Teresa's father. "I need you to talk to him. He needs to stop this. You have to make him stop this."

"Colonel, I am right here, and I can hear you," her father said. He turned his head toward Tanaka, his eyes steady and blank. "And I remember you. You were one of the first with me. You saw Mars die, and you were part of the remaking of it in the empire. This is the continuation of that. This is what we were fighting for all along. We will make all of humanity safe and whole and unified."

"Sir," Tanaka said, "we can do this without mindfucking everyone. We can fight this war and still be human beings."

"You don't understand, Colonel. But you will."

Teresa shook herself out of Jim's grasp. "You don't have to do this. You can come back." But she heard the despair in her own voice as she said it.

Her father's smile was beatific. "It's all right to let go. Holding on is only pain and weariness. You can let go."

Teresa felt a wave of nothingness swim through her, an emptiness where her self should be, and she shouted. It wasn't words or a warning or a threat. It was just her heart screaming because there wasn't anything else to do. She fired the suit thrusters, slamming herself into the black web that held her father, and she started ripping. Grabbing handfuls of the dark, spiraling filament and yanking it free. The smell of ozone came into the sweltering light like the threat of storms at the edge of a heatwave. Her father shouted and tried to push her away, but the strands held him.

Jim's voice seemed to come from a great distance. "Teresa! Get away from there! Don't damage the station!"

Her universe shrank to her body, her vac suit, her father's compromised flesh, and the alien thing consuming him. He writhed in pain as she tried to tear him free, and screamed for her to stop.

A force grabbed her like a vast, invisible hand and pulled her away. A million tiny, unreal needles bore into her flesh and began to rip her apart. *Oh,* she thought, *my father's going to kill me.*

And then, the pain eased. Jim was beside her, and for a moment someone else was too, but she couldn't see him. The glimmer in Jim's eyes was brighter, and his skin had gone waxy with an eerie opalescence under it. His teeth were bared in raw, animal effort.

"He's gone," Jim said. It was barely a grunt. "He's gone. If he's willing to kill you, it isn't him anymore. He's gone."

Her father—the thing that had been her father—was still held in the black threads. His mouth was open in pain and rage, but no sound came out. The blue fireflies danced along the torn threads like ants from a kicked hill.

"Holden," Tanaka said. "We have a problem."

Tanaka had her back to them. Over her shoulder, the wide, bright space was filling with bodies. From every corridor and passage, the alien sentinels were pouring in like smoke.

Chapter Forty-Five: Naomi

The closer the *Rocinante* and the *Falcon* kept to the station, the more cover the alien structure provided and the less of the field of battle was in her scopes. The *Roci* was able to build real-time reports by syncing with other ships in her little fleet by tightbeam and making a patchwork map with data from half a dozen different ships. She didn't like it, though. It left her feeling half blinded.

"Two more in," Alex said.

"Got them," Naomi shouted back. One from Argatha system, another from Quivira. She set the *Roci* to identifying their silhouettes and drive signatures. Neither one was running a transponder. There was no reason to. Everyone on the hive mind's side already knew who they were, and they weren't about to let her in on it.

On the far side of the ring space, three enemy ships were slowly dismantling her fighters. She'd lost the *Amador* and the *Brian and Kathy Yates.* The *Senator* had taken heavy damage and was venting air. More enemy ships were coming through the rings, wave after wave after wave. Some of them—many of them—were ships she'd called there. Laconian science and military ships, survey and support ships from the underground. The crews had answered to her or Elvi or Trejo, and now were something else entirely. A different organism.

When she had a moment to gather herself, she wondered how many people there were still left out there. Had Duarte invaded and co-opted the minds of everyone in all the systems, or was he targeting the ones on their way toward the rings? She imagined whole stations filled with silent bodies working in perfect coordination, the need for verbal communication replaced by the direct influence of brain on brain. A single hand with billions of fingers. If that was what humanity was now, there would never be another conversation, another misunderstanding or joke or shitty pop song. She tried to imagine what it would be like for a baby born into a world like that, not as an individual but an appendage that had never known itself as anything else.

"Naomi?" Alex said. "Three more, and one of 'em is a *Storm*-class."

"I see it. Tightbeam to the... the *Lin Siniang.*"

"It's yours," Alex said.

"And watch the dropship coming in from Torfaen system."

"Just waiting until she's in range."

Naomi pulled up their ammunition supply even though she didn't really have time to. They still had a decent number of torpedoes and rail-gun slugs. PDCs were a little low. And they were the back of the fleet, to the degree that a spherical battlefield had a back.

The connection came up. The woman on the other side of it had long, black hair pulled back in a functional bun and the old-school split circle of the OPA tattooed on her collarbone, though she looked too young to have been born when the OPA was still a real force. The *Roci* put her name up in a chyron for Naomi.

"Captain Melero, I need you to intercept and delay the

incoming ships. Take the *Duffy*, the *Cane Rosso*, and the *Malak Alnuwr*."

The young woman's eyes went flat and her face pale. She'd just been handed a death sentence, and they both knew it. *Belay that*, Naomi thought. *Get your people and run like hell. Live to fight another day.* Except there weren't any other days. This was the last day anyone had, and it was only as long as the time they could win for Jim and Teresa.

She tried not to think about Jim.

"Compra todas, sa sa," Melero said. "Count on us, ke?"

She dropped the connection. Naomi didn't think she'd ever met Captain Melero before, and she was certain she would never see or speak to the woman again. She wished they could put together a more coordinated defense, but the best she could manage was to set small groups together and give them leave to do what they thought was best. That and hope.

Her timer went off, and she took another pill out of her pocket and swallowed it dry.

You don't need to do that. There's no shame in letting go. It's going to happen eventually anyway. Naomi didn't push back at the thought. She had the impression that engaging with the other thoughts and memories, even to fight against them, made them stronger. The best she could manage was to let them rise up in her and fall away, and keep chugging down pharmaceuticals until her kidneys cried uncle. She wasn't worried about long-term damage. An outright overdose would be bad, but she didn't see much option there either. If she was swamped by other people's selves, lost in the chatter of minds that weren't her own, it would be just as good as dead. From a tactical standpoint, worse.

"Everyone brace," Alex said. "I'm taking the shot."

"Braced," Amos said over the comms as Naomi centered herself in her crash couch. The kick of the rail gun was almost subliminal, counteracted by a thrust from the drive, but if the timing went wrong, she didn't want to be bouncing around the deck like a bad throw in golgo.

She pulled up the scopes in time to see the dropship scattering into bright dust. There had been people on that ship. She wondered if they were dead now, or if their memories and opinions and senses of their own selves were stuck flickering through a billion different brains that weren't theirs to begin with. Or if they'd been dead before their bodies were destroyed. Maybe those were different ways of saying the same thing.

The comms chimed with a connection request from the *Falcon*. From Elvi. Naomi checked her timers. The window for the *Whirlwind*'s entry into the system was already open. Depending on how hard the *Magnetar* had burned and braked, it could pass through the Laconia gate at any time now. The end was about as nigh as they got. She accepted the connection.

Elvi looked even more exhausted than usual. Naomi had a flashbulb memory of a dark-skinned man with pale hair and soft, hooded eyes reciting *My candle burns at both ends. It will not last the night.* She didn't know if the recollection was hers or someone else's.

"Give me good news."

"Well," Elvi said. "It looks like the isolation chamber is effective in stopping the shared consciousness effect. Being in the catalyst chamber stops the hive mind, even after Tanaka's psychoactives have dropped to subclinical levels."

"How quickly can we expand that to something, say, the size of a gunship?"

"With enough labor and materials, we could probably pull it off in a couple years. Until then, you can pick the three, maybe four people you want to stuff in there until someone opens it and hauls them out again."

Naomi couldn't help laughing, but there wasn't any mirth in it.

"Yeah," Elvi said. "I know."

"Get me a report. How the isolation chamber works. Directions for building one. We'll put it on a torpedo, get it through some gates. It won't do us any good, but maybe someone out there can benefit from it."

"Can I start it 'Be sure, stranger, to let the Laconians know we rest here, obedient to their command'?"

"I won't stop you," Naomi said. "Sol, Auberon, and Bara Gaon. Where else do we send it?"

"We should send it everywhere. The big tech centers are where Duarte's most likely to concentrate. The smaller colonies might not have the supplies and manufacturing ready to go, but the knowledge will keep as long as there's anyone who's not part of the hive mind."

"If there is anyone. I've got thirty-one ships left, including us. I'm about to have fewer. I don't have thirteen hundred torpedoes, and every one of these messages we send is one less round we can use defending ourselves and Jim."

Elvi nodded. "I'll get you the data."

"Do it quickly," Naomi said. "We don't have long."

Elvi dropped the connection. On the tactical display, the *Lin Siniang* and the little battle group with it were engaging with the two new enemy ships. Four more enemy arrived simultaneously in different quadrants of the ring space. *They're pulling us apart*, she thought. *They're drawing us away from the station.* And it was working. Naomi's little fleet was falling apart before her eyes, and there was nothing she could do about it. As she watched, the *Cane Rosso* blinked from green to orange and vanished like an ember going cool. Thirty ships to defend one station with the full weight of thirteen hundred systems pouring down on her.

"Alex," she said. "We have four more friends who've come to the dance. Get me tightbeams to...the *Lastialus* and the *Kaivalya*."

"Coming up," Alex said, as calmly as if she'd asked him for a flight schedule.

He had been her pilot longer than anyone else in her life. They knew each other's moods and rhythms, and stress only made them work more smoothly together. Maybe group minds weren't that strange after all. In their way, the crew of *Roci* had developed something between them that, over the decades, had felt like more than the sum of its parts. It was cracked and fractured now—Bobbie gone, Clarissa gone, Jim gone, Amos changed—but with her and Alex, there was still the spark of it. The last smooth surface in a universe that had gone rough and biting.

"Well shit," Alex said. "Looks like last-dance time."

The alert came up on her tactical map as he spoke. A new ship had arrived through the Laconia gate. Its transponder was off, but that didn't matter. The silhouette was enough. Larger than anything besides the void cities and uncannily organic in its design, the *Voice of the Whirlwind* came into the ring space. It was almost a relief to see it. The dread of knowing it was coming had been terrible. Now the worst had happened, and all that was left was playing out the last few moves, and then packing up the board and seeing whether death was the end or something more interesting.

She started a recording. "This is Naomi Nagata. Concentrate all fire on the *Whirlwind*. When you're dry, evacuate the area on your own judgment. We will hold our post."

She grabbed the comms and set the *Roci* to deliver it to each of the remaining ships in turn. By the time she'd finished, the *Whirlwind* was visibly farther into the ring space. Its velocity was terrifying and its braking burn murderous. The *Roci* ran the numbers in an instant. The *Magnetar* was on course for the ring station, covering half a million klicks in a little more than twenty minutes. They were coming to protect Duarte.

"Hey," Amos said through the comms. "About how many rail-gun rounds do you think we could put in that thing before it gets here?"

"Only one way to be sure," Alex answered, and Naomi felt an overwhelming rush of affection for them both.

All across the ring space, the last vestiges of humanity, the few whose minds were still their own, threw the missiles and PDC rounds and rail-gun slugs that they had toward the incoming behemoth, clear in the knowledge that it wouldn't matter. Naomi watched as the torpedoes were shot down, the streams of fast-moving slugs dodged or ignored. They were gnats, and the *Whirlwind* could disregard them.

A message from Elvi came with the report on the isolation

chamber, and Naomi put it in the *Roci*'s torpedoes—a last message in her final bottles—and fired them out. The *Roci*'s loadout dropped to zero. *Well, you tried*, an old man said. *You did try.* She could picture his house—a little row house on a thin street in Bogotá—and the orange tabby who slept on his windowsill. Like she was falling into a daydream, she felt the other lives around her, felt herself forgetting Naomi Nagata and the pain and loss and anger of being her. And also the joy.

She checked her timer. It was still an hour before her next dose of the drugs was due. But by that time, it wouldn't matter. She opened the ship-wide comm. She tried to find her last words. Something that would fit the love she had for these men, this ship, the life she'd led. The *Whirlwind* was more than halfway to the station already, though the second stretch would be slower. Even at a quarter million kilometers away, the *Roci* was picking up the excess radiation from its drive plume.

The shout, when it came, literally defied description. It was an overpowering taste of mint or a vibrant purple or the shuddering sense of an orgasm without the pleasure. Her mind skipped and jumped, trying to make sense of something it had no capacity to understand, matching the signal to one sensation and then another and then another until she found herself on the float above her crash couch with no idea how much time had passed.

"Ah," Alex said. "Did you guys feel that?"

"Yup," Amos said.

"Any idea what it was?"

"Nope."

Naomi's tactical map was still up, and it had changed. The *Whirlwind* had cut its braking burn and was on its way to overshooting the station entirely. The other ships—both the enemy and her own—were in disarray. The comms lit up with a broadcast message, and she realized that the jamming had stopped. She accepted the message.

The woman on the screen was young, dark-skinned, with close-cropped hair, and Naomi had seen her once before.

"This is Admiral Sandrine Gujarat of the Laconian battleship *Voice of the Whirlwind*. I would very much appreciate someone telling me how the fuck I got here."

Naomi's finger hovered over Reply, while she tried to think of what to say. She was still there when another broadcast message came through, this one from the *Falcon*. Elvi's eyes were wide and bright, and her smile was so fierce it was almost a threat.

"This is Dr. Elvi Okoye, head of the Laconian Science Directorate, in cooperation with Naomi Nagata of the *Rocinante*. You have all experienced a cognitive manipulation. You may be disoriented or have inappropriately strong emotional reactions. No ships in this space pose any threat. Please stand down and remain safely in place. We will reach out to each of you shortly. Message repeats…"

Naomi turned off the comms. In the quiet of the *Rocinante*, she let her mind drift, and nothing drifted back. No outside memories. No voices. No sense of looming invisible presence.

"Naomi?" Alex called down. "I'm feeling weird up here."

"It's gone. The hive mind. It's gone."

"So it's not just me?"

Amos' voice was calm and affable. "Nobody's bumping into the back of my head either."

"He did it," she said. "I think Jim did it."

She closed her eyes and relaxed and something hit her, hard as a kick, from every direction at once. Her eyes shot open, and she couldn't quite understand what she was seeing. The ops deck hadn't changed at all—the comm display, the crash couches, the passage up to the flight deck and down to the rest of the ship. And also everything had been transformed. The comm display was a field of bright pixels, glowing and flickering too fast for the human eye to follow. The detail of each one made the shapes of words and buttons that they created too abstract to comprehend, like trying to see the curve of a planet from its surface. She raised her hand, and the skin on her knuckles was a range of crags and valleys as complex as anything that stone and erosion had ever managed.

When she cried out, the air fluttered with her breath, compression waves bouncing and curving, enhancing and annihilating.

She tried to find the clasp on the crash couch straps, but she couldn't make out the surface where one thing began and another ended. And streaking through the emptiness of things, the vacuum that still lived in the heart of matter, threads of living blackness, more solid and real than anything she'd ever seen. They writhed and swam, and behind them, everything swirled and came apart. With no one manning the lighthouse now, the elder gods returned.

Oh, she managed to think, *right*.

Chapter Forty-Six: Tanaka

Teresa!" Holden shouted at the girl. "Get away from there! Don't damage the station!"

Well, Tanaka thought, *aren't we just fucked?*

The girl ignored him, ripping at the black threads that were wired into the high consul's body. None of this was in her brief. None of it was going even remotely the way she or Trejo had intended or hoped. There was some independent judgment she was going to have to exercise very, very soon now.

The girl shuddered and jumped, but not in a way that made sense. Something had her, lifting her away from what had been Duarte. The raw panic on Holden's face told her that he knew what this was, and it wasn't good. The girl screamed without seeming to be aware that she was screaming, and Holden grabbed at her, pulled himself to her. For a moment, the girl looked like she was widening. Tanaka could almost imagine invisible angels pulling at her arms and legs. There had been an execution method like that once, she thought. Tie a horse to each limb of the prisoner and see which one kept the biggest chunk. But then Holden shouted and the angels all vanished, leaving the girl behind.

Jesus, you're disappointed? You're disappointed you didn't just see that girl killed? a man's voice said. *What is wrong with you? How do you live with yourself?* Then, something else—a man, a woman, something—was with her and she was in the administrator's office at Innis Deep and she was eleven. The administrator was explaining that her parents were dead. The overwhelming sense, unspoken but clear, was pity. This was why she's so broken. This is why she hurts people. This is why she only fucks men she can dominate, because she's always so frightened. Look at all the things that were wrong with her.

"I swear to God," she said, softly enough that Holden and the girl couldn't hear it, but not talking to herself. "I will put a bullet through my brain if you don't get out of me."

Holden was saying something to the girl. Tanaka didn't care. Winston Duarte's writhing, pale-fleshed body—still wrapped with black threads like someone had sewn them into him—was argument enough that the appeal-to-paternal-instinct plan wasn't going to work. The girl was useless. And her mission—bring the high consul back to Trejo—was impossible now too. Even if Duarte was capable of leaving this place, Trejo and Laconia didn't exist in any meaningful way.

Which meant her Omega status was meaningless. She had better than it. She had freedom. She had nothing to stop her from doing whatever she saw fit except whoever had the balls to try and stop her.

A sound plucked at her. A skittering, buzzing noise that was also like hearing soldiers on parade. At one of the openings in the bright, hot furnace of a chamber, one of the great insectile sentinels came out, and then another. And then a flood. Tanaka felt her eyes go wide.

"Holden, we have a problem."

He muttered an obscenity. The girl was crying. Blue fireflies swirled like sparks at a bonfire.

"If you hurt them, they'll take you apart. They literally use your body to fix the damage you do."

"You were able to protect the girl?"

Holden looked confused for a moment. His skin looked wrong. Like there was some mother-of-pearl version growing up from under his skin. "I...Yes? I guess I was?"

Tanaka switched the gun on her forearm to armor-piercing rounds. "Good. Now do that for me."

Her first shot was intended for Duarte, but her aim was fouled by the vanguard of the enemy slamming into her. The impact pushed her to the side and sent her spinning, but she kept a grip on the attacker. It was faceless, eyeless, more machine than organism. She put her fist to what passed for its thorax, resting her knuckles against the weird plates of its armor or exoskeleton, and opened fire. Even dampened by the strength of her power armor, the recoil felt wonderful. The sentinel twitched and went still, and then there were two more. She felt something tugging at her like a magnetic force that didn't register on her suit's sensor array, and a wave of pain washed over her like needles being driven into her body. One of the sentinels swung a scythe-like arm at her, the cutting edge skittering across her chest plate, and she caught a glimpse of Holden, shielding the girl with his body, his teeth bared in a rictus grin of effort.

The needles sensation faded, and she grabbed the scythe arm, braced her foot against the thing's body, and ripped the arm free. There were more around her now, slamming into her until her ears rang with the impacts. She lost herself for a moment in the glory of the violence, breaking what she could get hold of, shooting what she couldn't.

There were too many of them for her to have any hope of winning. One managed a lucky swing and left a sliver of its carapace stuck in her suit's left shoulder joint. Another wrapped itself around her right leg and didn't let go, even when she pumped a dozen rounds through its body. They swarmed her, threw themselves at her, died, and made way for a dozen more behind them. She switched back to incendiary rounds, and everything around her turned to fire, but they kept coming through the expanding balls of flame. Two of them grabbed her right arm, and between them, they bent the power armor back. Then two more had her left. She didn't know how many she'd killed, but it had to be more than a dozen. That's how long it had taken them to find a strategy against her that worked.

She kept firing, but they were in control of her aim now. The best she could hope was that a few of them would bumble into the line of fire and die there. Holden was wrapped around the girl, his eyes closed, sweat sheeting his skin. And beyond him, through the crowd of sentinels, Duarte.

The man she'd betrayed Mars for was flapping like a wet rag in a breeze. His bright, sightless eyes reminded her of nothing so much as Okoye's pet catalyst. Blue fireflies ran along the black threads, sewing him back in place. She didn't feel pity for him. It was now nothing but contempt.

The glowing eyes swung toward her, seemed to fix on her. *See* her for the first time. Something opened at the back of her consciousness, something was wrenched open, and Duarte flowed into her. The idea of Aliana Tanaka felt distant and small compared to the maelstrom of his—of its—awareness. An ant that defied the anthill was torn apart. No wasp betrayed the hive and lived.

The sentinels hauled her toward him and his black webbing, and she was abased. She felt an oceanic shame, and that shame was a punishment poured into her against her will—a manipulation, a proof that her own heart could be commanded against her— it didn't matter. Nearby, the girl was screaming for her father, and somewhere deep in the prison of her mind, a young Aliana Tanaka wept for the loss of her own parents and for the evil she had done in turning against her spiritual father, her true father, and the ideal of Laconia. Voices flooded her, wailing and angry and scouring as a sandblaster. She felt herself falling apart under their attention, until all that was left of her was sorrow. *Ongoing, intimate assault*, another voice said in the mind that was no longer truly her own. An invasion in her secret space. The thing that she kept apart, only for herself.

Then another voice came through. This one, not from Duarte or his hive, but from her. From her past. If it hadn't still hurt, she might not have heard it. Aunt Akari. *Are you sad, or are you angry?* And she felt the slap as a sting on her still-healing cheek. *Are you sad, or are you angry?*

I'm angry, Tanaka thought, and because she did, it was true.

She looked up. She wasn't more than eight meters from Duarte in his torn, dark cradle. She couldn't move. The sentinels had her well and truly restrained as they worked to tear her apart. But they were holding her power armor. No one was holding *her*.

The advantage of training in different forms of combat for as many years and as consistently as she had was simple: You moved past thought. There was no consideration, no weighing of what she should or shouldn't do, no planning. There was no need for them. The emergency blow of the power armor was like a flower bud blossoming; the plates and joints that the alien insect things were holding popped and fell away like petals. The insect things kept their grip on them, but Tanaka had already pushed off. The air against her skin, the lightness of her underarmor, the oppressive heat of the chamber. They were all flashes of experience. Flickers that she was aware of without the need to attend to. She knew that one good blow from any of the sentinels would open her to the bone if it connected, but she knew it without fear. It was one fact among many, and the calculations were all as reflexive as catching a tossed ball.

She crossed the gap to Duarte in an instant, sliding past him and over the webbing on the left side, where the girl had damaged it enough to leave a hole. One arm around his throat, bracing her legs around his waist. The heat of his body was almost painful, but she fit herself into place. From here, she could use the strength of her whole body, pulling through her back and twisting at the core, against the little vertebral joints in Duarte's neck. The girl screaming somewhere. Holden shouted something. Tanaka pulled, twisted. Duarte's neck snapped like a gunshot. She felt it as much as heard it. In gravity, his head would have lolled to the side, the weight of his skull drawing it down. Here, it might almost not have happened.

The sentinels shuddered, and Holden shouted again. Something stung her arm like a wasp. A strand of the black filament dug into her skin. A half sphere of deep-red blood was spreading out where it had bitten; she swatted it away, and Holden shouted again. This time, she understood the words.

He's not dead.

Between her still-braced legs, Duarte shifted. The noise in her brain ramped up to a scream. Instincts warred in her: push away and evade, or commit to the attack. She leaned into the attack.

Holden was on the float, turning slowly on all three axes, with the girl in his arms, her head curled into his neck to hide her eyes. His skin was mottled and bright and twisted with effort. The sentinels twitched, jumping toward her and then falling back. Tools with two masters, bouncing between conflicting commands. Her last battle, and she was locking shields with James fucking Holden.

Tanaka punched Duarte twice in the ribs. The second time, she felt the bones go. Another sting. Another thread, biting at her leg this time. She flicked it away. The girl had been trying to pull her daddy free from the web, and even her amateur thrashing had done some damage. Tanaka didn't know what the relationship was between Duarte and the threads, but she could recognize a weak point. It wasn't proper shuto-uchi, but she could improvise. She stayed braced with her legs and the arm around Duarte's broken neck, and brought the knife-edge of her hand in where the threads met his body. With every hit, a few more ripped free. Drops of black fluid stippled the free air, and she didn't know if they were coming from Duarte or the filament.

Duarte writhed against her, and his pain made her lock down harder. The inside of her thighs was burning like he'd poured acid on her, but the pain was only a message. She didn't have to care. She kept chopping away at the threads. By the time his side was free, his arms had started flapping back at her, punching her face and the side of her head. The shriek in her mind was constant now.

When she went to shift her position so she could attack the connection on Duarte's other side, the skin on her arm tore. Tiny extrusions were coming out of Duarte's throat, thick and wet as slugs. They'd burrowed through her sleeve and penetrated the flesh of her arm. When she tried to pull her legs free, she couldn't.

"Oh, fuck *you*," she said. Strategy vanished, and she beat her fist into Duarte's side, crushing bones with every strike. The thing that had been the leader of all humanity squealed in pain, and she took joy in the sound. Something pressed into her belly, squirming its way into her like a snake. She stiffened her fingers and pressed hard into the softness where Duarte's rib cage ended. His flesh ripped under the pressure. "Not as much fun when it's happening to you, is it, you fuck," Tanaka said. "Don't like it as much when it's happening to you."

Ink-black blood slickened her hand and stung the quick under her fingernails. Her fingertips pushed through a tough, resistant layer of muscle, and her hand was inside him. The snake thing in her gut whipped and writhed. The pain of it was transcendent. She pushed into him, fitting up to her wrist, pulling him in close against her. Something in his chest fluttered against her like a sparrow. She grabbed it, crushed it, and forced her way deeper.

Something happened, and everything went white. She lost herself, if just for a few seconds. When she came to, her mind was clear. It was her own for the first time since the *Preiss* came back from going dutchman. She coughed, and tasted blood.

The threads that were still sewn into the mess that was her body and his released, floating in the sweltering, furnace-hot air like smoke from hell. Tanaka's breath was shallow, and when she tried to force herself to breathe deeply, she couldn't. She pried her legs free of Duarte's corpse, and scoops of missing flesh the size of golf balls filled with her blood. When she tried to push him away, the snake thing snapped off, still stuck in her gut.

Duarte floated, rotating slowly. His empty eyes swept past her. For almost four decades, she had been an officer of the Laconian Empire, and she'd been good at it. For longer than that, she'd been herself.

Off to her left, Holden and the girl were still. A cloud of sentinels around them had turned to statues. Holden's eyes found hers. There was still enough humanity in him that she could see horror and disgust in his face. She wished she had a sidearm, so she could have put a round through both of them and watched them bleed out with her. She reached out her arm, index finger pointing forward, thumb raised, and sighted in on Holden's face.

"Bang, motherfucker," she said.

The last thing she felt was rage that he didn't die.

Chapter Forty-Seven: Jim

Don't look," Jim said. "Don't look, kid. I've got you. Don't look."
Teresa kept her head against him, her eyes down. Even with
his numbed arms, he could feel her hyperventilating. Her father's
body, not just mutilated but also transformed, floated slowly
away, a sheet of dark liquid clinging to it from surface tension.
Tanaka, covered by more traditional blood, was on the drift too.
The two bodies separated slowly.

He tried to imagine what it would have been like for him, seeing Mother Elise or Father Caesar or any of his parents die that
way. He tried to picture Naomi or Alex where Duarte was. He
couldn't do it. He couldn't imagine being sixteen years old and
watching his father, the center of his life and reality, who had been
taken from him and then teasingly almost returned, die that badly.

"It's going to be okay," he whispered to her as she sobbed and
wailed. "It's all right."

Miller swept off his hat and wiped metaphorical sweat off his unreal brow. He looked exhausted.

"Is he gone?" Jim asked.

Miller nodded. "Yeah, we're the only ones here now. Which is good. I was switching those goons off a hundred times a second, and he kept setting them back on 'murder everything.' "

Teresa raised her balled fists to her eyes. Miller shook his head. "I always hate this part. The bodies and the blood are gross sometimes, but the ones who are left holding the bag? Especially kids. I hate that part."

"What do I do?"

"Normally, I handed them a stuffed bear and called in the social worker. I don't know. How do you tell someone that it's just the way the game plays, and this time their number came up?"

Jim rested his chin on the top of her head. "It's going to be all right."

"Or lie to them," Miller said. "That works too. But there is a question we need to answer. I'm not sure how we get her out of here safe."

"We can clear a path, can't we? If Duarte's not reconfiguring the station, can't we do it?"

"Sure, probably. I seem to be an all-purpose remote as far as local things are concerned. But what are you going to put her on when she gets there?"

Despite the heat, Jim felt a chill. "Why not the *Roci*?"

Miller tilted his head like he was hearing an unfamiliar noise. "You're forgetting what got us here. All this is a complication on the real problem. When Colonel Friendly aced Duarte, she took his finger out of the dike. We're safe in here. This place has already taken the worst the bad guys could dish out and stayed solid. But everyone else out there?" He shook his head.

The coolness in Jim's chest bloomed into pain for a second, and then switched back off. He tried to catch his breath. "What do I do? How do I stop it?"

"Stop what?" Teresa asked.

"Hey," Miller said. "We've only got one brain here. If I know, you do too. It's like I told you last time. Walking around with a body on means you've got a certain level of status."

"Of access," Jim said.

"You're not making a remote connection. It's why he had to come here. Had to *be* here."

Jim felt a tension he didn't know he was carrying release. His arms were numb to the shoulder now, his legs up to the waist. His breath was shallow and his jaw ached. Miller shrugged. "You knew coming in here you weren't coming back out."

"I did. But I'd hoped. You know, maybe."

"Optimism is for assholes," Miller said with a laugh.

"Maybe what?" Teresa asked. "I don't know what you mean. Maybe what?"

He took her by the shoulders. The tears sheeting her eyes had turned her sclera pink and raw. Her lips trembled and shook. He'd known her since he'd first been sent to Laconia in chains. She'd been a child then, but she'd never looked as young as she did now.

"There's something I have to do. I don't know how it's going to work out exactly, but listen. I will not leave you here alone, okay?"

She shook her head, and he could tell she wasn't hearing him. Not really. Of course she was in shock. Who wouldn't be? He wished there was something more he could do. He fumbled, taking her hands in his. He had to watch his fingers to know where they were.

"I will take care of you," he said. "But I have to do this now. Right now."

"Do what?"

He drew back his hands, and turned toward the network of black filaments. The space where Duarte's body had been was empty apart from floating black fibers. They stirred in a breeze Jim couldn't feel. Something about the motion reminded him of sea creatures putting out feelers to catch their prey. A wave of nausea washed over him.

He held out his arms, fingers splayed, and let the threads touch

him. Glimmers of blue ran along them and swirled through the
air. He felt a gentle tug across his shoulders as the web pulled taut.
The ranks of inert sentinels floated randomly through the wide,
bright, empty air. The Laconian corpses, still drifting, drew farther away. The black threads snaked toward him like they were
following a scent and laced themselves into his sides when they
found him.

Teresa was watching him, stunned. Her eyes were wide with
horror and disbelief. He tried to think of something to say—a
joke that would break the tension and let her laugh at the nightmare. He couldn't come up with anything.

"Whatever he did, he did before," Miller said, beside him now.
"If there was any setup or arrangements that needed to be made,
Duarte already put them in place before the *Preiss* did its not-
vanishing trick. We'll have to navigate it a little."

"How am I supposed to find it?" Jim said. "I don't know how
any of this works. I don't know how to do anything but put
myself in the circuit and hope."

"It's like the doc said. This whole thing wants to do what it's
going to do. You're just here to let it. You're not building a gun,
just pulling a trigger."

"That's a lot less helpful than you think," Jim said.

The thing in his gut shifted. His heart did something violent
and not at all heart-like, and he was someplace else. Someplace
cool. He could feel his arms and legs again, and there was no pain
anymore. If he concentrated, he could still see the bright room,
the floating sentinels. He could still feel his body, wracked by the
threads and the changes the protomolecule was making to him. It
was like being on the edge of sleep, aware of his sleeping self and
his dream self at the same time.

Miller cleared his throat. "It's happening. You should hurry."

"How am I supposed to do that?"

Miller's face was an apology. "You're the station now. This is
your Eros, and you're what Julie was. Relax, and let it show you
what you want to know."

Naomi, Jim thought, aching. *I want to see Naomi again.*

And awkward as a child taking its first steps, his awareness broadened. It wasn't quite like seeing, and it wasn't quite like knowing something intellectually, but a mix of both. He felt Naomi at her place on the flight deck, recognized her distress. And as it bore down on her, scattering the molecules and atoms of his ship like a wind scattering dust, Jim saw the enemy clearly for the first time.

Instinctively, he reached out and pushed it back. The black thing from a different reality screamed and fought, pressing against him. Jim wanted to feel the struggle pushing against his hands, but that wasn't quite right. His sense of his body was very strange now. But he could feel the black thing making its way forward like it was swimming toward Naomi against a heavy current.

"You're going to need to think a little bigger," Miller said, and the scope of Jim's awareness expanded. The ring gates and the space between them exploded into his mind. Not just the physical space and the ships scattered through it, not just the crews of the ships and their candle-flame-bright minds, but the invisible structures of it: lines of subtle force that laced between the gates and the station, looping and reinforcing, coming together and apart in a complex sacred geometry. From this perspective, the intrusion of the enemy on the *Rocinante* and on all the other vessels was a single thing. A deformation in the lines of force that kept the ring space from collapsing back into nothingness.

He pushed back, trying to bring the nature of the ring space back to true, but the pressure working against him was implacable. It was omnipresent, and anyplace he resisted it, it flowed around him.

"Miller?"

"I'm right here."

"I can't do this. I can't stop it."

"That's a problem, then."

"Miller! They're going to die!"

Jim pressed back like he was trying to lift a blanket with a toothpick. He was too small, and the pressure, the deformation, was coming from everywhere at once. He felt the candlelight minds on a dozen ships starting to go out. Jim started to panic, flailing. Another few flickering lights went out. One of the ships changed from a single thing with a bright core of energy at its heart to a thousand tiny things, to nothing, as the enemy shattered it and the flow of the attack carried it outside the bubble of space.

"How do I stop this?"

"You know," Miller said. "I told you. You stop it the same way he did."

Jim reached out to the candle-flame minds, pushing into them, and with each one he touched, he felt himself growing wider. A man from Earth, born after the devastation, who joined the underground because he was angry with his father who had capitulated to Laconia became part of Jim. A woman whose mother was sick and might be dying at a medical center on Auberon. Someone who was secretly in love with their pilot. Someone who had been thinking of killing themselves. Jim washed through the minds of everyone in the ring space—Naomi, Alex, Amos—and what had been impossible became possible.

This, Miller said, but not aloud, *all of this was built by one kind of animal. An animal made from light that shared a single mind across more than a thousand systems. If you want to use their guns, you have to have hands the same shape as them.*

Hands? Jim tried to say, but there was so much to him now, he was so wide and bright and full it was hard to know whether he'd managed.

It's a metaphor, Miller said. *Don't get too stuck on it.*

Jim pressed out, and this time he was able to push everywhere at once. The pressure was terrible. The enemy was stronger than he was—than they were—but the structure of the rings and the space and the lines of subtle force were like a construction mech, amplifying his strength, protecting him. Slowly, achingly, he moved back. The crushing pressure outside the ring space was a furnace, an engine, a source of unimaginable energy. Like a judo master, the ring station took the near-infinite power of an entire universe trying to crush it and pivoted, turning its strength against it. The other, older universe just outside the sphere of rings moved past him, and he could feel the pain he caused it. He could feel its hatred. The wound in its flesh that he was.

It pushed, but he could hold it. The lines were in their places now, stable in a way that took less effort to hold in place until the ancient enemy rallied again. He felt it slithering against the slow zone, a black snake larger than suns.

All the energy we can use is from one thing that wants to be something else, Miller said. *Water behind a dam that wants to get to an ocean. Coal that wants to be ash and smoke. Air that wants to equalize pressure. This structure is stealing energy from another place like a turbine slows down the wind just a little. And the things from the other place will never stop hating us for it.*

Jim pulled back, extracting himself from mind after mind after mind. Making himself smaller, lesser, and weaker with each one. Making himself only himself.

"So," Miller continued, "they announced their let's-call-it-displeasure by finding ways to slaughter us. When by 'us' I mean the other things that grew up in our universe. Our galactic photo-jellyfish cousins or whatever. The bad guys took out a system here, a system there. We shut down the gates to try to keep them from killing us, but it didn't work. We tried to build tools that would stop them."

"But nothing could," Jim said.

"Nothing until now. See, now we've got a few billion murder-primates we can slot in where the airy-fairy angels of light used to be. I'm going to give us a better chance at that point."

"That was Duarte's plan."

"It was."

"I didn't go through all of this just to be him."

"Maybe you came through all this to understand why he did what he did. To get your head around it," Miller said, taking his hat off and scratching the back of one ear. "You do what you have to do to fight back, or you get slaughtered. Either way, you lose what being human used to be."

All through the ring space, people rushed. Fear and relief and the focused concentration of repair work being done while emergency klaxons sounded.

And beyond the rings, the systems. Billions of lives. Billions of nodes waiting to be strung together into a single, vast, beautiful mind. From here, Jim could see the great unity that humanity could become, and more than that, he could do it. He could finish the work Duarte had started, and bring something new and grand and strong into the universe.

It would be beautiful.

Miller nodded like he was agreeing with something. Which maybe he was. "Nerving yourself up to kiss your big crush for the first time? Or getting pissed off because the apartment one over has a nicer view than yours? Playing with your grandbabies, or drinking beer with the assholes from work because going back to an empty house is too depressing? All the grimy, grubby bullshit that comes with being locked in your own head for a lifetime. That's the sacrifice. That's what you give up to get a place among the stars."

For a moment, Jim let himself look forward through epochs to see the brightness that humanity could become spread through the universe, discovering and creating and growing in its chorus. Reaching beyond anything a single human mind could conceive. A blanket of light that rivaled the stars themselves. Back in the bright chamber, his physical body wept with awe.

And he sighed.

"It's not worth it."

"Yeah," Miller said. "I know. But what can you do?"

"They shut the rings down," Jim said, "but they kept the station. The slow zone. They left it all here so that they could come back to it. The Sol ring couldn't have worked if the station hadn't been here for it to connect with. They put a bandage over it without getting the splinter out first."

Miller frowned thoughtfully, but there was a glimmer in his eyes. Somewhere, Teresa was screaming Jim's name. He'd need to take care of that. There was another thing first.

"Amos," he said, and the big mechanic turned to look at him. The machine shop was in emergency lighting, and a swath of the deck was simply missing. Amos had a patch kit in one hand and a welding rig in the other. Muskrat, still in her crash couch, barked her greeting bark and wagged.

"Hey, Cap."

"How bad's the damage?"

Amos shrugged. "We've had worse. What happened to you?"

"A lot. Really a lot. I need you to do a favor for me."

"Sure."

"Tell Naomi to evacuate the ring space. Get everybody out. And wherever you go, be ready to stay there."

"How long are we talking?"

"Stay there," Jim said, and Amos lifted his eyebrows.

"Well. All right then."

At the edge of the ring space, the enemy shifted and pressed, sensing, maybe, that Jim's strength wasn't what it had been. "And tell her to hurry. I'm not a hundred percent sure how long I can hold this."

Amos looked around the machine shop, lips pressed together, then sighed and started stowing the patch kit. "You sure you don't want to tell her yourself?"

"I think we've already said what we needed to say," Jim said. "Another goodbye won't help."

"I can see that. Well, it's been good shipping with you."

"You too."

"Hey, Cap, about the rest of 'em?"

"Tanaka's dead. Duarte is too."

"Tiny?"

"Don't leave until she gets there."

"That's what I was waiting to hear."

Jim moved his attention back to the station, complex and active

as his cells. It all made sense to him now—the passages, the sentinels, the vast machines that broke rich light and opened the holes
in the spectrum. That generated the subtle lines. There was so
much that they'd never seen or understood. They'd all just bumbled through, using the gates as shortcuts and hoping for the best.
A species of beautiful idiots.

He shifted what he could, remade the passages. There was some
risk in it. The subtle lines shuddered, and the enemy circled, sniff-
ing at the gates. Jim opened his eyes.

The pain was astounding. Now that he was aware of his body
again, he didn't understand how he'd ignored it. The numbness
in his limbs had given way to a burning. The threads in his side
tugged and ripped. It was hard to see. His eyes were changing,
and the skin all down his front itched badly, but his arms were
restrained and he couldn't scratch.

Teresa was floating in a ball. He was aware that she'd been
screaming for him the way he knew the relative densities of different elements or the names of Greek gods. Intellectually, and without remembering where he'd learned it.

"Teresa," he said. His voice sounded wet and phlegmy. She
didn't respond. "Teresa!"

She started. Her face was blotchy. Her eyes were red and mis-
erable. She looked terrible. She looked achingly beautiful. She
looked so very human.

"I've cleared a path back to the ships for you," Jim said. "You
need to run..."

Chapter Forty-Eight: Alex

"...evacuate immediately. Assume whatever system you are enter-ing is where you will be from now on. Expect and assume no fur-ther contact after your transit, and do not reenter the ring space once you've left. This is not a joke. This is not a drill. Message repeats." Naomi ended the recording, sent it out, and then floated back from her control screen and swallowed a couple times. Alex felt the same. The hollowness in his gut.

"Well," he said. "Holy shit."

The ops deck around them wasn't in ruins, quite, but it was hurting. He'd been in the galley when the universe went strange and the black things had come swimming through it like mat-ter was a thin mist and they were the only things that were real. Which was just as well, seeing as half the pilot's crash couch was missing now. If he'd been in his usual spot, he wouldn't be worry-ing about any of this.

Naomi's right arm was in a sling, but she wasn't missing anything. The best they could reconstruct, she'd jumped back when one of the things had gone for her and slammed her shoulder against the bulkhead. A long stretch of the decking was gone, and there was a hole in the inner hull that Amos had thrown a quick patch on, the metal bright against the old foam-and-cloth covering.

"What do we need to be ready?" Naomi asked.

Amos went still the way he did ever since he'd gotten killed, then he shrugged. "There's a few things I should patch up. We lost one of the port PDCs, but as long as we're not planning to shoot anybody, that can wait. Make sure the water tanks aren't leaking and triple-check the reactor and the drive."

"How long?"

The big mechanic smiled. "If we're good, half an hour. If we're not, then it depends how bad we are."

"Get started, and I'll come assist as soon as I can."

"Copy that, Boss," Amos said. "And Tiny, right?"

"Not leaving without her," Naomi said. "But I may be cutting the *Falcon* loose."

"Let me go double-check the bridge then. You can fuck things up pretty good if you try folding those back in when they're broken."

"Thank you," Naomi said, then turned to Alex. "Preflight checks. All of them, top to bottom. And keep running the diagnostics until the second we're ready to go. If you can get through them five times, do them five times."

"You got it," Alex said, and hauled himself into an undamaged crash couch. "Don't worry. The *Roci*'s not going to let us down now."

"That's because we're not going to let it down," Naomi said.

On the tactical display, the ships still remaining in the ring space started ticking from yellow to green as their courses changed and their drives bloomed. On the comms, half a dozen connection requests were already queued—people asking for clarification or for help. He didn't know what to do for any of them.

Naomi ignored them for the time being and put in her own connection request to Elvi, which was accepted as soon as it was made.

"What's the *Falcon*'s status?" Naomi asked.

Alex started the diagnostic run, querying each of the maneuvering thrusters for power, reaction mass feed status, pressure, and control response.

Elvi's answer was equal parts mania and relief. "Fucked, flustered, and far from home."

"I'm going to need something a little more technical," Naomi said, but there was a smile in her voice. One of the port thrusters threw up an alert for low reaction mass. Alex started isolating the line and looking for pressure drops.

"We lost two crew. Harshaan Lee and David Contreras. I don't think you met David. He was a chemist. He had a wife on Laconia."

"Oh. Not Harshaan. I'm so sorry."

"We sustained some damage, but not as much as last time, because I've been through that twice now. I never wanted to do that again. I hate it."

"How long before you're good to go?"

"It'll take an hour," Elvi said. "And then, like a bat from the depths of hell."

Alex found the problem. A broken feed from the water tanks. In a perfect life, they'd fix it, but the *Roci* had been built for war. Multiple redundancies were in her nature. Her backups had backups had backups. He started flipping through alternate feeds while the diagnostic run went on ahead of him.

"Where are you going?" Naomi asked.

Alex felt a little twinge of concern at Elvi's sigh. "Sol," she said, quietly. "I haven't said so yet, but Sol."

"Not Laconia?"

"The *Whirlwind*'s heading that way. Even if Trejo decides to honor his amnesty, and there are literally no consequences for breaking his word, I'm pretty sure Admiral Gujarat has an enemies list. If I'm on it, and I am very much on it, a lot of my staff is going to be in for a hard run too. I'm breaking up some families, but I'm saving some lives. What about you?"

"Sol," Naomi said. "But I can't go until Teresa's out of the station. I won't make you wait for me. As soon as we can detach the ships, you get the fuck out of here."

"Don't need to say it twice," Elvi said, and dropped the connection. Alex identified a feed with no pressure drop and switched to it. Naomi pulled up the first message in the queue.

"This is Captain Loftman of the *Lagomorpha*. We are in need of assistance. Our drive cone has suffered catastrophic damage..."

Naomi fell to, finding rescuers for ships in need of rescue, answering questions for ships whose command staff were in panic, checking in with Amos now and again as he worked his way through the ship. On her screen, a small window was dedicated to the visual telescopy pointed at the station, the entrance.

Alex felt himself trembling before he knew what it was about. When he did know, he pulled his hands back from the controls. The *Roci* went on, checking the status of the air and water recyclers, the power grid, the Epstein drive.

"Naomi," he said, and something in his voice must have told her there was a problem, because she abandoned the comms at once and turned to him. For a moment, he remembered her the way she'd been when he first knew her back on the *Canterbury*, when the biggest problem he'd had was whether they could get from Ceres to Saturn and back fast enough to collect the on-time bonus. She'd been a quiet thing then. Always hiding behind her own hair and avoiding eye contact. The woman she'd become... Well, they were related, but they weren't the same.

"If this is what's happening," he said, thinking his way through each word as he said it. "If this is pick-the-last-place-you're-going-to-be...I know I've been a restless kind of guy, but Kit is in Nieuwestad system with his wife and their little boy. And I'm not young. If there's no chance of me ever seeing them again on one hand, and there's I'm-able-to-find-a-job-and-send-messages-and-swing-by-a-couple-times-a-year on the other? I don't know that I can go back to Sol. My family's not there."

There was a way that his last words could have been cruel, but he didn't know how else to say it. Naomi was family, and Jim was. And Amos. Even Teresa and her old dog, a little bit. He looked away, afraid to see hurt in Naomi's eyes.

"If it were Filip," she said, "I'd be going where he was."

"I'm sorry."

"You're a lovely man." She turned back to her comms, and a moment later Elvi was there. "Change of plans. I have to send the *Roci* someplace else. Can Amos and I hitch a ride?"

"Of course."

"We have a dog."

"That makes it the least problematic passenger I've had in years."

Naomi dropped the connection and made a different one.

"What's up, Boss?" Amos asked.

"Don't pull in the bridge to the *Falcon*. Get the *Roci* shipshape, get whatever you want to keep, and grab a berth on the *Falcon*. Muskrat's stuff too."

Alex leaned forward, looking for the right explanation. The right apology.

"Alex going to hang out with his kid?" Amos asked.

"Yup," Naomi said.

"It's not that I don't love you guys," Alex said.

"Sure, whatever," Amos agreed cheerfully. "If I'm not going to be on board to patch any leaks, I'll want to change some repair priorities."

"Use your best judgment," Naomi said, and let the connection drop. She stretched over, squeezed Alex's hand once, and let it go. "Get to work with the preflight. We're under some time pressure here."

Thirty minutes later, they were at the airlock. Naomi had a small bag under her arm. Amos had a bottle of liquor and part of Muskrat's customized crash couch. The rest had already been moved over to the *Falcon*. The dog, floating between them with her tail windmilling, seemed the most anxious of them, glancing from one to the other with wide, wet, brown eyes. It was hard to believe that after all the years on the *Roci*, all the lives they'd lived together there, it would be so easy to gather up everything and pack it out. And yet, there they were.

The inner airlock doors were open, and the control pad said that the bridge was pressurized. Alex gripped and released the handhold even though he wasn't drifting. *This is a mistake*, he thought. *We shouldn't be doing this. I was wrong.*

Then he thought of Kit, and of never seeing him or hearing his voice again, and he kept his mouth shut.

"I left a list in engineering," Amos said. "It's all the stuff you really need to get fixed soon. I mean, don't wait. And then a couple dozen things you ought to look at. But I'm pretty sure you're good. I don't know if they have a dry dock on Nieuwestad."

"They do," Alex said. "I checked."

Amos' black eyes shifted. They suddenly didn't seem eerie at all. "You probably ought to head there first. And don't use the rail gun. Cracked capacitor will probably blow if you charge it."

"Don't shoot anybody. Got it."

"Unless you have to," Amos said, then he tucked the dog under one arm and headed for the airlock door. Naomi, watching, smiled.

"He hasn't changed," Alex said. "Not really."

"He has," she said. "We all have."

"Before you go, I wanted to say..." Naomi shook her head gently, and he trailed off.

"It was good," she said.

"It was."

She touched a handhold, rotated, and slid through the still air and into the lock. Muskrat barked once, and Alex was going to tell them to say goodbye to Teresa for him, but the inner door slid closed. The outer door opened, and Naomi and Amos and the dog transferred onto the bridge and across it. He saw that they were speaking to each other, but he didn't know what they said. As the *Falcon*'s lock opened to accept them, the *Roci*'s outer door closed, and Alex was alone on the ship. He waited for a moment, telling himself that he was just listening to the hum of the docking bridge retracting. Making sure nothing went wrong. But even after it was folded in place and ready for travel, he floated there for a few more seconds before he headed back up to the controls.

It felt odd, piloting from ops. Not that he hadn't done it before, but when he had, it had been because there was someone with him there he wanted to talk to without shouting down. Despite all the times he'd run through the diagnostics with the others on board, he ran them again, saw nothing unexpected, and maneuvered away from the *Falcon*. When he lit the drive, the crash couch rose up under him, and he settled into the gel. The drive looked solid. He hadn't caught the *Falcon* in the plume. He shifted up to a third of a g, then a half. Then a full g. Then more. The ship creaked, and he told himself that it was only the normal sounds. They only seemed louder because he was the only one hearing them. Two gs and he injected himself with a half dose of the juice. He stopped there. He also didn't want to strain the ship before it could get a real once-over. He didn't want to have a stroke when no one could get him to the autodoc.

"Trade-offs," he said out loud. "It's always trade-offs."

No one answered. He took a moment, feeling the emptiness of the ship. Just him and the *Rocinante* and the starless void of the ring space. He opened the ship-wide comm.

"If anybody's in here, this is your last chance. Say it now, or you're part of the crew from now on."

It was just a joke, and he was the only one who could appreciate it. He checked the drive. It was running fine. The course was inside tolerance, but there was enough noise that he'd want to adjust a time or two before the transit. The time until he reached the gate...He upped the drive to three gs. His bones could handle it. He wasn't that old.

For the first half hour, he sat in the crash couch, shifting between diagnostic screens, waiting and watching for a sign of malfunction. Then he cut thrust to a third g for a few minutes, went down to the galley, and got a cup of tea. He wanted a beer, but maybe not until after the transit. But he could put on some music, so he did. Old Martian rai-fusion rang through the corridors and cabins. It was both beautiful and melancholy.

He got back in the chair and put the spurs in again.

It wasn't long before other ships reached the gates. The list of vessels in the ring space, formatted for reporting just the way Naomi had designed, lost one name. Then another. The rubric showed that it was safe to go, that they were at very low risk of going dutchman, with the profile ticking up almost imperceptibly with every ship that left. The *Duffy*, heading for Bara Gaon. The *Kaivalya* for Auberon. Even the poor, busted-up *Lagomorpha* with its bad drive cone made it through Sol gate. When the *Whirlwind* passed into Laconia, the model shifted for almost a minute, ready to warn any incoming ships to slow their approach. It would have been a good system.

Slowly, and yet with all due haste, the ring space emptied.

Pressed into his couch, he started thinking about what came next. Here he was, a pilot with an old, broken ship and no crew. He didn't know much about Nieuwestad, other than it was a corporate holding. That wasn't going to mean much. But there wasn't a large military presence. Having a gunship would either ensure his independence or make the local authorities anxious about him. But that was borrowing trouble before it came. The *Roci* was a good ship, and rated for atmosphere. Once he got it fixed up and found a crew, they could carry scientific survey teams through the system. Maybe do a little prospecting of his own. He imagined Kit and his wife shipping out with him on some microclimate engineering mission. Or something. Or just a little family vacation. He imagined being Grampa Alex, and grinned to himself. Then he imagined being Grampa Alex without Giselle there to make comments about his belly, and let himself smile just a little bit more. There were good lives out there for him. Possibilities.

The alarm sounded when he was still a hundred thousand klicks from the gate. A misfeed in the fuel supply to the reactor. Maybe nothing, maybe the first sign of a real problem. He pulled up the logs, running down them with a fingertip to help his eyes keep focus. This wasn't the time to miss anything. He was glad now he hadn't gone for the beer, or the ones after it.

"Come on," he cooed to the ship. "We can do this. Just a little further down the trail now."

Chapter Forty-Nine: Naomi and Jim

Somewhere, Holden was burning. Fever within his body. Heat without. Somewhere, he was in misery, but it wasn't here. Here, he was aware—seeing without sight—of the *Rocinante* shifting away from the *Falcon*, away from the station. Turning away and burning. If he'd made the effort, he could have gone closer. Known more. He let it go.

"Probably the smart move," Miller said. "Don't want to tire yourself out."

"Little late for that," Holden said.

The detective chuckled, and Holden's back spasmed. For an instant, he was in the bright room. The blue fireflies whirled around him, and there were words in their flickers that he could almost understand. He'd decode them, given time. Waves of nausea washed over him, and vertigo made the room spin like a top, but that was just his inner ears changing. He closed his eyes and willed himself elsewhere.

Deep in the station, Teresa was flying too fast. She'd missed the turn that led back to the surface, to the *Falcon*. He shifted the passageways in front of her, guiding her back the right way. He could see her jaw clenched tight, determination on her face that bordered on anger. He wished there was something more he could do.

The nature of space shifted, and the subtle lines fought to shift it back. Holden pushed, righting them. Space stayed just space. For the moment.

"You remember the first time we did this?" Miller said.

"We have never done this before."

"You know what I mean. Eros. We were sitting there waiting for the radiation to slough all our skin off. You were talking about some kids' show."

"Misko and Marisko."

"That's the one." Miller hummed the theme song, waving his hand like a conductor in front of an orchestra.

Holden smiled. "Haven't thought about that in years. I committed great sins in a past life to keep getting stuck with you when I'm dying."

"Nope. You are coming apart, but this isn't dying. Goes on a lot longer than dying."

"Unless something interrupts the process."

"Yeah," Miller agreed. "Unless that."

Teresa was coming close to the entrance. A few hundred more meters, and she'd be out. He hoped she remembered to put her helmet back on. Normally, he wouldn't have worried, but she was upset.

"That was the first time I told Naomi that I loved her," Holden said. "She handed me my ass on a plate."

"You had it coming. And hey, it ended better than it started."

Teresa reached the edge of the station, and then went beyond it. He could feel her hesitate, lose her way, and then find the *Falcon* and launch herself toward it. At the gates, ships transited out, first one and then a handful. The empty space became a little emptier. Teresa shifted closer to the *Falcon*. The things on the other side stirred like predators scenting something—smoke or blood. Unsure whether to attack.

Teresa reached the airlock and passed inside. Holden felt himself relax. He waited for the ship to move. For its drive to bloom. The minutes passed slowly. Painfully.

"Come on," he said. "Come on. Get out of here. Please don't stay. Please go."

The inner door of the airlock opened, and Teresa spilled inside. Her eyes were wild and tearstained. Her mouth was a square gape of rage.

"Where's my *ship*?!"

The *Falcon* was crawling with activity. The crew making last-minute repairs and preparations for the burn, Amos reassembling the dog's custom crash couch, Naomi coordinating the evacuation with the last stragglers. She almost hadn't come down to meet Teresa. Naomi could see the moment the girl recognized her. The combination of relief and the focus of finding a target was complex.

"Where did the *Roci* go?" Teresa shouted.

"Alex had to take it," Naomi said. "We'll be on the *Falcon* for now."

"No one said that was going to happen!"

"Hey, Tiny," Amos said, floating in from Naomi's right. "Thought you might—"

Teresa shrieked and launched herself at the mechanic. She slammed into his shoulder, wrapping her arms around his neck and her legs around his arm. Adrenaline hit Naomi's bloodstream like a hammer, and then she heard the girl sobbing. Amos steadied himself with his other hand as Teresa gripped him with her whole body. His flat, black eyes shifted to Naomi and he gestured. *What do I do with this?*

Naomi raised her shoulders. *I don't know.* Awkwardly, Amos reached over and patted Teresa's head. "It's okay, Tiny. You're safe now. We got you."

He looked utterly out of his depth, and as unmistakably human as she had seen him since his change. A moment later, Cara and Xan appeared, sliding through the air to Amos' side, touching Teresa's shoulder to let her know they were there, and then wordlessly embracing her. The one shattered girl enfolded and comforted by the three gray-skinned, black-eyed people. It looked like a painting. Alien and beautiful. Teresa's sobbing slowed, but her grip stayed tight.

"We may need a minute or two, Boss."

"When you can," Naomi said, and hauled herself out and back to the workstation Elvi had given her.

The evacuation was progressing well. Every ship that was able to move was moving. Every ship that couldn't had been docked with and their crews transferred off. Most were heading for the nearest exit. The *Falcon* and the *Roci*, at the center of the ring space, had the farthest to travel in order to reach a gate. Some few of the others were going across the ring space, heading for Bara Gaon or Sol or Auberon at the hardest burn they could manage.

"We're ready," Elvi said.

"That's an exaggeration," Fayez said. "We've reached an arbitrary level of fuck-it-good-enough. We're calling that ready."

Naomi turned. Fayez was fastened to the decking with mag boots; Elvi floated beside him. It made an illusion that he was in gravity and she, ethereal, was floating away like a balloon. Her thinness and atrophy helped sell it.

"We don't have enough of the submersion couches for everyone," Elvi said. "It's going to limit how fast we can accelerate safely."

Naomi looked at her tactical map one last time. There was nothing more she could do. She closed the display with the sense that it was her last moment as the head of the underground. She expected the relief she felt at the idea. The sorrow was more surprising.

"We can use submersion for the most vulnerable," she said.

Fayez looked to his wife. "She means you, honey."

"He's right," Naomi said. "I do."

"If we had time, I'd push back on that," Elvi said. "Five minutes to get everyone in place?"

"I'll get to my couch now," Naomi replied.

It was a standard enough design: a gel base on a gimbaled platform. It wasn't the same kind that the *Roci* had used. The Laconian gimbals were silent, and the gel had an odd warmth that Naomi understood was supposed to help maintain circulation under high gs but made the couch feel uncomfortably fleshy. There was a temperature control, though, so as soon as she strapped in, she turned it down to a cooler level.

She used her hand terminal to check in with Amos. The lag was suspicious until she realized it was still trying to route through the *Roci*'s system. She shifted it to the *Falcon*, and the connection request was instantaneous.

"Hey, Boss," the thing that had been Amos—that maybe sort-of still was—said.

"All of ours in place?"

"Yep. Muskrat's a little anxious about the whole thing. Between the new digs and Tiny freaking the fuck out. The medical guy gave Tiny a little something to take the edge off. She's sleeping now. He said she's traumatized?"

"Seems plausible."

"I don't know how I got this old without someone telling me they had pills for that," Amos said, and she could hear the disapproval in his tone. It reminded her of who he'd been before.

"There's a big toolbox," she said. "Everyone has to find their own way through."

"I guess. Anyway, I'm strapped in. Tiny's good. Dog's good. And that's us."

Fuck, Naomi thought. *That's us.*

"All right."

"How're you holding together?" Amos asked.

"I'll see you on the other side," she said, and let the connection drop.

A moment later, Elvi came over the ship-wide system telling

everyone to strap in and prepare for hard burn. Naomi pulled up the exterior telescope and set it to track the station. To track Jim. She knew that for the most part, he'd be lost in the drive plume, but she did it anyway.

The countdown came. The crash couch needles bit into her, the juice flowed into her blood, and the *Falcon* slammed up into her from below.

Holden felt the ships leaving the space, one and then another. The ones still in the bubble of false space shifted toward the escapes, going mind-numbingly fast and still too slow. Holden willed them to go faster. To get out. To be safe.

The brightness of the gates, the light they passed between them, was unfolding for him as he grew more fully into the mechanism. It reminded him of the way babies learn without seeming to try—soaking up information and discovering pattern as part of growing into the being they were going to become. Part of him wished that he could stay longer, see more, die knowing something.

"Hard to let go of a bad idea," Miller said as if he were agreeing. "I mean, I'm not the guy who can start throwing stones at someone for not wanting to give up the case, right?"

"But you're pretty good at dying if that's what it takes to make things right."

"Turns out that is a talent of mine," Miller said with a lopsided grin. "There's always new mysteries out there. We get those for free."

The dark things shifted again, deforming the space, reaching into it. Trying to change its nature, and this time, touching the ring gates. Pushing through them to the systems beyond. Their attention felt slick and muscular. Wet, somehow. Holden reached out to pull them back, and the effort was terrible.

"Harder to do on your own," Miller said.

"You could help."

And the feeling changed, as if there really were two of them and not just an illusion made from memories in a dying body. The thick, slimy reach of the things beyond the gates squirmed and resisted, pushing past Holden's will, trying to find one more way to end the intrusion.

"Just give me a little fucking time," Holden said, but if the enemy could hear him, it ignored him. Holden redoubled his efforts, and slowly, reluctantly, the invisible tentacle retracted into its own universe and left him spent and exhausted.

If an attack came again, he wouldn't be able to stop it.

"You left it all on the field," Miller said. "Whatever that means."

"Football."

"What?"

"It's a football thing."

"Oh," Miller said, and scratched his neck. "Yeah, that makes sense."

The *Rocinante* cleared the Nieuwestad gate. Two other ships passed through to Sol. The only things left alive in the ring space were Holden and the *Falcon*. He could feel Naomi on the ship. And Amos. His actual body shuddered and wept, and he did everything he could to ignore it.

"Kind of funny," Miller said. "You being here to do this."

"Yeah, it's hilarious."

"It actually is, smartass. Mister make-sure-everyone-has-a-voice. Fight against everyone who is making decisions for other people. Your whole fucking life has been that. Now here you are. Those colony systems aren't baked yet. A lot of them rely on trade. We do this, and some of them aren't going to make it."

"I know."

The dark things shifted, pressed. They weren't tired at all. Holden felt their hunger and didn't know if it was real, or just something he projected onto them. The *Falcon* drew nearer to the Sol gate. Each second, it moved faster than the second before. Falling toward safety and away from him faster than just falling would have done. *Go*, he thought. *Please be safe.* The rings sang their songs in light. The blue sludge in his veins plucked at him, changed him, offered ways that he could live and spread and *know*.

"I mean, don't get me wrong. My analysis of the situation is a lot like yours. But you got to see there's an irony in it. All the shit you gave me about giving people all the information and trusting them to do the right thing? Most of these fuckers aren't gonna know what happened. This decision you're making for the whole human race."

"Is there a reason you're needling me like this?"

Miller's expression went stern and sorrowful. "I'm trying to keep you awake, old fella. You're drifting."

Holden realized that was true. He made an effort to pull his mind back together. The *Falcon* was approaching the Sol gate. Not minutes now. Less.

"I absolutely believe that people are more good on balance than bad," he said. "All the wars and all of the cruelty and all of the violence. I'm not looking away from any of that, and I still think there's something beautiful about being what we are. History is soaked in blood. The future probably will be too. But for every atrocity, there's a thousand small kindnesses that no one noticed. A hundred people who spent their lives loving and caring for each other. A few moments of real grace. Maybe it's only a little more good than bad in us, but..."

The *Falcon* passed through the Sol gate. Nothing was left in the ring space but him.

"And yet," Miller said, "we're about to consign millions of people to slow deaths. That's just the truth. Are you sure this thing you're about to do is the right one?"

"I don't have a fucking clue," Holden said, and then did it anyway.

For an instant, there was a release of energy second only to the beginning of the universe. There was no one there to see it.

The ring gate faded. Its recent brightness went first, and then the distortion at its center...faded. Where there had been a mystery and a miracle, a gateway to the galaxy, now there were just distant stars framed by a dull loop of metal a thousand kilometers across.

And then it fell.

The *Falcon* was on a fairly gentle one-third g burn that would put it near Ganymede in a few weeks, and the whole staff—the brightest minds of a shattered empire—were watching the ring gate die, measuring it, collecting data from the corpse. Naomi, sitting alone in the galley with a bulb of tea, just watched it. For decades, it had been fixed in place, one of the farthest objects in the solar system. It didn't orbit. It didn't move. Now, it tumbled a little, pulled in toward the sun the way anything would be. The miracle, ended.

Her message queue was like a fire hose. Contacts from the underground, reporters from a hundred different outlets, politicians and Transport Union officials and the local traffic control authorities. Everyone wanted to talk to her, and however they phrased it, they all wanted the same questions answered. What does this mean? What happens now?

She didn't answer any of them.

The crew of the ship came and went. Some were injured, like her. Some were injured less visibly. She recognized some. It was almost the whole shift before Amos came in. His wide, rolling gait as familiar as her own voice. She wanted to believe it was really him, that her old friend had actually survived Laconia and not just become the raw material of an alien machine. She smiled and raised her bulb.

"Hey, Boss," Amos said. "How're you holding together?"

"A little weird," she said. "How's Teresa?"

Amos went to the dispenser, frowning at the unfamiliar control menu as he spoke. "She's seen better days. Whatever happened on that station, it fucked her up pretty good. I think she was really hoping she'd get her dad back." He found the menu he wanted and grunted with satisfaction. "Seems like her and Sparkles are hitting it off, though. I think Little Man's kind of jealous. I think he wants to be Tiny's bestie. There's some brother-sister dynamics. It'll work out."

The galley chimed and put out a little silver tube. Amos cracked the top, rolled over, and sat across from her. His gentle smile could have meant anything. He looked at Naomi's hand terminal. The tumbling ring.

"Fayez says it's going to fall into the sun," Amos said. "Says even all the way out here, it hasn't got enough sideways to it for an orbit. Just boom, right into the fireball."

"You think that's true?"

Amos shrugged. "I think a bunch of independent contractors are gonna strip-mine that shit before it gets to the Belt. They'll be lucky if there's a handful of dust left to hit the corona."

To her surprise, Naomi laughed. Amos' smile got maybe a degree more genuine.

"I think you're right," she said. "And if not, someone'll hire a tug to give it a little lateral impulse. Nothing humans can touch goes unmodified."

"A-fucking-men. What about you, Boss? What do you think about all this shit?"

He meant, *Are you all right? You've lost Jim. You've lost Alex. You've lost your ship. Are you able to live with that?* And the answer was that she could. But she wasn't ready to say it out loud, so she answered the other question instead.

"I think we got lucky. I think we were one little system in a vast, unreachable universe that was always on the edge of destroying itself, and now we have thirteen hundred chances to figure out how to live with each other. How to be gentle with each other. How to get it right. It's better odds than we had."

"Even if someone does, though. We'll never know. The alien roads are gone. Now it's just us."

The ring tumbled on her screen, and she looked past it to the stars. The billions upon billions upon billions of stars, and the tiny fraction that had other people looking back toward her.

"The stars are still there," she said. "We'll find our own way back to them."

Epilogue: The Linguist

Marrel expected reintegration to hurt, but it didn't. It didn't feel like anything. He didn't even have the grogginess of waking from sleep, which—thinking on it—shouldn't have been surprising, as he hadn't fallen asleep. Somehow, he was surprised all the same.

He had climbed into his transit pod on the crew deck of the *Musafir* along with everyone else, watched the countdown timer on the reinforced crystal wall in front of him go to zero, and then change to 31:11:43:27 as if that was the number that naturally followed zero.

Thirty-one days, eleven hours, forty-three minutes, and twenty-seven seconds had elapsed for his homeworld while Marrel and the twenty-nine other souls on board the *Musafir* existed only as energy and intention sliding along the membrane between universes. Thirty-one days as they vanished and reappeared at their destination, nearly 3,800 light-years from home. A long-held breath as they swam through the cosmic foam and re-emerged at a different place in the ocean.

"Yinvisa Merrel isme dorasil. Yi ie dovra?" the pod asked him in its carefully neutral voice.

"Caan Ingliz," Marrel said. "Ta-Connia atze a en-callase, per." *Common English. Post-Laconian expansion, pre-collapse, please.*

"Are you well?" the pod repeated.

"I am well."

"The transit from Dobridomov was successful," the pod informed him. "Welcome to Sol. The *Musafir* is currently twenty-four days from our destination at best speed."

"If the transit was unsuccessful," Marrel said, "would we exist?"

"It is theoretically possible for reintegration to occur at an unexpected destination, though it is statistically unlikely."

"May I see the contact report, please?"

The *Musafir* set down on a small hill some distance from an ancient city. The emptiness of the space around Earth was eerie. Like walking into a tomb. This was the ancestral home of all the Thirty Worlds, and yet it had fewer structures around its system than any contact before. Not that there were none. The emplacements of weapons were disguised, but not so well that the *Musafir* hadn't seen them. The hidden ships they had identified were almost certainly not the only ships that there were. Everywhere, there was a sense of threat.

The diplomatic team remained on the ship, but watched and listened as Marrel walked down the ramp to the grassy field that stretched off in every direction and took a deep breath of the air humanity had been born in. The ship had issued him prophylactics to ensure that the local pollen would not trigger an allergic reaction. If nothing else, Marrel could tell his future grandchildren this. He had stood on the grass of Earth. He had breathed its air.

The group that had come for him stood some distance off. Many of them carried obvious weapons. Marrel wasn't sure if they were an honor guard waiting for him to approach, or a strike team waiting to charge him and try to take the ship. He fumbled with the target pointer in his hand. If need be, the ship could turn the field in front of him into a molten lake. He prayed that wouldn't be the case.

A single figure detached from the knot and began walking in his direction with long, loping strides. It was tall, but Marrel had expected this. Dobridomov was of slightly heavier gravity than Earth, and the average height was a bit less. The figure was also broad, and thick limbed, with ebony skin and a wide, hairless head. As it approached, the color of its skin began to look less like a natural color and more like an artificial pigment. Marrel wondered if full-body tattooing or cosmetics were popular here. It might be some kind of caste mark.

The figure stopped a few meters away and waited. Up close, it appeared to be male.

"My name is Marrel Imvic, of the Dobridomov system," he said in ancient Chinese. He was prepared to repeat the message in a dozen different old languages until one was recognized. "I am a linguist, here to establish communication protocols so that our diplomatic group can begin a dialog."

"You got any English?" the man said with perfect pre-collapse intonation.

"Yes," Marrel said, stunned. "Yes, I do."

"Good, because my Chinese is pretty iffy. I'm okay in Belter, but I bet you guys forgot that one."

"I know what Belter is," Marrel said, thrilled at the idea that this man spoke a dialect considered dead for a thousand years.

"Cool," the man replied. "So it's been a rough millennium around here. We're starting to get our shit together, and I've been doing what I can to help with that, but it's slow going."

"Are you a leader of these people?" Marrel asked.

"I'm not into job titles. Name's Amos Burton. If we're good,

I'm just some asshole. If you're here to start some shit, I'm the guy you'll have to go through first. Tell 'em I said that."

He gave Marrel a vague smile and waited. The diplomatic group listened as Marrel translated for them.

"Great," Amos Burton said when he was done. "Now we got that shit out of the way, follow me. We'll grab a few beers and get reacquainted."

Acknowledgments

U sually, we start these by talking about how any book is, on some level, a collaboration. This time, we're talking about more than a book. The first volume of The Expanse was written a little over a decade ago, and between there and here, it has been a long, wild ride with us racking up debts and reasons for gratitude all along the way.

This series and all that came with it would not exist without the hard work and dedication of Danny Baror and Heather Baror-Shapiro, the whole brilliant crew at Orbit including (but by no means limited to) Bradley Englert (and his predecessors, Darren Nash, DongWon Song, Will Hinton, and Tom Bouman), Tim Holman, Anne Clarke, Ellen Wright, Alex Lencicki, and Lauren Panepinto. Special thanks are also due Carrie Vaughn, for her services as a beta reader, and the gang from Sakeriver: Tom, Sake Mike, Non-Sake Mike, Jim-me, Porter, Scott, Raja, Jeff, Mark, Dan, Joe, and Erik Slaine, who got the ball rolling.

The support team for this series has also grown to include the staff at Alcon Entertainment and the cast and crew of *The Expanse* television show. Our thanks and gratitude go especially to our showrunner, Naren Shankar, and the inimitable Dan Nowak, who were there from the beginning to the end. And an extra-special thank-you to Sharon Hall, who took a chance on our books and taught us how to make them into TV.

Also critical to the success of this project has been the consistently brilliant performance of Jefferson Mays, who, if you got this as an audiobook, is the voice you're listening to right now. If we're ever in the same bar, that man drinks for free.

And, as always, none of this would have happened without the support and company of Jayné, Kat, and Scarlet. We lost time with them in order to do this, and it wouldn't have been worth doing if they hadn't been there for us when we got back.By James S. A. Corey

The Expanse

Leviathan Wakes

Caliban's War

Abaddon's Gate

Cibola Burn

Nemesis Games

Babylon's Ashes

Persepolis Rising

Tiamat's Wrath

The Expanse short fiction

The Butcher of Anderson Station

Gods of Risk

The Churn

Drive

The Vital Abyss

Strange Dogs

James S. A. Corey is the pen name of fantasy author Daniel Abraham, author of the critically acclaimed Long Price Quartet, and writer Ty Franck. They both live in Albuquerque, New Mexico.

For the first time, all of the short fiction set in James S. A. Corey's *New York Times* bestselling Expanse series are available in this collection.

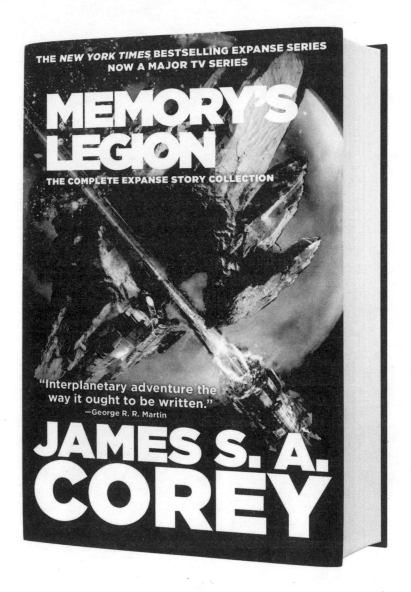

learn more at orbitbooks.net

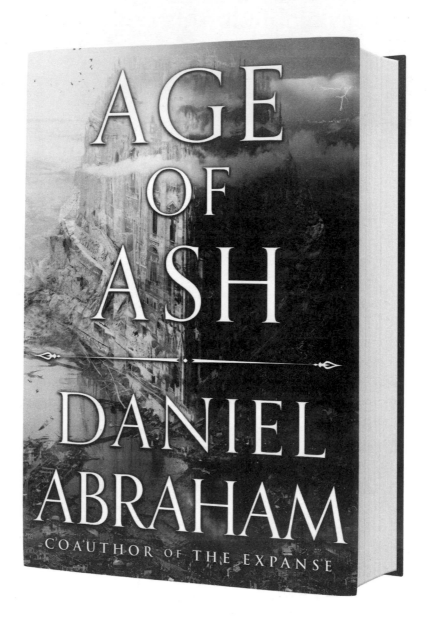